One in a Thousand
Or, The Days of Henri Quatre

by

G. P. R. James

Double9
BOOKS

One in a Thousand
Or, The Days of Henri Quatre
by G. P. R. James

Copyright © 2024

All Rights reserved.

ISBN: 978-93-64283-08-3

Published by

DOUBLE 9 BOOKS

2/13-B, Ansari Road
Daryaganj, New Delhi – 110002
info@double9books.com
www.double9books.com
Tel. 011-40042856

This book is under public domain

ABOUT THE AUTHOR

George Payne Rainsford James (1799-1860) was a British novelist and historical writer who gained considerable popularity during the 19th century. James was a prolific writer, known for producing over 100 novels, plays, and non-fiction works. His literary output covered a wide range of genres, including historical fiction, romance, adventure, and historical non-fiction. During his lifetime, James enjoyed considerable success and popularity as a novelist. His novels were widely read both in Britain and internationally, contributing to his reputation as one of the leading historical novelists of his time. James is best known for his historical novels, which often explored significant historical events, figures, and periods. His works were noted for their detailed historical research and vivid portrayals of characters and settings. Some of his notable works include: "Richelieu, Or the Conspiracy" (1829),"The Gipsy" (1835) ,"Darnley" (1830),"The King's Highway" (1830) ,"One in a Thousand, Or, The Days of Henri Quatre" (1844) ,"The Smuggler" (1845) . Although his popularity waned in the later decades of the 19th century, G. P. R. James's contributions to historical fiction and his impact on the genre were significant. His works continue to be studied and appreciated for their historical insights and literary merits.

CONTENTS

INTRODUCTION

George Payne Rainsford James, Historiographer Royal to King William IV., was born in London in the first year of the nineteenth century, and died at Venice in 1860. His comparatively short life was exceptionally full and active. He was historian, politician and traveller, the reputed author of upwards of a hundred novels, the compiler and editor of nearly half as many volumes of letters, memoirs, and biographies, a poet and a pamphleteer, and, during the last ten years of his life, British Consul successively in Massachusetts, Norfolk (Virginia), and Venice. He was on terms of friendship with most of the eminent men of his day. Scott, on whose style he founded his own, encouraged him to persevere in his career as a novelist; Washington Irving admired him, and Walter Savage Landor composed an epitaph to his memory. He achieved the distinction of being twice burlesqued by Thackeray, and two columns are devoted to an account of him in the new "Dictionary of National Biography." Each generation follows its own gods, and G. P. R. James was, perhaps, too prolific an author to maintain the popularity which made him "in some ways the most successful novelist of his time." But his work bears selection and revival. It possesses the qualities of seriousness and interest; his best historical novels are faithful in setting and free in movement. His narrative is clear, his history conscientious, and his plots are well-conceived. English learning and literature are enriched by the work of this writer, who made vivid every epoch in the world's history by the charm of his romance.

"The Man at Arms" tells the story of Jarnac and Moncontour, and ends with the fatal day of St. Bartholomew. "Henry of Guise" takes up the history of the Religious Wars, with sympathy chiefly for the Catholics, and closes with the assassination of that great soldier; then "One in a Thousand" resumes the tale just before the murder of Henry III. and the battle of Ivry. The two former are rather short and remarkably brisk in movement, this one is somewhat longer and much more elaborate. It has a complex plot, a large crowd of characters from both factious, and has evidently been worked out with, perhaps, less vivacity but more pains. "Willingly" says the novelist, "we turn once more from the dull, dry page of history ... to the more entertaining and instructive accidents and adventures of the individual characters which, with somewhat less skill than that of a Philidore, we have been moving about on the little chess-board before us."

There is an ironical undermeaning here; but so far as James suggests that his flagrant romanticism, mysterious dwarfs, princesses disguised as pages, and battles prefigured in the thunder-clouds are more interesting than his retelling of historical events and careful portraiture of historical people, we must venture to dissent from him. The fiction is simply his favourite story of a wealthy heiress held out as a bait by the heads of rival factions to attract the allegiance of two powerful nobles. We feel not the slightest anxiety as to the ultimate happiness of the fair lady and the blameless lover, or the appropriate fate of their enemies. On the other hand, the intimate picture of the Leaguers at Paris, of the headquarters of Henry Quatre, and more particularly the speaking likeness of the Duke de Mayenne, the head of the Guises, are keenly interesting and real contributions to the history of those times. Though the stage effects are well done, this shows far more talent. With all his fierce ambition, his lack of scruple, and his froward temper, the Duke stands out as a man, and is infinitely more alive than the purely romantic characters; furthermore, the family likeness between the various members of that powerful house, the Guises, is admirably brought out in this series of romances, and the figure of Henry of Navarre is not less well done, though he is a personage that we meet with less rarely either in James's novels or in those of other historical raconteurs.

CHAPTER I

Oh the confines of the two beautiful provinces of Maine and Touraine, lies one of the sweetest valleys that the foot of man ever trod. The hills by which it is formed are covered on one hand by a wood of venerable oaks, while the other side offers a green slope only broken occasionally by rocky banks; and on the summit of every eminence stands out, in bold relief, a group of two or three young trees, casting their deep, soft shadows on the velvet turf below.

The eye of a traveller, placed at the northern extremity of the valley, may trace its course winding on in varied beauty for nearly a league to the southward; till at length the hills between the acclivities of which it lies, seem to end abruptly in that direction, but still without meeting; the one side terminating in a high rugged rock, cutting clear and distinct upon the sky, and the other fringed by the branches and foliage of the trees. Far away beyond--enframed, as it were, by the opening of the valley--lies a rich, splendid landscape, showing bright Touraine, with its plains, and woods, and dells fading off in long misty lines of light and shade, till earth and heaven blend in the blue obscurity of distance.

Washing the roots of the trees on one side, and edged with a bank of soft green moss on the other, a small limpid stream runs swiftly along over a shallow bed of rocks and pebbles, and, like some spoiled child of fortune, winds rapidly on amidst a thousand sweets and beauties, still hurrying forward, careless of all the bright things that surround its path. Such is the picture of that valley as I have seen it within the last twenty years; but the tale I have to tell refers to a period more remote.

Down the steep, rugged bridle-road, which, descending sharply from the brow of the more exposed hill, crossed the course of the valley and the stream at nearly a right angle, and then, mounting the opposite slope, made its way through the forest;--down that road, somewhere near the end of April, 1589, a very handsome boy, seemingly about sixteen years of age, took his path on foot. He was just at the time of life when childhood and manhood meet--when sports, and pastimes, and sweet innocence are cast away like faded flowers, and when we first set the naked foot of inexperience on that burning and arid path through the fiery desert of desire and disappointment, which each man must tread, ere he reach the night's resting-place of the tomb. Not a shade of down yet tinged his upper lip with the budding of the long-coveted mustachio, and his face was smooth and soft; but there was a flash and a fire in his splendid dark eye, which told that the strong and busy passions that beset man's prime had already taken possession of his heart.

He was dressed in a vest of dark murrey-coloured cloth, bound with a light edging of gold, and in large trunk breeches descending to his knee, made of the same stuff, and ornamented in the same manner. His cloak, which was more ample than was usual in those days, or than the time of year required, was fastened by a buckle to the right shoulder, and, being brought round under his left arm in the Italian mode, was wrapped across his chest, without opposing any obstacle to the free passage of his hand towards the hilt of his dagger or his sword. He was, if anything, below the middle height, and slightly made; but in his countenance there were all those signs and features from which we are accustomed to argue the presence of high and daring courage: and, perhaps, it might have been a safer task to attack many a man of greater personal strength, and much more warlike appearance, than that slight boy, with his light active limbs, and quick remarking eye.

On the summit of the hill he paused for a moment, and gazed over the country which he had left behind, as if looking anxiously for some expected sight; and then, muttering the words, "Negligent varlets!" he resumed his path down the side of the hill. After wandering for a short space along the margin of the shallow stream, seeking for a place where he might cross its fretful waters, without wetting the light buskins that covered his feet, he sat down upon the mossy bank under the shade of a clump of oaks, seemingly wearied with his walk, and, pulling off his boots and stockings, dipped his feet in the rivulet to cool and refresh them. Laying his broad-plumed hat by his side, he leaned back against the broken bank, from which sprang the oaks that shaded him; and, with the water still rippling over his feet, and the chequered light and shade of the green leaves above playing on his broad fair brow, he seemed to give himself up to one of those fanciful dreams ever so busy with the brain of youth.

It was certainly a spot and an hour to dream in. It was the noon of a bright spring day. Every bird of the season was singing its sweetest song in the forest opposite or in the trees above his head; and his seat was carpeted with the meek-eyed wood anemone, the soft blue periwinkle, the daisy, the primrose, and the violet, together with a thousand other flowers, the sweetest children of the early year, whose very birth and being are one of the brightest themes that nature offers to imagination. And yet the youth's meditations did not appear to be pleasant ones. Whatever was the chain of thought that bound his mind, there was upon his countenance an expression of sad and painful gloom, which gradually changed, like the hues of a red and stormy sunset, to the deeper signs of wrath and indignation. Sometimes he gazed heavily upon the stream, with an eye all unconscious of the flashing waters before it; and then again, as some sterner feeling seemed to take possession of his heart, his brow would knit, his lip would quiver, and his eye would flash like a young tiger in its spring. Soon, however, the thoughts--whatever they were--which gave rise to such emotions, passed away; and, hanging down his head, sadder sensations seemed, in turn, to occupy his breast. A bright drop rose and glittered in his eye, and the quick blood mounted hastily into his cheek, as if ashamed of the passion he had shown, though he knew not that any one was near to witness its expression.

Whether the passing emotions by which he had been agitated were marked or not, his progress from the top of the hill to the spot where he sat had not been unobserved; and the next moment a rustling sound, proceeding from the bushes on the opposite side of the stream, startled him from his reverie. Bounding up like a frightened fawn, he fixed his eyes upon the trees in the direction from which the noise had proceeded; but the thick foliage concealed for the time the object which alarmed him; though, by the continuance of the sound, and the waving of the boughs, it was evident that some large body was making its way towards the side of the river. The next instant the figure of a man emerged from the wood, and then that of a horse, whose bridle, cast over the stranger's arm, afforded the means of leading it forward along the narrow footpath which they had been treading. The leisurely pace at which both man and horse proceeded gave no signs of intentions actively hostile towards any one; and although those were days in which dangers were to be found in every field and in every road, yet a moment's thought seemed to have made the youth ashamed of the timid start which the stranger's approach had occasioned. Colouring highly, he sat down again upon the bank, and applied himself busily to replace his boots and stockings, without vouchsafing a look towards the other side of the stream.

"When you have done, my fair youth," said the stranger, after gazing at him for a minute from the opposite bank, "will you answer me a question?"

"If it suit me, and if I can," replied the youth, looking up into the stranger's face for the first time.

That face was not one to be seen without exciting in those who beheld it, more and more agreeable sensations than are usually called up by the blank countenances of the great mass of mankind--too often unlettered books, where mind and feeling have scarcely written a trace. The features on which the lad now gazed were strongly marked, but handsome; the broad expanse of the high, clear forehead, the open unbent brow, the bright speaking eye, and the full arching lips, conveyed at once to the untaught physiognomist which watches and reasons at the bottom of every man's heart, the idea of a candid and generous mind. There was much intelligence, too, in that countenance--intelligence without the least touch of cunning--all bright, and clear, and bold.

The stranger was about the middle height, and, apparently, had seen four or five and thirty summers: they might be less or more; for circumstances, so much more than time, stamp the trace of age upon the external form, as well as upon the heart and feelings, that it is often difficult to judge whether the wrinkles and furrows, which seem to have been the slow work of years, are not, in reality, the marks of rapid cares or withering passions. In his face were several lines which might well have borne either interpretation; but still, neither his dark brown hair, nor his thick glossy beard, offered the least evidence of time's whitening hand. His dress was a simple riding suit, the green hue of which appeared to bespeak, either for profit or amusement, a devotion to the chase. The same calling seemed denoted by a small hunting-horn, which hung by his side; and his offensive arms were no more than such sport required. He wore, however, a hat and high white plume, instead of the close unadorned bonnet generally used in the chase; and his horse, too, a deep bay barb, had less the air of a hunter than of a battle charger.

"My question is a very simple one, good youth," he said, while a slight smile curled his lip, excited by a certain degree of pettish flippancy which the boy displayed in replying to his first address:--"Did you meet a troop of reitters just now, as you came over the hill? and which way did they take?"

"I did meet a troop of Dutch vagabonds," replied the boy, boldly: "villains that foolish Frenchmen hire to cut foolish Frenchmen's throats! and as to the way they took, God 'a mercy! I watched them not."

"But from yon hill you must have seen which road they went," replied the stranger. "I am one of those foolish Frenchmen whom you mention, and an inoffensive person to boot, whose throat would have but small security under the gripe of these worthy foreigners. One of them I might deal with-- ay, two--or three, perchance; but when they ride by scores, and I alone, I see not why the green wood should not cover me, as well as many a brave boar or a stout stag. I pray thee, therefore, good youth, if thou sawest the way they took, let me know it, for courtesy's sake; and if thou sawest it not, why, fare thee well! I must take my chance."

For a moment or two the boy made no reply, but measured the stranger from head to foot with his eye; somewhat knitting his brow, as he did so, with a look of some abstraction, as if his mind were too busy with what he saw to heed the incivility of his long-protracted stare. "Yes," said he, at length, speaking apparently to himself, "yes;" and then, addressing the stranger, he demanded abruptly, "whither go you?"

"Nay, good youth! nay!" replied his companion; "these are not times--nor France the country--nor this the spot of all France--in which a man would choose to trust the first person he meets, with where he goes or what he goes for. I ask you not your road--ask me not mine. If you can answer my question, whether the band of reitters took the path to Tours, or wound under the hill towards La Fleche, do so, and I will thank you; if not, once more farewell!"--and, without putting foot in stirrup, he sprang upon his horse's back.

"Answer your question I cannot," replied the boy, with a degree of calm earnestness that seemed to speak greater interest in the stranger than he had at first evinced; "but I can do more for you," he proceeded. "Where the reitters went I did not see, for I hid myself behind the rocks till they were past; but I can show you paths where no reitters will ever come. Often have I flown my hawk across those plains," he added in an explanatory tone, as if he wished to recommend his guidance to the stranger by showing how his acquaintance with the country had been acquired;--"often have I followed my hound through these valleys, in other days long gone; and I know their every turning better than my father's house."

"In other days!" said the stranger; "why thou art now but a boy!"

"True," replied the youth; "yet I may have known other days, and happier ones--but to my purpose. What I offer you, I offer knowing what I am doing:" and he fixed Ins eyes upon the stranger's face with a meaning, but not a disrespectful, glance, and then proceeded: "Tell me whither you would go. I will conduct you thither in safety, and will not betray you, upon my honour!"

"In faith, I believe I must even trust you," replied the stranger. "There are many who, with wise saws and cautious counsels, would fain persuade me to be as prudent, and as careful of my life, as a great-grandmother of eighty years and upwards. But life, at best, is but as gold, a precious thing given to be spent. Whip me all misers, whether of their purse or of their safety, say I; and, therefore, boy, you shall be my guide, though you should give me over to all the reitters that ever the factious house of Lorraine brought to back the treason which they call piety."

"I will give you over to no reitters," replied the boy; "so be your mind at ease."

"Odds life! it is seldom otherwise than at ease," rejoined the other: "my heart is a light one, and will not be heavy now, as I ride on beside thee; though I may have caught thy tongue tripping, my fair boy. Thou art no Frenchman, or thine accent sorely belies thee."

"Now do you think me both a German and a reitter, I warrant!" replied the youth, with a playful smile, and a toss back of his dark hair. "But cannot your ear distinguish between the hoggish twang of the Teutonic gutturals, and the soft music of the Italian liquids?"

"Methinks it can," replied the stranger; "but, whether German or Italian, Switzer, or even Spaniard, thou shalt be my guide. Knowest thou the chateau of the Marquis of St. Real?"

The youth started. "Do I know it!" said he, "do I know it!" then suddenly seeming to check, in full career, some powerful feelings that were in the very act of bursting from his heart to his lips, he added, more calmly, "I know it well! I know it well! Willingly will I show you your road thither, and, perhaps, may name my guerdon by the way; but it is too far a journey for me on foot in one day."

"We will buy thee a horse, my fair boy," replied the stranger: "I must be at St. Real this night, and at Tours ere noon to-morrow; so we will buy thee a horse at the first village where we can find one."

"An ass will serve my turn as well as the best Barbary steed," said the youth; "and the one will be more easily found than the other; for, what between the League and the Huguenots, there are more asses in France than any other kind of beast--so now let us on our way."

Returning into the road from which he had strayed to wash his feet, the boy stepped lightly, from stone to stone, across the stream, and soon stood on the same side with the traveller. He, on his part, as if unwilling to save himself fatigue by continuing to ride while the youth walked by his side on foot, once more dismounted; and they then turned their steps up the broad way which led through the forest to the top of the hill, descanting, as they went, on the fineness of the day, the beauty of the scene, and all the ordinary topics which furnish conversation to those who have few subjects in common; but each avoiding, as if by mutual consent, any allusion to the purpose or station of his companion.

It was, as we have said, as fair and sunshiny an April day as ever woke since first the beautifying will of the Almighty robed the hills with verdure, and spread out loveliness as a garment over earth. The trees that, springing from the high broken banks on either side, canopied the road with their green boughs, were living and tuneful with all the birds of spring. There is not a cheerful feeling in the heart of man that might not there have found some sweet note to wake it into harmony. The air was balm itself--soft, yet inspiring like the breath of hope; and the dancing light and shade, that chequered the long perspective up the hill, had something in it gay and sportive, which--joined with the song of the birds, and the sparkling glee of a small fountain that, bursting from the midst of the road, rushed in a little diamond rivulet down to the stream below--addressed itself to all the purer sources of happiness in the human breast, and spoke of peace and joy. Both the journeyers, however, were grave; although the one was in the early spring of youth--that bright season of man's life where every pulse is light; and although each line in the countenance of his companion spoke that constitutional cheerfulness which is the most blessed auxiliary that this world can afford to aid man in maintaining his eternal warfare against time and circumstance.

At the top of the ascent, a wide and magnificent scene lay stretched beneath their eyes. The hill was not sufficiently high, indeed, to afford one of those map-like views, in which we see all the objects spread out over a vast extent in harsh and unshadowed distinctness, like the prospect of life and of the world which we take, when in mature age, after having passed through the illusions of youth and the passions of manhood, we gaze upon the past and the present, and see the hard, cold, naked realities of existence without a softening shade or an enlivening hue. Still the elevation was sufficient to let the eye roam wide over scenes where line after line, in sweet variety, presented a continual change of beautiful forms, softening in tint, in depth of colour, and in distinctness of outline as the objects became more remote, and forming a view such as that which is offered to the eye of youth, when after having climbed over the light ascent of boyhood, the joys of existence, grouped together without its cares, are first presented to the sight, one beyond another, to the very verge of being, all lighted up by hope, and coloured by imagination.

"Run your eye," said the youth, "over that ocean of green boughs which lies waving below us, to that tree-covered mound which starts high above the rest. In a straight line beyond you catch the spire of Beaumont en Maine, at the distance of nearly four leagues; and a little farther to the right, upon a woody hill, you may see the dark towers of the chateau of St. Real."

His companion gazed on in the direction which he pointed out, and then replied, "I once knew this land well, and could have marked out in it many a fair field either for the chase or the battle; but other scenes have made me forget it. Our memory is but like a French crown-piece, since so many kings have been called, one after another, to rule this unhappy land. First, one figure is strong upon it; then it goes to the mint, and a new king's head drives out the other, and keeps its place, till something fresh is stamped upon it again; while, all the time, traces of former impression may be seen below, but indistinct and meaningless. Ay! there is Beaumont en Maine, and there the chateau of St. Real; I remember them now: but what is that massive building, with that large square keep, still farther to the right?"

The youth fixed his eyes upon it, and remained silent for more than a minute: he then replied, abruptly, "That chateau belongs to the Count d'Aubin. Let us on!"

CHAPTER II

Memory is like moonlight, the reflection of brighter rays emanating originally from an object no longer seen; and all our retrospects towards the past times, as well as our individual remembrances, partake in some degree of the softening splendour which covers small faults and imperfections by grand masses of shade, and brings out picturesque beauties and points of interest with apparently brighter effulgence than even when the full sunshine of the present beaming upon them, suffers at the same time the eye to be distracted, and the mind otherwise engaged by a thousand minor particulars. Nothing gains more, perhaps, from the impossibility of close inspection than the manners, the customs, and the things of the past; and, in some instances, even Nature herself, and Time, that enemy of man's works, in general so remorseless, seem to take a fanciful pleasure in assisting the illusion. That which was in itself harsh and rude in form, acquires as it decays, a picturesque beauty which it never knew in its prime; and the rough hold of the feudal robber, which afforded but small pleasure to behold, and little convenience to its inmates, is now seen and painted with delight, fringed with wild flowers scattered from Nature's bountiful hand and softened with the green covering of the ivy.

The old chateau of St. Real, to which the two travellers we have just left were bending their steps, and to which, for a moment, we must now shift the scene, was one of those antique buildings, few of which have outlasted the first French revolution--buildings which, however we may love to look upon any that do remain, from the magical illusion regarding former days to which I have just alluded, were, nevertheless, much better suited to the times in which they were built, than to the more luxurious present.

Tumults, feuds, insurrections, civil wars, rendered every man's house his castle in no metaphorical sense; and thus the old chateau of St. Real, which had been originally built more than 400 years before the opening of this history, and had been repaired and improved at least a hundred times during the intervening ages of strife and bloodshed, was naturally, in almost all respects, much better calculated for defence against assault than for comfortable habitation. The woody chase, which swept for many a mile round the base of the little hill on which it stood, was cleared and opened in the immediate vicinity of the chateau; and the various avenues were defended with all the accuracy to which the art of war had arrived in those times. The very garden was a regular fortification; the chateau itself a citadel. From the reign of Louis VI., in which its walls had first been raised from the ground, to the reign of Henry III. with which this tale begins, although repairs and improvements had, as we have said, been often made, they were solely military, and nothing had in the slightest degree been permitted which could change the antique aspect of the place. Indeed, its proprietors, the Marquises of St. Real, springing from the most ancient race of French nobility, clung to the antiquity of their dwelling as if it formed a part and parcel of the antiquity of their family. Their habits, their manners, their characters, smacked all of the ancient day; and it was ever with pain that they suffered any of their old customs to be wrenched from them by the innovating hand of improvement.

At their gate, even in the times I speak of, hung, for the purpose of summoning the warder to the wicket, the last horn which, perhaps, was ever used on such occasions in France; and, though the mouthpiece had been renewed, and the chain frequently mended, the horn itself was averred to be the very same which had been hung there in the days of Philip Augustus. But if the lords of St. Real still maintained some tinge of the rudeness of their ancestors, it must by no means be forgotten that it was to the nobler and brighter qualities of former times that they adhered most strongly. They were a proud but a chivalrous race, bold, hospitable, courteous, generous, unswerving in faith and in honour. Their talents, which were by no means inconsiderable, had been principally displayed in the field; and some of the sneerers of the court had not scrupled to call them the *Simple St. Reals*: but, notwithstanding a degree of simplicity, which certainly did characterise them, they had ever been distinguished, from father to son, by that discriminating discernment of right and wrong which is worth all the wit in the world. Never had their word been pledged without being redeemed; never had their voice sanctioned a bad action; never had their sword supported an evil cause.

The present Marquis of St. Real, who was an old man who had borne arms under Francis I. had during the whole of the wars of the League remained obstinately neuter. He had declared, at the commencement of these unhappy wars, that he would not unsheathe his sword against his lawful sovereign, though friendly to the King of Navarre, and allied remotely to the house of Bourbon; but at the same time he added, that nothing should ever induce him to join in an unjust and cruel war against a portion of his countrymen, who were but defending one of the dearest and most unalienable rights of mankind--their religious liberty.

Too powerful for either party to entertain the hope of forcing him from his neutrality by any violent measures, both the League and the Huguenots spared no means of conciliation, which either wisdom or cunning could suggest, to win him to their side; for vast domains, in which the feudal customs of former times remained in full force, rendered his alliance a thing to be coveted even by the strongest. He remained unmoved, however; and neither a strong personal friendship which existed between himself and the Duke of Mayenne, nor the instigations and artifices of his confessor, could induce him to join the League, any more than gratitude to the King of Navarre for several personal favours, horror at the crimes of Saint Bartholomew, or even a strong belief that the Protestants were right in their warfare, if not in their religion, could bring him over to the party of the Huguenots.

To avoid wearisome solicitation, he had entirely abandoned the capital, and remained in the solitude of his paternal estates, wholly occupied in the education of his son, into whose mind, as principles, he endeavoured to instil, not knowledge of the world, or of courts, but all the firm and noble feelings of his own heart. He succeeded; the Chevalier de St. Real grew up to manhood everything that his father's fondest hopes could have anticipated: bold as a lion, skilled in all warlike exercises, and full of every sentiment that does honour to human nature. But yet, in many things, he was as simple as a child. Cut off from the general society of Paris, he wanted entirely that knowledge of the world which was never more necessary than in the days in which he lived.

On one occasion, indeed, when the infamous Catherine de Medicis, and her beautiful but licentious train, had visited the chateau of St. Real for the purpose of winning its lord to the party she espoused, more than one of her fair syrens had striven, by various arts, to initiate the handsome Chevalier of St. Real into the libertine mysteries of that debauched court; but he met them uniformly with that perfect simplicity which, though joined with much natural good sense, raised many a secret laugh at his expense, and yet guarded him effectually from their worst artifices.

The general current of his time flowed on in the various amusements of the country, as they existed in that age. The chase of the boar, the stag, and the wolf afforded active exercise for the body, while the large and ancient library of the chateau--a rare treasure in those days--yielded occupation to a quick imagination and an energetic mind, in poring over many a printed tome and many an illuminated manuscript. Besides these employments, however, both the old lord of St. Real and his son felt a keen interest in pursuits seldom much attended to by the feudal nobility of France. They not only lived in the country, and amongst their peasantry, but they also loved the country and their peasantry, and delighted in watching and superintending all those agricultural operations which formed the daily relaxation of many of the noblest Romans, but which were, in general, looked upon with indifference, if not contempt, by the new class of chieftains who sprung from the *élite* of their barbarous conquerors. The lords of St. Real delighted in all: they held to the full the opinion of the old orator, when he exclaimed--"Nec vero segetibus solum et pratis, et vineis, et arbustis res rusticæ lætæ sunt, sed etiam hortis et pomariis, tum pecudum pastu, apium examinibus, florum omnium varietate;" and, though they followed not precisely all the directions of Liebaut in his *Maison Rustique,* the garden that lay within the flanking walls of the castle, the orchard which extended from the outer balium to the barbacan, and the trellised avenue of vines which ran to what was called the lady's bower, showed taste as well as skill in those who had designed and executed them.

During several years previous to the precise epoch at which we have commenced our tale, the old lord of St. Real had seldom, if ever, slept a night without the walls of his own dwelling. His son, however, when either business, or that innocent love of a temporary change, which every man may well feel without meriting the charge of being versatile, afforded a motive for his absence from home, would often spend a day or two in the great city of Tours, or at the castles of the neighbouring nobility. Some communication with the external world was thus kept up; but the chief companionship of the Chevalier of St. Real was with his cousin-german the Count d'Aubin, who, though attached to the court, and very different in mind and character from his relations, often retired for a while from the gay and busy scenes in which he mingled, to enjoy the comparative solitude of his estates in Maine, and the calm refreshing society of his more simple cousin.

The character of Philip Count d'Aubin was one that we meet with every day. Endowed with passions and talents naturally strong, his passions had been pampered, and his talents misdirected, by an over-indulgent parent. A doubt had been at one time entertained of the legitimacy of his birth, but no one had contested his title; and the early possession of wealth, power, and influence, with the unrestrained disposal of himself and of the property which the death of his father left in his hands, had certainly tended in no degree to curb his desires or extinguish his vanity. His heart had, perhaps, been originally too feeling; but the constant indulgence of every wish and fancy had dulled the former brightness of its sensations; and it was only at times that the yet unextinguished fight shone clearly up to guide him through a maze of errors. His very talents and shrewdness often led him onwards in the wrong: for, possessing from education few fixed principles of action, the energies of his mind were generally turned to the gratification of his passions; and it was only when original rectitude of heart suggested what was good, that reason too joined her voice to urge him on the road of virtue. He was, in fact, the creature of impulse; but, as he had unfailing gaiety, and wit at will, and as a sudden turn of feeling would often lead him to some noble or brilliant action, a sort of false, but dazzling, lustre hung about his whole conduct in the eyes of the world: his powers were overrated, and his weaknesses forgotten. He was the idol and admiration of the young and unthinking, and even the old and grave often suffered the blaze of some few splendid traits to veil the many spots and blemishes of his character.

On the night following that particular day at which it has appeared necessary to commence this history, the two cousins spent some time together pacing up and down the great hall of the chateau of St. Real. The Count d'Aubin had come hastily from Paris, on receiving tidings of the severe illness of his uncle; and their conversation was of a wandering and discursive nature, originating in the increasing sickness of the old Marquis, who was then, for the first time during many days, enjoying a few hours' repose.

"Faith, Huon, thy father is ill," said D'Aubin, as they descended the stairs to the hall, "far worse than I deemed him till I saw him."

"He has, indeed, much fallen in strength during the day," replied the Chevalier de St. Real; "yet I hope that this slumber which has come upon him may bring a change for the better."

The Count shook his head. "I know not," said he; "but yet I doubt it. Your father, Huon, is an old man, and old men must die!" His cousin bent his eyes upon the ground, and slightly contracted his brow; but he did not slacken his pace, and the Count d'Aubin went on: "Yes, Huon, however we may love them, however we may wish that they could live to govern their own vassals and enjoy their own wealth, till patriarchal longevity were no longer a wonder; and I know," he added, pausing, and laying his hand upon his cousin's arm--"and I know, that if the best blood in your noble heart could add to your father's life, you would pour it forth like useless water;--still, whatever ties may bind them to us, still they are, as the old men amongst the ancients did not scruple to call themselves, *pabulum Acherontis*--but food for the tomb: and none can tell when death may claim his own. I say this because I would have you prepared in mind for an event which I see approaching; and I would also have you prepared to take some quick and immediate part in the great struggle which every day is bringing towards its climax in this land. Your father's neutrality has lasted long enough-- nay, too long; for it is surely a shame that you, as brave a youth as ever drew a sword, should have lived to five-and-twenty years without ever having led his followers to any nobler strife than the extermination of those miserable *Gaultiers* who came to ravage our fair plains. True, they were ten times your number--true that you defeated them like a very Orlando; but that is only another reason why your valour and your skill should not lie rusting in inactivity. Should your father die, give sorrow its due; then call your vassals to your standard, and boldly take one part or another. Faith, I care not which it be--Harry of Navarre and his Huguenots, Harry of France and his chevaliers, or Mayenne's brave Duke and the factious League: but for Heaven's sake, Huon, should fate make you Marquis of St. Real, cast off this idle, sluggardly neutrality."

Huon de St. Real had listened attentively to his cousin, though every now and then the flash of some painful emotion broke across his countenance, as if what he heard contained in each word something bitter and ungrateful to all his feelings. "Philip! Philip!" said he, pausing in his quick progress through the hall, as soon as the other had ceased speaking, "I know that you wish me well, and that all which you say proceeds from that wish; but let us drop this subject entirely. My father is ill--I feel too bitterly that he is in danger; but the bare thought of what I would do with his vassals, in case of his death, has something in it revolting to every feeling of my heart. Let us change the topic. Whatever misfortune Heaven may send me, I will endeavour to bear like a man, and whenever I am called to act, I will endeavour to act rightly. When that time comes, I will most willingly seek your advice; but I trust it will be long, very, very long, before I shall need the counsel of any other than of him who has heretofore guided and directed me."

The lip of the Count d'Aubin slightly curled at this reply; and, glancing his eye over the tall, graceful form of his cousin, while he compared the simple mind and habits of St. Real, with his own worldly wisdom, and wild erratic course, he mentally termed him an overgrown baby. Nevertheless, although he was often thus tempted to a passing scoff or an ill-concealed sneer, yet there was a sort of innate dignity in the very simplicity of the Chevalier of St. Real, which had its weight even with his world-read cousin; and, whenever temporary disappointment, or disgust, or satiety weaned D'Aubin awhile from the loose society in which he mingled, gave time for quiet thought, and re-awakened better feelings, leading him to seek, in the advice of any one, support against the treacherous warfare of his own passions, it was to none of his gay companions of the capital, nor to monk, nor priest, nor confessor, that he would apply for counsel; but rather to his simple, frank-hearted, unsophisticated cousin, St. Real.

"Well, well," said he, "let us change our theme;" and then, after taking two or three more turns in the hall, he went on; though there was mingled in his manner a certain natural hesitation with an affected frankness, which might have shown to any very close observer of human nature that the Count d'Aubin was touching upon matter in regard to which, desire was in opposition to some better principle, and that he feared to hear even the opinion which he courted. "I spoke but now," he continued, "of Mayenne and the League; and you will think it strange when I tell you, that I--I, who have ever been as staunch a royalist as Epernon, or Longueville--would now give a chateau and a pint of wine, as the vulgar have it, to change my party and go over to the League, did not honour forbid it."

He spoke slowly and meditatively, fixing his eyes upon the ground, without once looking in his cousin's face; yet walking with a firm, strong step, and with somewhat of a sneer upon his lip, as if he scoffed at himself for the reprehension which--while he acknowledged wishes that he felt to be wrong--his proud spirit suffered by comparison with the calm, upright integrity of the Chevalier.

"I do not see that anything could justify such a step," replied St. Real, far more mildly than the other had expected. "However wrongly the King may have acted, however unwarrantable the manner in which he has put to death the Duke of Guise, yet--"

"Pshaw!" interrupted his cousin: "Guise was a traitor--a great, brave, noble, ambitious, unscrupulous traitor! And though the mode of his death was somewhat unceremonious, it little matters whether it was an axe or a dagger which did the work of justice: he was born for such a fate. I thought not of him; it was of Eugenie de Menancourt I thought."

"Ha!" exclaimed St. Real, with a start; "no one has injured her?"

"Injured her! No, i'faith!" replied the Count. "Why, my good cousin, by your grim look, one would deem you her promised husband, and not me. No, no; had she been injured, her injury had been well avenged by this time. However, she is in the hands of the League. Her father, as you know, was wounded on the day of the barricades, and died soon after the flight of the court. His daughter, of course, would not leave him while he lived, and, at his death, the Duchess of Montpensier would fain have had her at the Hotel de Guise; and, though Eugenie wisely stayed in her father's own house, they would not suffer her to quit Paris, where she still remains--treated with all honour and courtesy, mark you, but still a sort of honourable prisoner."

His cousin paused in thought for a moment, and then replied, "But, surely, if you were to demand her from the Duke of Mayenne, informing him of the engagement between her father and yourself, she would be given up to you at once."

"I have done more," replied the Count; "whenever I heard of her situation, I required, of course, that she should be placed in the hands of the King, as her lawful guardian, till such time as her marriage with myself could be celebrated. After many an evasion and delay, the Duke replied to my application, that the throne of France was vacant, by a decree both of the Sorbonne and the Parliament of Paris; that, by the same authority, he himself was lieutenant-general of the kingdom till such time as a meeting of the three estates should regulate the government; and that, therefore, none other was for the time the lawful guardian of Eugenie de Menancourt. In the same letter he informed me, that the recent death of the young lady's father would prevent her from thinking of marriage for some time."

D'Aubin paused, shutting his teeth and drawing in his lips, evidently unwilling to show the full mortification and anger which these remembrances awoke; and, yet apparently leaving his tale unfinished.

"In regard to the latter part of the Duke of Mayenne's reply, it seems to me reasonable enough," answered the Chevalier de St. Real; "the loss of such a father is not to be forgotten in a day."

"Tut, man!" exclaimed his cousin, impatiently. "Wilt thou never understand a little of this world's ways? Huon, Huon! shut up in these old walls, thou art as ignorant of the present day as if thou hadst been born in the times of the first crusade. Nothing modern dare blow that rusty horn at thy gate--far less walk into the hall. Know, then, my most excellent, simple cousin, that since the ninth century a great quarrel has taken place between words and realities, and that they have separated, never to meet again; that now-a-days promises are of air, honour is a name, virtue a bubble, religion a mask; and while falsehood, hypocrisy, and folly walk about in comely dresses, and make bows to each other in every street, truth lies snug in the bottom of her well, secure in the narrowness of her dwelling, and the depth that covers her. The first thing that every one thinks of now is his own interest; and, sure that if he secures that, the world will give him credit for all high qualities, he works straight for that one object. Interest, interest, interest, is his waking thought and his sleeping dream. Mark me, Huon! Mademoiselle de Menancourt is an heiress--one of the most wealthy in France; young, beautiful!--you know how beautiful, Huon; for, by my faith, I could once have been almost jealous of you."

"Of me!" exclaimed the other, stopping suddenly, and looking full in his cousin's face, while a flush of surprise and indignation, all unmixed with shame, spread scarlet over his cheek and brow. "Of me! Philip, you do me great injustice! By my honour, if my hand or my word could advance your marriage by a single day, you would find both ready for your service. Tell me, when did I ever give you a moment's cause for jealousy?"

"Nay, nay! you are too quick!" replied the Count; "I said not that I was jealous of you; I merely said I could have been so, had I not known you better. I speak of the time when our late excellent and easy-virtued queen was here with her ladies. Many a bright eye was bent upon you, and many a sweet lip was ready to direct you through the tangled but flowery ways of love, without seeking to plunge you into the mire of matrimony; yet, in all our rides, there were you, always at Eugenie's bridle rein."

"Because she was the only pure thing present," interrupted St. Real, quickly; "and because, Philip--if you will press me--I thought that she might feel hurt that her promised husband should make love before her face to one of an infamous queen's infamous followers. Ay, even so, Philip! Frown not on me, good cousin; for such was the only interpretation that even I, who am not apt to see actions in their worst light, could place upon your conduct to Beatrice of Ferrara."

"Beatrice of Ferrara," replied the Count d'Aubin, with a degree of vehemence which might have made some of his loose companions smile to hear him use it in the vindication of any woman's virtue under the sun--"Beatrice of Ferrara was no infamous follower of an infamous queen; she was, I believe from my soul, as pure as snow, notwithstanding all the impurity that surrounded her. I knew not that I had shown her any such marked attention as you tell me; but let all that pass," he added, musing, "let all that pass: what were we speaking of before? O! I remember. To return, then, to my tale: Eugenie de Menancourt is an heiress, with a dowry of beauty and sweetness far beyond even her wealth; and wily Mayenne well knows that her hand is a prize for the first man in France. Now, think you, my good Huon," he continued, growing more and more eager, while the bright flashing of his eye told that he was moved by some stronger passion than the mere scorn with which he attempted to clothe his lips--"now, think you, my good Huon, though he talks so loudly about religion and zeal, and the state's welfare, that Mayenne has one other wish, one other object, than to vault into an empty throne, or play *maire du palais* to the old idiotic Cardinal de Bourbon! Ambition--'tis all-snatching ambition, Huon! that is the idol he worships; and whoever serves him in his schemes shall have the hand of Eugenie de Menancourt, notwithstanding her father's plighted word to me."

"But Eugenie will never consent," replied St. Real, calmly. "Doubt it not, Philip! I have known her from her childhood, as well as you; and I have often remarked, that, notwithstanding her gaiety--notwithstanding her seeming lightness of feeling, there was, when she knew herself to be right, an unchangeable determination in all her resolves, even in her childhood, that nothing could shake."

"Fie! you know nothing of human nature," replied D'Aubin, with a scoff; "or rather, I should say, of woman's nature. They are light--light, Huon, as a dry leaf borne about upon the breath of every wind that blows. The best of them, believe me, is firm in nothing but her caprices. Mark me, Huon!" he added, laying his hand upon his cousin's arm, and speaking with bitter emphasis, "within these ten days I have seen Mademoiselle de Menancourt. I demanded a pass from Mayenne; he granted it without a scruple, and free speech also of his fair ward, as he called her. He was sure of the impression he had made, and, therefore, kept up all fair seeming. I saw Eugenie; and she calmly and coldly refused to ratify the promise that her father had made me. Do you hear? She refused me! She rejected me! She told me she did not, she could not love me!" And, giving way to a violent burst of passion, totally opposed to the calm and contemptuous tone in which he had before been speaking, he dashed his glove angrily down upon the floor, as if it were the object that offended him.

His cousin looked down in silence. He imagined, and not without probability, that Mademoiselle de Menancourt must have seen the licentious manner in which D'Aubin had trifled with the ladies of Catherine's libertine court, and that she had resented it accordingly. But, however culpably he might deem that his cousin had acted, he would not have pressed it on him then for the world; and, besides, there were sensations in his own bosom, at that moment, which forcibly called upon his attention, and both surprised and alarmed him.

It is a strange thing the human heart; and, amidst the multitude of its inconsistencies and its weaknesses, there is none stranger than that principle which, as a French wit has remarked, is always ready to point out to us, in the sorrows and misfortunes of our friends, some topic of consolation for ourselves. As a general rule the sneer is unjust, though with many it holds good always, and with most at times, even with the highest and the most conscientious. Good, noble, generous, with chivalrous ideas of honour and virtue, the Chevalier of St. Real would sooner have laid his head upon the block than entertained a thought of doing anything to his cousin's detriment; and yet there was a degree of vague, undefined satisfaction in his feelings, when he heard the declaration made by Eugenie de Menancourt, that she did not and could not love the Count d'Aubin--satisfaction of which he himself felt ashamed. "Good God! was it for him," he thought, "to rejoice in his cousin's mortification? What matter for pleasure ought he to find in the pain of a person he loved? None, surely none. What is it, then, I feel?" he asked himself; "is it the triumph of having foreseen that Eugenie de Menancourt would resent the slight put upon her? Oh, no! Such a vanity can surely afford no gratification to any reasonable being." Such was the interrogation which St. Real rapidly addressed to his heart; but an instinctive apprehension of finding unknown and dangerous matter at the bottom of his own sensations prevented him from going deep enough.

Whatever it was that he felt, the blood rushed into his face as if he were committing some evil action; and he remained silent. The keen, suspicious eyes of the Count d'Aubin fixed upon him, in surprise at emotions that he did not comprehend; but he said nothing; and just as St. Real was struggling to speak, the whole place echoed with two such blasts upon the old horn at the gate, as had not rung amongst those halls for many a year.

"By heavens! that must be some drunken huntsman, St. Real," exclaimed the Count, "blowing the horn at the gate, as if he was sounding for his dogs."

"No, no! it is the ill-favoured dwarf you gave me," replied his cousin. "He heeds no decencies, and, I verily believe, would blow a flourish if we were all dying. Many a time have I thought to fell him with my gauntlet for his insolence; but he is so small, that it would seem a cruelty to crush such an insect."

"Nay, nay; crush him not, I beseech thee," replied the Count d'Aubin. "Remember, Huon, it was agreed between us, that when he seeks to quit thee, or thou growest tired of him, he comes to me again."

"I believe, in truth, the creature loves me," answered St. Real; "and, were it not for his stupid insolence, I might love him too; for there are traits of good about him which would redeem many a dark spot."

The Count's lip curled; but he replied, "Call it not *stupid* insolence, good cousin--call it, rather, clever insolence, for, on my soul, he was occasionally too clever for such a service as mine, and such a place as Paris. I know not well how it happened, but many a deep secret of my bosom seemed somewhat too familiar to his high ugliness; and so I gave him to you, who had no secrets to trust or to conceal."

"Thank God for that, at least!" answered St. Real, "for they are ever a heavy burden. But here comes the incubus:" and as he spoke, the low door of the hall was opened by a personage of whom it may be necessary to speak more fully.

CHAPTER III

The personage concerning whom the last sentences were spoken, and who now entered the hall, was not more than three feet six inches in height,[1] but perfectly well formed in every respect, except that the head, as is very usual with persons of his unfortunate description, was somewhat too large for the size of the body it surmounted. His former lord had spoken of his ugliness; but although his face was certainly by no means handsome, yet there was nothing in it approaching deformity. Between "the human face divine" and that of the monkey, our great original, there are a thousand shades and varieties of feature; and the countenance of the dwarf, it must be admitted, was at the very far extreme of the chain, and at the end nearest the ape. A pair of sparkling black eyes, and two rows of very fine white teeth, however, rendered the rest of his features less disagreeable, but by no means diminished his resemblance to the animal. Whether from a consciousness of this likeness, and a desire to hide it as far as possible, or from a sort of conceited foppery not uncommon, the dress of this small man was as scrupulously elegant as the taste of that day would admit. His beard and mustachios, which were soft and silky, were most accurately trimmed. His hair, thrust back from his face, exposed his large and somewhat protuberant forehead; while his pourpoint, composed of deep blue cloth, was slashed with primrose silk, to favour a somewhat dingy complexion. Sword and dagger he wore at his girdle; and all the chronicles of those days bear witness that he well knew how to use--and to use fearlessly--the weapons intrusted to his small hands.

His whole appearance produced a strange and not pleasant effect upon those who saw him. The want of harmony between his size and his form was constantly forcing itself upon attention. Could one have magnified him, he would have appeared a very well-dressed cavalier, according to the fashions of the times; and, had there not been something in his whole form and air that bespoke manhood, one might have looked upon him as a smart child; but, as it was, one felt inclined to smile as soon as the eye fell upon him, though there was in his demeanour but few of those absurdities by which many of his class of beings render themselves ridiculous. He had neither strut nor swagger, smirk nor simper; and the only thing which in any degree tended to render his aspect peculiar, besides the fact of his diminutive form, was a certain cynical smile which ever hung more or less about his lips, as if, from a consciousness of superior talent or superior cunning, he scorned the race which, for their superior corporeal qualities, he hated; or rather, perhaps, as if he were ever prepared to encounter their contempt for his inferior size by contempt for their inferior acuteness.

He entered the hall with ease, if not with grace; but, perhaps, with more of what may be termed boldness than either. To St. Real, as his actual master, he bowed low, and to the Count d'Aubin still lower, accompanying the inclinations of his head, in this instance, with a keen and significant glance, which, had the Chevalier de St. Real been of a suspicious nature, might have made him place but little confidence in an attendant of his cousin's recommending. But he himself had nothing to conceal, and, as yet, feared not that any one should see his inmost thoughts; for he was one of those few men who know no other use for words than to express their feelings.

"Why did you blow the horn so loud, Bartholo?" demanded St. Real, "when you well knew that my father lies so ill?"

"I did it, noble sir," replied the dwarf, "lest the cooks, and the pages, and the concierge at the door should lose a jest and fit of laughter--rare things in the castle of St. Real. I knew full well that some one would cry out, 'Hear what a great sound can be made by a little body!' and it would be unjust to disappoint the poor fools in the offices, for fear of disturbing the rich gallants in the hall. But, by my faith, I had another reason, too, which is worth looking to. There was a traveller came with me, and an ass, and an ass's burden."

"Was it the surgeon for whom I sent you?" asked St. Real, eagerly; "the new surgeon from Tours?"

"Seeing that my eyes and the surgeon are innocent of all intercourse," replied the other, "I cannot tell you, noble sir, whether it be he or not. The man was not in his dwelling when I reached it, so I left my message, and rode further; and, as I came back, what should I see, half a mile hence, but the white feather of this man's hat waving in the dark night, and not knowing its way to the chateau of St. Real. I asked him what party he was of, whither he was going, and if he had passport or safe conduct. He answered, short enough, that he belonged to his own party, had no passport but his sword and his right hand, and was coming hither. So, whether he were surgeon or not, let those judge that are wise! I asked no further, but brought him hither, and left him in the green arras room, as he seemed no way dangerous, and wished to see either the Marquis or the Marquis's son in private."

"It is either a reitter seeking service, or a quack-salver seeking the sick," cried the Count d'Aubin. "Go to him--go to him quick, Huon! He will whip you the gold lace off the hangings, either for his pocket or his crucible. So go to him, and leave me the dwarf to jest withal."

With the quick and impatient step which anxiety produces in the young and active, St. Real bent his steps towards the chamber to which he had been directed by the dwarf, hoping, notwithstanding the description which had been given of the person who awaited him, that he might prove the surgeon who had been sent for in aid of the ordinary medical assistance attending upon his father.

The room which he now entered was a small one, hung with arras of a dark-green hue, that served to absorb the greater part of the light afforded by a single lamp. The stranger had cast himself into a large chair at the farther end of the chamber, and, in the half obscurity, his person and features were but faintly seen; but nearer, and in the full light, sat the youth whom we first found washing his feet in one of the neighbouring streams. He seemed fatigued with journeying, and leaning listlessly against a small table under the lamp, suffered his head to rest upon his hand, showing a profusion of jetty curls falling thick round his brow, while the cap and feather which he had worn without was now thrown upon the ground beside him. The person whom he had accompanied, however, retained his hat and high white plume, and made no movement to rise as St. Real entered.

The eyes of the young noble first rested upon the boy; but immediately turning towards the elder of his two visitors, he advanced towards him, without noticing the apparent incivility of his demeanour. When he had taken two steps forward, however, St. Real paused; and then, with an exclamation of surprise, was again advancing, when the stranger rose, saying, "Ha, Monsieur St. Real, I did not know you at first. Ventre Saint Gris! I had forgot that ten years makes a boy a man."

"If I am not mistaken, I see his Majesty of Navarre," said the Chevalier; "and only grieve that my father is not capable of bidding him welcome, with all the goodwill that we entertain towards himself and his royal house."

"Henry of Navarre, indeed!" replied the monarch; "as poor a King as lives, St. Real, but one who grieves sincerely at your father's illness. I trust that it is not dangerous, however, and that I shall yet see him ere I depart; for to that purpose I have been forced to steal me a path amidst bands through which I should have found it hard to cut me a way, and to do that singly which I dared not attempt with many a stout soldier at my back."

"My father sleeps, my lord," replied St. Real; "'tis the first sleep that he has known for many a day, and I would fain----"

"Wake him not--wake him not for me!" interrupted the King. "To-morrow I must hie me back to Tours; but in the meanwhile I can well wait his waking, and will crave some refreshment for myself and this good youth, who has guided me hither, and who seems less able to bear hunger and long riding than Henry of Navarre."

"I will order such poor fare as our house affords to be placed before your Majesty directly," replied St. Real, "though I fear me much that the two surgeons and a priest, together with a *gentilhomme serjent* from La Fleche, are even now busy in despatching all that is already prepared."

"Let us join them! let us join them by all means!" cried the King; "by my faith I would never choose to dine where better cheer is usually to be found, than in company with surgeons and with priests. The first are too much accustomed to the care of other people's bodies to neglect their own; and the others, though they limit their special vocation to the preparation of souls for the other world, are not without care for the preservation of the corporeal part in this. But our horses, St. Real--they stand in the court-yard: that is to say, my horse, and this good youth's more humble charger in the shape of an ass."

St. Real turned his eyes upon the youth while the King spoke; and after having replied that he would give instant orders for Henry's equipage of all kinds to be attended to, added, still looking at the boy, "Your Majesty's page, I suppose?"

"If so, but the page of a day," replied the King; "but, nevertheless, though of so short an acquaintance, I can say that he seems as good a boy as ever lived, has guided me here through many dangers, with more wit and more courage too than most would have shown, and is by far too wise to prefer the service of a poor king to that of a rich lord. In short, St. Real, it seems that he was coming here when I met with him; and as his sole guerdon for the pains he has taken, he required me to advocate his cause with your father, to have him received as a page in your household."

"My father," said St. Real, in reply, "has a mortal aversion to pages, ever since the Queen was here with more than half a score, and will only suffer two in his household--his own stirrup page, and mine, a dwarf given me by my cousin Philip."

"Nay, nay, you must not refuse my first request, St. Real," said the King; "for I have many another to make ere I have done, and if I halt at the first step, I shall never be able to walk through the rest of the list."

"Oh! I never dreamed of refusing your Majesty so trifling a thing," replied the other; "but we must give him some other name than page. What will you be, my boy? You are too young and too gay-looking for a valet in such a dull house as this."

"And too noble," added the youth, "or too proud, if you will. I seek not, sir, to take wages of any man; but I seek to pass a time in some house where the hearts are as noble as the blood they contain, where old feelings are not forgot in new follies; and I would fain that that house were the chateau of St. Real."

"You speak well, good youth, and more like a man than a boy; but somewhat too haughtily too," replied St. Real.

"I will speak more humbly when I am your follower," answered the youth, colouring a good deal; "to those who would raise me up, I can be as humble as the dust, and to those who would cast me down, as proud as a diamond. I sought to be your father's page, my lord," he added, in a softer tone; "because I heard much of him, and because all that I did hear showed him as a man blending so equally in his nature goodness and nobility, that love and reverence must be his followers wherever he bend his steps."

Something very like a tear rose in St. Real's fine clear eye, and the youth proceeded. "I am grieved that aught should have grieved you, sir, on his account; but still let me beseech you to take me into his service. You know not," he added, eagerly, "how kindly I can tend those I love; how I can amuse the weary hours of sickness, and while away the moments of pain. I can read him stories from ancient lore, and from many a language that few pages know. I can tell him tales of other lands, and describe places, and things, and nations that he has never seen. I can sing to him sweet songs in tongues that are all music, and play to him on the lute as none in this land can play."

"Enough! enough!" cried Henry; "by my life, St. Real, if you do not conclude your bargain with the boy quickly, I will step in and try to outbid you in your offers; for if he but perform his undertaking with you as well as he has done with me, you will have a page such as never was since this world began."

"He was ours, my lord, from the first moment that your Majesty expressed a wish that he should be so," replied St. Real. "There is my hand, good youth, and it shall ever give you aid and protection at your need. But tell me, what is your name? for although, as in the old times, we let our guests come and go in the chateau without question; yet, of course, I must know what I am to call *you*."

"Leonard," answered the youth; "Leonardo, in my own land; but here in France, men call me Leonard de Monte."

"I thought I heard a slight Italian accent on your lips," said St. Real; "but tell me, have I not seen you as one of the pages of Queen Catherine's court?--a court," he added, almost regretting that he had yielded to the King's request, "a court, not the best school for----" But there again he paused, unwilling to hurt the feelings of any one, and seeing a flush come over the boy's face, as if he already anticipated the bitter censure that court so well deserved. The youth's answer made him glad that he had paused.

"I know what are in your thoughts, sir," he replied; "but I beseech you speak no evil of a mistress who is now dead, and who was ever kind to me. Let her faults lie in the grave where she lies, and let men forget them as soon as they forget virtues. As for myself, I may have faults too; but they have never been those of the persons amongst whom I mingled; I have neither learned to lie, nor to flatter, nor to cheat, nor to run evil messages, nor give sweet hints. If, then, I have lived amidst corruption and come out pure----"

"You are gold tried in the fire," rejoined St. Real, laying his hand upon his shoulder; "and I will trust you, my good youth, as much convinced by the tenderness of your speech towards her who is no more, as by your defence of yourself----. But this matter has kept your Majesty too long," he added, "and by your permission I will now conduct you to the lesser hall, where these four persons are at supper; though I cannot but think that you had better suffer me to order you refreshments here."

"Nay, nay, I will sup with chirurgeons by all means," replied Henry, laughing, "and we will forget that there is such a thing as a king, if you please, St. Real; for I would not have it blazed abroad that I am wandering about without an escort, or I might soon find myself in the castle of Amboise. Call me Maitre Jacques, if you please, for the present time, and let us make haste; for if I am to gauge the appetite of those worthy doctors by my own, they will have devoured the supper ere we reach the hall."

"Permit me, then, to show the way," replied St. Real; "seek out my dwarf, Bartholo, good youth," he added, turning to the page, "and bid him find you lodging and refreshment, as he values my favour. But I will see more to your comfort myself shortly; for the villain is sometimes insolent, and may be spiteful too, like most of his race, though I never have marked it."

The youth bowed his head without other reply, and St. Real proceeded to conduct Henry of Navarre, afterwards so well known as the frank and gallant "Henri Quatre," along the many long and dimly lighted passages of the chateau of St. Real, towards a small hall in one of the farthest parts of the building.

"Maitre Jacques! remember I am Maitre Jacques!" said Henry, as the young noble laid his hand upon the lock; "and you must not only make your words call me so, but your demeanour also, St. Real."

"Fear not! fear not!" answered St. Real, in a low tone; "I will be as disrespectful as you can desire, sire."

Thus saying, he opened the door, exposing to view the interior of what was called the little hall, which presented a scene whereon we may dwell for a single instant; for, though the picture which it displayed of the callous indifference of human nature to the griefs and sufferings of others, is not an agreeable one, it was not new enough even then to excite wonder, and is not old enough now to be omitted. The master of the house was dying, and his family full of sorrow at the approaching loss of one who had been a father to all who surrounded him; but there, in the little hall, was collected, in the persons of the surgeons, the priest, and the lawyer, attendant upon the dying man, as merry a party as it had ever contained. The hall, though it was called little, was only so comparatively; for its size was sufficient to make the table at which the feasters sat look like a speck in the midst. Nevertheless, it was well lighted; and St. Real and his royal companion, as they entered, could plainly see the man of law holding up a brimming Venice glass of rich wine to one of his two shrewd eyes, while the hall was echoing to some potent jest that he had just cast forth amongst his companions. Even the carver at the buffet, and the serving man who was filling up the wine for the rest, were shaking their well-covered sides at the joke; and the priest, though repressing as far as possible the outward signs of merriment, was palating the *bon mot* with a sly smile, and had perhaps a covert intention of using it himself secondhand, whenever he could find occasion. For a minute or two the party at the table did not perceive the entrance of any other persons, or concluded that those who did enter were servants; and their conversation went on in the same light tone which had evidently predominated up to that moment.

As soon, however, as St. Real and his guest appeared, matters assumed a different aspect; and solemn ceremony and respect took the place of merriment. Seats were soon placed; and Henry, while engaged in satisfying the hunger that a long day's journey had occasioned, failed not by some gay and sportive observations to bring back a degree of cheerfulness: but the natural frank liveliness of the King's heart was controlled, or rather oppressed, by many an anxious thought for himself, and by feelings of kindly and sincere sympathy with the young noble who sat beside him. St. Real, on his part, did not affect to feel aught but deep anxiety; and, after their entrance, the merriment of the party in the hall was very much sobered down from its previous elevated tone, giving way, indeed, in the breasts of the lawyer and the surgeons, to many a shrewd conjecture in regard to the profession and object of their new comrade Maitre Jacques.

In the meantime, the page stood where St. Real and the King had left him, supporting himself against the table in an attitude of much grace, but one which spoke deep and somewhat melancholy thought. His head leaned upon his bosom, his hand fell listlessly by his side, his eyes strained with the deep and intense gaze of anxious meditation upon one unmeaning spot of the marble floor; and thus, without the slightest motion, he continued so long in the same position, that he might have been taken for some fanciful statue tricked out in the gay dress of that time, had not every now and then a deep sigh broke from his bosom, and evinced the conscious presence of life and all its ills.

Near a quarter of an hour elapsed without his taking the slightest notice of the lapse of time. The steps of his new master and the prince had long ceased to sound through the passages, other noises had made themselves heard and died away again; but the youth remained apparently unconscious of everything but some peculiar and absorbing facts in his own situation. His reverie was, however, at length disturbed, but apparently not unexpectedly, though the stealthy step and silent motions with which the dwarf Bartholo advanced into the room in which the youth stood, had brought him near before the other was aware of his presence. For a moment after their eyes had met neither spoke, though there was much meaning in the glance of each; and at length the youth made a silent motion of his hand towards the door. The sign was obeyed at once; and the dwarf, closing the door cautiously, returned with a quick step, suddenly bent one knee to the ground, and kissed the hand the boy extended towards him.

"So, Bartholo," he said, receiving this somewhat extraordinary greeting as a thing of course, "so! you see that I am here at length!"

"I do," replied the dwarf, rising; "but for what object you are come I cannot conceive."

"For many objects," answered the youth; "but one sufficient to myself, is that I am near those that I wish to be near; and can watch their actions-- perhaps see into their thoughts. If I could but make myself sure that St. Real really loves the girl! that were worth all the trouble."

"But the risk! the risk!" exclaimed the dwarf.

"The risk is nothing, if my people are faithful to me," answered the youth sharply; "and woe be to them if they are not! Why came you not as I commanded, but left me to wait and wander in the neighbourhood of Beaumont, and nearly be taken by a party of reitters, in the pay of Mayenne?"

"I could not come," answered the dwarf; "for I was sent to seek a chirurgeon from Tours for the old man, who lies at the point of death. I made what haste I could; but missed you, and could not overtake you till you had nearly reached the chateau."

"And is the old Marquis, then, so near the end of a long good life?" asked the youth. "There are some men whose deeds are so full of immortality, that we can scarce fancy even their bodies shall become food for worms. But so it must be with the best as well as with the worst of us."

"Even so!" answered the dwarf; "but as to this old man, I have not seen him with my own eyes for this many a day; but the report runs in the castle that he cannot long survive."

"His death would come most inopportunely for all my plans," replied the youth; "it would place me in strange circumstances: and yet I would dare them, for I have passed through still stranger without fear. I feel my own heart strong--ay, even in its weakness; and I will not fear. Nevertheless, see you obey my orders better. You should have sent some other on your errand, and not have left me to the mercy of a troop of reitters."

"Crying your mercy," said the dwarf, with a significant grin, "I should have thought that your late companion might have proved as dangerous."

"Dare you be insolent to me, sir?" cried the youth, fixing his full dark eye sternly on the dwarf. "But, no; I know you dare not, and you know me too well to dare. But you are wrong. Whatever may be the faults of Harry of Navarre--all reprobate heretic as he is--nevertheless he is free from every ungenerous feeling; and although I might think I saw a glance of recognition in his eyes, yet I harbour not a fear that he will betray me or make any ill use of his knowledge, even if he have remembered me."

"Are you aware, however," asked the dwarf, lowering his voice and dropping his eyes--"are you aware that the Count d'Aubin is here?"

"No, no!" cried the youth, starting. "No, no! Where--where do you mean? I know that he is in Maine, but surely not here."

"In this very house," answered the dwarf--"in the great hall, not a hundred yards from the spot where we now stand."

"Indeed!" said the other, musing. "Indeed! I knew that he was near, and that we should soon meet; but I did not think to find him here. Look at me, Bartholo! look at me well! Think you that he would recognise me? Gold, and embroidery, and courtly fashions, are all laid aside; and I might be taken for the son of a mechanic, or, at best, for the child of some inferior burgher."

"I knew you at once!" answered the page emphatically.

"Yes, yes; but that is different," replied he whom we shall take the liberty of calling by the name he had given himself, although that name, it need scarcely be said, was assumed; "but that is different," replied Leonard de Monte. "You were prepared to know me; but I think that I am secure with all others. Why, when I look in the mirror, I hardly know myself."

The dwarf gazed over the person of him who was evidently his real master, however he might, for some unexplained purposes, affect to be in the service of others--and after a moment, he replied, with a shrug of the shoulders, "It may be so indeed. Dusty, and travel-soiled, and changed, perhaps he would not know you; and were you to put on a high fraise, instead of that falling collar, it would make a greater difference still in your appearance."

"Quick! get me one, then" cried the youth; "I will pass before him for an instant this very night, that his eye may become accustomed to the sight, and memory be lulled to sleep. See, too, that all be prepared for me to lodge as you know I would."

"I have already marked out a chamber," answered the dwarf, "and have curried favour with the major-domo, so that he will readily grant it to the new page at my request."

"Where is it?" demanded the youth. "You know I am familiar with the house."

"It is," replied the dwarf, "one of the small chambers, with a little ante-chamber, in the garden tower."

"Quick, then! Haste and ask it for me," exclaimed Leonard de Monte. "The young lord bade me apply to you for what I needed; so you can plead his order to the master of the chambers. Then bring me the fraise speedily, ere I have time to think twice, and to waver in my resolutions."

With almost supernatural speed the dwarf did his errand, and returned, bearing with him one of those stiff frills extended upon whalebone which are to be seen in all the portraits of those days. The youth instantly took it from his hand; and, concealing the falling collar of lace, which was for a short period the height of the fashion at the court of Henry III., and which certainly did not well accord with the simplicity of the rest of his apparel, he tied the fraise round his neck, and advanced to a small mirror in a silver frame that hung against the arras. "Yes, that does better," he exclaimed-- "that does better. Now, what say you, Bartholo?"

"That you are safe," answered the page--"that I should not know you myself, did I not hear your voice."

"Well, then, lead through the hall, if Philip of Aubin be there." replied the youth; "and when I am in my chamber, bring me a wafer and a cup of wine; for I am weary, and must seek rest."

The dwarf opened the door, and led the way, conducting his young companion across the great hall, up and down which the Count d'Aubin was pacing slowly and thoughtfully.

"Who have you there, Bartholo?" demanded the young noble as they passed.

"Only a page, my lord," replied the dwarf; and they walked on. The Count looked at the page attentively; but not the slightest sign of recognition appeared on his face; and, though the youth's steps faltered a little with the apprehension of discovery, he quitted the hall, satisfied that his disguise was not seen through. As soon as they reached the door of the small chamber, which was to be thenceforth his abode, Bartholo left him, to bring the refreshment he had ordered; and as the dwarf passed by the door of the hall once more, and heard the steps of the Count pacing up and down, he paused an instant, as if undecided. "Shall I tell him?" he muttered between his teeth, "shall I tell him, and blow the whole scheme to pieces? But no, no, no; I should lose all, and with him it might have quite the contrary effect. I must find another way;" and he walked on.

CHAPTER V

The Chevalier de St. Real, according to the ideas of hospitality entertained in those days, pressed the King of Navarre to his food, and urged the wine upon him; but scarcely had Henry's glass been filled twice, ere the sound of steps hurrying hither and thither was heard in the hall, and the young noble cast many an anxious look towards the door. It opened at length, and an old servant entered, who, approaching the chair of his young lord, whispered a few words in his ear.

"Indeed!" said St. Real; "I had hoped his sleep would have lasted longer. How seems he now, Duverdier?--is he refreshed by this short repose?"

"I cannot say I think it, sir," replied the servant; "but he asks anxiously for you, and we could not find you in the hall."

"I come," answered St. Real; and then turning to the King, he added, "My father's short rest is at an end, and I will now tell him of your visit, sir. Doubtless he will gladly see you, as there is none he respects more deeply."

"Go! go! my young lord," cried Henry; "I will wait you here, with these good gentlemen. Let me be no restraint upon you. Yet tell your father, my good lord, that my business is such as presses a man's visits on his friends even at hours unseasonable, else would I not ask to see him when he is ill and suffering."

The young lord of St. Real bowed his head and quitted the apartment; while Henry remained with the other guests, whose curiosity was not a little increased in regard to who this Maitre Jacques could be, by the great reverence which seemed paid to him. They had soon an opportunity of expressing their curiosity to each other, in the absence of the object thereof; for in a very few minutes the Chevalier of St. Real returned, and besought Henry to "*honour* his father's chamber with his presence." The King followed with a smile; and when the door of the little hall was closed behind them, laid his hand upon St. Real's arm, saying, "You are no good actor, my young friend."

"I am afraid not," replied St. Real, in a tone from which he could not banish the sadness occasioned by his father's illness; "yet I trust what I said may in no degree betray your Majesty."

"No, no," answered Henry, "I dare say not; and should you see any suspicions, St. Real, you must either--in penance for having shown too much reverence for a king, in an age when kings are out of all respect--you must either keep these gentry close prisoners here till I have reached Tours, and thence made a two-days' journey Paris-ward, or you must give me a guard of fifty men to push my way through as far as Chartres."

"It shall be which your Majesty pleases," replied St. Real; "but here is my father's chamber."

The spot where they stood was situated half way up a long passage traversing the central part of the chateau of St. Real, narrow, low, and unlighted during the day by anything but two small windows, one at each extreme. At present two or three lamps served to show the way to the apartments of the sick man, at the small low-framed doorway of which stood an attendant, as if stationed for the purpose of giving or refusing admittance to those who came to visit the suffering noble. The servant instantly threw back the plain oaken boards, clasped together by bands of iron, which served as a door, and the next moment Henry found himself in the ante-chamber of the sick man's room. The interior of the apartment into which he was now admitted was much superior in point of comfort to that which one might have expected from the sight of such an entrance. The ante-chamber was spacious, hung with rich though gloomy arras, and carpeted with mats of fine rushes. One or two beds were laid upon the ground for the old lord's attendants; and on many a peg, thrust through the arras, hung trophies of war or of the chase, together with several lamps and sconces which cast a considerable light into the room. The chamber beyond was kept in a greater degree of obscurity, though the light was still sufficient to show the King, as he passed through the intermediate doorway, the faded form of the old Marquis of St. Real, lying in a large antique bed of green velvet, with one thin and feeble hand stretched out upon the bed-clothes. At the bolster was placed one of those old-fashioned double-seated chairs which are now so seldom seen, even as objects of antiquarian research; and, from one of the two places which it afforded, an attendant of the sick rose up as Henry entered, and glided away into the ante-room. St. Real paused and closed the door between the two chambers; and Henry, advancing, took the vacant seat, and kindly laid his hand upon that of his sick friend.

"Why how now, lord Marquis?" he said, in a feeling but cheerful tone; "how now? this is not the state in which I hoped to find you. But, faith, I must have you better soon, for I would fain see you once more at the head of your followers."

The Marquis of St. Real shook his head, with a look which had neither melancholy nor fear in its expression, but which plainly conveyed his conviction that he was never destined to lead followers to the field again, or rise from the bed on which he was then stretched. Nor, indeed, although the young monarch spoke cheerful hopes--did he entertain any expectations equal to his words. The Marquis of St. Real was more than eighty years of age; and though his frame had been one of great power, and in his eyes there was still beaming the light of a fine heart and active mind, yet time had bowed him long before, and many a past labour and former hardship in the Italian wars had broken the staff of his strength, and left him to fall before the first stroke of illness. Sickness had come at length, and now all the powers of life were evidently failing fast. The features of his face had grown thin and sharp; his temples seemed to have fallen in; and over his whole countenance--which in his green old age had been covered with the ruddy hue of health--was now spreading fast the grey ashy colour of the grave.

"Your Majesty is welcome!" he said, in a low, faint voice, which obliged Henry to bend his head in order to catch the sounds; "but I must not hope, either for your Majesty or any one else, to set lance in the rest again. I doubt not," he continued, after a momentary pause--"I doubt not that you have thought me somewhat cold-hearted and ungrateful, after many favours received at your hands, and at those of your late noble mother, that I have not long before this espoused the cause of those whom I think unjustly persecuted. But I trust that you have not come to reproach me with what I have not done, but rather to show me now how I can serve you in my dying hour; without, however, even then forgetting the allegiance I owe to the crown of France, and my duty to her monarch."

"To reproach you I certainly have not come, my noble friend," answered Henry; "for I have ever respected your scruples, though I may have thought them unfounded. Nevertheless, what I have now to tell you will put those scruples to an end at once and for ever. The cause of Henry of Navarre and of Henry III. of France are now about to be united. My good brother-in-law, the King, has written to me for aid----"

"To you!--to you!" exclaimed the Marquis, raising his head feebly, and speaking with a tone of much surprise.

"Ay, even to me," answered Henry. "He found that he had misused a friend too long, that too long he had courted enemies; and, wise at length, he is determined to call around him those who really wish well to him and to our country, and to use against his foes that sword they have so long mocked in safety. I am now on my way to join him with all speed, while my friends and the army follow more slowly. As I advanced, I could not resist the hope that enticed me hither--the hope that, when justice, and friendship, and loyalty are all united upon our side, the Marquis of St. Real, to whom justice, and friendship, and loyalty were always dear, will no longer hesitate to give us that great support which his fortune, his rank, his renown, and his retainers enable him so well to afford."

"When Henry of Navarre lends his sword to Henry of France, how should I dream of refusing my poor aid to both?" answered the Marquis. "When *you* refuse not to serve an enemy, sir, how should *I* refuse to serve a friend? But my own services are over. This world and I, like two old friends at the end of a long journey, are just shaking hands before we part; but I leave behind me one that may well supply my place. Huon, my dear son, are you there?"

"I am here, sir," said the young lord, advancing: "what is your will, my father?"

"My son, I am leaving you," replied the Marquis. "I shall never quit this bed; another sun will never rise and set for me. I leave you in troublous times, Huon, in times of difficulty and of sorrow; but that which now smoothes my pillow at my dying hour, and makes the last moments of life happy, is the fearless certainty that, come what may, my son will live and die worthy of the name that he inherits; and will find difficulty and danger but steps to honour and renown. So long as injustice stained the royal cause, and cruelty and tyranny drove many a noble heart to revolt, I would take no part in the dissensions that have torn our unhappy land; though God knows I have often longed to draw the sword in behalf of the oppressed; but now that the crown calls to its aid those it once persecuted, in order to put an end to faction and strife, my scruples are gone, and, were not life gone too, none would sooner put his foot in the stirrup than I. But those days are past; and on you, my son, must devolve the task. A few hours now, and I shall be no more; yet I will not seek to command you how to act when I am gone. Your own heart has ever been a good and faithful monitor. Let me, however, counsel you to seek the Duke of Mayenne ere you draw the sword against him. Show him your purposes and your motives; and tell him that he may be sure those who have been neutral will now become his enemies--those who have been his friends will daily fall from him, unless he follow the dictates of loyalty and honour."

The old man paused, and a slight smile curled the lip of Henry of Navarre. His nature, however, was too frank to let anything which might pass for a sneer remain unexplained; and he said, "You know not these factious Guises well enough, my friend. They strike for dominion; and that game must be a hopeless one indeed, which they would not play to gratify their ambition. But let your son seek Mayenne! More! If he will, let him not decide whose cause he will espouse till he have heard all the arguments which faction can bring to colour treason. I fear not. Strong in the frank uprightness of a good cause, and confident both of his honesty and clear good sense, I will trust to his own judgment, when he has heard all with his own ears. Let him call together what followers he can; let him march them upon Paris; and, under a safe conduct from the Duke and from the King, visit both camps alike. True, that with Henry of Valois he will find much to raise disgust and contempt; but there, too, he will find the only King of France, and with him all that is loyal in the land. With Mayenne, and his demagogues of the Sixteen, he will find faction, ambition, injustice, and fanaticism and I well know which a St. Real must choose."

"Frank, noble, and confiding, ever, sire!" said the Marquis, "nor with us will your reliance prove vain. Oh, that we had a King like you! How few hearts then could, by any arts, be estranged from the throne!"

"Nay, nay," said Henry, smiling, "you forget that I am a heretic, my good lord--a Huguenot--a *maheutre!* They would soon find means to corrupt the base, and to persuade the weak against me, were I King of France to-morrow--which God forfend!--and, by my faith, were I a great valuer of that strange thing, life, I should look for poison in my cup, or a dagger in my bosom at every hour."

"And yet, my lord, you are going to trust yourself where daggers have lately been somewhat too rife," said the Chevalier de St. Real; "and that, too--if I understood you rightly--with but a small escort."

"As small as may be," answered the King, "consisting, indeed, of but this one faithful friend, who has never yet proved untrue;" and he laid his finger on the hilt of his sword, adding, gaily, "but no fear, no fear: my cousin brother-in-law could have no earthly motive in killing me but to make Mayenne King of France, which, by my faith, he seeks not to do. He knows me too well, also, to think that I would injure him, even if I could; and, perhaps, finds now, that by making head against the Guises, and their accursed League, I have been serving him ever, though against his will."

"Would it not be better, my lord," asked the old man, in a feeble voice--"would it not be better to wait till you are accompanied by your own troops?"

"No, no," replied Henry; "Mayenne presses him hard. He is himself dispirited, his troops are more so. Still more of the *Spanish catholicon*--I mean Spanish mercenaries--are likely to be added to the forces of the League; and I fear that, if some means be not taken to keep up his courage, more speedily than could be accomplished by the march of my forces, he may cast himself upon the mercy of the enemy, and France be lost for ever."

"The Duke of Guise went as confidently to Blois as your Majesty to Tours," said the Chevalier; "and the Duke of Guise was called a friend: you have been looked on as an enemy."

"But Guise was a traitor," answered Henry, "and met with treachery, as a traitor may well expect. He went confiding alone in his own courage, but knowing that his own designs were evil. I go, confiding both in myself and in my honesty; and well knowing, that in all France there is not one man who has just cause to wish that Henry of Navarre were dead."

"He has violated his safe conduct more than once," said the Marquis, "and may violate it again."

"It will not be in my person, then," answered the King; "for safe conduct have I none, but his own letter, calling for my aid in time of need. Two drops of my blood, I do believe, spilled on that letter, would raise a flame therewith in every noble bosom that would set half the land a-fire. But I fear not: kings have no right to fear. My honesty is my breastplate, my good friend; and the steel must be sharp indeed that will not turn its edge on that."

"And the hand must be backward indeed," said the Marquis, "that would refuse its aid to such a heart. However, my lord, I give you my promise, and I am sure that my son will give you his, that the followers of St. Real shall be in the field within a month from this very night. Willingly, too, would we promise that they should join the royal cause; but, it is better, perhaps, as you have offered, that he who leads them should go free, till he shall have spoken his feelings freely to the leaders of the League."

"So be it! so be it, then!" answered Henry. "I apprehend no change of feeling towards me. My cause is that of justice, of loyalty, and of France. So long as I opposed your king in arms, I could hardly hope that a St. Real would join me, however great the private friendship might be between us; but, now that his cause is mine, and that the sword once drawn to withstand his injustice is drawn to uphold his throne, I know I shall meet no refusal. But I weary you, lord Marquis," he continued, rising; "and, good faith, I owe you no small apology for troubling you with such matters at such a time. Yet, I will trust," he added, laying his hand once more on that of the sick man--"yet I will trust that this is not our last meeting by very many, and that I shall soon hear of you in better health."

The Marquis shook his head. "My lord," he said, "I am a dying man; and though, perhaps, were the choice left to us, I would rather have died on the battle-field, serving with the last drops of my old blood some noble cause: yet, I fear not death, even here in my bed; where, to most men, he is more terrible. I have lived, I trust, well enough not to dread death; and I have, certainly, lived long enough to be weary of life. For the last ten years-- though they have certainly been years of such health and strength as few old men ever know--yet, I have daily found some fine faculty of this wonderful machine in which we live, yielding to the force of time. The ear has grown heavy and the eye grown dim, my lord; the sinews are weak and the joints are stiff. Thank Heaven! the great destroyer has left the mind untouched: but it is time that it should be separated from the earth to which it is joined, and go back to God, who sent it forth. Fare you well, sir; and Heaven protect you! The times are evil in which your lot is cast; but if ever I saw a man who was fitted to bring evil times to good, it is yourself."

"Fare you well! fare you well, my good old friend!" answered Henry, grasping his hand; "and though I be a Huguenot, doubt not, St. Real, that we shall meet again."

"I doubt it not, my lord," replied the old man, "I doubt it not; and, till then, God protect your Majesty!"

Henry echoed the prayer, and quitted the sick man's chamber, followed by the young lord of St. Real. He suffered not his attendance long, however; but, retiring at once to rest, drank the sleeping cup with his young friend, and sent him back to the chamber of his father. He had judged, and had judged rightly, that the end of the old Marquis of St. Real was nearer than his son anticipated. After the King had left his chamber, he was visited by the surgeon and the priest, and then again slept for several hours. When he awoke there was no one but his son by his bed-side, and he gazed upon him with a smile, which made the young lord believe that he felt better.

"Are you more at ease, my father?" asked the young man, with reviving hopes.

"I am quite at ease, my dear Huon," replied his father. "I had hoped that in that sleep I should have passed away; but, by my faith, I will turn round and try again, for I am drowsy still." Thus saying, he turned, and once more closing his eyes, remained about an hour in sweet and tranquil slumber. At the end of that time, his son, who watched him anxiously, heard a slight rustle of the bedclothes. He looked nearer, but all was quiet, and his father seemed still asleep. There was no change either in feature or in hue; but still there was an indescribable something in the aspect of his parent that made the young man's heart beat painfully. He gazed upon the quiet form before him--he listened for the light whisper of the breath; but all was still--the throbbing of the heart was over, the light of life had gone out! St. Real was glad that he was alone; for, had any other eye than that of Heaven been upon him, he might not have given way to those feelings which would have been painful to restrain. As it was, he wept for some time in solitude and silence; and then, calling the attendants, proceeded to fulfil all those painful offices towards the deceased which in those days were sadly multiplied. When these were finished, the morning light was shining into the dull chamber of the dead; and St. Real, retiring to his own apartments, sent to announce his loss to his cousin and to the King of Navarre. The first instantly joined him, and offered such consolation as he thought most likely to soothe his cousin's mind. Henry of Navarre, however, was not in his chamber; and, on further inquiry, it was found that he had taken his departure with the first ray of the morning light.

CHAPTER VI

A month and some days succeeded--full of events important to France, it is true, but containing nothing calculated to affect materially the course of this history; and I shall, therefore, pass over in my narrative that lapse of time without comment, changing the scene also without excuse.

There is in France a forest, in the heart of which I have spent many a happy hour--which, approaching the banks of the small river Iton, spreads itself out over a large tract of varied and beautiful ground between Evreux and Dreux, sweeping round that habitation of melancholy memories called Navarre, filled with the recollections of Turennes and Beauharnois. Over a much greater extent of ground, however, than the forest, properly so called, now occupies, large masses of thicket and wood, with, occasionally, much more splendid remnants of the primeval covering of earth, show how wide the forest of Evreux must have spread in former years; and, in fact, the records of the times of which I write compute the extreme length thereof at thirty-five French leagues; while the breadth seems to have varied at different points from five to ten miles.

In the space thus occupied, was comprised almost every description of scenery which a forest can display; hill and dell, rock and river, with sometimes even a meadow or a corn-field presenting itself in different parts of the wood, which was also traversed by two high roads--the one leading from Touraine, and the other from Alençon, Caen, and the northern parts of Normandy. These high roads, however, were, from the very circumstances of time, but little frequented; for the eloquent words of Alexis Monteil, in describing the state of France in the days of the League, afford no exaggerated picture:--"France, covered with fortified towns, with houses, with castles, with monasteries enclosed with walls within which no one entered, and from which no one issued forth, resembled a great body mailed, armed, and stretched lifeless on the earth."

Nevertheless, interest and necessity either lead or compel men to all things; and along the line of the two high roads already mentioned were scattered one or two villages and hamlets--the inhabitants of which had little to lose--and a number of detached houses, the proprietors of which were willing to risk a little in the hopes of gaining much. The fronts of these houses, by the various signs and inscriptions which they bore, gave notice to the wayfaring traveller, sometimes that man and horse could be accommodated equally well within those walls; sometimes that the human race could there find rest and food, if unaccompanied by the four-footed companion whose greater corporeal powers we have made subservient to our greater cunning. According to the strict letter of the existing laws, we find that the *auberge* for foot passengers was forbidden to lodge the equestrian, and that the *auberge* for cavaliers had no right to receive the traveller on foot. But these laws, like all other foolish ones, were neglected or evaded in many instances; and he who could pay well for his entertainment was, of course, very willingly admitted to the mercenary hospitality of either the one or other class of inns, whether he made use of the two identical feet with which nature had provided him, or borrowed four more for either speed or convenience.

Notwithstanding the turbulent elements which rendered every state of life perilous in those days, the landlord of the *auberge*, however isolated was his dwelling, did not, in fact, run so much risk as may be supposed; for by a sort of common consent, proceeding from a general conviction of the great utility of his existence, and the comfort which all parties had at various times derived from his ever-ready welcome, the innkeeper's dwelling was almost universally exempt from pillage, except, indeed, in those cases where the party spirit of the day had got the better of that interested moderation in politics which is such a distinguishing feature of the class, and had led him to espouse one of the fierce factions of the times with somewhat imprudent vehemence. Nevertheless, it need hardly be said, that between the several villages, and the several detached houses which chequered the forest of Evreux, large spaces were left without anything like a human habitation; and the traveller on either of the two highways, or on any of the multifarious cross-roads which wandered through the woods, might walk on for many a long and weary mile, without seeing anything in the likeness of mankind. Perhaps, indeed, he might think himself lucky if he did find it so; for--as there then existed three or four belligerent parties in France, besides various bodies who took advantage of the discrepancy of other people's opinions upon most subjects, to assert their own ideas of property at the point of the sword--there was every chance that, in any accidental rencontre, the traveller would find the first person he met a great deal more attached to the sword than to the olive branch.

A little more than a month, then, after the funeral of the old Marquis of St. Real, in a part of the forest where a few years before the axe had been busy amongst the taller trees, there appeared a group of several persons, two of whom have already been introduced to the notice of the reader. The spot in which they were seated was a small dry grassy strip of meadow by the side of a clear little stream, which at a hundred yards distance crossed the high road from Touraine. From the bank of the stream the ground rose very gradually for some way, leaving a space of perhaps fifty yards in breadth free of underwood or bush. It then took a bolder sweep, and became varied with manifold trees and shrubs; and then, breaking into rock as it swelled upwards, it towered into a high and craggy hill, diversified with clumps of the fine tall beeches which the axe had spared, and clothed thickly, wherever the soil admitted it, with rich underwood, springing up from the roots of larger trees long felled. On the other side again, the ground sloped away so considerably, that had the stream flowed straight on, it would have formed a cataract; and as the eye rested on the clear water, winding in a thousand turns within a very short distance of the edge of the descent, and seeming to seek a way over without being able to find it, one felt as we do in gazing upon a child in a meadow looking for something it has lost, which we ourselves see full well, yet cannot resolve to point out, lest the little seeker should desist from all the graceful vagaries of his search. Various bends and knolls, however, confined the rivulet to the course it had taken; but still the whole ground on that side was low, and at one point sunk much beneath the spot where the travellers before mentioned were seated, affording--over the green tree-tops--a beautiful view of a long expanse of varied ground, lying sweet in the misty light of summer, with many a wide and undulating sweep, fainter and more faint, till some grey spires marked the position of a distant town, and cut the line of the horizon.

The party here assembled consisted of five persons: the first of whom was the page already described under the name of Leonard de Monte, and who, now stretched upon the ground, seemed making a light repast, while the dwarf Bartholo, standing beside him, filled a small horn cup with wine from a gourd he carried, and presented it to the young Italian with a low inclination of the head. The other three personages who made up the group were evidently servants. The colours of their dress, however, were very different from those of the Marquis of St. Real, and they were also armed up to the teeth, though their garb bespoke them the followers of some private individual, and not soldiers belonging to any of the parties which then divided the land. Besides the human denizens of the scene, five horses were browsing the forest grass at a little distance. Three of these were equipped with saddles; while two still bore about them the rough harness, if harness it could be called, by means of which they had been attached to a small vehicle, somewhat between a carriage and a car, which, with its leathern curtains and its wicker frame, might be seen peeping out from amongst the bushes hard by.

While the page concluded his repast, two of the servants--the other seemed the driver of the carriage--stood behind him with their arms folded on their bosoms, but still in an attitude so common in those times of trouble as to have found its way into most of the pictures which have come down from that epoch to the present. The same movement which crossed the right and left arms over the chest had easily brought the hilt of the sword, and the part of the broad belt in which it hung, up from the haunch to the breast, where the weapon was supported by the pressure of the left arm and the right hand, and was ever ready for service at a moment's notice. The youth, however, who was the principal person of the party, and the dwarf, who seemed to ape his demeanour, wore their swords differently, following the extravagant court fashion of the day, and throwing the weapon which, in those times, might be needed at every instant, so far behind them, that the hilt was concealed by the short cloak then worn, and would have been out of the reach of any but a very dexterous hand.

When the page had concluded his repast, he wiped his dagger on the grass, and returned it to the sheath; and then, making the dwarf mingle some water from the stream with the wine he offered, he asked, ere he drank, "Are you sure, Bartholo, right sure, that we have passed them?"

"Certain! quite certain!" answered the dwarf; "unless, noble----"

"Hush!" cried the youth, holding up his hand impetuously; "have I not told thee to forget, even when we are alone, that I am any other than Leonard the page. Some day thou wilt betray me; and, by my troth, thou shalt repent it if thou dost. Go on! go on! What wert thou saying?"

"Nothing, then, Signor Leonard," answered the dwarf, with his usual sardonic grin; "but that I am certain we have passed them, quite certain: for I saw each day's march laid down before they set out; and though we were two days behind them, and had to take a round of ten leagues to avoid their route, yet we have done five leagues more than they each day that we have travelled."

"Well, then, well!" said the youth; "dine, and make these varlets dine. If I am in Paris three days before them, it is enough. Yet lose no time; for I would fain be on far enough to-night to be beyond their utmost *fourriers* ere I stay to rest. I go up yon hill to look over this woody world. When all is ready, whistle, and I will come." Thus saying, he turned away with a slow step, and, climbing the banks, was quickly lost amongst the trees and underwood.

As soon as he was gone, the dwarf beckoned to the servants; and, making them sit down beside him on the grass, did the honours of the feast, but still taking care to maintain that air of superiority with which a master might be supposed to portion out their meal to his domestics, on some of those accidental expeditions which level, for the time, many of the distinctions of rank. The servants, too, submitted to this sort of assumption as a matter of course; and though the eye of each might be caught running over the diminutive limbs of the dwarf with a glance in which the contempt of big things for little was scarcely kept down by habitual deference, yet, in their general demeanour, they preserved every sort of respect for their small companion, keeping a profound silence in his presence, and treating him with every mark of reverence.

Scarcely had they concluded their meal, however, and were in the act of yawning at the horses they were about to harness, when the rustling of the bushes on the hillside, and the fall of a few stones, gave notice of the approach of some living being. The moment after, the light and graceful form of their young master appeared, bounding down the slope like a scared deer, with his cheek flushed, and all the flashing eagerness of haste and surprise sparkling in his dark eye. "Quick!" he cried, as he came up, "quick as lightning! Draw the carriage into that brake, and lead the horses in amongst the bushes. Scatter as far as possible, and come not hither again till you hear my horn."

"But the carriage!" cried the dwarf, looking towards the spot to which the page pointed--"the brake is deep and uneven."

"We must get it out afterwards as best we may," replied the youth; "do as you are bid, and make haste! They are not half a mile from us, when I thought they were leagues. I saw them coming up, on the other side of the hill, and they will be here in five minutes. Quick! quick as lightning, Bartholo!"

The dwarf and his companions obeyed at once, and in a few moments the carriage was drawn into a woody brake that completely concealed it from view; the horses were led into the forest; Bartholo betook himself one way, and the attendants another; and their young lord, climbing the hill, sought himself out a place amongst the shrubs and larger trees, where he could see all that passed upon the high road, without running any risk of being seen himself. A quick and impatient spirit, however, gauging all things by its own activity, had, as is often the case, deceived him as to the movements of others; and instead of five minutes, which was the utmost space that his imagination had allowed for the arrival of the persons he had beheld, full half an hour had elapsed ere any one appeared.

At length, however, the trampling of horses sounded along the road; and the moment after, winding round from the other side of the hill, was seen a party of six horsemen, each bearing in his hand a short matchlock, with a lighted match, while three other weapons of the same kind hung round at the different corners of the steel saddle with which every horse was furnished. After a short interval, another small party appeared; and, succeeding them again, might be seen, first moving along above the interposing shoulder of the hill, and then upon the open road, the dancing plumes of a large body of officers and gentlemen, in the midst of whom rode the young Marquis of St. Real, and his cousin, the Count d'Aubin. The eyes of Leonard de Monte fixed eagerly upon that party, and followed its movements for many a minute, till a new bend of the road concealed it from his sight; and he turned to gaze upon the strong body of troops that then appeared. Two companies of infantry, each consisting of two hundred men, came next; and a gay and pleasant sight it was to see them pass along with their shining steel morions, and tall plumes, and rich apparel, in firm array and regular order, but all gay and cheerful, and singing as they went. Amongst them, but in separate bands, appeared the various sorts of foot soldiers then common in France; the musketeer with his long gun upon his shoulder, and the steel-pointed fork, or rest, used to assist his aim in discharging his piece, while, together with the broad leathern belt which supported his long and heavy sword, hung the innumerable small rolls of leather, in which the charges for his musket were deposited. The ancient pikeman, too, was there, with his long pike rising over the weapons of the other soldiers, and one or two bodies of arquebusiers, armed with a lighter and less cumbersome, but even more antique kind of musket, here and there chequered the ranks. A troop of cavalry, still stronger in point of numbers, succeeded, consisting of two companies of men-at-arms, which old privileges permitted the two houses of St. Real and D'Aubin to raise for the service of the crown, and of about four hundred of more lightly armed horse of that description which, from having been first introduced from Germany and Flanders, had acquired the name of reitters, even when the regiment was composed entirely of Frenchmen. The first body contained none but men of noble birth, and consisted principally of young gentlemen attached to the two great houses who raised it. Each carried his lance, to which weapon the men-at-arms of that day clung with peculiar tenacity, as a vestige of that ancient chivalry which people felt was rapidly passing away before improved science, but from which they did not like to part. Each also was splendidly armed; and gold and polished steel made their horses shine in the sunbeams.

The reitters, however, were more simply clothed, and were composed of such persons from the wealthier part of the *classe bourgeoise* as the love of arms, the distinctions generally affixed to military life, or feudal attachment to any particular house, brought from the very insecure tranquillity then afforded by their paternal dwellings, to the open struggle of the field. This corps, however, was not distinguished by the lance: a long and heavy sword, which did terrible execution in the succeeding wars, together with a number of pistols, each furnished with a rude flint lock, composed the offensive arms of the reitter. His armour, too, and his horse were both somewhat lighter than those of the man-at-arms; but his movements were, in consequence, more easy, and his march less encumbered.

The whole body wound slowly on with very little disarray Of confusion, till, one by one, the several bands turned the angle of the wood, and disappeared in the distant forest. A few scattered parties followed; then a few stragglers, and then all was left to solitude, while nothing but a cloudy line of dust, rising up above the green covering of the trees, and two or three notes of the trumpet, told that such a force was near, or marked the road it took. Leonard de Monte gazed from the place of his concealment upon each party as it passed, and then waited for several minutes, listening with attentive ear till the trumpet sounded so faintly that it was evident his own small hunting-horn might be winded unheard by the retiring squadrons. He descended, however, in the first instance, to the bank of the stream where he had been previously sitting, and then gave breath to a few low notes, as of a huntsman recalling his dogs. The sounds were heard by his attendants, and instantly obeyed. The horses were led forth from the wood; and, while the two servants bestirred themselves to draw out the carriage from the brake in which it had been concealed, the youth beckoned the dwarf towards him, demanding--"Now, Bartholo! now! what think you of this?"

"Why, I think it a very silly trick, sir," replied the dwarf: "I could forgive a raw youth like the Marquis for leading his men through such a wood as this; but how an experienced soldier, like my good lord the Count, could let him do it, I cannot fancy. Why, the League might have taken them all like quails in a falling net!"

"You are wrong," said the youth; "you are wrong, Bartholo. He knows full well that the League, close cooped in Paris, have not men to spare, and that Longueville and La Noue keep Aumale in check near Compeigne. St. Real is no bad soldier. At least, so I have heard. But it was not of that I spoke. What are we to do now? You told me that they were a day behind, and now they are right on the road before us. They must have changed their route. What must we do?"

"Why, we must turn back," answered the dwarf, calmly; "and then at Dreux seek out the *maître des postes*, leave these slow brutes behind us, and on to Paris with all the speed we can."

"But should there be no horses?" said the youth, "as was the case at La Fleche; what must we do then?"

"Oh, beyond all doubt, we shall find horses there," the dwarf replied; "and if the post be broken up, we can but apply to the master of relais, whose horses will take us on for fifteen leagues, while these tired brutes will scarce carry us to Dreux: better go with beasts that have dragged a cart, than halt half way on the road."[2]

The youth paused and pondered; and though his intention was at first directed to the exertions of the servants with the carriage, yet the moment after, his glance began to stray abstractedly over the forest; and it is more than probable that his thoughts wandered much farther than the mere trifling embarrassment in which he found himself; for his brow became clouded and melancholy, his lip quivered, and his eye, which was now again straining vacantly upon the grass, seemed as if it would willingly have harboured a tear. The dwarf gazed at him earnestly with his quick black eyes, while the habitual sneer upon his lip seemed mingled with other feelings, which somewhat changed its character, but rendered it not less dark and keen. Whatever were his own thoughts, however, he seemed perfectly to comprehend that his young lord's mind had run beyond the situation of the moment. "You are sorry you undertook it at all!" he said, keeping his eyes still fixed upon the face of the other.

"Out, knave!" cried Leonard de Monte, turning sharply upon him. "Out! Did you ever know me hesitate in a pursuit that I had once determined, or regret a deed when once it was done? Firm in myself, I am firm to myself, and, whether good or ill happens, I never regret. No, no; think you that I am such a fool or such a child as to start from the first trifling obstacle? To whimper, because I am forced to lie on a hard bed, or fly off indignant because some saucy serving-man breaks his jest upon *the page?* No, no! I was thinking of my father's house, and of a picture there which some skilful hand had painted of just such a scene as this. There was the little sparkling stream, and there a sweet and tranquil grassy bank like that, with the bright sunshine--even as it does now--streaming through the bushes, and touching the rounded turf with gold. Often, very often, have I stood and gazed upon that landscape, and my fancy has rendered the dull canvass instinct with life. I have dreamed that I could see through those groves, or climb the hill, and wander amongst the rocks; and in infancy--that time of happy hearts--imagination, as I stood and looked, has shaped me out a little paradise in such a scene as that. The palace and its cold splendour has faded away around me, and I have fancied myself wandering in the midst of Nature's beauties, with beings as bright and as ideal as my dream: and now, Bartholo--and now--what are all those visions now?"

The dwarf cast his eyes to the ground, and for a moment, a single moment, the cynical smile passed away from his lip. "You," he said--"you have made your fate! You have sought the bitter well from which you are forced to drink. You have chosen sorrow, and the way to sorrow; for the love of any human thing is but the high road thither, and you must tread it to the end."

"How now, sir!" cried the youth, proudly tossing back his head; "school'st thou me?"

"Nay, I school you not," answered the dwarf; "and less than all sought to offend you. I would have given you consolation. I would have said that you, for a great prize, had played a stake as weighty:--I mean that knowingly, willingly, you had risked happiness for love; and, seemingly having lost, are sorrowful; but still you have the satisfaction of knowing that your fate has been your own deliberate act."

"Would not that make it all the more painful, thou bitter medicine?" asked the youth.

"Not so!" answered the dwarf, "not so! Think, what must be his feelings who is *born* to disappointment and to scorn; whose heart may be as fine as that which beats in the bosom of the lordliest warrior in the land, and yet whose birthright is contempt, and degradation, and slight; whose mind may be as bright as that of prelate, or of lawgiver, and yet whose doom is to be despised and neglected? Think what must be his feelings, who has no refuge from disappointment, but in the hardness of despair; who has no warfare to wage against insult, but by hurling back contempt and defiance!"

"I am sorry for thee, from my heart," answered the youth. "Indeed, I am sorry for thee."

"*Your* pity I can bear," replied the dwarf, "because I believe it is of a nobler kind; but the pity of this base degraded world is poison to every wound in my heart. No more of myself, however," he added, resuming at once his usual look; "I have spoken too long about myself already. I cannot change my state, were I to reason on it till the sun grew old and weary of shining; but you can do much to change yours; and, in honesty, it were better to try a new plan, for this is a bad one."

"Care not thou for that," replied the other; "its wisdom or its folly rests upon me. Thou canst not say that there is either sin or crime therein; and till then, be silent."

"You spoke of your father's house," still persevered the dwarf. "Why not return thither, where now, since your uncle's death, peace, and repose, and a princely fortune await you?"

"Return thither!" replied the youth, with a sigh. "Return thither! and for what? to find the voices I used to love silent; the forms that used to cheer it gone; to see in every chamber a memorial of the dead, and in each well-known object a new source for tears. Oh, no! I loved that place once with love far beyond that which we give in general to inanimate things; but it was because the living, and the good, and the kind, were mingled up with every scene and every object; but now they are gone: the fairy spell is broken; the rich gold turned dross; and no place of all the earth is so painful in my sight as that--my father's house."

"Nevertheless," urged the dwarf somewhat anxiously; but the other went on: "But that is not all, Bartholo," he said, "that is not all; though that were fully enough. No, when I last saw my father's halls my bosom was as light as air, and all the thoughts that filled it were as the summer dreams of some sunny, happy child. Since then how many a bitter lesson have I learned; how changed is the aspect of life, and fate, and the world!--No, no! The sunshine that shone in my father's halls is gone for ever--the sunshine of a happy heart; and I will carry back with me a new star to light them, or never see them more."

"Nevertheless," repeated the dwarf, "nevertheless--"

"No more in that tone!" interrupted the youth, "let me hear no more! My resolutions are fixed beyond change. My fate is upon the die in my hand, and I will cast it boldly, let the chance be what it will. Say no more! for no more will I hear! Quick! hasten those laggards with the horses, and let us begone: each word of opposition but makes me the more eager to run my course to the end."

The dwarfs lip curled into a more bitter smile than ever, but he made no reply; and proceeded to obey the orders he had received to hasten the preparations for departure. Those preparations were soon concluded; for while the conversation detailed above had been proceeding, the servants, with the aid of the horses, had dragged the carriage out of the brake. With some difficulty, and some danger of overturning it, it was at length brought to the high road. Leonard de Monte entered; and, wrapping himself in a large cloak, cast himself back with an air of gloomy thought. The rest mounted their horses, and, as fast as the nature of the rude vehicle, and the state of the roads would permit, the little cavalcade wound away towards Dreux, leaving the forest once more to silence and solitude.

CHAPTER VII

In one of the old houses between the Louvre and the Place Royals, is still preserved in its original state a fine antique saloon of the times of Henry II. No gorgeous hall, no spacious vestibule, impresses you at once with the grandeur of the mansion; but, winding up a narrow and incommodious stair, you find yourself upon a small landing-place, whence two steps--each the segment of a circle, and both turning considerably, as if they had once formed part of a spiral staircase--conduct you, through a deep but narrow passage in the wall, to a door of black oak. On opening this, you find yourself at the threshold of a room some two-and-thirty feet square, panelled with dark and richly carved wood, and possessing a ceiling of the same. At the farther end of the saloon, opposite to the door, is a deep recess, or, rather, a sort of bay, at the entrance of which the floor rises with a high step, forming a sort of little platform capable of receiving a table and two or three chairs. From the distance of about three feet and a half above the ground up to the ceiling, the greater part of this recess or bay is of glass, with only just so much Gothic stone and wood work as serves to support the large casements, which afford the sole light of the room. The form which this projection takes on the outside of the house presents three sides of a regular octagon, and, in ornament and lightness, is not unlike one of the windows of the new part of St. John's, Cambridge, though certainly not near so beautiful as any part of that exquisite specimen of Gothic architecture.

Though, as I have said, from this window is derived the sole light which the room possesses; nevertheless, that light is enough, especially as the sunshine seems to regard that casement with particular favour, and never fails to linger about it when the bright beams visit earth.

At the time to which we must now go back, the floors were not so dingy, the oak was not so black, as they are at present; but the full summer sunshine was pouring through the large oriel, chequering the wood work of the raised flooring with the golden light of the rays and the dark shadows of the leaden frames in which the glass was set. A stand for embroidery appeared on the little platform; and before it sat a lady plying the busy needle and the shining silks; while a maid, seated near, read to her from a book--the Gothic characters of which were fast merging into the round letters of the present day--and another female attendant, a little farther off, followed the industrious example of her mistress, and busied herself at her frame. The principal person of the group was habited in deep mourning, which, in the fashion of that day, was, perhaps, the most unbecoming dress that the vanity of man ever permitted. The sombre hue of the garment was relieved by nothing that could give lightness or grace; and the heavy black veil, hanging from the head, seemed designed purposely to cast a gloomy, unsoftened shadow over the face. But that lady was one of those whom we see sometimes, and dream of often, so lovely by the gift of nature, that art can do nothing either to add to the beauty or diminish it; and she looked as transcendently lovely in the dark wimple and the sable stole, as if she had been clad in jewels and in lace. She was as fair as the morning star, with eyes of the deep, deep blue of the evening sky, full and soft, and overhung with a long fringe of jetty eyelashes, which sometimes made the eyes themselves seem black. Her cheek bore the rosy hue of health, though the colour was by no means deep, and was so softly diffused over her face, that it was scarce possible to say where the warm tint of the cheek ended, and the brilliant fairness of the forehead and temples began. The features, too, were as lovely as if the brightest fancy and the most skilful hand had combined to personify beauty; but they had nothing of the cold, still harshness of the statue, and one looked long in admiration ere one could pause to trace the graceful lines that went to form so fair a whole. The form was in no way unworthy of the face; and even the stiff, heavy folds of the mourning robe were forced into graceful falls by the symmetry of the limbs they covered. All, however, was calm and easy, and every part of the figure was concealed, as far as possible, except the tip of one small foot, and the soft rounded delicate hands, which, with a thousand graceful movements, urged the needle through the embroidery.

Such was Eugenie de Menancourt, whom her father's death in Paris had left one of the richest heiresses of France, and had cast into the hands of the faction called the League, which then ruled in the capital, while the King waged war against it in the field. The possession of Eugenie de Menancourt, indeed, was no slight advantage to that party, for those who have much to bestow will always be followed; and the reward of her hand, and all the wealth that accompanied it, was one well calculated to lure many an aspiring noble to the faction who had the power of awarding it. This the Duke of Mayenne felt fully, and made, indeed, no slight use of his advantage: not that he held out the hope of obtaining her to any one directly, except to the Count d'Aubin, to whom she had been promised by her father, and whom Mayenne was most anxious to gain over from the royal cause; but, nevertheless, he took good care that, when any of his agents busied themselves to bring over an opposite, or confirm a wavering, partisan, the list of the good things which the League could bestow should not be left unmentioned, and amongst the first was the hand of Eugenie de Menancourt, the heiress of near one half of Maine. There was many another poor girl in the same condition; but as, in those days, inclination was the last thing consulted by parents in the marriage of their daughters, there was but little difference between their fate in the hands of the League, and in the hands of their more legitimate guardians. Nevertheless, the circumstances by which she was surrounded, her isolated situation in the house wherein her father had died, and which had been assigned to her by the League as her abode during the time of her honourable captivity in Paris, and the prospect of being forced to wed a man she did not love, all contributed to heighten the gloom which her parent's recent death had cast over her, and to make melancholy the temporary expression of a countenance which seemed by nature born for smiles.

One only consideration tended to make her situation feel more light: the Count d'Aubin was deeply engaged on the side of the King; and on his late journey to Maine, had even been entrusted with the high task of keeping in check that province, and some of the neighbouring districts. So long as he adhered to the King, Eugenie well knew that Mayenne would never consent to his marriage with herself; and though she sometimes doubted the steadiness of D'Aubin's loyalty, she trusted the artful game which she knew that the Duke was playing, in order to detach him from the royal cause, would insure her not being pressed to give her hand to any one else. She hoped, therefore, for a degree of peace till such time, at least, as some change in the political affairs of France delivered her from the chance of force being employed to compel her obedience to a choice made by others.

On such facts and such speculations her mind was often forced to dwell; but Eugenie de Menancourt was too wise to yield full way to painful remembrances or anticipations that could produce no change; and she studiously strove to occupy her thoughts with other things: either reading herself during all the many hours she spent alone, or making one of her maids read to her, when she was employed with any of those occupations which engage the hand without absorbing the attention.

Thus, then, was she employed plying her needle in the sunshine, and listening to some of the poetry of Du Bartas, while, though she attended, and she heard, some melancholy feeling or some gloomy thought, springing from the depths of her own heart, would mingle insensibly with the other matter which engaged her mind, and make all she heard associate itself with the painful circumstances of her situation. In the midst of the reading, however, the door of the saloon opened, and a person entered, of whom we must pause to give almost as full a description as we have been beguiled into writing in regard to Eugenie de Menancourt herself.

The figure that appeared was that of a lady as beautiful as it is possible to conceive, but in a style of loveliness as different from that of her she came to visit as the ruby is different from the sapphire. She might be three or four and twenty years of age, but certainly was not more; and the full rounded contour of womanhood was exquisitely united in her figure to the light and easy graces of youth. Her hair was as jetty as a raven's wing, and her full bright eyes also were as dark. Her skin was fair, however, and her teeth, of dazzling whiteness, were just seen through the half-open lips of her small beautiful mouth. The soft arched eyebrow, the chiselled nose, the rounded chin, the gentle oval of the face, the small white ear, and the broad clear forehead, made up a countenance such as is seldom seen and never forgotten; and to that face and form she might well have trusted to command admiration, had such been her object, without calling in "the foreign aid of ornament." Dress, however, and splendour had not been neglected, though her rich garments sat so easily upon her, that they seemed but the natural accompaniment of so much beauty, worn rather to harmonise with than to heighten the splendid loveliness of her face and person. Her whole apparel, except the mantle and the sleeves, was of the lightest kind of gold tissue, consisting of a small stripe of pink, and a still smaller one of gold. The bodice, or stays, was laced with gold; and the body, or *corps de robe*, shaped not at all unlike those in use at present, came much higher over the bosom than was customary at a libertine court, and in a libertine age. The sleeves, which were large on the shoulders, and suddenly contracted till they fitted close to the round and beautiful arms, were of white satin, as was also the mantle, which round the edge was richly embroidered with pink and gold. Her girdle was of gold filigree worked upon white velvet; and through it was passed a chaplet of large pearls, with every now and then a sapphire or an emerald, to mark some particular prayer. Jewels were in her ears too, and on the bosom of her dress, though it was but mid-day; and in her hand she held one of the small black velvet masks, which the fair dames of those days very generally wore when in the streets, even in their carriages, under the pretence of guarding their complexions from the sun and wind, but, in fact, more for the sake of fashion than from over-tenderness, and often with views and purposes which might well shun the day.

The lady, however, who now entered, bore no appearance of one likely to yield to the luxurious softness, or the weak vices of the day. There was a light and a soul in her dark eyes, a play and a spirit about her ever-varying lip, a firmness and determination on her fine clear brow, that might, perhaps, speak of passion intense and strong, but could hardly admit the idea of weakness. As soon as Eugenie de Menancourt beheld her, she started up with a look of joy; and, advancing to meet her, pressed her kindly in her arms, exclaiming, "Dear, dear Beatrice! are you better at length? Why would you not let me see you?"

"Well! quite well now, Eugenie," replied the other, returning her embrace as warmly as it was given "but my illness, they said, was contagious; and why should I have suffered you to risk your valued and most precious life for such a one as I am?"

"Oh! and your life is precious too, Beatrice," replied her friend; "most precious to those who know you as well as I do."

"But how few do that, dearest friend!" replied Beatrice of Ferrara; for, strange as it may seem, it was she whose name has once before been mentioned in this work, who now stood beside Eugenie de Menancourt, on terms of the dearest intimacy and affection. "How few do that! Do you know, Eugenie, that I regard as one of the greatest and sweetest triumphs of my life, the having conquered all your prejudices against me; having won your love and your esteem, and taught you to know me as I am."

"But indeed, indeed, as I have often told you," replied Eugenie, "I had no prejudices against you."

"Nay, nay," replied the other, with a smile; "you beheld me surrounded by the profligate and the base; you beheld me mingling with the idle and the vain: you beheld the seducers and the seduced of a corrupt court worshipping this pretty painted idol that you see before you; and, doubtless, thought in your own secret heart that it was with pleasure that I bore it all."

"No, no, indeed," replied Eugenie; "quite the reverse! Wherever I went I heard you mentioned as the exception. The malicious and the scandalous were silent at your name; and not even the braggart idlers, whose vanity is fed by their own lies against our sex, ventured to say you smiled upon them."

"They dared not, Eugenie!" said Beatrice, her dark eye flashing as she spoke; "they dared not! There is not a minion in all France who would dare to cast a spot upon my name! Not because they fear to speak falsehood, be it as gross and glaring as the sun; but because they know I hold, that where the honour of Beatrice of Ferrara is assailed, she has as much right as any punctilious man in all the land to avenge herself as best she may. Nay, start not, dear friend! but send away your women, and let us have a few calm moments together, if the idle world will let us."

The women, who had been in attendance upon Eugenie de Menancourt, required no farther commands; but, the one laying down her book, and the other covering up her embroidery-frame, left the room.

"You started but now, Eugenie," continued Beatrice, advancing towards the little platform in the bay window, and seating herself beside her friend; "you started but now, when I said that women have as much right to avenge themselves, when their honour is assailed, as men; but I say so still--ay, and even more right. I have long thought so, and shall ever think so, Eugenie; though Heaven only knows how I should act, were such a case to happen. I might be as weak as women generally are, and let the traitor escape out of pure fear: but I think not, Eugenie--I think not. I believe that I would rather die the next minute after having avenged myself, than live on in the same world with one who had slandered that fair fame which, in spite of circumstances, and my own wild thoughtlessness, I have maintained unstained in the midst of this foul court."

"Nay, but consider, Beatrice," cried Eugenie, earnestly, "this world is not all."

"I know it well, sweet friend," replied Beatrice; "but I think, if there be pardon in heaven for any offence, it would be for that Men claim the right, and die without a fear; and why should not we have the same privilege? They, when their honour is assailed, could clear themselves without revenge; they could call their comrades to judge of their conduct; but, with us, the very whisper is destruction; and no proof of innocence ever gives us back that pure, untarnished name which is our only honour; we can have no exculpation, we can have no redress, and vengeance is all that is left us."

Eugenie was silent, and Beatrice gazed upon her, for a moment or two, with a smile, adding, at last, "But no--no, Eugenie, such thoughts and such feelings are not for you. Your nation, your education, your country, will not let you feel as I feel, or think as I think; and yet, Eugenie, we love each other," she added, twining her graceful arm through that of her fair friend, "and yet we love each other--is it not so?"

"Indeed, it is!" replied Eugenie de Menancourt, turning towards her with a warm smile. "Your company, your affection, your sympathy, dear Beatrice, have been my only consolations since I came within the walls of this hateful city; and all I wish is that I could on some points make you think as I do. I wish it selfishly, and yet for your sake, Beatrice; for, if I could succeed, I should not tremble every moment for your happiness and for your peace, as I do now."

"Thank you, thank you for the wish, dear friend!" replied Beatrice, with more melancholy than mirth in her smile; "thank you, most sincerely, for the wish! but still it is in vain. You can never, with all your kind eloquence, make a wild, ardent, passionate Italian girl, a calm, gentle, yielding being like yourself, all charity and half Huguenot. It is in vain, it is in vain. But you speak of happiness, Eugenie, as if I knew what happiness is. Now listen to me, and you shall hear more of Beatrice of Ferrara than ever you have yet done. There is a subject, I know, on which we have both thought often, and on which we have wished often to speak--I know it, Eugenie! I know it! I have heard it in half-spoken words; I have read it in your manner, and in your tone; I have seen it in your eyes--that, often, often, when we have talked of other scenes and other days, you have longed to ask what is Beatrice of Ferrara to Philip d'Aubin, and what is he to her? Nay, I dream not that you love him, Eugenie; I know better--I know that you love him not; and I feel that Philip d'Aubin, with all his splendid qualities, with all his energies of mind, and graces of person, is the last man on earth that Eugenie de Menancourt could love."

She paused a moment, gazed thoughtfully in her friend's face, and then, leaning her head upon Eugenie's shoulder, while she took her hand in hers, she added, in a low tone and with a deep sigh--"But it is not so with Beatrice of Ferrara!"

A bright blush rushed over her cheek, as she spoke the words which gave to her friend the full assurance of a fact that she had long suspected, perhaps we might say had long known; and she closed her dark bright eyes, as if to avoid seeing whatever expression that confession might call into the countenance of Eugenie. The moment after, however, she started up, exclaiming eagerly, "But mistake me not! mistake me not! I have not loved unsought; I have not called upon my head the well-deserved shame of being despised for courting him who loved me not. No, Eugenie, no! although the blood that flows in these veins may be all fire, yet in my heart there is a well of icy pride--at least, so he has often called it--which would cool the warm current of my love--ay, till it froze in death!--ere the name I bear should be stained even by such a pitiful weakness as that. No! he sought me, he courted me, he lived at my feet, till the proud heart was won. Yes, Eugenie, he lived at my feet, he seemed to feed upon my smiles, till, at length, ambition and interest opened wider views, and vanity was piqued to think that Eugenie de Menancourt could be dull to such high merits as his own----"

"If ambition and interest swayed him," said Eugenie;--but her friend interrupted her ere she could finish. "Hear me out!" she cried, "hear me out, Eugenie! Ambition and interest had much to do therewith. When I and my young brother first sought this court to find protection against the injustice of my father's brother, I possessed little but a small inheritance in France, the dowry of my mother. This he well knew; and though, if there be any truth on earth, he loved me, yet, with men, Eugenie, there are passions that make even love subservient--ambition, interest, vanity, Eugenie, are men's gods!"

"But is it possible, Beatrice," cried Mademoiselle de Menancourt, "that, thinking thus of all men, and of him in particular, you can either esteem or love him, or any of his race?"

"Oh, yes, Eugenie! oh, yes!" she replied. "Love is a tyrant--not a slave: we cannot bind him to the chariot wheels of reason; we cannot make him bow his neck beneath the yoke of judgment. On the contrary, we can but yield and obey. There is but one power on earth that can restrain him, Eugenie--Virtue! but everything else is vain. And, oh! how many ways have we of deceiving ourselves! The sun will cease to rise, Eugenie--summer and winter, night and day, forget their course, ere love, in the heart of woman, wants a wile to cheat her belief to what she wishes. Even now, Eugenie, even now, I believe and hope; and I fancy often that, though misled by things whose emptiness he will soon discover, the time will come when Love will re-assert his empire in a heart that is naturally noble. It may be all in vain!" she added, with a deep sigh; "it may be all in vain! yet, who would willingly put out the last faint, lingering flame that flickers on Hope's altar?"

"Not I!" said Eugenie, echoing her friend's sigh; "not I, indeed!--Would that he were worthy of you, Beatrice! Would that he were worthy of you!" she added, after a momentary pause; during which, perhaps, her mind was struggling back to the real subject of their conversation from some path of association, into which it had been led by her companion's last words. "Would that he were worthy of you! but if his fickle and wayward nature could never be endured by me, who can bear much, how much less would it suit you, Beatrice, who, I am afraid, are calculated to bear but little!"

"You know not how much I have already borne, Eugenie," replied Beatrice; "you know not how much love can bear: though, yes, perhaps you do," she added, in a lighter tone; "at least, there are those who know well how much--how very much--they could bear for love of Eugenie de Menancourt."

The warm blood spread red and glowing over Eugenie's fair face. "I know not whom you mean, Beatrice," she said, gravely: "I know none that love me; and few that are capable of loving at all--if you speak of men."

"Nay, ask me not his name!" said Beatrice, the gaiety of her tone increasing, as she marked, or thought she marked, a greater degree of confusion in her friend's countenance than the subject would have produced in other persons brought up regularly in the sweet and pleasant pastime of deceit. "Nay, ask me not his name! I am no maker of fair matches, nor half so politic, as this world goes, to endeavour to marry my friend to the first person that presents himself, solely to rid myself of the presence of her beauty."

"Nay, but dear Beatrice," replied Mademoiselle de Menancourt, "I know no one who has even seen that beauty, if so it must be called, for many a month: so indeed you are mistaken."

"Nay, nay, not so," answered Beatrice, smiling; "a few hours, a few minutes, a single instant, are enough, you know, Eugenie: and for the rest, indeed I am not mistaken. I would stake my life, from what I have seen-- from signs infallible--that you are loved deeply, truly, with all the ardour of a first passion in a young--a very young heart."

"Pray God, it be not so!" cried Eugenie; "for it were but unhappiness to himself and to me."

"Are you so cold, then, Eugenie, that you cannot love?" asked Beatrice, with a smile; "or is that sweet heart occupied already by some one who fills it all?"

Eugenie smiled too, and shook her head; but there was once more a deep blush spread over her face; and though it might be but the generous flush of native modesty, Beatrice read in it a contradiction of her words, as she replied, "No, no, not so, indeed! Perhaps I may be cold; as yet I cannot tell, for no one has ever yet spoken to me of love whose love I could return. But, even could I do so, Beatrice, would it not be grief to both, as here I remain in the hands of others, unable to dispose of myself but as they please?"

"Out upon it, Eugenie!" cried Beatrice; "'tis your own fault if you are not your own mistress in an hour. Never was there a time in France when woman--the universal slave--was half so free."

"But what would you have me do?" demanded Eugenie. "With a thousand eyes constantly upon me, I see not how I could obtain more freedom, or dispose of myself, were I so inclined."

"As easy as sit here and sew," cried Beatrice. "Here is the King claims the disposal of your hand, and the League claims it too; and, between them both, you can give it to whom you will. Fly from Paris! Betake yourself where you will, but not to the court of Henry; for his tyranny might be greater than even that of the League. Then, make your choice. Give your hand to him you love; and be quite sure, that the party that your good lord shall join will sanction your marriage with all accustomed forms."

"But if I love no one?" said Eugenie, with a smile.

"Why then, live in single simplicity till you do," replied Beatrice, with an incredulous shake of the head. "But, at all events, fly from the yoke they now put upon you."

"Fly, Beatrice?" answered Eugenie; "fly, and how? How am I to fly, with a city beleaguered on all sides; a watchful Argus in the League, with its thousand eyes all round me: having none to guide me, and not knowing where to go;--how am I to fly?"

"By a thousand ways," answered her friend, laughing at her embarrassment. "Change your dress, in the first place: put on a petticoat of crimson satin embroidered with green, together with a black velvet body and sleeves, cut in the fashion of the Duchess of Valentinois, of blessed memory!--a cloak of straw-coloured silk, a *capuche* of light blue cloth broidered with gold, a mass of grey hair under a black cap, and a *vertugadin* of four feet square. Dress yourself thus, and call yourself Madame la Presidente de Noailles; and, by my word, the guards will let you pass all the gates, and thank God to get rid of you! Or, if that does not suit you, take the gown and bonnet of a young advocate," she continued in the same gay tone; "hide those pretty lips and that rounded chin under a false beard from Armandi's; and be very sure the guards would as soon think of stopping you as they would of stopping the prince of darkness, who, after all, is the real governor of this great city. Nothing keeps you here but fear, my Eugenie! Why, I will undertake to go in and out twenty times a day, if I please."

"Ay, but you have a bolder heart than I have," answered Eugenie de Menancourt; "and I know full well, Beatrice, that a thing which, executed with a good courage, is done with ease, miscarries at the first step when it is attempted by timidity and fear. The very thought of wandering through the gates of Paris alone makes me shrink."

"But I will go with you, Eugenie," replied Beatrice, "and will answer for success whenever you like to make the attempt."

Eugenie paused, and thought for several moments, fixing her fine eyes upon vacancy with a faint smile and a longing look, as if she would fain have taken advantage of her friend's proposal, yet dared not make the attempt. "Not yet, dear Beatrice--not yet!" she answered: "I dare not, indeed, unless some sharp necessity happens to give me temporary courage. As long as they refrain from urging me to wed one I can never love, and from pressing on me any other in his room, so long will I stay where I am."

"But see that your decision come not too late, Eugenie," answered her friend. "They may soon begin to press you on the subject; and, when once they find you reluctant, they may take measures to prevent your flight."

"I do not think they will press me," answered Eugenie. "First, in regard to Philip d'Aubin, they will never favour him, as he is of the party of the King; and, in regard to any other, they know full well that I could, if I would, urge my father's promise to him."

"But you would not do it!" exclaimed Beatrice.

"No, Beatrice, no!" answered Eugenie, laying her hand kindly upon hers; "no, I would rather die!"

"But hear me," said Beatrice, somewhat eagerly; "think of all that may happen. A thousand things may tempt D'Aubin to quit the royal party. He may come over to the League--he may urge your father's promise--he may obtain the sanction of Mayenne:--what will you do then?"

"Fly to the farthest corner of the earth," replied Eugenie, "sooner than fulfil a promise that was none of mine, and against which my whole heart revolts on every account. Listen, Beatrice; I do believe that, in the moment of need, I shall not want courage, and certainly shall not want resolution. Should I have any reason to fear compulsion, but too often used of late, I will take counsel with none but you; you shall guide me as you think fit, and I will fly anywhere, rather than give my hand to one I cannot love."

"Write me but five words," replied Beatrice, "write me 'Come to me with speed,' and send it by a page when you want assistance, and doubt not but I will find means to deliver you, were you at the very altar. But, hark! I hear steps upon the staircase, and horses before the house; and I must resume all my bold and haughty bearing, and put on the mask, which I have laid aside to Eugenie de Menancourt alone."

As she spoke, she drew her chair a little further from that of her friend; and, placing it in the exact position which the ceremonious intercourse of that day pointed out, she remained with the glove drawn off from one fair hand, which, dropping gracefully over the arm of the *fauteuil*, continued to hold her small black mask, twirling it as listlessly round and round as ever the fair hand of fashionable dame in our own days played with a glove, to show her skin's whiteness or her brilliant rings. Eugenie de Menancourt's eyes sought the door with an expression of anxiety; but Beatrice, on the contrary, gazed vacantly through the window towards the buildings on the opposite side of the river; and the visitors had entered the room, and were already speaking to her friend, before she appeared to be conscious of their presence, or condescended to notice them. Turning her head at length, she fixed her eyes upon a square-built, powerful man, with a somewhat heavy, but not unpleasing, countenance; who, richly dressed, and followed by two or three gentlemen, in a more gay and smart, but not more magnificent, costume, was speaking to Mademoiselle de Menancourt, with all that courteous respect which chivalrous times, then just passing away, had left behind them.

"Good morrow, my lord Duke!" said Beatrice, as the visitor turned towards her: "I anticipated not the pleasure of seeing your Highness here to day. Good faith! have you so much ease in a beleaguered city, as to exercise your horses in visiting ladies before noon? On my honour, I will be a soldier, for 'tis the idlest life I know, and only fit for a woman."

"I came but to ask briefly after your fair friend's health," replied the Duke; "and knew not that I should have to risk with you, gay lady, one of our old encounters of sharp words. I trust, however, your health is better."

"Did you ever see me look more beautiful, Duke of Mayenne?" asked Beatrice, with a gay toss of her head; "and can you ask if I am ill? But as to my *friend's* health, if you would that she should be well, and keep well, let her go out of Paris, home to her own dwelling; and keep her not here, where one is surrounded, night and day, with the sound of cannon and arquebuses. Do you intend that it should be said, in future, that carrying on the war against women and children was first introduced into modern Europe by the Duke of Mayenne and the Catholic League, that you keep a lady here a close prisoner in your beleaguered capital?"

"Not as a prisoner, fair lady," answered the Duke of Mayenne; "God forbid that either I or she should look upon her situation as one of imprisonment; but, being lieutenant-general of the kingdom, and, consequently, her lawful guardian and protector, till marriage gives her a better, I should be wanting both in duty and in courtesy, were I to leave her in a distant and distracted province, in a time of unfortunate civil war."

"Well explained and justified, my good lord Duke," cried Beatrice, who, both in right of rank and beauty, treated the ambitious leader of the League as equal to equal. "And yet, after all, my lord, has not that same marriage that you mention some small share in your tenacious kindness? Did you ever hear, my lord, of a rat-catcher giving the rats the bait out of his trap, from pure affection for the heretic vermin?"

The Duke of Mayenne first reddened, and then smiled; either more amused than angry at the gay flippancy of his fair opponent, or judging it best, at least, to appear so. "Your similes savour of a profession that I know not, fair lady," he replied; "but if you mean, Lady Beatrice, that hereafter I may dispose of your fair friend's hand in such a manner as seems to me most conducive towards her happiness--if you mean that," he repeated, in a marked tone, "I deny not that you are right. Yet I would fain know who has a better right to do so than the lieutenant-general of the kingdom?"

"Oh! no one, surely!" answered Beatrice, in the same tone of mingled pride and gaiety--"no one, surely, my lord, except the King of that kingdom, or the poor frightened girl herself."

"Come, come, fair lady," cried Mayenne, laughing; "you carry your jest so far, that I will bid you take care what you say farther, lest I should dispose of your hand for you, too, for the purpose of showing you--to use your own figure--that I have more baits than one to my rat-trap."

"Indeed, lord Duke, you count wrongly, if you reckon that I am one," replied Beatrice. "You know too well that the task would neither be a very safe nor very easy one, to try to wed me to any one against my will. You may be lieutenant-general of the kingdom, and I, for one--being not of this kingdom, and thinking much better of you than of the crowned Vice at St. Cloud--will not deny your right; but you are not lieutenant-general of Beatrice of Ferrara; and you might find it more difficult to govern her than half the realm of France; and so, good morrow! Love me, Eugenie; and do not let these men persuade you that they are half such powerful and terrible things as they would make themselves appear. Fare you well!"

Each of the gentlemen in the prince's suite stepped forward to offer his hand to the gay, proud beauty, whose tone of light defiance had something in it more attractive to the general youth of those excited times, than all the retiring graces and gentle modesty of Eugenie de Menancourt. Beatrice scarcely noticed them while her friend took leave of her, but as soon as the embrace was over, she ran her eye over the three or four cavaliers who stood round, and, singling out one, gave him her hand, saying, "My lord of Aumale, I believe you are the only one here present, except my lord Duke, who never whispered that you loved me; and therefore I doubt not that you *do* love me enough to--hand me to my carriage."

The young noble, to whom she addressed herself, answered with all those professions which the formal gallantry of the day not only permitted, but required, and led her down to the rudely formed, but richly decorated, vehicle, which was the carriage of those days.

In the meanwhile, Eugenie de Menancourt remained waiting in some suspense, to hear the real object of the visit paid her by the Duke of Mayenne, the purport of which she could not conceive was merely to inquire after her health. Whether, however, the great leader of the League judged that his conversation with Beatrice of Ferrara was not the most favourable prelude to anything he had to say to the young heiress, or whether he really came but to trifle away a few minutes in a visit of ceremony, it is certain that he said nothing which could induce Eugenie to imagine that he had any immediate view of pressing her to a marriage with any one. After spending about ten minutes in ordinary conversation, upon general and uninteresting subjects, and expressing many a wish for the comfort and welfare of his fair ward, as he did not fail to style Mademoiselle de Menancourt, Mayenne rose, and left her to the enjoyment of solitude and her own reflections, which, for the time, were sweetened by the hope, that the evils to which her situation might ultimately give rise were yet remote.

CHAPTER VIII

The carriage which contained Beatrice of Ferrara rolled on with slow and measured pace through the narrow and tortuous streets of old Paris, till at length, as it was performing the difficult man[oe]uvre of turning a sharp angle, it was encountered by a small party of horsemen, in the simple garments of peace, which, at that warlike period, was a less common occurrence than to see every one who could bear them clad in grim arms. The right of staring into carriages, when the velvet curtains were withdrawn, was already established in Paris; and it needed but a brief glance to make the principal cavalier of the group draw in his bridle rein, beckon the coachman to stop, and, springing to the ground, approach the *portiere* of the vehicle wherein Beatrice was placed. As usual in those days, she was not alone; but, while a number of lackeys graced the outside of her carriage, two or three female attendants were seated in the interior of the machine, leaving still a space within its ample bulk for many another, had it been necessary. More than one pair of eyes were thus upon her; and yet Beatrice, though brought up in a court--where feelings themselves were nearly reckoned contraband, and all expression of them prohibited altogether--could not repress the very evident signs of agitation which the approach of that cavalier occasioned. Her cheek reddened, her breathing became short, and she sank back upon the embroidered cushions of the carriage, as if she would fain have avoided the meeting. The agitation lasted but a moment, however; and as soon as he spoke, she was herself again: perhaps gaining courage from seeing that his own cheek was flushed, and that his own voice trembled as he addressed her.

"A thousand, thousand pardons, lady!" he said, standing bareheaded by the door, "for stopping your carriage in the streets; but these unfortunate wars have rendered it so long since we have met, that most anxious am I----!"

"My lord Count d'Aubin," replied Beatrice, raising her head proudly, "the time of your absence from Paris has not seemed to me so long as to make me rejoice that it is at an end!"

"I have no right to expect another answer," replied D'Aubin, in a low voice; "and yet, Beatrice, perhaps I could say something in my own defence."

"Which I should be most unwilling to hear," replied the lady, coldly. "I doubt not, sir Count, that you can say much in your own defence: I never yet knew man that could not, but a plain idiot, or one born dumb. But what is your defence to me? I am neither your judge nor your accuser. If your own heart charges you with ambition, or avarice, or falsehood, plead your cause with it, and, doubtless, you will meet with a most lenient judge. Will you bid the coachman drive on, sir? this is a foolish interruption, and a narrow street."

"Oh, Beatrice!" exclaimed the Count d'Aubin, piqued by her coldness, "at least delay one moment, till you tell me you are well and happy: I have just heard that you have been ill--very ill."

"I have, sir," she replied; "I caught the fever that was prevalent here; but I am well again, as you see, and should be perfectly happy, if I did not hear King Henry's artillery above once a week, and if people would not stop my carriage in the streets."

"And is that all you will say to me, Beatrice?" asked the Count, in the same low tone which he had hitherto used--"is that all you will say, after all that has passed?"

"I know nothing, sir, that has passed between us," replied Beatrice aloud, "except that once or twice, in a fit of wine or folly, you vowed that you loved Beatrice of Ferrara better than life, or wealth, or rank, or station; and that she received those vows as she has done a thousand others, from a thousand brighter persons than Philip Count d'Aubin, namely, as idle words, which foolish men will speak to foolish women, for want of better wit and more pleasant conversation; as words which you had probably spoken to a hundred others, before you spoke them to me, and which you will yet, in all probability, speak to a hundred more, who will believe them just as much as I did, and forget them quite as soon. Once more, sir, then, will you order the coachman to drive on, or let me do so, and retire from the wheel, lest it strike you, and the Catholic League lose a valiant convert by an ignoble death?"

"Nay, there at least you do me wrong!" replied the Count d'Aubin: "the Catholic League has no convert in me; I am here, under a safe conduct, on matters of no slight importance to my good cousin St. Real: but to his Majesty will I adhere, so long as he and I both live!"

"Indeed!" cried Beatrice, with a light laugh. "Is there anything in which the fickle Count d'Aubin will not be fickle? Nay, nay, make no rash vows; remember, you have not yet heard all the golden arguments which his Highness, the lieutenant-general of the kingdom and the League can hold out. Suppose he offer you the hand of some rich heiress; could you resist, sir Count? could you resist?"

D'Aubin coloured, perhaps because Beatrice had gone deeper into the secrets of his inmost thoughts than he felt agreeable. He answered, however, boldly, "I could resist anything against my honour."

"Honour!" exclaimed Beatrice, with a scoff: "honour! Marguerite, tell the coachman to drive on. Honour!"

D'Aubin drew back, with an air at once of pain and anger, made a silent sign to the coachman to proceed, and, springing on his horse, galloped down the street, followed by his attendants, at a pace which risked their own necks upon the unequal causeway of the town, and which certainly showed but little consideration for the safety of the passengers. The emotions of Philip d'Aubin, however, were such as did not permit of consideration for himself or others. He felt himself condemned, and he believed himself despised, by the only woman that, perhaps, he had ever truly loved. The better feelings of his heart, too, rose against him: he knew that his conduct was ungenerous; and he felt that, had the time been one when faith and honour towards woman were aught but mere names, his behaviour would have been dishonourable in the eyes of mankind, as well as in the stern code of abstract right and wrong: and unhappy is the man who has no other means of justifying himself to his own heart but by pleading the follies and vices of his age. D'Aubin did plead those follies and vices, however, and he pleaded them successfully, so far as in soon banishing reflection went; but there was a sting left behind, which was the more bitter, perhaps, as mortified vanity had no small share in the pain that he suffered. He had believed that he could not so soon be treated with scorn and indifference; he had fancied that his hold on the heart of Beatrice of Ferrara was too strong to be shaken off so easily; and though he had no definite object in retaining that hold, though other passions had for the time triumphed over affection, and placed a barrier between himself and her which he was not willing to overleap, yet still the lingering love that would not be banished was wounded by her bitter tone; and, joined to humbled pride and offended vanity, made his feelings aught but pleasing.

In the meantime, the carriage of Beatrice of Ferrara bore her on with a heart in which sensations as bitter were thronging; though, as we have seen in her conversation with Eugenie de Menancourt, her feelings towards her lover were less keen and scornful than her words might lead him to believe. On the state of her bosom, however, there is no necessity to dwell here, as many an occasion will present itself for explaining it in her own words; and it may be better, also, to let her thus speak for herself, because in endeavouring to depict abstractedly, by means of cold descriptions, that varying and chameleon-like thing, the human heart, one is often led into seeming contradictions, from the infinite variety of hues which it takes, according to the things which surround it.

The carriage rolled on and entered the court-yard of the splendid mansion in which she dwelt. Here Beatrice alighted; but she did not go into the house, for a hand-litter or chair,--one of the most ancient of French conveyances,--waited under the archway, as if prepared by her previous order, with its two bearers, and a single armed attendant; and this new conveyance received her as soon as she set foot out of the other. The door was immediately closed, and the blinds, filled with their small squares of painted glass, were drawn up, Beatrice merely saying to the attendant who stood beside her as she shut out the gaze of the passers-by, "To Armandi's!"

The bearers instantly lifted their burden, and began their course at the same peculiar trot which has probably been the pace of chair-men in all ages; nor from this did they cease or pause till they reached one of the most showy, if not one of the richest, shops in the city. Standing forth from the building, under a little projecting penthouse, to secure the wares against both sun and rain, was along range of glass cases, containing every sort of cosmetic then in vogue, from the plain essence of violets, wherewith the simple burgher's wife perfumed her robe of ceremony, to the rich ointment compounded from a thousand rare ingredients, wherewith the King himself masked his own effeminate countenance against the night air whilst he slept. Behind these cases was the shop itself, hanging in which might be seen a crowd of various objects for the gratification of vanity and luxury,--the black velvet mask, or loupe, the embroidered and many-coloured gloves, the splendid hair-pins and enamelled clasps, the girdles of gold and silver filigree and precious stones, together with many another part of dress or ornament, some full of grace and taste, some fantastic and absurd, and some scarcely within the bounds of common decency. Beyond the shop, again, but separated from it by a partition of glass, covered in the inside with curtains of crimson silk, was the inner shop, or most private receptacle for all those peculiarly rich or fragile wares which Armandi, the famous perfumer of that day, did not choose to expose, to tempt cupidity, or lose their freshness, in the more exposed parts of his dwelling. Here, too, report whispered, were concealed those drugs and secret preparations, his skill in compounding which, it was said, had been much more the cause of his great favour with Catherine de Medicis than his art as a perfumer, which was the ostensible motive of her calling him from Italy to take up his abode in her husband's capital. However this might be, certain it is that, after the sudden death of the Queen of Navarre, the suspicions of the Huguenots turned strangely against Armandi, to whose diabolical skill they very generally attributed the loss of their beloved princess: and it is more than probable that he would have fallen a victim to their indignation, whether just or unjust, had not the horrors of St. Bartholomew shortly after delivered him from the presence of his adversaries in Paris.

Nevertheless, although suspicion might be strong, and the man's character as infamous as such suspicions could render it, yet the shop of Armandi was not less the resort of the beautiful and the fair, and even of the gentle and good: for it is most extraordinary how far female charity will extend towards those who contribute to the gratification of vanity and satisfy the thirst for novelty. The newest fashions, the most beautiful objects of art and luxury, the freshest and most costly rarities were nowhere to be found but at his shop; and no one chose to believe that Armandi dealt in poisons--but those who wanted them.

Thither, then, the chair, or *litiere encaissee*, as it was called, of Beatrice of Ferrara, was borne at an hour when the greater part of the gay Parisians were busy with that employment which few people love better, namely, that of eating the good things which their own gastronomic art produces. The bearers halted not at the steps which led into the shop, but proceeded till the chair was brought parallel to a door in the partition, between the outer and the inner chamber, so that she could pass at once from the one into the other. Her countenance, however, bore but little the expression of one going to buy trinkets, or to amuse oneself by turning over the light frivolities of such a place as that in which she stood. The usual fire of her eye was somewhat quelled, and a degree of melancholy, perhaps of anxiety, unusual with her at any time, had, since her meeting with the Count d'Aubin, pervaded her whole countenance. The doors of the partition and that of the chair had been both thrown open as soon as the gilded lions' feet of the latter touched the floor, and there stood the Signor Armandi, dressed in silks and velvets of rose colour and sky blue, with his mustachio turning up almost to his eyes, and a small jewelled dagger occupying the place of the sword, which his calling did not permit him to wear in Paris. His face was dressed in sweet complacent smiles; and, as he bowed three times to the very ground before his lovely visiter, his head was certainly "dropping odours;" for no one held his own perfumes in higher veneration than he did himself.

"Enchanted and honoured are my eyes to see you once again, lady most fair and chaste!" said he, in high-flown Italian. "I heard that you had been upon that sad couch, where the head is propped by the thorns of sickness, rather than by the roses of love."

"Hush, hush, Armandi!" cried Beatrice, with an impatient wave of the hand; "you should know me better than to speak such trash to me. I neither use your cosmetics, nor will hear your nonsense. I have come upon more weighty matters."

"For whatever you have come, most beautiful of the beautiful," replied the other, affecting to subdue his exalted tone; "you have come to command, and I am here to obey. Speak! your words are law to Armandi."

"When followed by the necessary seal of gold, I know they are," answered Beatrice, gravely. "Now hear me, then. I wish--I wish--" she paused and hesitated, and the perfumer, accustomed to receive communications of too delicate a nature to bear the coarse vehicle of language, hastened to aid her.

"You wish, perhaps," he said, in a soft voice, "to see some friend, and require the magical influence of Armandi to bring him to your presence----"

"Out, villain!" cried Beatrice, her eyes flashing fire. "For whom do you take me, pitiful slave? Do you fancy yourself speaking to Clara de Villefranche, or Marguerite de Tours en Brie, or, higher still in rank and infamy, Marguerite de Valois? Out, I say! Talk not to me of such things;--I wish--I wish--"

"Perhaps you wish to see some friend no more," said the soft voice of the perfumer, apparently not in the least offended by the hard terms she had given him, and equally disposed to do her good and uncompromising service of any kind. "Perhaps you wish the magical influence of Armandi to remove from your sight some one who has been in it too long, and troubles you?"

A bitter and painful smile played round the beautiful lips of Beatrice of Ferrara, while, bowing her head slowly, she replied, after a moment's thought, "Perhaps I do."

"Then I am right at last," said Armandi, softly, rubbing his hands together. "I am right at last; and you have nothing to do, fair lady, but to name the person, and the time, and the manner, and it shall be done to your full satisfaction; though I must hint that all the preparations for rendering disagreeable people invisible are somewhat expensive; and the amount depends greatly upon the mode. Would you have it slow and quietly, that he or she should disappear? That is the best and easiest plan, and also the least expensive--for there is the less risk."

"No!" replied Beatrice, firmly, "I would have it act at once--in a moment, and so potently, that no physician on the earth can find skill sufficient to undo that which has been done."

"Of the latter be quite sure," replied the perfumer. "But with regard to the former, it is much more dangerous, as a sudden catastrophe leads instantly to examination. Now, a few drops of sweet *aqua tophana* has its calm and tranquillizing effects so gradually, that no doubt or suspicion is awakened; and you can surely wait patiently for a month, or a fortnight, to give it time to act?"

"You mistake," replied Beatrice, thoughtfully; "you mistake: yet say, how are such things managed? Let me hear, that I may judge."

"Why, lady," replied Armandi, with a mysterious smile, "there are secrets in all things on this earth, from the fine composition of a lady's heart, to the simples of poor Armandi. Nevertheless, although the mysteries of the art must remain hidden in my own bosom, as I enjoy the blessing of having been born in the same land with one so beautiful, and as I know that you were deeply beloved by my late royal and honoured mistress, though somewhat frowning on the soft pleasures of her court, I will, without reserve, reveal to you how your purpose may be best effected."

Thus saying, he took a small silver key from his pocket, and opened a Venetian cabinet, that stood near. "See here!" he said, producing a small gilded phial, containing, apparently, a quantity of a perfectly limpid fluid; "see here! the water that Adam found in the first fountain he met in Eden was not more clear than this; and yet the fruit of the tree that stood near it was not more certain death. No odour is to be discerned therein: to the eye it has no colour; to the lip no taste; and yet, like many another thing, with all this seeming simplicity, it is the most potent of all things, having power unlimited over life and death. Three drops of this, in the simplest beverage, will ensure that slow and gradual decay, which, at the end of a year, shall leave him who drinks it a clod in his mother earth. A larger dose will shorten the time by one half; and a larger still will reduce the time to a few weeks or days. The only difficulty is how to give it: but that I will find means for when I know the person."

"It will not do!" replied Beatrice; "it will not do! it is not quick enough. Have you no other means?"

"Many, lady! many!" replied the perfumer, smiling; "but, in good sooth, you are as impatient as a young lover. All our art has been tasked to render the means at once slow and secure, so as, in cases of necessity, to effect our deliverance from enemies without calling suspicion on ourselves. See here! this artificial rose, so like the natural flower, that the eye must be keen, indeed, which, at the distance of half a yard, could detect the difference. The scent, too, is the same----"

"But why do you keep it under that glass ball?" demanded Beatrice, interrupting the long description with which he was proceeding.

"Because, lady," replied the Italian, "that rose, placed in as fair a bosom as your own, and worn there for one half-hour, would lose its scent, and the wearer health and life within a week. Its odour, therefore, is too valuable to trust to the common air."

"And those gloves?" asked Beatrice; "those gloves, so beautifully embroidered, for what purpose are they designed?"

"Heaven forbid that I should see them on your hands!" replied Armandi; "though I have heard that they were once worn by a queen--who is since dead. But you spoke of quicker means. Here is this small box of powder, containing a certain salt that, in the twinkling of an eye, extinguishes the fire of the heart, and the light of the mind, and leaves nothing but the ashes behind. We often use it, diluted with other things, for other purposes; but I would not administer one dose of that, to any one of note, for a less sum than ten thousand golden Henrys, though the whole box is scarcely worth a hundred crowns. But so quick is its effect, and so marked the traces that it leaves behind, that the chirurgeon were a fool who did not at once pronounce the cause of death in him who took it."

"Give me yon *bonbonnière*," said Beatrice, pointing to a painted trifle on one of the tables. "And now," she continued, as the man gave it her, "is that enough for one dose?" and as she spoke, she emptied part of the powder from the box which contained it into the *bonbonnière*--"Is that enough for one dose?"

"It is enough to kill the King's army!" replied the man. "But what mean you, lady? What do you intend to do?"

"The person for whom I mean this drug," replied Beatrice, "shall receive it from no hands but my own. You shall risk nothing. There is a jewel, worth one half your shop," she added, drawing a ring from her finger, and casting it upon the table; "and the powder is mine."

"But, lady! lady!" cried the perfumer, regarding the diamond with eager and experienced eyes, and yet trembling for the consequences which his fair visitor's strong passions might bring upon himself; "but, lady, if you should be discovered! You are young and inexperienced in such matters. They must be performed with a calm hand, and a steady eye, and an unquivering lip: and if you should be discovered, and put to the torture, you would betray me."

"However I may contemn thee, man," answered Beatrice, "there is no power on earth that could make me betray thee. But rest satisfied; I take the powder from thee, whether thou wilt or not;--but I will make thee easy, and tell thee, that if one grain thereof ever passes any human lip, that lip will be my own. It is well to be prepared for all things--to have ever at hand a ready remedy for all the ills of life--to possess the means of snatching ourselves from the grasp of circumstance: and, in the path which I may be called to tread, the time may well come when I shall wish to change this world for another. I leave to better moralists to decide whether it be right or not, courageous or cowardly, to shake off a life that we are tired of. For my part, I will bear it to the utmost; and, when I can endure it no longer, then will I try another path."

"If such be your purpose, lady," answered the perfumer, with a sweet smile, and a low inclination, "far be it from me to oppose you. Every one, as you say, should be prepared for all things; and I hold that man not half prepared who does not possess the means of limiting the power his enemies have over him to simple death, a fate that all must undergo. Men think far too much of death: it is but cutting off a few short hours from a long race of pain and anxiety: far oftener is it a mercy than a wrong. Men think too much of death!"

"You think little enough of it in others, at least," answered Beatrice, looking upon him with curiosity and hate, not unmingled with that peculiar kind and degree of admiration, which wonder always more or less produces. "Have I not heard that you were busy amongst the busiest on the night of St. Bartholomew?"

"Not I, lady! not I!" exclaimed the perfumer, with a look of disgust and horror at the very name of that fearful massacre. "Not I, indeed! not for the world would I have borne a part, either in that shameful affair, or in the late brutal murder of the great Duke and the Cardinal de Guise."

"Why, how now!" cried Beatrice. "Would you, who hold life so lightly, and take it so carelessly from others; would you affect scruples at slaying those you consider heretics, or at putting away ambitious tyrants?"

"Lady, you mistake it altogether," answered the dealer in poisons, with a grim smile. "The Huguenots are heretics, and damnable heretics, since such is your good pleasure and the Pope's: but in that capacity I have nought to do with them. The Guises were tyrants if you will; though Heaven forbid that any ears but yours should hear me say so! But they tyrannised not over me. What I objected to, was the manner of the thing; and it is the manner that, in this world, makes the only difference between crime and virtue. What is murder in one manner, is war and glory in another; what is fraud in a merchant, is skill in a minister; what is base when done in a burgher's coat and with a simpering smile, is noble when done in royal robes and with a kingly frown. Now, what could be more beastly, or brutal, or indecent, than to cut the throats of some hundreds of men in their beds, stain all their pillows with blood, and throw the old admiral himself, half-naked, out of a window? What could be more cruel than to put them for hours in mortal terror; inflict upon them excruciating wounds, and, in some instances, leave them half dead, half-living, when the whole might have been effected without pain, without fear, without bloodshed, in the midst of some gay banquet, or some pleasant carouse: where they would all have died as if they were going to sleep! Nay, nay, lady! our late royal mistress made there a great and a cruel mistake; and as for the Guises--Pho! was ever anything so stupid and so filthy as to swim the King's own closet with gore, and have a man reeling and tumbling about in the midst, under the strokes of half-a-dozen daggers! I cannot conceive how the King, who is as delicate a gentleman as any in all France, could consent to such an indecency."

Beatrice of Ferrara listened, but she thought deeply too; for there was something in the character of the man who spoke--such a blending of frivolity and foppery with cold-blooded villany, that it led her thoughts far on into the wilds of speculation; and was not without its moral for herself. She saw, from his example, how easy it is for any one to persuade oneself of anything on earth, however much opposed to reason, or to virtue. She saw that there are no bounds to self-deceit, that it is illimitable, and that there was never yet a crime so base, so horrible, so revolting, for which it will not find a pleasant mask and a gay robe;--she saw it, and she began to doubt whether all her own reasonings in regard to self-destruction had not derived their strength from the same source. She resolved that, ere she ever thought again of attempting such an act, she would consider well, and scrutinise her own feelings minutely; but still, with the usual weakness of human nature, she would not lose her hold upon the means of doing that which she more than half believed to be wrong. Without replying to the perfumer's dissertation, she turned thoughtfully towards the door; but, as she did so, she took the poison which she had purchased from the table, and concealed it in her bosom.

Armandi hastened to open the door between the inner and the outer shop, and, with low reverence, presented the tips of his delicate fingers to lead the lady to her chair; but at that very moment the clatter of many horses' feet, and the rush and murmur of a passing crowd, made them both pause, and turn their eyes towards the street. The matter did not remain long unexplained. A considerable body of those mercenary soldiers, who, from their blackened arms, were called the black reitters, were passing along before the house: but their march through the streets of Paris was so common an occurrence, that it would have attracted no crowd to gaze, in the present instance, had not some additional circumstance given another kind of interest to their appearance on this occasion. In the midst of them, however, well mounted, but disarmed, appeared a handsome and noble-looking young man--no other than the Marquis of St. Real--followed by about twenty retainers, also disarmed, and bearing those black scarfs which were, at that time, symbols of military mourning. There was nothing either depressed or anxious in the countenance of St. Real; and he gazed about at the many interesting objects which the streets of the capital presented, with the calm and inquiring glance of a person mentally at ease: but, at the same time, on either side of the file in which he and his followers rode, appeared a body of the reitters, with their short matchlocks rested on their knees, their hands upon the triggers, and their matches lighted; evidently showing, that those they guarded were brought into Paris in the condition of prisoners.

The moment this spectacle met her eyes, Beatrice of Ferrara called to the armed attendant who had accompanied her chair, and who, like his mistress, had now turned to gaze upon the cavalcade as it passed by. "Quick!" she cried, "follow them quick, Bertrand! follow them quick, and leave them not till you see their prisoner safely lodged. Make sure of the place, and then bring all the tidings you can gather to me."

The servant, accustomed to comprehend and to obey at once the orders of a mistress whose mind was itself as rapid as the lightning, sprang from the door, without a word, and, mingling in the crowd, followed the reitters on their way. Beatrice remained in silence till the last had passed, and then, entering her chair, was borne back to her own dwelling.

CHAPTER IX

We must now turn to trace the proceedings of Philip Count d'Aubin, who, riding on at full speed, drew not his bridle rein till he reached the magnificent Hotel de Guise; where, pushing through the mingled crowd of attendants and petitioners, that swarmed, round the *porte cochere* of the dwelling, in which, for the time, resided all the power of Paris, if not of France, he advanced, with hasty steps and abstracted look, to the foot of the great staircase. He had even proceeded some way up the stairs ere he noticed, or even seemed to hear, the reiterated inquiries regarding his name and business, which were addressed to him by the various grooms and porters in his progress. When, at length--called for a moment from his fit of absence--he did condescend to speak, he merely mentioned his name, without indicating in any manner which of the many persons that the house contained was the object of his present visit.

Although unacquainted with his person, the valet, who had at length obtained an answer, happening to recall some of the court scandal of former times, instantly, by an association not unnatural, connected the coming of the Count d'Aubin with the presence of the Duchess de Montpensier, the sister of the Duke de Mayenne, in the house at that moment; and he proceeded forthwith to show the Count to her apartments. D'Aubin entered the splendid saloon in which the Duchess was sitting with the same thoughtful and abstracted air which had been left behind by the strong and turbulent passions, that had just been excited in his bosom by his interview with Beatrice of Ferrara. Madame de Montpensier, surrounded by a group of the gay idlers of the capital, who even at that time mingled in their character that degree of levity and ferocity which marked with such dreadful traits the first French revolution, was engaged in the seemingly puerile employment of cutting out a paper crown with a huge pair of scissors, the sheath of which, black, coarse, and disfiguring, was passed through the silken girdle that spanned her beautiful waist.

Shouts of laughter were ringing through the hall, when the valet opened the door, and announced the Count d'Aubin. The Duchess instantly looked up, with a smile of pleasure; but, remarking the ruffled aspect of the Count, she instantly exclaimed--"Why, how now, D'Aubin! how now! After so long an absence, do you come back to our feet, not like a penitent suing for pardon, but rather like a harsh husband, full of scoldings and tempests?"

The cause of those gloomy looks, which she remarked, was not one which Philip d'Aubin would willingly have communicated to the gay, satirical Duchess de Montpensier, who, to the libertine freedom common to the whole court, added many a wily art, and many a vindictive passion, derived from the angry political factions of the time. The immediate cause of his visit to Paris, however, afforded him a ready motive to assign for his dark brow and agitated look. "Well may I be disturbed, madam," he replied, after a hasty word of salutation, "when my noble cousin, St. Real, confiding in an authentic pass, from the hands of your Highness's brother, has been entrapped in the neighbourhood of Senlis, and is now, as I am informed, a prisoner in Paris!"

"Nay, but why bear such a countenance into our presence, Count d'Aubin?" rejoined the Duchess; "I am guiltless of entrapping your cousin, or of even trying to entrap yourself; though, once upon a time," she added in a low tone, "I may have seen the Count d'Aubin a tassel not unwilling to be lured;" and she looked up at him with a glance in which reproach was so skilfully mingled with playfulness and tenderness, that D'Aubin, although he knew that full two-thirds of the pageant which daily played its part on her countenance, was mere artifice, could not refrain from smiling in his turn.

"Ever willing to be lured, dear lady, where the lure is fair!" he replied; "and though I certainly came to speak reproaches, they were not to you. I know not why your blockhead groom," he added, "brought me hither, unless he divined, indeed, how much the sight of your Highness softens all wrath. My business was with your brother, the Duke of Mayenne."

The Duchess muttered to herself--"That will never do! If he see Mayenne, he will spoil the whole! I appeal to you, fair ladies and gentlemen all," she exclaimed aloud, with one of those quick and happy turns of artifice, which no one knew better how to employ, "if this is not a high crime and misdemeanour in the court of love and gallantry, to tell a lady, whom he dare not deny to be fair, that he came for any other purpose on earth than to see herself?"

"Blasphemy! blasphemy! utter blasphemy!" cried half a dozen voices. "Judge him, fair lady, for his great demerits!"

"Philip d'Aubin!" exclaimed the Duchess, putting on a theatrical air, "you are condemned by your peers; but, under consideration of your having been thoroughly brutalized, by a two months' residence at the distance of a hundred leagues from Paris, we are inclined to show you lenity: kneel down here, then; humbly, at our feet, confess your crime! and swear upon this paper crown, which we have cut expressly for the royal Henry's head, never to commit the like iniquity again!"

D'Aubin had entered the apartment, not very well disposed to jest, but yet the feelings which had oppressed him were of such a nature, that he was quite willing to forget them; and the smiles of the Duchess de Montpensier, as well as the tone of tenderness she assumed towards him, together with the remembrance of many gay moments, spent in her society long before, made him gladly enough take up the part that she assigned him. Bending his knee gracefully before her, then, he made confession of his crime, declared his penitence, and, vowing, in the terms she had dictated, never to offend again, he stooped his head to kiss the paper crown which she held upon her knee. At the same moment the Duchess bent forward, as if to receive his vow, and, as she did so, she whispered, rapidly, "Stay with me, D'Aubin, and I will soon send these fools away."

The Count replied nothing, but rose; and, still holding the paper crown playfully in his hand, demanded, in his ordinary tone, what was the real intent and purpose of that fragile mockery of the royal symbol.

The Duchess saw that he had heard, understood, and was prepared to obey her whisper; and she replied, "'Tis exactly as I have told you, most incredulous of men. When, by the fate of war, or by the blessing of God, Henry, calling himself the Third, shall be brought in chains into Paris, it might be expected that the sister of the murdered Guise"--and as she spoke, her eye flashed for a moment with all the fiery spirit of her race;--"it might be supposed that the sister of the murdered Guise should not bound her wishes for revenge, till she saw the assassin's blood flow like water in the kennel. But she is more charitable, or, rather, he is too pitiful a thing to be worthy of severe punishment. With these scissors shall be cut off his royal locks, ere he quits the courtly world for the world of the cloister; and on his head shall he bear this crown, from the door of Notre Dame to the abbey of St. Denis, when he goes to take the vows that exclude him for ever from the world."

D'Aubin laughed. "So, this crown is for King Henry!" he exclaimed: "and have you never thought, madam, of cutting out another, from some different materials, for your noble brother of Mayenne?"

"It must be an iron crown, then," replied the Duchess, tossing her head proudly; "and he must hew it out for himself, with his good sword."

"Rather a Cyclopean labour," remarked D'Aubin; "rather a Cyclopean labour I suspect! especially since Harry of Valois, to whom you deny the crown, has chosen to turn up his hat with a Huguenot button."

"We shall see, we shall see!" replied the Duchess: "I know, sir Count, you laugh at all parties; so I understand not why you should cling so fondly to the rabble of accursed murderers and heretics, who lie out there at St. Cloud, like vipers in a garden."

D'Aubin laughed outright at the Duchess's vehemence, and reminded her that some of her near relations were amongst the rabble she so qualified.

"They are none the less vipers for that," she replied: and the conversation taking a turn neither very wise nor very decent, may as well be omitted in this place. It lingered on, however, from minute to minute, without the Duchess making any apparent effort to fulfil the promise she had made to D'Aubin, and send away the idlers by whom she was surrounded. Too long accustomed to the intriguing society of Paris, and too well acquainted with the character of the wily woman with whom he had now to deal, not to be armed at all points against every art and deception, D'Aubin began to suspect that the Duchess was trifling with him for some particular purpose, and was seeking to occupy him with other matters, till some moment of importance, to himself or his cousin, was irretrievably lost.

"Hark!" he exclaimed, as this thought crossed his mind; "there is the clock of St. Gervais striking one, and I must really seek my lord the Duke."

"I hear no clock," replied the Duchess--nor could she, for none had struck--"I hear no clock! But not yet, D'Aubin, not yet; I am not yet going to slip the jesses of my *faucon gentil*, after having just recovered him from so long a flight. Stay you with me, D'Aubin, and I will send and see if my brother be within. You go, Mont-Augier," she added, turning to one of the young cavaliers, who instantly sprang to obey her; but, ere he reached the door, the Duchess, by a sudden movement, placed herself near him; and, while D'Aubin was for a moment occupied by some other person present, she said, in a low voice, "Do not return, do not return: we must keep the Count away from Mayenne, or they will together spoil some of our best schemes."

D'Aubin's eye turned upon her; and his quick suspicions might have gone far to counteract her purposes, had not Madame de Montpensier, almost as soon as Mont-Augier's back was turned, contrived, on various pretences, to dismiss the rest of her little court. Left thus alone with a fascinating and beautiful woman, who condescended to court his society, D'Aubin could not resist the temptation to trifle away with her half an hour of invaluable time, though he knew all her arts, and even suspected that, on the present occasion, they were employed against him for insidious purposes. He was on the watch, however, and, ere long, the clatter of many horses' feet in the court-yard caught his attention, and led him instantly to conclude that the Duke of Mayenne was about to go forth, without having seen him. It was now all in vain that Madame de Montpensier, who likewise heard the sounds, and attributed them to the same cause, endeavoured to occupy his attention by every little art of coquetry. D'Aubin started up, and, in gay, but resolute terms, expressed his determination of seeing the Duke ere he left the house.

To what evasion Madame de Montpensier would have had recourse, is difficult to say; but, ere she could reply, the door opened, and a lady entered, whom we will not pause here to describe. Suffice it, that she was the widow of the murdered Duke of Guise, and that, though her person wore the weeds, her face betrayed few of the sorrows, of widowhood.

"Catherine! Catherine!" she exclaimed, entering; "there is our slow brother of Mayenne just returned, and calling for you so quickly that one would think he were himself as nimble as Harry of Navarre."

"Returned! I knew not that he was absent!" replied the Duchess de Montpensier, with an air of irrepressible mortification, on finding that all her arts had been thrown away, and, instead of preventing D'Aubin from seeing her brother ere he went forth, had only tended to keep the Count there till he returned. A meaning smile, too, on the lip of D'Aubin, served to increase her chagrin; and she exclaimed, with a slight touch of pettish impatience in her tone, "Well, well, I go to him; and you, my fair sister, had better stay and console this tiresome man, till my return."

The Duchess of Guise saw that something had gone wrong; but D'Aubin laughed, and replied, as Madame de Montpensier turned towards the door, "May I request you to tell his Highness that the tiresome man waits an audience; and, as his business will be explained in few words, he will not detain the Duke so long as he has detained Madame de Montpensier,--or as, perhaps, I might say, more truly, Madame de Montpensier has detained him,--probably under a mistake;" and he made her a low and significant bow, to which she only replied by shaking her finger at him as she passed through the doorway.

"Where is the Duke?" she demanded eagerly of the pages in the corridor, who started up at her approach; and then, scarcely listening to their answer, she hurried on to the room in which she expected to find him, and opened the door without ceremony. The Duke was seated at a table, hastily sealing some letters, while a courier, booted, spurred, and armed, stood by his side, ready to bear them to their destinations as soon as the packets were complete.

"Why, how now, Catherine!" he exclaimed, turning towards her as she entered, and, in so doing, spilling the boiling wax over his broad hand, without suffering the pain to produce the slightest change of expression on his heavy, determined countenance; "why, how now, Catherine! you have been tampering, I find, with things wherein you have no right to meddle. What is this business about the young Marquis of St. Real? Is it not bad enough that that rash boy, Aumale, should lose me a battle beneath the walls of Senlis, without my sister losing me my honour?"

"Tush, nonsense, Duke of Mayenne!" replied his sister; "Nonsense, I tell you! If you intend that packet for Senlis, you may spare the wax, and your trouble, and your fingers, for it shall never go!"

"Indeed!" said the Duke, pressing firm upon it the broad seal of his arms; "indeed! and why not? Do you not know me better than that, my fair sister? Do you not know that my word, or my safe-conduct, was never in life violated by myself, and never shall be violated by any one else with impunity?"

"All very true! all very true, Charles of Mayenne!" she replied; "but, in the first place, I tell you that your safe-conduct cannot be said to be violated, because some friends of mine choose to help this young St. Real to pursue his journey on the very road for which the safe-conduct was given; and, in the second place, there is no use of sending to Mortfontaine or Nanteuil either, for within an hour St. Real will be, I trust, in Paris."

"Then within an hour he shall be set at liberty!" replied the Duke; "for I shall suffer no quibbling with my honour: he shall be free to come and free to go, till the term of the safe-conduct expires."

"Nonsense, nonsense, Charles!" replied the Duchess; "do not talk like the man in the mystery. Send this fellow away, and let me speak with you calmly; for here is the Count d'Aubin already in the house; and, if you go on vapouring in this way, you may miss a golden opportunity of gaining more than the battle of Senlis has lost."

The Duke made a sign for the courier to withdraw. "I know your skill well, Kate!" he said, as the man left the room, "and am far from wishing to counteract your views; but neither must you meddle with my schemes, nor affect my honour. Now let me hear what it is you have done, and what you propose to do."

"For the done first, then," replied Madame de Montpensier: "what I have done is simply this:--Hearing from good authority that this St. Real had left his troops under the command of his Lieutenant, and, while his cousin D'Aubin went to join Longueville, at Chantilly, had shown a strong inclination to seek the camp of the Henrys before he came to Paris, I thought it much better to change his destination, and bring him hither, well knowing that the first step is all. So much for the past! and now for the future. Leave him but in my hands two days; and if, in that time, I do not find a way, by one means or another, to make him put his hand to the Union, and draw his sword for Mayenne, why, set him free, in God's name! and then talk of your honour and your safe-conducts as much as you like. He shall be well and kindly treated, upon my word!"

The Duke smiled. "I doubt not that, Catherine," he said; "you and your fair sister of Guise, who, I suppose, has some hand in the affair, are not such hard-hearted dames, I know, as to use harsh measures, when tender ones will do."

"Well, well, Mayenne," she answered, "if we bestow our smiles to promote your interest, you, at least, have no occasion to complain, good brother: but you consent, is it not so?"

"On condition that no harshness is used--that I know not where he is--that I see him not--and, that he finds no means for applying for liberation to me: for on the instant I set him free!"

"Manifold conditions!" replied his sister; "but they shall be all complied with. And now for the Count d'Aubin. If we can but win St. Real, I will promise you D'Aubin; for I know one or two of the good Count's secrets, which give me some tie upon him."

"I hold him by a stronger bond," replied the Duke; "the bond of interest, Catherine; for, by my faith, if he quit not soon him whom Beatrice of Ferrara calls the crowned Vice at St. Cloud, I will give the hand of Eugenie de Menancourt to some better friend of the League. I am glad he is come, for I may give him a gentle notice to decide more speedily."

At the name of Beatrice de Ferrara, the cheek of Madame de Montpensier reddened, and her brow contracted; and, without noticing the concluding words of her brother, she replied, "I hate that woman, that Beatrice of Ferrara!" and as she spoke, she moved absently towards the door. The Duke marked her with a smile, and followed, saying, "Well, well, where is this Count d'Aubin?"

The Duchess led the way to the apartment in which he had been left with the Duchess de Guise, and where she still found him, bandying repartees with the fair widow, and with the Chevalier d'Aumale, who had lately been added to the party. The entrance of the Duke of Mayenne, however, at once put a stop to the light jests which were flying thick and fast; and the Duke, without preface, entered upon the subject of D'Aubin's journey to Paris.

"Good morrow! Monsieur le Comte," said he, with an air of unconsciousness, which his somewhat inexpressive countenance enabled him easily to assume. "Right glad was I of your application for a safe-conduct last night, doubting not that, by this time, you are heartily tired of consorting with the effeminate rabble of painted minions and Huguenot boors gathered together at St. Cloud, and are come to support the Catholic faith, with a sharp sword, that has been somewhat too long employed against her."

"Your Highness's compliment to the sharpness of my sword," replied D'Aubin, "does not, I am afraid, extend to the sharpness of my wit; for the occurrences which have taken place within the last five days are surely not calculated to bring over a cousin of the Marquis of St. Real to the party of the Catholic League, or to raise very high the character of dealers in Spanish Catholicon."

The Duke of Mayenne turned a sharp and somewhat angry glance upon Madame de Montpensier; but to D'Aubin he replied coldly, "You seem angry, Monsieur le Comte d'Aubin; and as it is far from my wish to give just cause for anger to a French nobleman, whose good sense, I am sure, will, sooner or later, detach him from a party composed of all that is either infamous or heretical, if you will explain the subject of your wrath, I will do all that is in my power to satisfy you, if I shall find your complaints just and reasonable."

"My complaint is simply this, my lord Duke," replied D'Aubin, smiling at the air of unconsciousness which Mayenne assumed:--"If my imagination have not deceived me, somewhat less than a month ago, Charles, Duke of Mayenne vouchsafed, under the title of lieutenant-general of the kingdom, to grant a regular safe-conduct to a noble gentleman called the Marquis of St. Real, in order that the said Marquis might visit, in safety, the capital of this country, as well as the court of King Henry, in order to judge between the factions which strangle this unhappy land, and take his part accordingly."

"True," said the Duke of Mayenne, bowing his head, "true, we did so."

"Well, then, my lord," continued D'Aubin, "is it not equally true that, when my cousin, St. Real, thought fit to leave his forces at a sufficient distance from either army to give him an opportunity of joining which he pleased hereafter, and was advancing calmly to confer with the King, he was entrapped by false information, surrounded by a party wearing the green scarfs of the League, and carried off, in direct contravention of the safe-conduct you had given him?"

"I will not affect to deny, Monsieur d'Aubin," replied the Duke,--and Madame de Montpensier looked in no small anxiety while he spoke; "I will not affect to deny, that the rumour of some such skirmish as you speak of has reached me--"

"Skirmish, my lord Duke!" exclaimed D'Aubin; "there has been no skirmish in the business; the simple facts are these:--My cousin, with only twenty gentlemen in his train, was surrounded by a party of two hundred men; and, of course, offered no resistance. He produced your safe-conduct, however; but it was set at nought and the leaders of the band gave him very sufficiently to understand, that they had your own authority for what they did. Such, at least, is the account brought to me by one of my cousin's attendants, who contrived to effect his escape; and I now make the charge boldly and straightforwardly, in order that you may have the opportunity of clearing yourself at once; or, that the spot of darkness, which such a transaction must affix to the character of the Duke of Mayenne, may be stamped upon it in characters which no aftertime can efface."

The Duke reddened, and bit his lip. "You make me angry, sir!" he said--"you make me angry!"

"No cause for anger, my lord Duke," replied D'Aubin, "if you be clear of this transaction. It is I who am a friend to the character of the Duke of Mayenne, by giving him an instant opportunity of clearing it;--and let me say, my lord, if you be not free from share in this business," he added, sternly and boldly, "you may find that you are not the only one who is made angry: for, putting aside all respect to your high rank, and to the station which you hold, I shall urge the matter against you as noble to noble, and gentleman to gentleman."

"Was ever the like heard?" exclaimed Madame de Montpensier. "Heed him not, Brother of Mayenne! heed him not; the man is mad, raving mad!"

"Not so mad, nor so foolish, lady," replied D'Aubin, his lip bending into a slight smile, "as to be turned from my purpose, either by sweet words, or angry ones. My lord Duke," he continued, approaching nearer to the Duke of Mayenne, who had taken a hasty turn in the room, as if to give his passion vent before he spoke; "my lord Duke, I mean not to offend you; but my cousin has suffered wrong, and that wrong must be redressed."

"You have spoken too boldly, Count d'Aubin," replied Mayenne, to whom the considerations of policy had by this time restored the calmness of which personal anger had deprived him: "but I must make excuses for the warmth of affection which you seem to bear your cousin; and, in reply to your charge, I have merely to say, that the first correct information respecting this event"--and he turned a somewhat reproachful glance upon Madame de Montpensier--"has been received from yourself; that the capture of your cousin was unauthorized by, and unknown to me; that I know not precisely in whose hands he is; and, that I promise you, upon my honour, he shall be set free as soon as ever I meet with him. Farther still, I pledge myself to find him and liberate him before three days have expired, and to punish, most severely, those who are concerned, in case he have met with any ill-treatment whatever."

"Your promise goes farther than even I could expect, my lord Duke," replied D'Aubin, in a softened tone; "and I most sincerely thank you for having met so candidly a charge which I may, perhaps, have urged too boldly, as your Highness says. Forgive my hastiness, my lord; for, on my honour, in these times of indifference, it is sometimes necessary to give way to a little rashness, in order to show that we have some heart and feeling left."

"We esteem you all the more highly for it," answered the Duke, "and only regret, Monsieur d'Aubin, that one who can so well feel what is right and noble, in some points, should attach himself to a party stained with murder, treachery, falsehood, and many a vice that I will not number; while sense, and wisdom, and good feeling should all induce him to take the more patriotic part that we are in arms to maintain."

"And, let me add, his own interest also," said Madame de Montpensier, "should lead him to join us here."

"Wisely reserving the best argument for the last!" joined in the Chevalier d'Aumale. "The great God Interest, first cousin to the little God Mammon, is powerful both with Catholic and Huguenot, Leaguer and Royalist; and doubtless, beautiful priestess, if you can show that the Deity favours the League more than its opponents, you will soon bring over Monsieur d'Aubin to worship at his shrine."

"That can be easily shown," rejoined the Duke of Mayenne, following the idea of the Chevalier d'Aumale, half in jest and half in earnest: "Has not the god already put at our disposal sundry Huguenot lands and lordships, purses well stuffed with gold, and, above all, the hand of more than one fair heiress? On my word! Monsieur d'Aubin," he added, assuming a more serious and feeling tone, "far would it be from me to hold out to you views of interest, in order to bring you over to the party of the Faith, did not those views of interest coincide entirely with your honour, your reputation, and your duty."

D'Aubin mused for a moment, and then answered laughing, "I never yet did hear, my lord, that interest did not bring a long train of seeming virtues, to give greater strength to her own persuasions: and yet, I do not see how my honour could be raised by abandoning my king at a moment of his greatest need; how my reputation could be increased by quitting a party which I have long served; or how my duty is to be done by breaking my oath of allegiance to my legitimate sovereign."

"Thus, Monsieur d'Aubin," replied the Duke:--"if you are a man of honour,--and most truly do I hold you to be such,--you will flee the society of those who have none; if you have a fair reputation, you will quit a court whose very breath is infamy; and, if you hold sincerely to the Catholic faith, you cannot refuse to turn your sword against its most inveterate enemies."

"No, no, my lord!" replied D'Aubin; "King Henry holds the Catholic faith as well as yourself; and, indeed, loves monks and priests rather better than either you or I do. To him, also, have I sworn fidelity and attachment, as my lawful sovereign; and I will neither break my oath, nor forget my allegiance."

"Thank God, that the thread of a tyrant's life is spun of very perishable materials!" said Madame de Montpensier, with a significant glance at the Duchess de Guise; "and were this Henry dead, we might well count upon you, D'Aubin: is it not so?"

D'Aubin replied not for a moment; and the soft sleepy-eyed Duchess of Guise could not refrain from pursuing the subject jestingly; although her sister-in-law endeavoured, by a chiding look, to stay her, till D'Aubin had answered. "Perhaps the noble Count may be a Huguenot himself." she exclaimed: "who knows, in these strange changeable times----"

"Or, perhaps, this dearly-beloved cousin of his may have been one these twenty years," said the Chevalier d'Aumale; "for shut up in that old castle of theirs, these St. Reals may have been Turks and infidels, for anything that we can tell."

"I wish there was as good a Catholic present as St. Real," replied D'Aubin; "and as for myself, though not very learned in all its mysteries, I hold the faith of my fathers, and will not abandon it. My lord of Mayenne, I would fain speak with you for one moment, in this oriel here," he added.

The Duke of Mayenne instantly complied; and, advancing with the Count into the deep recess of one of the windows at the farther end of the room, he listened to what D'Aubin had to say, and then replied gravely. The Count rejoined; and, though the subject which they discussed seemed to interest them highly, it might be inferred, from the laughter which occasionally mingled with their discourse, that their conversation had taken a turn towards some topic less unpleasant than that which had been broached at the beginning of their first interview.

In the meantime, however, a new personage had been added to the party at the other end of the room. He was a tall gaunt man, of about five-and-forty, with aquiline features, a keen kite-like eye, fine teeth, and curly hair and beard: in short, he was one of those men who are called handsome by people in whose computation of beauty the expression of mind, and soul, and feeling make no part of the account. His dress was not only military, but of such a character as to show that his most recent occupation had been the exercise of his profession. The steel cuirass was still upon his shoulders, the heavy boots upon his legs; and, though some attempt had been made to brush away the dust of a journey, a number of long brown streaks, on various parts of his apparel, evinced, that whatever toilet he had made had been hasty and incomplete.

As soon as Madame de Montpensier caught the first glance of his person entering the saloon, she made him an eager sign not to come in; but he either did not perceive, or was unwilling to obey the signal, and proceeded, with an air of perfect assurance, till the Duchess, starting up, advanced to meet him; trusting, apparently, that the eager conversation which was going on between D'Aubin and the Duke would prevent either of them from remarking her man[oe]uvres at the other end of the room.

"What, in misfortune's name, brought you here?" she said, giving a hasty glance towards the oriel, and perceiving at once that she must make the best of what had occurred, for that D'Aubin's eye had already marked the entrance of the stranger; "what, in misfortune's name, brought you here just now? Here is D'Aubin himself inquiring furiously after this young kestril, that we have taken such pains to catch; and Mayenne, like a fool, standing on his honour, has promised to set him free as soon as ever he finds dim. So you know nothing about the matter: pretend utter ignorance; and swear you have never seen the young Marquis."

"That I can well swear," replied the other, in the same low tone, but with a slight Teutonic accent; "that I can well swear, most beautiful and charming of princesses! for I took especial care to keep out of the way while the poor bird was being limed; and have ridden on before to tell you that, by this time, he must be safe in my house, in the rue St. Jacques."

"Keep him close and sure, then," replied Madame de Montpensier, "at least till his shrewd cousin is out of the city; for Mayenne will let us keep him but two days; and we must work him to our purpose before that time expires." She had just time to finish her sentence, ere Mayenne and D'Aubin quitted the recess of the oriel window; and the latter, advancing towards the place where she stood, addressed her companion as an old acquaintance.

"Ha! Sir Albert of Wolfstrom," he said, with an ironical smile, "faithful and gallant ever! Receiving the soft commands of this beautiful lady with the same devotion as in days of yore, I see! But I have reason to believe that you are lately become acquainted with one of my cousins, and have laid him under some obligations."

"No, no;" replied Wolfstrom, with a grin, which showed his white teeth to the back; "no, no: if you mean Monsieur de Rus, we have been very intimate ever since that night when we three played together at Vincennes, and when I won from you ten thousand livres, Monsieur d'Aubin."

"Well, well, I will win them back again," replied D'Aubin, "the first truce that comes."

"I don't know that," rejoined the German; "you are always unlucky with the dice, D'Aubin: you should be more careful, or, by my faith, the Jews will have all your fine estates in pawn."

D'Aubin coloured deeply; for, as Wolfstrom well knew, the hint that he threw out of excessive expenses, and consequent embarrassments, went home. Mayenne, however, who by those words gained a new insight into the situation of the Count, smiled, well satisfied; assured, from that moment, that those who had it in their power to grant or to withhold the hand of the rich heiress of Menancourt would not be long without the support of Philip d'Aubin.

The Count recovered himself in a moment; and, turning the matter off with a pointed jest, which hit the German nearly as hard, he prepared to take his leave before anything more unpleasant could be said.

"I shall look for the performance of your promise, my lord Duke," he said, as he turned to depart; "and three days hence, shall hope to hear that my cousin has been liberated."

"Come, to make sure of it, yourself," replied Madame de Montpensier, holding out her hand, which he raised in gallant reverence to his lips; "come and make sure of it, yourself. Sup with me at Rene Armandi's, our dearly beloved perfumer, who has a right choice and tasteful cook; and, though the profane rabble insist upon it that he used to aid our godmother, of blessed memory, Catherine, mother of many bad kings, in sending to heaven, or the other abode, various persons, to prepare a place for her, we will ask him, on this occasion, to give us dainties, and not poisons."

"You must send me a safe-conduct, however," replied D'Aubin, laughing, "and I will come with all my heart."

"A safe-conduct you shall have," answered Mayenne, "and as many as you like. But, remember, I do not make myself responsible for Armandi no, nor Catherine, either," he added, with a smile.

"Oh! I will trust her Highness," replied D'Aubin: "the only thing I fear are her eyes;" and, with a low bow, and a glance which left it difficult to determine whether the gallant part of his speech was jest or earnest, he took his leave, and, mounting his horse, rode away towards the gates of Paris.

"He teases me, that Count d'Aubin," said Madame de Montpensier: "I don't know whether to love him, or to hate him."

"Oh! if he teases you, you will love him, of course," replied the Chevalier d'Aumale.

"I think you may love him, Kate," replied the Duke. "At all events, one thing is very certain, that Philip Count d'Aubin is varying fast towards the League; and if you, Catherine, by some of your wild schemes, do not spoil my more sober ones, we shall soon have him as one of our most strenuous and thoroughgoing partisans: for you know, Wolfstrom," he added, laying his broad hand significantly upon the iron-covered shoulder of the German, who, together with three thousand lansquenets, had deserted from the party of Henry III. on the pretence of wanting pay; "for you know, Wolfstrom, there is no one so zealous as a renegade!"

CHAPTER X

Those were busy days in Paris! So manifold were the intrigues, so frequent the changes, so rapid the events, of that time, that it would have required almost more than mortal strength and activity, in those who played any prominent part amongst the factions of the day, to accomplish the incessant business of every succeeding hour, had not that levity, for which the Parisians have been famous in every age of history, stood them in better stead than philosophy could have done, and taught them to consider the fierce turmoil of party, the eager anxiety of intrigue, and even the appalling scenes of strife and bloodshed in which they lived, rather as playthings and as pageants, than as fearful realities.

No sooner had the conference terminated, of which we have given an outline in the last chapter, than Madame de Montpensier, leaving her brother of Mayenne to break his somewhat bitter jest upon the leader of the lansquenets, hurried from the room; but, ere the conversation which succeeded was over, though it lasted but a very brief space, she reappeared, covered with what was then called a penitent's cloak, and holding her mask in her hand, as if prepared to go forth.

Beckoning Wolfstrom towards her, she spoke with him for a few moments, in an under tone; and then, concluding with, "Well, be as quick as possible, and bring me some certain tidings," she again quitted the apartment, without making Mayenne, who was conversing upon lighter matters with the Duchess de Guise and the Chevalier d'Aumale, a sharer in her plans and purposes.

We shall not follow the progress of her chair through the long, tortuous, busy streets of Paris; nor record how her attendants cleared the way through many a crowd, gathered together round the stall of some great bookseller, or before the stage on which some itinerant friar, like a mountebank of modern times, sold his treasure of relics, or chaplets, or authentic pictures of saints and martyrs, or the still-valued indulgence, which the church of Rome did not fail to grant to those who had money and folly enough to purchase either the right of eating flesh, while others were doomed to fish, or the gratification of any other little carnal inclination, not held amongst irremissible sins. Suffice it that--amidst stinks, and shouts, and bawlings, mingled now and then with the "shrill squeaking of the wry-necked fife," and various savoury odours were wafted from the kitchens in which cooks, and traiteurs, and aubergistes prepared all sorts of viands, from the fat quail, and luscious ortolan, to good stout horse-flesh and delicate cat--the Princess's vehicle bore her on, till wide at her approach flew open the gates of the Dominican convent, in the rue St. Jacques, and, entering the first court, the Duchess set down, under the archway, on the left-hand side.

After whispering a word to the *frere portier*, the errant daughter of the noble house of Guise was led through the long and narrow passages of the building, not to the parlour which usually formed the place of reception by the priors of the convent, but to a small room, which had but one door for entrance, and but one narrow window to admit the needful light. The furniture was as simple as it could be, consisting of five or six long-backed ebony chairs, a table, a crucifix, a missal, and a human skull, not, as usual, nicely cleaned and polished, so as to take away all idea of corruption from the round, smooth, meaningless ball of shining bone, but rough and foul as it came from the earth, with the black dirt sticking in the hollows where once had shone the light of life, and the green mould of the grave spreading faint and sickly over the fleshless chaps.

Standing before the table, with his arms crossed upon his breast, and his dark gleaming eye fixed upon the memento of the tomb, stood a tall pale man, habited in the black robe of a prior of the order of St. Dominick, with the white under-garment of the Dominicans still apparent. He raised his eyes as the Duchess entered, but fixed them again immediately upon the skull; and, ere he proceeded to notice in words the approach of his visitant, he muttered what appeared to be a brief prayer, and bowed towards the cross.

"Welcome, madam!" he said, at length; "I have been eagerly expecting you; for it will not be long ere vespers, and we have much to consider."

"I have been forced to delay," replied the Duchess, "in order to save some of our very best schemes from going wrong. But is not Armandi come? He should have been here an hour ago."

"He is here, though he has not been here so long," replied the Prior. "I made them keep him without till you came; for I love not his neighbourhood."

"I ought to pray your forgiveness, father, for bringing him here at all," said the Duchess; "but, in truth--"

"Make no excuse, lady, make no excuse!" answered the Prior. "We labour for the holy church--we labour for the faith; and there is no weapon put within our reach by God, but we have law and licence to use it against the rank and corrupted enemies of the church militant upon earth. Did not the blessed St. Dominick himself say, 'Let the sword do its work, and let the fire do its work, till the threshing-floor of the house of God be thoroughly purged and purified of the husks and the chaff which pollute it?' Did not he himself lead the way in the extirpation of the heretics of old, till the rivers of Languedoc, from their source even to the ocean, flowed red with the foul blood of the enemies of the faith? And shall we, his poor followers, halt like fastidious girls at any means of pursuing the same great object, of obtaining the same holy end? As I hope to reach the heaven that has long received our sainted founder, if this Armandi can find means of accomplishing our mighty purpose, I will embrace him as a brother, and pronounce with my own lips his absolution from all the many sins of his life, on account of that worthy act in defence of the Catholic faith. Shall I call him in?"

"By all means!" said the Duchess, seating herself near the table: "by all means! let us hear what he has devised."

The Prior of the Dominican, or rather, as it was called in Paris, the Jacobine, convent, proceeded to the door, and made a sign to some one, who, standing at the end of the long passage, seemed to wait his commands; and, after a momentary pause, an inferior brother of the order appeared, introducing the perfumer, habited in the same silks and velvets wherewith we have seen him clothed when visited by Beatrice of Ferrara, about an hour before. With a courtly sliding step, inclined head, and rounded shoulders, Armandi advanced towards the spot where the Duchess was seated; and, after laying his hand upon his breast, and bowing low and reverently, drew back a step beside her chair, as if waiting her commands, with a look of deep humility. The Prior of the Jacobines seated himself at the same time, and looked towards the Duchess, as if unwilling himself to begin the conversation with the worthy coadjutor who had just joined them. Madame de Montpensier, whose acquaintance with Armandi was of no recent date, had not the same delicacy on the subject, but at once began, in the familiar and jocular tone which the light dames of Paris were but too much accustomed to use, towards the smooth minister of evil that stood before her: "Well, pink of perfumers," she said, "let us hear what means your ingenious brain has devised for accomplishing the little object I mentioned to you some days ago."

"Beautiful as excellent, and bright as noble!" replied Armandi, in his sweetest tone; "adorable princess, whose charms the lowest of her slaves may reverently worship, sorry I am to say, that the enterprise which you have been graciously pleased to propose to me, I--luckless I!--am unable to undertake."

The Duchess heard all his rhodomontade upon her charms--although the very broadness of Armandi's flattery savoured somewhat of mockery--with more complaisance than had been evinced towards him by Beatrice of Ferrara; but the Prior listened with impatience to his waste of words, and seemed to hear his concluding declaration with disappointment and indignation.

"How is this?" cried he, "how is this? Surely thou, unscrupulous in everything, affectest no vain qualms in regard to the tyrant at St. Cloud! If thou holdest dear the Catholic faith,"--and the keen eyes of the Prior fixed searching upon the soft smiling countenance of the poisoner--"if thou art not infidel, or atheist, or Huguenot, thou wilt clear away thy many sins, by exercising a trade, hellish in other circumstances, in the only instance where it is not only justifiable and praiseworthy, but where, by the great deliverance of the church, it may merit you hereafter a crown of glory. Or is it, perchance," he added, "that thou fearest because this tyrant is a king, and the son of thy former patroness? I tell thee, that were he thine own brother, as a good Catholic, thou shouldest not hesitate."

Armandi listened to the vehement declamation of the monk with his usual composed air, and half subdued smile, and at the end replied, with every apparent reverence--"No, holy Father Bourgoin; you mistake entirely your humble and devoted servant. I am not so presumptuous as to think, that what such a holy man as you tells me to do can be against either right or religion; and, besides, I would humbly beseech you to give me absolution for anything I might do at your command; so that, being a sincere and devoted Catholic, my conscience would be quite at ease." There was the slightest possible curl on Armandi's lip as he spoke, which in the eyes of the Dominican looked not unlike a sneer; but his manner, as well as his words, was in every other point respectful, and he went on in the same tone:--"Neither is it, reverend father, that the royal object of the ministry which you wish me to practise, has had more than one crown put upon his head, which makes me halt; for I never yet could discover that the holy oil with which he is anointed has the least resemblance to that elixir of life which forbids the approach of death; or that in the golden circlet with which his brows are bound lies any antidote for certain drugs that I possess. Nor am I moved by considering that his most Christian Majesty is the son of my dear and lamented mistress; for, taking into account the troublous world in which we live, and the many difficulties, dangers, and disasters which surround Henry at this moment, truly it would be no uncharitable act to give him a safe and easy passport to another world."

"Then why, why," demanded the Duchess, "why do you hesitate to do so?"

"Sweet lady! it is because I cannot," answered Armandi: "the King's precautions put all my arts at fault. Not a dish is set upon his table, but a portion of it is tasted two hours before; his gloves themselves are made within the circle of the court; his own apothecary prepares the perfumes for his toilet; and the cosmetic mask Which he wears in bed, to keep his countenance from the chill night air, is manufactured by his own royal hands."

Madame de Montpensier and the Prior looked at each other with somewhat sullen and disappointed looks; and Armandi added, "Unless you can get me admitted to his household, I fear my skill can be of no avail."

"We have no such interest with the effeminate tyrant," replied Madame de Montpensier, "and so this scheme is hopeless," she added. "But I fear me, Armandi, that, from some love to this tyrant, or to his minions, your will is less disposed to find the means than the means difficult to be found."

"No, as I live, beautiful princess!" answered the poisoner, with more eagerness than he often displayed. "No, as I live! I had once a daughter, lady, as beautiful as you are; and it was her father's pride that she should be wise and chaste: when one mid-day, in the open streets of Paris, my child was met by the base minion, Saint Maigrin, hot with pride, and vice, and wine. He treated her as if she had been an idle courtesan; and how far he would have carried his brutality, none but the dead can tell, had not a gentleman, whose name I know not, rescued her from his hands: although so hurt and terrified, that, ere long, she died. I called loudly for justice, lady--I called with the voice of a father and a man; but I was heard by this Henry, who has never been a father, and is but half a man. He mocked me openly: but the house of Guise, in revenging their own wrongs, revenged mine; and you may judge whether I would not willingly aid you to remove from the earth one who has cumbered it too long."

"Then you absolutely cannot do it?" demanded the priest.

"I cannot," answered Armandi; "but, if I may say so, reverend father, I think you can."

"Ay, and how so?" asked the Prior, eagerly: "if it rests with me, it is done; for, so help me Heaven! if this right hand could plant a dagger in his heart, I would not pause between the conception and the act: no, not the twinkling of an eye!--no, not the breathing of a prayer! so sure am I that, by so doing, I should better serve the Catholic faith, than had I the eloquence of St. Paul to preach it to the world. How can I do it?"

"Very simply, I think," replied the poisoner. "I have often remarked, standing by the gate of your convent, or kneeling at the shrines at Notre

Dame, a dull, heavy-looking man, pale in the face, strong in the body, and having but little meaning in his eye, except that when before some relic, or the image of some favourite saint, a wild and uncertain fire is seen to beam up but for a moment, and go out again as soon. He seems about twenty years of age; and I met him now just going forth as I came hither."

"Oh, yes! I know him well," replied the Prior: "you mean poor Brother Clement; a simple, dull, enthusiastic youth, whose strong animal passions now, most happily for himself, all centre in devotion."

A dark and bitter smile curled the lips of René Armandi as he listened to the Prior's account of the person on whom he himself had fixed as a fit instrument for the foul and bloody schemes that were agitated so tranquilly in their strange conclave. "Yes," he said; "yes, stupid he is; wild, visionary, and enthusiastic, he seems to be; and the same animal passions, which once plunged him in brutal lusts and foul debauchery, may now act as a stimulus to drive home the dagger in the cause of the Catholic faith!"

The gleaming eyes of the Prior fixed sternly upon the countenance of the poisoner while he spoke; and it seemed that no very Christian feelings were excited in the bosom of the monk by the bitter and sneering tone which the Italian employed. The suggestion, however, which his words had implied, rather than expressed, instantly caught his attention, and diverted his mind towards more important matter. "Ha!" he exclaimed; "ha! think you he could be prevailed upon?"

"I have often remarked, reverend father," replied Armandi, who had caught the transitory look of wrath as it had passed over the monk's countenance, and who, being but little disposed to make an enemy of one both powerful and unscrupulous, now spoke in a milder and more deferential tone--"I have often remarked, reverend father, that there are men in whose souls the animal part seems to be so much stronger than the intellectual, that mere appetite drives them on to coarse extremes in everything, however opposite and apparently incompatible. Thus, do we not see," he asked, lowering his tone, as if he suspected that the case he was about to put might be that of his auditor; "do we not see that men, who, in their youth, have given themselves up somewhat too freely to gallantry, and to those fair sins which the church condemns in vain, in after-years wear the bare stones with their bended knees, and tire all the saints in the calendar with penitence and prayer?"

"Thou speakest profanely," said the Prior: "is it not natural and just that men, who have great sins to atone for, should do the deeper penance when their conscience is awakened to repentance? But what if it were even as thou wouldst sneeringly imply? How does this affect our Brother Clement?"

"If I reason wrongly," replied Armandi, "my reasoning affects him not; but if my view is right, it matters much. I doubt, good father, that it is always true repentance which brings the libertine to the altar. My conviction is, that it is but one appetite gone, and another risen up in its place; and amongst such men, had I some good and reasonable cause,--some powerful motive to stir them up to action,--it is amongst such men, I say, that I should seek for one to undertake fearlessly, and execute resolutely, such a deed as that which has been proposed to me: and let me say too," he continued, a natural tendency to sneer at his companions getting the better of the moderation he had assumed; "and let me say, too, that I would seek for one whose reasoning powers, in the nice balance of the brain, would kick the beam when the opposite scale were loaded with animal passion and vagrant imagination. Do you understand me?"

The Prior made no reply; but, starting up from his seat, walked up and down the room with his hands clasped, his head bent, and his lips muttering. In the meanwhile, Madame de Montpensier beckoned Armandi towards her, and held with him a brief conversation in an under tone. His communication with her, however, seemed to be much more free and unrestrained than it had been with the monk; for jest and laughter appeared to take the place of shrewd and somewhat bitter discussion; and, though looks of intelligence and significant gestures made up fully one half of what passed, the lady and the poisoner seemed to understand each other perfectly. Their conversation ended by Madame de Montpensier exclaiming aloud, "Oh, never fear, never fear! To attain that object I will act the angel myself, and go any lengths in that capacity."

"Reverend father," continued the Princess, "this scheme is a hopeful one, easily executed, and involving no great risk."

The Prior paused, and turned to listen to the Duchess, who knew much better how to treat him than Armandi. "What is the scheme, lady?" he demanded: "as yet I have heard of none, except vague hints regarding a brother of the order, mingled with sneers at religion and religious men, which, in better days, would have had their reward."

"No, no, good father," replied the Duchess; "poor Armandi means no evil. Answer me one or two questions: think you not that Henry,--the excommunicated tyrant, the sacrilegious murderer of one of the prelates of the holy church, the friend of heretics, who is at this moment doing all that he can to spread heresy and destroy the Catholic faith in France;--think you not that he is without the pale of law, and that any means are justifiable to stop him in his damnable course, and save the holy church and the Catholic population in this country?"

"Not only do I think so," replied the Prior, vehemently, "but I think that he who does stop him in his course will gain a crown of glory, and would obtain, should death befall him in the act, the still more glorious crown of martyrdom."

"That is enough, that is enough!" replied the Duchess; "I will explain to you the whole scheme when we are alone. You, Armandi, go and prepare everything that you spoke of,--the rose-coloured fire, and the dress, and the wings, and come to me to-night, that we may arrange all the rest."

With profound and repeated bows, the perfumer was in the act of taking his departure from the apartment where this iniquitous conference had taken place, when three soft taps on the door arrested his progress, and the next moment the same monk who had ushered him thither on the arrival of the Duchess, announced that a noble gentleman without craved to speak with Madame de Montpensier, according to her own appointment.

"Give him admittance, father! give him admittance!" cried the Princess; "it is our faithful friend Wolfstrom, who brings me news of other feats accomplished in the same good cause that occupies us here."

The order for his admission was immediately given by the Prior; and as Armandi passed out, the leader of the lansquenets entered, exchanging glances of recognition with the poisoner, the circle of whose acquaintances had extended itself, by one means or another, to almost every one possessing any degree of rank, wealth, or influence in Paris.

"Well, lady!" said the soldier of fortune, after a formal bow to the Prior, "the stag is safely housed, and we wait but your commands to follow up the sport."

"But have you learned any particulars of his mind and character?" demanded the Duchess, eagerly; "have you discovered which way we best may lead or drive him to the point? Remember, our time is but short, and much remains to be done in those brief three days."

"Good faith! there seems but little to be learned, lady," replied the soldier. "As I promised, I took care that he should have companionship with none but those who would take up every light word, to let us see into the dark nooks of his heart, and report all truly that they learned; but, by the Lord! it seems that there are no dark nooks to be found out! All is open and clear--he seems simple as the day, religious in the true Catholic faith, sir Prior, bold and calm, but having little to take hold of, if it be not his devotion."

"Of whom speak you?" demanded the Prior, while Madame de Montpensier fixed her fine dark eyes thoughtfully on the ground; "is it of the young St. Real, of whom our noble lady here spoke some days since?"

Albert of Wolfstrom nodded; and the Prior also fell into a fit of meditation, seeming to revolve, like the Duchess, the means of dealing with one of those characters, whose right simplicity of nature renders them much more difficult to manage than even the wily, the worldly, and the shrewd.

"We must think of this matter, Sir Albert," said the priest, "we must think of this matter. Is he in safety at your house, do you think?"

"Why, by my honour, that is doubtful," answered the German. "My lansquenets have active duty to perform; people are coming in and out at all hours; and I never know when his Highness the lieutenant-general himself may not make his appearance there."

"That will never do!" said the Duchess; "that will never do--we must send him to the Bastile. Mayenne will never venture there; for he knows very well that within those walls he would meet many a sight which his fine notions of honour and justice would compel him to inquire into, to the mortification of his policy, and the destruction of his prospects. We must have him to the Bastille."

"Your pardon there, madame," said the soldier, somewhat uncourteously; "my prisoner goes not to the Bastille, wherever he goes! That foul burgher demagogue Bussy le Clerc shall hold at his good pleasure no prisoner of mine."

Madame de Montpensier's dark eye flashed, and her cheek reddened as she listened to the bold tone of the mercenary leader; but all the tangled and complicated political intrigues in which his services were necessary, and perhaps some more private considerations also, rendered her unwilling to break with one whose faith and integrity were somewhat more than doubtful. She smothered her anger, therefore, and, after a few moments' thought, replied, "I have it, I have it! He shall be brought here. You say, Sir Albert of Wolfstrom, that, notwithstanding the intimacy of his father with the Huguenots, he seems to hold fast by the Catholic faith. You, reverend father, shall try your oratory upon him; and, if possible, we must make him benefit by all that we do to lead on Brother Clement to the point we desire. You object not to this plan; do you, Sir Albert?"

"It is more hopeful than the Bastile," replied the soldier; "and I will bring him here with all my heart: but yet," he continued, with a doubtful shake of the head: "but yet--though I cannot tell why--but yet I have some fears that you will not find this young roebuck so easy to manage as you imagine. There is something about him, I don't know what, that makes me doubt the result."

"Oh! but we have means that you know not of," replied the Duchess, "which, if he be in faith and truth a son of the holy church, must bring him over to the Union for her defence."

"Well, well, I will bring him here," said the mercenary leader; "and you, fair lady and reverend father, must do the rest."

"Away, then, quick! and you will find me here at your return," replied the Duchess; "but take care that you meet not with Mayenne by the way, for he will set him free to a certainty; and then all that we have done will only tend to drive him over to the other party, instead of gaining a powerful adherent for the League."

"No fear, no fear!" replied Wolfstrom. "The distance is but a hundred yards; and I will post scouts at the end of the street before we set out." So saying, the leader of the lansquenets took his departure, leaving Madame de Montpensier with the Prior of the Jacobine convent, with whom an eager and interesting conversation instantly took place, the consequences of which we may have to detail hereafter.

CHAPTER XI

We must now turn once more to the young Marquis of St. Real; and, although the events which had befallen him since the death of his father may have been gathered by the reader from what has passed in the chapters immediately preceding, it may not be unnecessary to recapitulate here, as briefly as possible, the occurrences which had placed him a prisoner in the midst of Paris.

According to the promise which Henry of Navarre had obtained from the old Marquis of St. Real on his death-bed, that nobleman's son, as soon as possible after the last rites had been paid to his father's memory, had prepared to take the field in behalf of one of the great contending parties which then struggled for mastery in France. He had applied for and obtained, both from King Henry III. on the one part, and from the Duke of Mayenne on behalf of the League, a safe-conduct to visit the camp and the capital, accompanied by twenty retainers. The rest of his forces, it was expressly stipulated, were to remain at the distance of fifteen leagues from the royalist army; and the position of the two kings, as they advanced to lay siege to Paris, had compelled him, in compliance with this stipulation, to deviate from his direct road to Paris, and accompany, for a short way, his cousin, who was advancing to reinforce the troops of Longueville and La Noue. Although strongly pressed by messengers from those two generals to decide at once in favour of the royal cause, and join the partisan force which they commanded, St. Real steadily refused to do so, till, according to the determination he had expressed, and in consideration of which he had obtained a safe-conduct from Mayenne, he should have visited the head-quarters of the king and of the League.

As soon as he had obtained such a position for his forces as enabled him to leave them in perfect security, he set out with his small train, purposing to proceed first to the camp of the two Henrys, as the nearest at the moment, and then to visit Paris. He had scarcely advanced, however, half a day's march on his way, when he was suddenly surrounded by an immensely superior body of reitters and lansquenets, who had been sent forth from Paris for the express purpose of obtaining possession of his person. How Madame do Montpensier had gained such accurate intelligence of all his movements, was a matter of surprise even to her own immediate confidants;

but it was very well understood that the orders, in consequence of which this bold stroke was executed, emanated from her; and the leaders of the mercenaries, who captured St. Real, were not only furnished with the exact details of his line of march, but also with a ready answer to the indignant appeal which he instantly made, on his arrest, to the safe-conduct he possessed under the Duke of Mayenne's own hand. That safe-conduct, they replied, had been given him in order to facilitate a peaceful visit to Paris; while he, on the contrary, had not only led his troops into such a position as to enable him to give strong support to the Duke of Longueville, but had even detached a body to aid that nobleman in the battle of Senlis.

It was in vain St. Real explained to his captors, that the troops which had left him were the immediate retainers of his cousin, the Count d'Aubin, over whom he had no authority, and that he himself had positively refused to take part with the Duke of Longueville. His remonstrance was without effect; and, although he well knew his own innocence, he could not but admit that the reasoning against him was specious. In reply to all his explanations, the captain of the lansquenets simply urged that he had no power to release him, and that his justification must be made to the Duke of Mayenne himself. To submit, therefore, was a matter of necessity; and, as he was in every respect well treated, the young Marquis did submit without any very angry feelings, concluding that he might as well reverse the order of his proceedings, and first visit Paris instead of the royal camp.

On his arrival in the capital, he demanded to be carried instantly to the presence of the Duke of Mayenne; but this application was evaded, it being boldly asserted by those who held him in their hands that the Duke was absent from the city. Hitherto his attendants had been permitted to bear him company; and as he had ridden through the crowded streets of the city, he had felt less as a prisoner than as a voluntary visiter of the great metropolis; but when, after having been detained for some time at the house of Albert of Wolfstrom, he was told that he must accompany his captor to the convent of the Dominicans, whither only one servant could be permitted to attend him, he began to suspect that the bonds of his imprisonment were being straitened; and he remonstrated with calm but firm language, reiterating his demand to be brought before the Duke of Mayenne, and expressing his determination to hold the name of that nobleman up to the reprobation of all honourable men, if he suffered any of his adherents to violate the safe-conduct from his hand with impunity.

Wolfstrom, however, who on more than one occasion had shown himself but little tender of his own fair fame, could not be expected to feel much solicitude for that of another; and, although he held the potent Duke in some degree of awe, he had become hardened by the impunity which every sort of falsehood enjoyed in the good easy times of civil war, and doubted not that, in the end, he should find means of extricating himself from the consequences of the present intrigue, as he had done in regard to many which had preceded, namely, by the unlimited command of impudence, shrewdness, and three thousand mercenaries.

He turned a deaf ear, therefore, to the complaints of St Real; and the young Marquis was conducted to the convent of the Jacobins, in the midst of precautions which he did not fail to mark, and from which he augured little good in regard to the intentions of his gaolers.

The distance from the dwelling of the mercenary leader to the convent was but short; and the people of Paris were well accustomed to see parties of soldiers pass through their streets: but the indescribable pleasure of staring, in this instance, as in all others, collected a little crowd round the centre of bustle; and the gates of the Jacobins, as they opened to receive St. Real, were surrounded by between twenty and thirty persons of different conditions. To those who have eaten sufficiently of the tree of good and evil in a great capital to know *that they are naked*, the presence of a gaping mob to witness the fact of their being dragged along like culprits by a party of rude soldiers, would be a subject of annoyance. St. Real felt injured, but not ashamed or afraid; and fixing his eye upon the most respectable personage of the crowd, he suddenly stopped where he stood, and, ere any one could prevent him, exclaimed, in a loud and distinct voice, "My friend, if the Duke of Mayenne be in Paris, you will serve both him and me by telling him that the Marquis of St. Real is here detained, contrary to the Duke's safe-conduct and his honour."

"You will tell him no such thing, as you value your ears!" shouted Albert of Wolfstrom, fixing his eyes upon the Parisian with a marking glance, which seemed to intimate that he would not be easily forgotten by the wrath of the German leader in case of disobedience. The Parisian drew back, determined from the very first to practise that sort of wisdom which those long resident in great cities, and much habituated to scenes of contention and intrigue, do not fail to acquire; namely, to meddle with nothing that does not personally concern them. There was another person present, however, whose diminutive stature, and the simplicity of garb which he had assumed, combined to conceal him from the notice of either St. Real or the mercenary leader; no other, indeed, than the young Marquis's dwarf page, Bartholo; who, peeping through the open spaces between the other personages that formed the little crowd, saw and heard all that passed without attracting notice himself. Slipping out at once from amongst the rest, he made his way down the street, holding one of his usual muttered consultations with himself.

"Now, shall I tell Mayenne," he said, "that the great baby is caught, and shut up here in the Jacobins, like a young imprudent rat, in a politic rat-trap; or shall I let him lie there for his pains, till that spoilt boy, D'Aubin, has married the other fair-haired baby, and that matter is irrevocable?"

He paused for a moment at the end of the street, revolving the question he had put to himself in silence. "No, no," he added, at length; "no, no, there I might outwit myself; these Leaguers are too cunning for that. If they can't get St. Real on any other terms, they may marry him to this Eugenie de Menancourt, and spoil all my schemes at once. If Mayenne hears publicly where he is, he must set him free, for his honour's sake. Then will he go off, in the heat of his anger, to the people at St. Cloud; D'Aubin will come over to the League, marry the girl, and all will be safe. Yes, yes, to Mayenne! I will to Mayenne!"

In consequence of this determination, he proceeded as quickly, but as quietly as possible, to the Hotel de Guise, and demanded to speak with the Duke of Mayenne,--a privilege which every one in Paris claimed in regard to that leader, whose power was principally based upon his popularity. The Duke, however, had by this time set out to watch the progress of the skirmishes which were taking place almost hourly in the Pré aux Clercs, and the dwarf, not choosing that the tidings he had to communicate should be given in any other than a public manner, refused to intrust them to Mayenne's retainers, and retired, resolving to repeat his visit early the next morning.

In the mean time St. Real was hurried into the convent, the gates were shut, and, preceded by two or three of the Dominicans, he was led along the dark and gloomy passages of the building, towards the apartment in which the Prior and Madame de Montpensier were still in conference. Here, however, he was stopped at the door; and Albert of Wolfstrom, entering alone, held a brief but rapid conversation with the Prior. It ended in St. Real being led back again across the great court to a distant part of the monastery, where, after climbing two flights of steps, he was ushered into a corridor extremely narrow, but of considerable length. In the whole extent of wall, however, which this corridor presented, there only appeared three doors, besides the low arch by which he entered. Two of these opened on the left, and were close together; the other was at the further end of the passage.

Albert of Wolfstrom and his soldiers paused at the entrance; but the monks led St. Real on, and, in a moment after, the Prior himself followed. He seemed to regard the young stranger with some degree of interest, and addressed him with mildness and urbanity. "I am told, my son," he said, "that it is necessary, for reasons into which I have no authority to inquire, to hold you as a prisoner till the decision of the lieutenant-general of the kingdom is known in regard to your destination; but at the same time the members of the holy Catholic Union, whose object is solely to maintain the faith and liberties of the people, and to oppose the progress of tyranny and heresy, desire that you should not be treated as a common prisoner of war, but rather should have every comfort and convenience till your fate is otherwise decided. For this purpose, they have consigned you to our care rather than to the rude durance of the Bastille; and, instead of assigning you one of the common cells of the brotherhood, I have directed that you should be placed here, where you can have more space and convenience. Yonder door, at the farther end of the corridor, belongs to a cell fitted for your attendant; this first door on the left leads to an apartment which we shall assign to one of our brethren of St. Dominick, through whom you can communicate with the convent and the world without. This is your own apartment--"

As he spoke, he opened the second of the two doors, which stood close together on the left, and led St. Real into a spacious and well-furnished chamber. It was airy, but somewhat dim, as it derived its only light from a window, which appeared, by its great height and Gothic shape, to have once formed part of some church or chapel. At the present moment, such arrangements had been made--amongst the various alterations which the old building must have undergone--that this single window, which reached from the ceiling to the floor, served to give light both to the room in which St. Real stood, and to the other immediately by its side, which together must have once formed but one large chamber. The thin partition of woodwork which separated the one room from the other, was supported, from the floor to the roof, by the strong stone pillar that divided the Gothic window into two parts; and thus, though the two chambers were completely distinct, they both had an equal share of light.

"This chamber is somewhat obscure," continued the Prior; "but in the alterations which were made in this building, some twenty years ago, we could not arrange things better. What are now sleeping rooms were then part of the old chapel, and this high window looked out to the Prior's dwelling." So saying, he advanced and opened the casement, a great part of which, swinging back on its creaking and clattering hinges, gave admittance to the free air of summer from without, and showed to St. Real the heavy walls of another body of the building rising up before the window, at the distance of scarcely five feet. Running along upon the same level as the chamber in which he stood, might be seen one of those Gothic passages of fretted stone-work, which, in churches, are called monks' galleries; while, at the distance of about twenty feet below, appeared between the two buildings the narrow paved alley which united the inner to the outer court of the Dominican convent.

The Prior proceeded with some more excuses for the dimness of the chamber; but as soon as he had concluded, St. Real, who had listened calmly, replied, "I complain not of the apartment, father, I have slept in worse; but I complain of imprisonment, when my safety and freedom were guaranteed to me by the Duke of Mayenne himself. However, let me warn you, that I am aware, from some circumstances which occurred at the gate of the convent, that his Highness of Mayenne is purposely held in ignorance of my imprisonment. I acquit him therefore of all dishonourable conduct: but how you, and others, will answer to him for bringing his honour and good faith in question, you must yourself consider."

"For my actions," replied the Prior, somewhat sternly, "I am prepared, my son, not only to answer to him, but to God. Those of others I have nought to do with. It suffices for me, that I have authority from those who have a right to give it, to detain you here till I am assured that the lieutenant-general thinks it fit that you should be set at liberty. You are ungrateful, my son, for kindness felt and shown: you might have undergone harsher treatment, had you been consigned to the Bastille."

"Father, I am not ungrateful," replied St. Real, whose simple good sense was no unequal match for even monkish shrewdness; "but when an act of injustice is committed, it is somewhat hard to require that the sufferer should be well pleased that that act of injustice is not greater than it is. To confine me here is wrong--to confine me in the Bastille were worse; but, surely, I cannot be expected to feel grateful to the thief who cuts my purse, simply because he does not cut my throat also!"

"Your language is hard," replied the Prior, "and your similes are indecent towards a minister of the religion you profess to hold; I shall, therefore, waste no more words upon you, young sir. Your conduct, however, makes no change in my purposes. The treatment you receive shall be as gentle and as good as if you were grateful for kindness, and courteous towards those whom you should respect. You will one time know me better; and you may be sure, even now, that I have no purposes to serve by your detention; as you will find by our intercourse, be it long, be it short, that I shall strive for nothing but, if possible, to lead you in that course in which your honour, your happiness, and your best interests, here and hereafter, are alone to be found."

St. Real made no reply; and the Dominican, bowing his head with an air of conscious dignity, withdrew from the apartment, and, proceeding through the doorway by which he had entered, left the young Marquis and his attendant alone. The sound of turning keys and drawing bolts succeeded, and St. Real for the first time found himself a prisoner indeed. Now "The soul, secure in its existence, may smile at the drawn dagger, and defy its point;" yet there are many things which may happen to the body, that defy the soul to preserve her equanimity, although they be much less evils, in comparison, than that irretrievable separation of matter and spirit, which we are accustomed to look upon with more indifference. For a moment or two, St. Real lost his calmness, and, striding up and down the room with his arms folded on his breast, gave way to that bitterness of spirit, which every noble heart must feel on the loss of the great, the incomparable, the inestimable blessing of liberty. His more philosophical attendant, who had been selected in haste from among the rest of his followers, without any great attention to his mental qualities, consoled himself, under the privation which so painfully affected his master, by examining every hole and corner in the apartments to which they were consigned; and comforted himself not a little, under all their woes and disasters, by the sight of soft and downy beds, rich arras, and velvet hangings. Before his perquisitions were well complete, however, and just as his master was reasoning himself into calmer endurance of an event he could not avoid, the door once more opened, and admitted a brother of the order, on whose appearance and demeanour we must pause for a moment.

He was younger than any of the friars that St. Real had yet seen,--pale in countenance, heavy in expression, with a certain degree of sadness, if not wildness, in his eye, and that close shutting of the teeth and compression of the lips, which, in general, argues a determined disposition. A little above the middle height, he was powerful in limb and muscle; but the appearance of strength and activity, which his form would otherwise have displayed, was contradicted by a certain slouching stoop, which deprived his demeanour of all grace; while the habit of gazing, as it were, furtively from under the bent brows which almost concealed his eyes, gave his dull countenance a sinister expression, not at all prepossessing.

"Benedicite!" said the friar, as he advanced towards St. Real; "benedicite!"

St. Real made some ordinary answer in Latin; but the dull unreplying countenance of the monk showed that his stock of Latinity did not extend even to the common phrases in use amongst persons of his profession; and the young Marquis proceeded in French: "You are, I presume, the brother appointed to keep watch over us in our confinement?"

"The Prior has given me, for a penance," replied the monk, "the task of lying in a down bed, and waiting your will in communicating with the parlour and the refectory, till to-morrow morning. I am commanded to ask you if you will have supper: it grows late."

"I am here, father," replied St. Real, with a smile, "as a bird in a cage, and you must feed me at what hours you please: it matters but little to me."

The monk gazed on him, for a moment, in sullen silence, as if he hardly attended to his reply, or hardly understood its meaning; and then, as his slow comprehension did its work, he turned away with a few muttered, half-intelligible words, and left the apartment, going apparently to command the meal of which he had spoken. It was soon after brought in; and, during its course, the Dominican sat by, turning over the leaves of his breviary in silence, from time to time reading a few sentences, and filling up the intervals in gazing vacantly upon the pages, seemingly occupied in dull and gloomy dreams.

The meal did not occupy much time; and after it was concluded, St. Real, anxious to hear something more precise concerning the state of the capital, and to obtain some information in regard to his own situation, endeavoured to enter into conversation with the monk; but the course of all their thoughts lay in such different lines, that he soon perceived the attempt would be in vain. The Dominican sat and listened, and replied either by monosyllables, or by long fanatical tirades, in general totally irrelevant to the topic which called them forth; and, as twilight began to grow upon the world, the young Marquis abandoned the endeavour, and intimated, by his silence, a desire to be left alone. It was long before the other gratified his inclination in this respect, however, but sat mute and absent, still turning over the leaves of his breviary, and gazing, from time to time, upon the face of his companion. Nor was it till St. Real expressed his desire to have a lamp, and to be left to his own thoughts, that the monk deemed it advisable to retire.

Fatigued in body and mind by the events of the day, St. Real soon cast himself down to rest; and sleep was not long in visiting his eyelids. His slumber was profound also; and he awoke not till various sounds in the immediate vicinity of his chamber disturbed his repose somewhat rudely.

The nature of the first noises that roused him he could not very well distinguish, for slumber, though in flight, still held, in some degree, possession of his senses. They seemed, however, as far as he could remember afterwards, to have proceeded from some smart blows of a hammer upon a wooden scaffolding; but, before he was well awake, those sounds had ceased, and a buzzing hum, like that of a turner's wheel, or a quickly moved saw, had succeeded. St. Real listened attentively; and, having convinced himself that the noises, by whatever they were occasioned, were not produced by anything in his own chamber, but rather seemed to proceed from some part of the building opposite his window, he addressed himself to sleep again, and not without success.

But his repose was not so full and tranquil as before. His former slumbers had been profound, forming one of those dreamless, feelingless, lapses of existence, which seem given us to show how the soul, even while dwelling in the body, can pause with all her powers suspended, unconscious of her own being, till called again into activity by some extraneous cause. The sleep which succeeded, however, was very different: dreams came thick and fast; some of them were confused and wild, and indistinct, but some were of that class of visions in which all the objects are as clear and definite as during our waking moments,--in which our thoughts are as active, our mind is as much at work, our passions are as vehemently excited, as in the strife and turmoil of living aspiration and endeavour--dreams which seem given to show us how intensely the soul can act, and feel, and live, while the corporeal faculties, which are her earthly servants, are as dead and useless as if the grave's corruption had resolved them into nothing.

At one moment it seemed that he was in the battle-field, amidst the shout and the cry, and the clang of arms, and the rush of charging squadrons; and then he was in the flight of the defeated army, and he knew all the bitter indignation of reverse, and all the burning thirst to retrieve the day, and he felt all the vain effort to rally the flying, and the hopeless and daring effort to repel the victor; and then again, when all was lost, and not the faint shadow of a despairing hope remained, he was hurrying his rapid course across some dark and midnight moor; and, while he spurred on his own weary horse, he held in his hand the bridle rein of another, who bore one for whom he felt a thousand fears which he knew not for himself; and ever and anon, as he turned to look, the soft sweet eyes of Eugenie de Menancourt would gaze upon him with imploring earnestness. Then, suddenly, the figure changed, the rein dropped from his hand, and, armed all in steel, with lance couched and visor up, as if galloping to attack him, appeared his cousin, Philip d'Aubin; and, with a feeling of horror and a sudden start, St. Real woke.

The sounds that he now heard--for as yet the night had by no means assumed her attribute of quietness--were certainly not calculated to produce the painful sensations that he had just undergone. There was music on the air--soft and delicate music,--not gay, and yet not sad, but with a certain wild solemnity of tone, that well accorded with the hour, and seemed calculated to raise the thoughts to high and unearthly aspirations. At first, the music was solely instrumental; but, in a moment or two afterwards, two sweet voices were heard, singing, with a peculiarly thrilling softness of tone, that seemed to have something supernatural in its clear melody.

St. Real listened; and, though the sounds must have proceeded from some distance, yet the words were pronounced so distinctly, that he lost not a syllable of the song they poured upon the night.

SONG.

First Voice. Blessed! blessed! art thou,

Amongst the sons of men!

For angels are wreathing for thy brow

Flowers that fade not again!

Second Voice. A crown, a crown of glory for the brave!

First Voice. Blessed! blessed! are those

That sleep the sleep of the good!

Blessed is he whose bosom glows

To shed the tyrant's blood!

Second Voice. Glory to him whom the Church shall save!

First Voice. Amongst the saints in Paradise,

In glory he shall dwell!

And angels shall greet him to the skies,

When to earth he bids farewell!

Second Voice. Joy, joy, joy to the champion of the Lord!

First Voice. His arm is now endued with might,

The foes of the Faith to destroy!

To sweep the tyrant from God's sight,

To crush the worm in his joy!

Second Voice. Death, death, death to the tyrant abhorred!

Both Voices. Blessed! blessed! blessed art thou

Amongst the sons of men!

For angels are wreathing for thy brow

Flowers that fade not again!

It was no longer doubtful whence these sounds proceeded; for, in consequence of the closeness of a hot August night, St. Real had left his window open; and he now distinctly perceived that the music issued from a spot in the monks' gallery, very nearly opposite. Springing out of bed as soon as the sounds had ceased, he advanced to the window, and looked out; but he could perceive nothing. The night was somewhat obscure, the moon by this time was down, and it was with difficulty that he distinguished the fretted stonework of the gallery from the rest of the dark mass that rose before him. He paused for a moment, to consider what all this could mean. Though a sincere Catholic, and habituated to make a marked distinction between the doctrines of the religion he professed and the absurdities, superstitions, and corruptions with which knaves and fools had endeavoured to disguise it, still the Reformation had disclosed too much, and the young noble was of too inquiring a disposition for him to be unaware of the multitude of tricks, intrigues, and deceptions, which some of the more bigoted members of the Roman church thought themselves justified in practising for the attainment of an end desired. The sounds he had just heard, therefore, he attributed at once to their right cause, looking upon them as part of some piece of monkish jugglery. Almost as rapidly joining this conclusion in his mind to his own arrest without the knowledge of Mayenne, to his detention in the Dominican convent, to his separation from the rest of the community, and to the peculiar position of the apartments assigned to him, he was led to believe--though wrongly--that he himself was the object of the somewhat absurd stratagem which he had just witnessed.

"These monks must surely deem me a very great fool indeed!" he thought, as he stood and gazed out upon the building opposite, longing to give the persons who had been singing an intimation of his consciousness of their arts, and of the contempt in which he held them. But, while considering whether it would not be more dignified to let the matter pass over in silence, a new trick was played off. A sudden light burst through the apertures of the stone-work, and was poured, as it were, in a full stream upon the window at which he stood, but not on the part contained in his own chamber, being directed entirely upon that portion of the casement which was beyond the partition, and which gave light to the chamber assigned to the young monk who had been given him as an attendant. The first ray of light that St. Real perceived was of the ordinary hue, though of a dazzling brightness; but the next moment it assumed a bright rose-colour, and proceeded to pour on, changing to a thousand varied and beautiful tints, which the young noble thought certainly very admirable, but not at all supernatural. The next moment, however, he heard through the partition the murmuring of voices in the neighbouring chamber; and, thinking that the jugglery had been carried quite far enough, he determined, if possible, to put an end to it. Throwing his cloak round him, therefore, he approached the door, intending to enter the chamber of the young Dominican, and tell him in plain language, that he was not to be deceived; but, when he attempted to draw the lock, he found that the key had been turned upon him from without; and, with a curling lip, he cast himself again upon his bed, and soon forgot, in tranquil slumber, events which had excited in his mind no other feeling than contempt.

CHAPTER XII

It was late in the morning when St. Real awoke; and so profound had been his slumbers during the latter hours of their course, that the door of his chamber had been opened without his knowing it; and, on looking round, he found the young Dominican sitting at the farther end of the room, employed, as usual, in turning over busily the leaves of his breviary. In his eye there was more wild and gloomy fire than St. Real had remarked on the preceding evening; and the young noble, who could not help connecting the monk with the trick that had been played off upon him during the night, resolved to speak upon the subject at once, in the hope of discovering what was the real object of the friars.

"Good morrow, father!" he said, as their eyes first met; "I trust you have slept more soundly than I have."

"Why should *you* sleep unsoundly?" demanded the Dominican in return. "You have no mighty thoughts! you have no heavenly calling! you have no glorious revelations to keep you waking! Why should you sleep unsoundly?"

"Simply, because foolish people took the trouble to disturb me," replied St. Real. "Heard you not the singing, and saw you not the light?"

"Foolish people!" cried the friar, with his grey eyes gleaming: "call you the angels of Heaven foolish people? Yes, profane man, I saw the light, and I heard the singing; and that you heard and saw it too, shows me that it was no dream, but a blessed reality! But you saw not what I saw! you heard not what I heard! You saw not the winged angel of the Lord that entered my cell, bearing the sword of the vengeance of God! you heard not the message of Heaven to poor Jacques Clement, bidding him go forth in the power of faith, and smite the Holofernes at St. Cloud--the oppressor of the people of the Lord, the enemy and contemner of the will of the Highest!"

"No, indeed!" answered St. Real, "I neither heard nor saw any of these things; but I now perceive, father, that the vision was addressed to you, not to me, as at first I believed it to be. But tell me, good father, you surely are not simple enough to take all this that you have seen for--"

Ere St. Real could conclude his sentence, the door, which the Dominican had left ajar, was thrown wide open, and the Prior of the convent entered the room, and approached the bed where the young gentleman had remained resting on his arm while he maintained this brief conversation with Father Clement. "Good morrow, my son!" said the Prior. "What! still abed! Brother Clement, thou mayst withdraw."

The friar immediately obeyed; and the superior went on: "I bring you tidings, my son, which you will be glad to hear. The lieutenant-general of the kingdom has been informed of your arrest; and, notwithstanding some circumstances of a suspicious kind which justified that measure, trusts so much to your good faith and honour, that he has ordered your liberation, and recognises the validity of your safe-conduct. Some of his officers wait below; your own attendants are now collected in the court; and all is prepared in order that you may immediately visit him. In the meantime, however, while you rise and dress yourself, I would fain speak a few words of warning and advice."

"Willingly will I attend, reverend father," replied St. Real, who was disposed to show every sort of respect to the teachers of his religion, although he could not but believe that there was a good deal of double-dealing, even in the very speech by which the Prior announced the tidings of his liberation. "Happy am I to hear that the Duke of Mayenne, however he may have learned my detention, is more awake to a sense of his own honour, than that detention itself seemed to imply. But let me hear: what is it you would say, good father?"

"As a vowed teacher of the true faith, and a preacher of the holy Gospel," replied the Dominican, "I would warn you, my son, against any hesitation in those particulars where your eternal salvation is concerned. In matters of faith, as in matters of virtue, there can be but one right and wrong: there is no middle course in religion; and, if you are a true Catholic, holding the doctrines of the apostolic church, and reverencing that authority which the Saviour of mankind transferred to blessed St. Peter and his successors, you must hold the enemies of that church, who oppose its doctrines, and strive for its overthrow, as blasphemous and sacrilegious heretics, whose existence is an ulcer in the state, whose very neighbourhood is dangerous, and whose companionship is a pest. You must hold those who, pretending to be apostolic Catholics, support, maintain and consort with the enemies of that religion, as even worse than those enemies themselves, inasmuch as they add hypocrisy and falsehood to heresy and sacrilege; and when you perceive that every vice which can degrade human nature characterises those who are thus apostates to the church, and protectors of heresy, you will see the natural consequences which fall upon such as disobey the injunctions of the church they acknowledge, and the punishment that will attend all those who uphold a foul and evil cause,--disgrace, dishonour, loss of their own esteem, crimes that they once regarded with horror; in this life infamy, misfortune, and reverse; speedy death; and then eternal condemnation."

In the same strain the Prior proceeded for some time, enlarging, and not without eloquence, upon all the common topics with which the preachers of the League were accustomed to stir up the fanatical spirit of their auditors. He touched also upon St. Real's own situation, his power of choosing, at that moment, between good and bad: he spoke of the unquestionable honour and high repute of many of the leaders of his faction; he painted in the most dark and terrible colours the vices and the crimes that stained the court of Henry III.; and he artfully glossed over, or passed in silence, all that could be detrimental to his own party in the opinion of an honourable and an upright gentleman. He said nothing of the ambition, the rapacity, the debauchery, the prostitution of feeling, honour, virtue, patriotism, to the basest party purposes and the most sordid self-interests, which disgraced the faction of the League.

While he proceeded, St. Real went on with the occupations of his toilet, and, somewhat to the annoyance of the Dominican, heard his oration in favour of the League with a degree of calmness that set all his powers of penetration at defiance. He expressed neither assent nor dissent; neither wonder at all the charges which the Prior brought against the King and his minions, nor admiration of the characters which he attributed to the leaders of the League. He listened, but he did not even take advantage of any pause to answer; and, when the Prior had completely concluded, he merely said, "Well, father, I shall soon see all these things with my own eyes, and shall then determine."

Somewhat piqued to find that all his oratory had produced so small an effect, the Prior rose, and, with an air of stern dignity, moved towards the door. As he approached it, he turned, drew up his tall figure to its full height, and, lifting his right hand, with the two first fingers raised, he said, in an impressive tone, while he fixed his keen eyes upon the figure of the young Marquis, "Remember, my son, what Christ, your Saviour himself, has said: 'He that is not for me, is against me;'" and, without waiting for a reply, he turned and quitted the room.

Unmoved by what he considered, rightly, a piece of stage effect, St. Real soon followed, and found the door of the corridor left open; while the servant, who had been suffered to accompany him to the convent, was seen in the little ante-room beyond, speaking with some persons in rich military dresses, with whose faces St. Real was unacquainted. The moment he approached, however, one stepped forth from the rest, and addressed him by his name.

"I am commanded, Monsieur de St. Real, to greet you on the part of his Highness the Duke of Mayenne, lieutenant-general of the kingdom, and to inform you that the arrest under which you have suffered, took place without either his knowledge or consent, by a mistake on the part of a body of reitters, who seem to have confounded you in some way with the troops attached to Monsieur de Longueville. I am further directed to conduct you to the presence of his Highness, who will explain to you more at large how these events have occurred. Your own attendants and horses are already prepared below: and, if it suits your convenience, we will instantly set out."

"At once, if it so please you, sir," replied St. Real. "I am so little used to imprisonment, that every minute of it is tedious to me."

Proceeding, therefore, to the door of the ante-chamber, at which stood one of the Dominican friars, St. Real and his companions were led down to the court, and there mounted their horses. As he was turning his rein towards the gate, however, his eye fell upon the form of the Prior, standing at an oriel window above; and, raising his hat, he bowed with all becoming reverence. The Prior spread his hands, and gave his blessing in return, adding--"May God bless thee, my son, and give thee light to see thy way aright!"

On the present occasion, there appeared to be not only dignity, but even sincerity, in his tone. Nor, indeed, did St. Real doubt the purity of his intentions throughout; but, in the wars and factions that had preceded the time of which we now speak, the young noble had, as we have said, acted the part of a looker-on; and thus he had learned many a lesson in the art of appreciating the character of such men as Prior Edmé Bourgoin--men who, devotedly sincere themselves in their attachment to the party they espouse, and convinced by passion's eloquent voice of the justice of their cause, think every means justifiable to attain its objects, or to bring over converts to its tenets. St. Real felt sure that the Prior entertained not a doubt of the rectitude of his own motives, and the propriety of everything he did in behalf of the League; but he felt equally sure, that the Dominican would think right and just a thousand means and stratagems, to obtain his purposes, which he, St. Real, would look upon as base, dishonourable, and even impious. Whatever end, therefore, had been sought by confining him in the Jacobin convent, the effect had been anything rather than increased affection for the League; and, as he rode away from its gates towards the Hotel de Guise, his only reflection was, "Well, if such be the means by which the League is supported, and such the stratagems by which its adherents are gained, I, at least, will not be one of the crowd of fools whereof its followers must be composed."

At the Hotel de Guise a different scene awaited him, and different means of attraction were played off in order to win him to the faction. All that had passed at the Jacobins had apparently been minutely reported to Madame de Montpensier; and, with a profound knowledge of human nature, and a perfect command of art, she at once read the principal points of St. Real's character, and adapted her own behaviour to suit it. The mistakes which she committed, as we shall presently see, were not from misapprehending the traits of his disposition, but from not perceiving their depth.

On alighting from their horses, the young officers who had conducted St. Real from the Dominican convent, led him at once towards the audience chamber of the Duke of Mayenne. At the door, however, they were informed by an attendant that the Duke was busy on matters of some deep importance, but that he would be at leisure in a few minutes. Another attendant then stepped forth to usher him to some waiting-room; and, ere he was aware of it, St. Real was in the presence of two beautiful women,--the Duchess of Guise, and the Duchess of Montpensier,--who appeared busy with the ordinary morning occupations of ladies of that day, and seemed surprised at the intrusion; though it need scarcely be said, that the whole man[oe]uvre had been conducted upon their own positive orders. The attendant, who led the young cavalier thither, seemed also surprised to find that chamber engaged; and, begging St. Real to follow him again, was retiring, with many profound reverences and apologies to the two ladies, when Madame de Montpensier demanded the gentleman's name; and, glancing her eye over his person, with a smile not at all unnatural, added, before the man could answer, that, as all the other chambers were occupied, the stranger might, if he so pleased, remain there till her brother was disengaged, as he did not seem so ferocious a person as to make war upon a bevy of women, though Henry of Valois had shown that even the sacred robe of the church was sometimes no protection.

St. Real's name was then given by the attendant; who, without further question, retired, leaving the young cavalier to play his part with the two artful women in whose society he was placed, as best he might. The Marquis, however, did not play that part ill. Graceful by nature and by education, his manners were embarrassed by no kind of bashfulness; for although his acquaintance with society was but limited, yet there were two feelings in his bosom which gave him ever perfect self-possession without presumption. The first of these feelings was a slight touch of the pride of birth, which taught him, when in company with the high or the proud, never to forget that he was himself sprung from the noblest of the land; the second, was the consciousness of perfect rectitude in every thought, feeling, and purpose. Besides all this, the St. Reals had been, as I have said, from age to age, a chivalrous race; and their representative had strong in his own bosom that species of chivalrous gallantry, which made him look upon woman's weakness as a constant, undeniable claim to deference, to courtesy, and to those small attentions, which give greater pleasure very often than even greater services.

Madame de Montpensier was surprised and pleased; and the Duchess de Guise, perhaps, inwardly determined to add St. Real to her train of admirers. At all events, both bent their efforts, in the first place, to gain him for the League; and the sister of the haughty house of Lorraine pursued her plan with the calm and steady purpose of a great diplomatist. In her communion with the young Marquis, she scrupulously avoided aught of coquetry--she suffered not a touch even of levity to be apparent in her manner--she put a guard upon her tongue and upon her eyes, and suffered not even an idle jest to pass those lips with which such things were so familiar. At first, affecting even a degree of distant coldness, she suffered the softer and more blandishing manners of the Duchess of Guise to smooth away all the difficulties of an accidental introduction; and then, as the conversation proceeded, she affected to become more interested, spoke wisely and cautiously, and assumed the tone of virtue and deep feeling, which she knew would harmonise with his principles; though, if all tales be true, that tone was the most difficult for her to affect.

She soon contrived to discover a fact, of which she seemed to be ignorant till St. Real told her; namely, that he was the cousin of the Count d'Aubin; and then, acting upon one of those vague intuitions, which women are occasionally gifted with in regard to matters of the heart, she turned the conversation suddenly and abruptly to Mademoiselle de Menancourt, and the subject of her detention in Paris. St. Real was taken by surprise: there had been some warring in his bosom too, of late, in regard to the fair girl, who had been the companion of his early youth: it was the only point on which his thoughts were not as free and light as the sunshine on the waters; and, at the name of Eugenie de Menancourt, so suddenly pronounced, the blood mounted for a moment into his cheek, and glowed upon his brow.

Madame de Montpensier saw, without seeming to see; and instantly understood the whole: but she fancied even more than she understood. Even though the purity of St. Real's nature forced itself upon her conviction, the evil and subtlety of her own character affected the impression which his left upon her mind, and changed it from its natural appearance. It was like a beautiful face seen in a bad mirror--the traits the same, and yet the aspect changed. She fancied that she saw in the feelings of St. Real towards Eugenie de Menancourt the secret of his hesitation between the League and the Royalists: not, indeed, that she believed that he wished to bargain for his services, as so many had done, or that he designed to attempt to deprive his cousin of the hand of her he loved; but she imagined that secret, and perhaps unconscious, hopes of some fortuitous circumstance, proving favourable to his wishes, might be the cause of a lingering tendency towards the party who could bestow the hand of Eugenie de Menancourt, when his political feelings led him to support the royal cause. Upon these suppositions she shaped her plans, and proceeded to speak of the young heiress with all the tenderness and consideration of a sister. She commiserated her situation, she said,--promised by her father to a man that she could not love, and then left an orphan in the midst of such troublous times. It was happy, indeed, she added, that the young lady had fallen into the hands of one in every respect so noble and considerate as the Duke of Mayenne; for Monsieur d'Aubin must, by this time, have learned, that the lieutenant-general, endeavouring to exercise his power for the happiness of all, would not suffer any restraint to be put upon the inclination of Mademoiselle de Menancourt, but would bestow her hand upon any one that she could really love, provided his rank and station, presented no invincible obstacles.

St. Real was, for a moment, silent; but he at length replied, that he could not conceive upon what ground Mademoiselle de Menancourt's present objections to a union with the Count d'Aubin could be founded. During her father's lifetime, he said, she had not apparently opposed the alliance; and, as far as he had heard, D'Aubin had given her no new cause of offence.

The subject was one on which St. Real found it difficult to speak, not from any feelings he might experience towards Eugenie de Menancourt-- for, by a strong sense of honour, and a great command over his own mind, he crushed all sensations of the kind as soon as he found them rising in his breast,--but his difficulty proceeded from a consciousness that D'Aubin was to blame, and from a wish to say as much as possible in favour of his cousin, without deviating from that rigid adherence to truth, which was the constant principle of his heart. What he said was true, indeed. Eugenie de Menancourt had evinced no strenuous opposition to the proposed alliance, so long as her father lived; and yet it was during his lifetime that St. Real had principally remarked those errors in the conduct of his cousin which he thought most calculated to give offence to that cousin's future bride. He did, therefore, wonder what new motive had given such sudden and strong determination to one whom he had always remarked as gentle and complying; and, although he doubted not he should find Eugenie in the right, he did long to hear from her own lips the reasons upon which her conduct was founded.

Madame de Montpensier remarked the restraint under which he spoke, but attributed it to wrong motives, and shaped her answer accordingly. "Perhaps," she said, with a significant smile, "Mademoiselle de Menancourt may have perceived that there are other people, more worthy of her heart; and, as soon as she finds that her duty to her father no longer requires obedience, she may yield to her own inclinations, especially where she finds they are supported by reason."

"I do not think that, madam," replied St. Real. "I do not think Eugenie de Menancourt is one to love easily; though, where she did love, she would love deeply."

There was a degree of simplicity and unconsciousness in this reply, that somewhat puzzled Madame de Montpensier, and put her calculations at fault. She did not choose to let the subject drop, however; and she replied--"You seem to know this young lady well, Monsieur de St. Real: have you been long acquainted?"

"I know her as if she were my own sister," replied St. Real. "We have been acquainted since our infancy; and, indeed, we are distantly related to each other."

"Not within the forbidden degrees, I hope?" said the Duchess or Guise, with a smile.

"She will scare the bird from the trap with her broad jests!" thought the more cautious Catherine de Montpensier, as she saw the colour come up again to St. Real's cheek; but he replied, with his usual straightforward simplicity, "I really do not know, madam: I never considered the matter; but the relationship is, I trust, sufficiently near to justify me in asking his Highness of Mayenne to grant me an interview with Mademoiselle de Menancourt, as I wish to see whether I cannot remove any false impression she may have formed of my cousin, and induce her to fulfil an engagement on which his happiness depends."

Madame de Montpensier gave a sharp eager glance towards the Duchess of Guise, to prevent her from pressing St. Real too hard; and she herself replied, "My brother will doubtless grant you the interview, Monsieur de St. Real; but I am afraid you will be unsuccessful. One thing, however, you may be sure of, that Mayenne himself will in no degree press Mademoiselle de Menancourt to such a union, for he is fully convinced that her objections are but too well founded: and although, perhaps, the party that we espouse might be benefited by holding out to your cousin the prospect of our support in this matter, yet it can in no degree be granted, unless some great change takes place in the feelings of Mademoiselle de Menancourt herself."

As St. Real was about to reply, an attendant again appeared, and announced that Mayenne was, for a few moments, free from those weighty affairs with which the situation of his party overwhelmed him. The young Marquis rose to obey the summons: but Madame de Montpensier was not at all inclined to abandon her unconcluded schemes to the chances of a private interview between her more candid brother and the object of her wiles. That which had at first been the mere desire of gaining a powerful acquisition to her party, and of depriving the Royalists of a strong support, had now become, under the opposition and difficulties she had met with, the eager struggle of compromised vanity. Her reputation for skill and policy were even dearer to her, at that moment, than her reputation for beauty and wit had ever been; and, at the mere apprehension of missing her stroke in a matter where she had risked so much, and employed such means, she called up before the eyes of imagination the calm, half-sneering smile with which Mayenne would mark her failure, and the galling compassion with which all her dear friends and favourite counsellors would commiserate her disappointment.

"I have a petition too to present to my all-powerful brother," she said, rising at the same time; "and, therefore, with your good leave, Monsieur de St. Real, I will accompany you to his high and mighty presence." St. Real, perhaps, would have preferred to see Mayenne alone, but no choice was left him; and, offering his hand, he led her through the long galleries and corridors of the Hotel de Guise to the audience-chamber of the lieutenant-general.

CHAPTER XIII

Oh entering the cabinet of the Duke of Mayenne, Madame de Montpensier and her companion found him still engaged in listening to the reports of several military men. He instantly made a sign, however, for the purpose of enjoining silence as his sister approached; and turning to St. Real, he pointed to a seat. "The Marquis de St. Real, I presume?" he said, with an air of plain and unaffected dignity. "Your mourning habit, sir, reminds me that I should condole with you on the death of one of the noblest gentlemen that France has ever known. He would not, it is true, take part with those who wished him well; but, even had he drawn his sword against us, I should have lamented his death as a star gone out that may never be lighted again."

There was a brief pause--for St. Real would not trust his voice with a reply--and the Duke, after having dismissed the officers by whom he had been surrounded, proceeded: "I trust, Monsieur de St. Real, that you know enough of him who speaks to you to believe, even without my saying it, that Charles of Mayenne is utterly incapable of such an act as that by which my safe-conduct was violated in your instance. For my own part, the persons who captured you allege, in their excuse, some dispositions of your troops, which gave cause to suspect an inclination to support our adversary, the young Duke of Longueville; but I--judging your sentiments by my own-- absolve you from all such suspicion."

"You do me justice, my lord," replied St. Real; "I am incapable of taking advantage of your pass in order to injure you; and, though in the first heat of anger at my arrest, I might cast the blame on you, I have since learned to judge better, and to know that it was the purpose of those who detained me to keep you in ignorance of my imprisonment. At least, I conclude so from the fact that, on my desiring one of the lookers-on, as I was carried through the streets, to bear the tidings to you, the commander, as he seemed, of the reitters threatened to cut the man's ears off if he obeyed. How the news was at length brought to you I know not, and would willingly hear."

"'Twas a little misshapen dwarf," replied Mayenne, "whom I remember well about the court some years ago, that brought the tidings, and bellowed them forth just as I was mounting my horse to ride out this morning."

"'Tis one of my own pages, doubtless," replied St. Real. "I fancied that the little pigmy could ill bear the fatigues of our long march, and I sent him on hither in a chariot, with another young lad, to prepare a lodging for me while in Paris."

"I knew not, sir Marquis," replied Mayenne, "that you, who affect so much retirement in the provinces, took such pains to follow the modes of the court. What! you have dwarfs for pages, too, have you? And doubtless, in such a household as yours, you equal this Henry of Valois, and have the *tailleur aux nains*, as well as the dwarf's valet."

A fear crossed the mind of Madame de Montpensier, lest her brother should be pressing St. Real somewhat too hard for his own interests; and she accordingly joined in the conversation at once. "No, no!" she exclaimed; "depend upon it, Charles, Monsieur de St. Real has obtained this dwarf through some accident. I am a better judge of nature than you, Mayenne; and I will answer for it that St. Real is not one to ape the follies of a vicious court, and have his dozen or two of dwarfs and buffoons."

"You are quite right, madam," replied St. Real, who could not but feel pleased to hear himself so boldly defended by such lovely lips. "This dwarf was given me, when I needed a page, by my cousin of Aubin, who prophesied that one day he would serve me at my need--a prophecy which you see has been happily fulfilled, by the unexpected service he has rendered me to-day; and I only trust that his Highness of Mayenne will punish as severely those who have abused his authority, as I will reward largely the activity of my little page."

Mayenne's brow darkened a little: for, of course, the contrivers of the scheme by which St. Real had been brought to Paris he could not punish; and the executors of that scheme were too necessary to his own purposes to admit of any severity being exercised towards them, even had a sense of justice not pointed out that they were mere instruments in the hands of his sister. He was embarrassed therefore; for he felt that the mind of the young Marquis of St. Real was too clear and too straightforward not to detect and appreciate any evasive reply: but Madame de Montpensier came to his aid.

"Nay, nay, Monsieur de St. Real," she said, half playfully, half sadly, "let us not talk of punishments to-day. The miseries and the pangs which are inflicted by either party on the other are sufficient, Heaven knows, without requiring us to be very severe upon our own. But you talked," she added, changing the subject abruptly, "of your page seeking you a lodging in Paris. Now, this is the Hotel de Guise; and I, as a daughter of that house, will take upon me to bid you make it your dwelling while you stay; though my brother, here present, might have had the courtesy to do so before now."

"Nay, Catherine," answered Mayenne, "I wished to put no restraint upon Monsieur de St. Real. He came to the capital to act and to judge for himself; to examine our cause, to mark the demeanour of those who support it; and, though anxious--most anxious--to have so noble a name joined to all those who already uphold the Catholic faith against the apostate and excommunicated tyrant who would destroy it, yet on no account would I bias for a moment the judgment of our noble friend, which, indeed, he might think I wished to do if I pressed him to dwell here."

There was a dignified simplicity in the demeanour of the Duke of Mayenne which pleased St. Real much; but still he wished in no degree to commit himself with the League, till he had ascertained that there was some strong and imperative cause for quitting the path which loyalty and his allegiance pointed out for him to follow. "I thank you, my lord, for your consideration," he replied; "but it was my purpose, after this interview, and having obtained one boon at your hands, to take my leave for the time, in order to proceed to St. Cloud, as I at first intended."

A cloud came over the brow of the Duke; but Madame de Montpensier again interfered. "Monsieur de St. Real," she said, laughing, with something of a double meaning, "you are strongly inclined to spoil all my best plans in your favour; but I do not intend to let you do so. Positively, for this day at least, you shall make your habitation in the Hotel de Guise. The morning you shall spend as you please--see all our faults and failings, and spy out the nakedness of the land. At night you sup with me, to which supper I also bid my lord Duke, here; and I will take care, that in the course of the evening, you shall have an opportunity of urging your cousin's suit upon the ear of Mademoiselle de Menancourt, as long and as privately as you please."

Mayenne cast an inquiring glance upon his sister; but she only replied, "Ay, Charles, even so: your fair ward, Eugenie de Menancourt, with whom Monsieur de St. Real desires to speak in favour of the Count d'Aubin. However, to this plan I will have no objections, my lord Marquis; so, on your gallantry, I call you to obey without murmuring, remembering that, as it is impossible for a young, gay, handsome cavalier like yourself to have a private interview with a beautiful girl like Eugenie de Menancourt at her own dwelling without notorious scandal, this is your only chance. No reply!" she added, with an air of playful imperiousness; "no reply! but obedience! Herbert!" she continued, raising her voice loud enough to be heard in the ante-room, "command the *maître d'hôtel* to conduct this gentleman to such a suite of rooms as may be sufficient for himself and his attendants, and suited to his high quality."

It would have needed a heart very stern and stoical to disobey commands so pleasantly given, and coupled with such temptations. St. Real, therefore, signified his assent, and, following the officer who had come to Madame de Montpensier's call, was conducted to an apartment in the Hotel de Guise, where he was soon joined by his own attendants, bearing the various articles of baggage which he had brought with him on quitting his little camp near Senlis, and which, to their singular honour be it spoken, the reitters had left with no very important abstractions, though plunder was no uncommon part of their military avocations.

Madame de Montpensier, although she had in reality neither boon nor question to demand of her brother, lingered for a moment after St. Real was gone, looking archly in the grave face of the Duke of Mayenne. "Well, Charles," she exclaimed, "do you not thank me for my assistance? have I not got you nicely out of a scrape?"

"After having wildly got me into one," replied the Duke. "But tell me, Kate, what is this business about Mademoiselle de Menancourt? I will not suffer you to trouble the course of events there."

"Nor do I purpose to do so," replied Madame de Montpensier; "but I see farther than you do, Charles, and, at all events, for this day will have my own way. So, you look to your plans, and I will look to mine, and may come to help you again when you get into difficulty." Thus speaking, and without waiting for any farther questions, she turned away, leaving the Duke to pursue the military arrangements in which he had been previously occupied.

CHAPTER XIV

St. Real, whose toilet at the convent of the Jacobins had been, from the circumstances in which he was placed, both hasty and unceremonious, now proceeded to change a dress suited alone to a journey, and both deranged and soiled by all that he had lately passed through. While thus occupied, a loud but well-known voice made itself heard in the ante-room, exclaiming, "Make way, make way! Paul Thiebaut and Pierre Langlois, if you do not get out of my way, I will break your pates with the hilt of my dagger! I will break your pates, though they may be as thick, and as hard, and as heavy as the leaden pummel of my old lord's double-handed sword! Out of the way, I say: do you think one can walk through your great hulking bodies?"

"No," replied one of the attendants, in a gruff voice, "no! but you could walk between our legs, I suppose, little Master Bartholo."

What was the dwarf's reply did not appear; but it would seem that it was somewhat of a manual nature, for a loud oath and stamp of the foot followed; and the door of the chamber opened so unceremoniously as to evince that Bartholo was in some haste to escape from the vengeance that his replication, whatever it had been, was likely to call down upon his head. Banging the door in the face of those behind, he instantly recovered his tranquillity when he found himself in the presence of his master; and advancing towards St. Real with graceful ease, bent his little knee to the ground, kissed his lord's hand, and gave him joy on his arrival in the great capital.

St. Real replied something kind to his first salutation, and then added, "But how now, Bartholo! you claim no merit for the service you have rendered me this morning?"

"I never like to claim merit," replied the dwarf, in his usual cynical tone: "I never like to claim merit, especially with people who think themselves generous; because, if they have forgot my merit, and do not intend to reward me, my claim is a reproach which they never forgive; and if they remember my merit, and design to thank me, my claim is a disappointment."

"It would be well, my good Bartholo," replied St. Real, "if every one else acted upon the same principle--not alone to those who think themselves generous, as you say, but to all men. It would, I believe, save many a disappointment, and many a bitter aggravation of ingratitude; for I have remarked that, as you say, those who are simply forgetful of services hate those who serve them when they are called on to be grateful. But where is Leonard de Monte? Could not he find out his master's abode as well as you, Bartholo? or is he one of those whose memory of kindness does not outlive the act?"

"Good truth, I do not know, my lord!" replied the dwarf. "I never judge of folks on brief acquaintance. His memory of kindness may be as short-lived as a jest at the gallows, or a widow's mourning, or a court lady's constancy--the sincerity of Madame de Montpensier, or the smiles of Monsieur de Mayenne, or any other short thing in this short life, for aught I know; but, in regard to the reason why Leonard's black eyes did not find you out here, it is that they are even now looking for you at St. Cloud. As you were two or three days later than your appointed time, the silly boy took fright, and set out late last night to seek for you. He would fain have persuaded me to go too; but I was not to be wheedled into such an errand. I know well that every fool finds his way to Paris, and that you, therefore, could not well miss it. So I remained quiet, watching every corner till you appeared; and then, as I found you guarded more strongly than necessary, and lodged more holily than I judged you would like, I made bold to bear the tidings to the Duke of Mayenne, begging him to deliver you forthwith from the preaching friars, for fear you should be tired of the friars' preaching."

"You did well and wisely, Bartholo," replied St. Real; "and, as this is the first piece of real good-will that I have ever seen you display to any one, it shall not go without reward. There is my purse, good Bartholo; and now, while I dress, give me the news of Paris; for you are sharp enough and shrewd enough, I take it, to discover and to mark all that is passing in this great city."

According to his master's desire, Bartholo proceeded to detail all the gossips, the scandal, and the real news of the capital, commenting, as he went on, on every anecdote that he related with the keen shrewdness and sagacity which peculiarly distinguished him. His observations, indeed, might derive a peculiar turn from his own particular views and purposes; but, in this curious and complicated world in which we live, every part fits into the other with such exact nicety, that the great depend upon the little nearly as much as the little depend upon the great: the intrigues of the mighty and the powerful, the schemes of the noble and the high, are almost always to be affected in their course--to derive their success or receive their overthrow--from the most mean and despised things that crawl almost unseen around their presence. Thus, in the present instance, all the art, the tortuous policy, the consummate acting of Madame de Montpensier was rendered nearly unavailing by the keen and sarcastic observations, the knowledge of parties, and the insight into real motives and actions, of even so insignificant a person as the dwarf. In the course of the half hour that succeeded, he gave to St. Real a completely new view of the state of the League, and the motives and characters of its supporters; and, without one direct assertion, without one attempt to controvert his opinions, or one apparent effort to obtain a particular object, he showed his master, that frank simplicity might be assumed as the best cloak for art, just as much as religion and patriotism might be affected for the purpose of concealing selfishness and ambition.

As soon as he was dressed, St. Real went forth on foot, followed, as was customary in those days, by two or three armed attendants, and guided by the dwarf, who took care that he should see everything which the capital contained that could disgust him with the proceedings of the League: though why he wished to drive his master into the royal party was somewhat difficult to discover. He first led the young Marquis into the large open space in the neighbourhood of the University, upon the pretence of showing him that building from which the light of knowledge had been so frequently poured forth upon France; but it would seem that he had calculated upon another and more important object presenting itself by the way: nor was he disappointed: for, immediately on entering the great square, St. Real's eyes encountered a considerable crowd; and, making his way forward through the press to a spot where he could see what was proceeding, he immediately beheld one of the many curious scenes which were then taking place in the French capital--such as no city in the world, at any period of its history, has presented, except Paris in the days of the League. Covered with steel corslets, armed with sword, and pike, and musketoon, and with their shaven heads covered with that species of iron caps called a *salade*, appeared a dense body of about 1500 men, man[oe]uvring with that close and serried discipline which was peculiarly attributed to the Spanish infantry. They seemed, indeed, at first, a very strong body of regular troops, though somewhat singularly clothed; but nearer inspection showed the large hanging sleeves and long flowing gowns of various communities of monks and friars protruding from under the iron panoply of war.

As soon as St. Real had satisfied himself that his eyes had not deceived him, he turned away disgusted, and, led by the dwarf, proceeded onward to the Bastille, where, entrance being refused to all but those who came against their own will, or those who had something to do with the act of bringing them thither, St. Real and his attendants stood without, while the dwarf commented in a low voice, but in bitter terms, upon the uses to which that prison was for the time applied. While thus engaged, a party of horsemen, followed by a small guard of cavalry, came up at full speed; and their leader, as he sprang to the ground at the gate of the fortress, turned to give a hasty glance at St. Real, exposing as he did so, the features of the Duke of Mayenne.

As soon as the Duke perceived who it was that was gazing up to the building, he beckoned to him to approach, saying, in the same bold and candid tone which he usually employed, "If you will come in with me, Monsieur de St. Real, you shall see the inside as well as the outside of this famous prison; and may also see--" he added, knitting his brows, "and may also see to what evil purposes power may sometimes be applied in troublous times, and how difficult it is for one who endeavours to guide aright the outburst of popular indignation to insure that his name and authority shall not be abused by others, even while he is labouring night and day himself to re-establish order and justice, and promote the public weal."

St. Real readily agreed to his proposal, as his desire was to see all that he could during his short stay in the capital. Every gate opened at the appearance of the Duke; but, as if by previous orders, he was not alone accompanied by his own immediate suite, but was also followed by at least one-half of the cavalry forming his escort: who, dismounting from their horses, gave their bridles to their companions, and kept close to the heels of Mayenne as he advanced. The guards and warders at the second and third gates looked suspiciously upon the number of soldiers thus introduced into the fortress, and seemed to hesitate in regard to giving them admission. Mayenne walked on; and, before his bold and determined aspect, all opposition at once gave way. A man at the second gate, indeed, made a sudden movement, as if to communicate the fact of the Duke's arrival to others in the interior of the building; but in a stern though low tone, Mayenne commanded him to stay where he was, and advanced rapidly unannounced. It would seem, indeed, that his coming took the demagogues then in possession of the Bastile by surprise. In the inner court a knot of several persons might be observed standing under a beam, which was thrust out of one of the loophole windows of an angular tower, and from which beam dangled a strong cord, formed into that ominous ellipsis, the sight of which has made many a stout heart turn cold. One of the group assembled below was in the very act of demonstrating to his fellows that it would be necessary to fetch a bench or table in order to bring their pastime to a crisis, inasmuch as the rope was too short, and the noose fully eight feet from the ground, when the appearance of Mayenne stopped his oration in the midst.

The speaker raised his hat at the approach of the Duke; but the glance that he gave was certainly not one of welcome or of love. "What are you doing, Monsieur le Clerc?" demanded Mayenne, sternly eyeing the fatal preparations before him. "All this seems very like an intention of again overstepping your authority."

The person he addressed was a shrewd bold-looking man, with an expression of quick eager cunning, not unlike that of a monkey. "We were going, my lord Duke, to do what, I trust, you will be well pleased to witness," replied Bussy le Clerc: "we were going to execute a traitor, a rebel to lawful authority, and an enemy to the apostolic League and to the Catholic faith-- him who was formerly called the President Blancmesnil."

"And how did you dare, sir," exclaimed Mayenne, in a tone that cowed even the bold plotter before him, "how did you dare to stir in such a matter without my authority? I ask you not where you got the impudence, for that you lack not for any feat; but where did you get the courage for such a deed? Am I, or am I not, lieutenant-general of the kingdom? and am I man to pass by such an act without punishment?"

"You are, my lord--you are lieutenant-general of the kingdom," replied Bussy le Clerc, in a humble tone; but the next moment he muttered between his teeth, "You are lieutenant-general of the kingdom; but those who made can unmake."

Notwithstanding the low tone in which he spoke, Mayenne seemed to catch his words; for, grasping him suddenly and firmly by the arm with his left hand, he pointed to the instrument of death, which Le Clerc had prepared for others, and, shaking the forefinger of his right in the pale countenance of the bloody man before him, he fixed his eyes upon him with a look of dark and stern significance, the meaning of which was not to be mistaken. He said not a word, but the glance was sufficient; and there was no one present who did not read therein a threat to make the demagogue taste of the portion he assigned to others, if he pursued his bloody course any further--a threat which did not fail to receive its accomplishment at an after period.

Mayenne held him in his powerful grasp for nearly a minute; then, letting his arm drop, he turned, and, while Le Clerc slunk away amongst his creatures, exclaimed aloud, "Bring forth the President de Blancmesnil!"

Several of the officers hastened to obey; and an old man, whose noble countenance and silver hairs might well win respect and pity, was brought out into the court, while two or three of the governor's satellites hurriedly untied the cords which had pinioned his hands behind.

"Ah! my good lord of Mayenne!" he exclaimed, as he approached, "I am happy to see your face."

"I had nearly come too late, Monsieur de Blancmesnil," replied Mayenne; "but still I am in time to tell you, that by the authority in me reposed, you are set free from this moment; and that whatever proceedings have been taken against you, in whatever court, whether legal or illegal, are null and void, so far as I can render them so."

The old man cast himself at Mayenne's feet and embraced his knees. "Thank you, my lord!" he said: "I thank you, and God will reward you for saving a guiltless man, on whose life some hopes and some affections are still fixed by those he loves; but yet, my lord, one boon--grant me one boon more, and let the cup of your generosity overflow! You have given me life--give me also liberty, and suffer me to retire from a city where each day shows me something either to condemn or to regret, and retire to the court of my lawful sovereign, where alone I can serve my country as I ought."

Mayenne paused for a moment, and his countenance, though not of the most expressive character, gave evident marks of a strong internal struggle; the quick glance of displeasure, and the open expansion of more generous feelings, succeeding each other rapidly, like the quick light and shade flying across a landscape in an autumn day, as the clouds are borne over the bright sky by the hasty wind. The sunshine, however, at length predominated. "Be it so; Blancmesnil, be it so," he replied, "be it so. I had hoped that your wisdom, your attachment to the faith, and your love of virtue would have kept you from a court of fools, of heretics, and of villains; but I will not stay you, if you love such men."

"My lord," said Blancmesnil in a tone almost of sorrow, "it would be ungrateful in me to answer you. Suffer me alone to say, that the most imperative and absolute sense of duty alone would induce me to repeat the request which I have made. None would more willingly spend his last few hours of this brief life in the service of one so noble and so generous as yourself than old Blancmesnil; but it cannot be, my lord, without the sacrifice of all those principles which have won me the esteem of your Highness."

"Well, well!" replied Mayenne, conscious that the impression produced by any further discussion of this kind in the hearing of St. Real would be very opposite to that which he could desire; "well, well! far be it from me to withhold any man from the path on which he thinks that duty prompts him. A bold enemy I love next to a faithful friend: it is only traitors to either cause that deserve punishment. Go! Blancmesnil, go! and do not forget that as much as we hate the vices which we are armed to crush, so much do we love virtue, even in an enemy!"

Mayenne felt that he had regained his advantage; and, turning to St. Real, he said, "Well, Monsieur de St. Real, you will return with me, for it grows late, and my sister will soon expect us. I will bear you company on foot. Sometimes I love to ramble amongst the people for a while, and hear the unvarnished opinions of the streets. Greatness, caged in gilded saloons, knows too little of the world around it, and needs now and then to take a flight amongst the wide universe of other beings, to learn how many varied and different aspects the state of all things can assume to the myriads of eyes that are looking on each passing event. You, Longjumeau," he continued, "take the horsemen, and guard Monsieur de Blancmesnil safely to his house. Wait there with him till all his preparations are made; and then, with a white flag, pass him safely to the outposts of the Huguenots at Meudon. Fare you well, Blancmesnil!" he added, turning to the old man; "I must embrace you once more, though you will be my enemy."

"Perhaps more your friend, my lord, in quitting you, than I should have been in staying with you," replied the President. Mayenne answered nothing, but, turning away, led St. Real from the Bastile, and took his way back to the Hotel de Guise, followed on foot by the principal part of the gentlemen of his household who had attended him to the state prison. No matter of any importance occurred during their walk; and St. Real was pleased to find, that far from attempting in any degree to influence him against his better judgment, the Duke confined his conversation solely to indifferent topics, commenting upon all the many objects of attention which all great cities present with as much liveliness as his nature permitted. More than one interruption occurred as they passed on, springing from the various duties and functions with which the Duke had charged himself, or with which the people chose to burden him. It was now an officer from the outposts, who stopped them on the way to demand orders and directions for the night; then a bare-footed friar, of not the most prepossessing appearance, approached the princely Mayenne, and held with him a whispering conversation of several minutes in the open street; then again a high officer, belonging to one of the courts of law, with his bonnet in his hand, presented some papers relative to the proceedings against the President de Blancmesnil; and then an old woman, thinking that she had as good a right as any other citizen of Paris to her share of the great Duke, hobbled across his path, and presented her dirty *placet* regarding a stall in the Fauxbourg de l'Université, and reinforced her petition by a torrent of that peculiar eloquence possessed by old apple-women in all civilised countries.

Mayenne gave her some mild but evasive reply; and turning with a smile towards St. Real, as they walked on, he said, "You see the post I occupy is not without its cares, and those cares so nicely balanced as to be all equally weighty; for you may judge, by that old woman, that, if the greater cares are more oppressive, the lighter are the more importunate."

All these interruptions of their onward progress had occupied no small time; so that the western sky began to look rosy with the summer sunset ere they reached the Hotel de Guise. "Quick! Monsieur de St. Real," said Mayenne, as they entered the vestibule; "quick! for in less than half an hour my sister will expect us at her supper-table."

St. Real accordingly retired to his apartments, and changing his dress with all speed, sent down one of his followers to seek out some of the attendants of the Duchess de Montpensier, and discover to what chamber, of all the many in that wide and rambling mansion, he was to bend his steps. Almost immediately after a servant of the Duchess appeared to conduct him; and he was led down the stairs, and through the manifold passages and turnings of the Hotel de Guise, at that particular moment of the day ere factitious light has supplied the place of the blessed sunshine, and when such rays of the set orb as still linger in the sky and find their way through the windows--though as rosy as those of the morning--are melancholy rather than gay. At length the servant opened the door of a small cabinet, and passing through, led St. Real into a larger room beyond, where he left him.

Standing near one of the windows at the farther end, and apparently gazing forth with some attention, appeared the figure of a lady in deep mourning. The light was not sufficient for St. Real to distinguish who she was; but her garb showed that it was not Madame de Montpensier, and St. Real was sure that it was not the Duchess de Guise. His heart beat quick, far quicker than he liked--for the heart is sometimes a prophet--and, for a moment, he paused in the midst of the room. The next instant, however, he again advanced: the lady turned as he approached, roused from her reverie by the sound of his footsteps, and St. Real suddenly found himself alone in the chamber with Eugenie de Menancourt. He was not surprised--at least he had no right to be so--for he was prepared to meet Mademoiselle de Menancourt at the Hotel de Guise that night; but it were vain to say that he was not agitated. He knew not why, and he was angry with himself for feelings which he could not, which he would not, perhaps, account for to his own understanding.

With Eugenie it was different. She was both surprised and agitated; for the last person she had expected, yet the person she had most wished to see, was the Marquis of St. Real. It was natural enough, too, that she should desire to see him: she had known him from her infancy; she had learned, in the early habits of unrestrained intercourse, to look upon him as a brother; she had found him always kind and gentle in his affections, clear and just in his opinions, and firm and noble in his principles; and, in the friendless and orphan state in which she was now left, there was no one to whom she so longed to apply for advice, assistance, and protection as to Huon of St. Real. At one time, indeed, in her utter ignorance of the selfishness of faction, she had contemplated applying to the Duke of Mayenne for permission to retire to the castle of the old Marquis of St. Real, whose neutrality between the contending parties of the day, she had fondly fancied, might obviate the objections which the leader of the League would entertain to any other asylum not within the immediate grasp of his own power. There was, however, in her bosom a vague unacknowledged consciousness of feelings, which she wished not to render more distinct--a sort of apprehension lest the world should attribute to her motives that she would have shrunk from entertaining --which made her hesitate so long in regard to giving voice to her request, that ere she decided the tidings reached her that the old lord was dead, and that the refuge which she might otherwise have hoped to find in his dwelling was consequently shut against her forever. Her thoughts, then, had often been busy with St. Real; she had often longed to see him, to speak with him, to confide her situation, her fears, her anxieties, her danger, to one in whom she was sure to find a kind and feeling auditor. With these wishes, however, no hopes had been combined. She knew, or believed she knew, that St. Real's principles would lead him to join the royal party; and that, therefore, unless he entered Paris as a victor or a prisoner, there was little chance of his visiting the capital. Madame de Montpensier, in summoning her to the Hotel de Guise, had given her no information of the object for which she was called thither; and she had obeyed with some degree of alarm, which had not been decreased by an apparent inattention and want of courtesy on the part of the Duchess, evinced by leaving her for nearly half an hour unnoticed in the wide and solitary chamber to which she had been ushered on her first arrival. Her sensations, therefore, on beholding St. Real, were purely those of surprise and pleasure; but they reached the height of agitation.

She spoke not; but, as the last light that lingered in the sky shone upon her beautiful countenance through the open window, St. Real beheld the warm blood rush up into her cheek and forehead, a beaming lustre dance in her eyes, and a bright irrepressible smile play about her lips, that plainly told he was no unwelcome visiter. The hand that was instantly extended to him he took in his; and he thought it no treason to his cousin to press his lips upon it. All that Eugenie and St. Real first said was too hurried and confused, too shapeless and unconnected, to bear much meaning if written down in mere cold words, without the looks, and the gestures, and the feelings, that at the time gave life and soul to those words themselves. They had a thousand things to speak of. Since their last meeting each had lost a father, each had lost a friend; and the affection that either had borne to the dead parent of the other was matter of deep sympathy and feeling between them. All their thoughts, their sorrows, their regrets, were in common, and their conversation, for some time, was one of those deep, touching, artless, unrestrained communications of mutual ideas, which--full of the reciprocation of bright sentiments--more than aught else on earth knit heart and heart together.

At length St. Real remembered that he was losing moments which he had destined for another purpose; and some of the servants entering to light the lamps and sconces in the apartment, at once showed him that he had no time to lose, and gave him an opportunity of changing the topic. As soon as they were left once more alone, he spoke of his cousin, the Count d'Aubin, and approached, without directly speaking of the subject of his pretensions, to Mademoiselle de Menancourt.

Eugenie turned as pale as death, and then again the red blood mounted to her cheek with a quick vehement blush: she too felt that there was an infinity to be said, and feared that there might be little time to say it. There was much--she felt there was much--to be staked upon the conversation of the next few instants; and she determined that, whatever report of her sentiments St. Real might bear his cousin, it should be such as to put an end for ever to his hopes of her affection.

"And would you, St. Real," she said, "would you, who know both him and me, would you press me to fulfil an engagement, in making which I myself bore no part, and which, even on the side of my father, was, as far as I can learn, but conditional? No, St. Real, no! sooner than disobey my father's commands, I would have sacrificed happiness, perhaps life itself: but he left me free, and pointedly, with his last breath, bade me, in the difficult circumstances in which I should be placed, use my own judgment. That judgment will never lead me to become the wife of one who can act as you and I have seen Philip d'Aubin act."

"But, believe me, Eugenie," replied St. Real, "Philip has changed. He loves you deeply, sincerely; and that love will teach him to seek your happiness by gaining your esteem."

"No, no! St. Real," replied Eugenie with a sigh, "no, no! he loves nothing but himself. I know him better than you do. While I thought that, at some time, I was to become his wife, I strove to love him as great an effort as woman can strive to direct the feelings of her own heart. In striving to love him, I strove to know him; and thus I learned all the baseness, all the selfishness, of his character. Forgive me, St. Real, for using such harsh language: you know it is not in my nature to speak or to feel thus, except in a case where all my happiness is concerned: but I wish you to understand at once, and for ever, that I will not marry Philip d'Aubin--because I do not love him."

"But might not time, and assiduity, and nobler deeds, teach you to love him?" demanded St. Real: "for, believe me, Eugenie, better qualities lie slumbering in his heart, which a great object might awake and strengthen. Might he not teach you to love him?"

"I would not love him for a universe," replied Eugenie; "for the woman who loves him is sure to be miserable. But press me no more, St. Real, press me no more: my resolution is taken--my mind and my heart are fixed. I do not love Philip d'Aubin--I never have loved him--I never can love him; and, sooner than become his wife, I would resign all that I have on earth but the dowry of a nun; quit the world, and seek peace in the cloister."

St. Real replied but by a sigh; and although that sigh might be one of sorrow for the disappointment of his cousin, yet it called up in the bosom of Eugenie de Menancourt varied emotions, that, for a moment, sent another bright flush across her cheek, which, fading away again, left her as pale as death. Ere the soft natural hue had returned, and ere St. Real had time to separate his mingled feelings from each other, and give to those he thought it right to express, the door opened, and Madame de Montpensier appeared alone.

Strange is it to say, but no less true, that though Eugenie de Menancourt and Huon de St. Real had both longed for such a moment of calm and unobserved communion, the approach of a third person was, at that moment, a relief to both. Nor was the manner of Madame de Montpensier at all calculated to lessen that sensation: it was the same which she had assumed in the morning towards St. Real, and which she had found succeed so well, that she determined not to abandon it till he had quitted Paris. She was, perhaps, even calmer and more tranquil in her demeanour now than she had appeared before: for reading, with deep knowledge, the secrets of the human heart, she knew that such a demeanour was best in harmony with the feelings which she wished St. Real and Eugenie to experience towards each other. Approaching, then, slowly and tranquilly, she welcomed Mademoiselle de Menancourt cordially, and then proceeded to speak of various indifferent subjects with wit and grace, but with very tempered gaiety, until the appearance of the Duchess of Guise, and then of the Duke of Mayenne, gave a different turn to the conversation. Supper was almost immediately announced; and, during the meal, all passed in the same calm tone. Eugenie, for the first time in her life, thought Madame de Montpensier as fascinating in manners as she was generally reported to be; and although she could not help feeling, with a degree of discomfort, that the eyes of the princess were frequently upon her with an inquiring, or rather, investigating, glance, yet the minutes went by more pleasantly than any she had known for many months. St. Real, too, felt the time brief and sweet; but, arguing from the costly apparel of the Duchess and her sister, that they were either going forth to figure on some more splendid scene, or were about to receive other guests at home, he judged that the moments allowed to such conversation as he then enjoyed would be but few; and he tormented himself by remembering a thousand things he wished to say to Mademoiselle de Menancourt, which he had forgotten at the only time when they could have been said.

At length the party rose; and, if the sound of rolling wheels, and shouting attendants, and trampling horses, augured true, the members of the house of Guise were even somewhat late in preparing to receive the noble guests who were invited that night to meet together in gaiety and splendour, though the morning had passed with many in strife and bloodshed, and though iron war was thundering with his cannon at the gates.

On the first signal of their design to quit the supper table, the attendants, who stood round, threw open the doors of the hall, and Madame de Montpensier, taking Eugenie by the hand, led the way into another chamber, which was already brilliantly lighted, and evidently prepared for some occasion of splendour, but into which, as yet, no one had been admitted. Passing through that and several rooms beyond, they at length approached a saloon, the door of which was open, and from which proceeded the busy hum of many voices; while various figures were seen passing to and fro across the aperture of the doorway, like the painted shadows cast by a phantasmagoria. Some of those guests, however, who watch for great men's steps, and observe their looks, soon perceived the approach of the family of Guise; and the words, "The Duke, the Duke! His Highness the lieutenant-general!" pronounced by several voices within, created, for the moment a brief bustle among the guests, and then the silence of expectation, till the party entered the room.

The number already assembled might amount to nearly fifty, of whom the greater proportion were officers and soldiers, either personally attendant upon the Duke of Mayenne, or eager to pay court to him whose fortunes were for the time in the ascendant. For them, governments, commands, and the many military employments which gave profuse opportunity of squeezing a divided people, formed the attractions towards one at whose disposal were placed all the good things of at least one half the empire. The rest of the party who occupied the saloon were made up of the lower classes of the French nobility, male and female, principally the *noblesse de la robe*, who, with the same views as the others, though directed in a different line, sought to be amongst the first at the Hotel de Guise.

Not long after, however, another class began to arrive, who, willing to associate with Mayenne, to partake of the influence of his good fortune, to share what he chose to delegate of his power, and to obtain for their younger children the various benefices in his gift, were yet desirous of distinguishing themselves from even the democracy of their own order, by making the hour of their visit somewhat later, that they might not be confounded in the first rush of the subservient crowd. Last of all, as if in mockery of the pride of their immediate predecessors, came the fops, the coxcombs, the witlings, the debauchees of Paris, heedless of all interests but the dear first all-absorbing interests of their own vanity, and ready to laugh or sneer at everything and everybody, from the great Duke himself, down to the last new-made *procureur*, who claimed a right to bear arms and call himself *gentilhomme*.

On his arrival in the hall, the Duke advanced and bowed round him with the dignity, and perhaps with a little more than the pride, of a legitimate monarch. Though his eye had not much of the fire and energy which characterized that of his father and his brother, it was sufficiently quick and marking to observe in the room all those who are likely to be serviceable, either individually to himself, or more generally, to the state; and to each of these he took care to address some word of more particular favour and encouragement. Some he passed with a mere inclination of the head; some he noticed not at all. Madame de Montpensier, however, though in her heart prouder than her brother, was one of those--of those few persons--capable of feeling the master passions of human nature in all the terrible energy in which they can display themselves. Hatred, revenge, and ambition, were for the time, predominant in her heart: and these are idols to which, as to the Moloch of the Ammonites, pride will even sacrifice its children. Knowing and feeling that the meanest man present might accelerate or retard the objects of her desire, casting aside all her natural vanity, and all the haughtiness of her race, Madame de Montpensier mingled with the crowd, and--while her languishing sister, the Duchess of Guise, sat coquetting with her own particular admirers--she spoke with every one, smiled upon every one, and left each with increased prepossession in her favour, and renewed attachment to her cause.

As the crowd increased, and the rooms became full, the party separated into groups, classing themselves by the various standards of rank, opinions, wit, or tastes. For all, amusement was provided in case conversation should not be sufficient to fill up the time; and many took advantage of such arrangements to favour or to conceal the purposes and the views with which each came thither more or less preoccupied. In one chamber the dice rolled upon the board, while one of the most vehement players was every now and then seen to hold a brief conversation with various persons who came and went in the room. At other tables again, those flat, dull pieces of mischievous pasteboard called cards were dealt and played in solemn silence, except when some biting jest, or well-directed and premeditated sneer, found a hook to hang itself upon, even in so insignificant a thing as the foolish names assigned to different cards. Then, again, in a vast and brilliant hall beyond, music of the sweetest kind hung upon the air; while the dance offered its protection to every sort of scheming, from the soft business of innocent love, to foul intrigue and tortuous policy.

In the midst of all this, St. Real, in the simplicity of his heart, saw nothing but very innocent amusement. Eugenie refused to take a part in the dance; and how or why he knew not, St. Real found himself generally by her side. Such a scene, of all others on the earth, affords the greatest opportunity of private communication; but, if the thoughts, the wishes, and the purposes of the speakers be not intimately known to each other, it may become the most dangerous place for such communion also. The half-spoken sentence is so often interrupted at the very point where it is the most interesting, and where it most needs explanation--so much must be said in haste, or not said at all--so much must be left to fancy--so great is the treasure turned over to imagination--that he who plays with hearts should be very sure of his game before he ventures boldly in such a scene as that. St. Real and Eugenie de Menancourt conversed, at first, upon subjects of every-day import and of general reference; but there were between them so many stores of private feeling and thought, that, upon whatever topic they began, the conversation soon flowed back to matters in regard to which their own hearts were in unison respecting either the past or the present. They found it vain to struggle against the stream of sympathies that either sooner or later drew their communion apart from the things that surrounded them; and as the evening went on, they more and more gave way to what they felt; endeavouring, indeed, to avoid speaking of their own sentiments in an individual manner, but still only covering their personal feelings under a thin veil of general observations. This veil, too, was so often rent by accidental interruptions--the termination of a phrase which was intended to give it its general character so often remained unspoken, that every minute, as it flew, left the hearts of Eugenie de Menancourt and Huon of St. Real with deeper and more agitating feelings than either of them had ever felt before: and yet, like all other people who have loved where it would have been wiser not, they were unconscious of what they were encouraging in their own hearts. Eugenie was agitated, but was not alarmed. St. Real was delighted, but only fearful, when he saw the eye of any one marking the close position that he occupied by Eugenie's side, lest it should be supposed that he was making love to her who had been promised to his cousin; but he never believed--he never dreamed--that he was making love--that he was winning her heart, and yielding his own. The very efforts he had made that very night in favour of his cousin were sufficient to blind him entirely, and to lead him, like a general deceived by his guides, into the cunning ambush which the keen archer Cupid so skilfully lays for the advanced parties of the human heart.

At length, towards midnight--that enchanted hour, when all the powers of the imagination, the fairies of the microcosm within us, are up and revelling in the greenest spots of the human heart--at length, towards midnight, when music, and conversation, and gay sights, and happy faces all around, and pleasant words, and the bright eyes of the sweet and beautiful, had left St. Real's fancy as excited as ever was Bacchus' self by the juice of the Achaian vine, Madame de Montpensier stood by his side; and, laying the jewelled forefinger of her right hand upon his arm, called his attention while she said, "I have a message to give Monsieur de St. Real from my brother, who cannot detach himself from that group to speak with you in person, and who fears that you may be absent to-morrow, ere he can see you. I will not detain you one instant."

St. Real obeyed the summons at once, giving but one look, as he turned to follow Madame de Montpensier, towards Eugenie de Menancourt, and another towards a young cavalier, who hastened to fill up the place he abandoned at her side. The Duchess also gave a glance to each, and a third to St. Real; and then, with a smile, led the way across the ball-room, and through two or three chambers beyond, to the utmost verge of the long suite of apartments, which was that night thrown open to the public.

There, looking round her to see that she was unobserved, she paused, and turned towards the young cavalier. "Monsieur de St. Real," she said, in a calm, sweet, but impressive tone, "when you came to Paris, you came undecided whether to join the friends and supporters of the Catholic faith, or its enemies. I think that you have seen enough of us now to judge and to decide; and I have not the slightest doubt of what your decision will be; nay, what it is! But, setting all that apart, I have an offer to make you, which the noblest amongst all yon glittering throng would give his right hand to hear addressed to himself. Mark me, Monsieur de St. Real! A woman's eyes are keen: you love Mademoiselle de Menancourt! Nay, stop me not; but hear! Eugenie de Menancourt loves you! I, in the name of the lieutenant-general of the kingdom, offer you her hand. Take it, and be happy! Spare my brother a world of anxiety and difficulty on her account; spare her the pain of importunity; relieve her from the helpless exposure of her present situation; and make the loveliest creature of all France happy, in the protection of him she loves!"

Pausing for a moment, she gave one glance at the countenance of her auditor, and then added, "Say not a word to-night! but breakfast with me *tête-à-tête* to-morrow, when all difficulties and obstacles shall be removed for ever!"

She turned away, and left St. Real standing alone in the room, feeling that the casket of his heart was opened to his own sight, and its deepest secrets displayed, never to be concealed again by any of the thin and glistening veils with which human weakness cloaks itself so effectually against the purblind eyes of self-examination. He cast himself into a seat, and for some minutes remained in bitter commune with his own heart, while the music and the dancing, and the gay society of the capital, were as unmarked as if they had not existed. Then remembering, painfully, that his demeanour had been already but too accurately watched, he rose, and, with a flushed cheek and contracted brow, returned to the chief saloon. As he approached Eugenie de Menancourt, however, he perceived that she was preparing to depart with a lady of high rank and advanced years, under whose especial care Madame de Montpensier had placed her. Eugenie paused as he came near. The crowd of gay gallants, who were pressing forward with the formal courtesy of the day to offer their services in conducting her to the carriage, drew back as he approached, as if already warned of the purposes of Mayenne in regard to the rich heiress. St. Real felt what was expected of him, and at once offered his hand; but it was with an air of restraint and absence that instantly caught the eye of her to whom he spoke. She suffered him to lead her through the rooms in silence; but, as a turn on the staircase left them for a moment alone, her anxiety prevailed, and, with an unsteady voice, she said, "You seem suddenly unhappy, Monsieur de St. Real. Has anything occurred to pain you?"

St. Real was not a good dissembler; and Eugenie had not dissembled. He heard in the soft, scarce audible tone--he felt in the trembling of the hand that lay in his--he saw in the soft and swimming eyes that looked on him--the truth of one part of what the Princess had said; and in his own heart he felt but too strongly the truth of all the rest. St. Real was not a good dissembler; and all he could reply was, "Oh, Eugenie!" but it was enough.

CHAPTER XV

St. Real entered not again the lighted halls in which the leaders and partisans of the League were assembled; but he paused for a moment in the open air, after the carriage which bore Eugenie de Menancourt towards her solitary home had driven out of the courtyard and passed away down the echoing streets. A momentary burst of artillery and small arms came, borne upon the wind, from a distance, as the indefatigable Henry of Navarre roused the Parisian garrisons with an *alerte* from the side of Meudon: but the mind of St. Real was too deeply busied with other thoughts for the thunder of the cannon to awake in his heart the martial and chivalrous spirit that lay within. The discovery which he had made of his own feelings was, in every respect, painful; and the insight which he had gained into those of Eugenie de Menancourt herself--although there is ever a sweet and soothing balm in the consciousness of being loved--was hardly less bitter. The idea of entering into rivalry with his cousin--of attempting to deprive one who confided in him of the hand of his promised bride--the idea of seeking, or even receiving happiness himself at the expense of that of Philip d'Aubin, found not harbour in the bosom of St. Real for one single moment. Deeply and severely did he blame himself for having suffered such feelings to grow up in his heart as the occurrences of that night had discovered to his own sight; and still more bitterly did he reproach himself for having allowed his feelings to carry him away as they had lately done. Even the degree of regard with which he saw that Eugenie de Menancourt looked on him was an additional reproach; for he well knew that that regard could not have been obtained without conduct on his own part which, although involuntary, he looked upon as a betrayal of his cousin's confidence.

St. Real was not a man, however, to waste upon fruitless regrets those powers of mind which should be employed in forming and executing noble resolutions. He grieved bitterly for what was past, but he grieved only with the purpose of shaping his conduct differently for the future; and, as he turned again to enter the Hotel de Guise, it was with the full determination of never seeing Eugenie de Menancourt again, till the fate of Philip d'Aubin, as far as it was connected with hers, was fixed beyond all recall.

This resolution was joined with another, which rendered the first not difficult to execute. With all her art, with all her skill, with all her knowledge of human character, and with all her insight into that of St. Real, Madame de Montpensier had overreached herself. She had been able to comprehend and appreciate the simplicity and purity with which he was attached to Eugenie de Menancourt, without perceiving the nature of his own feelings; but the quality of her own mind prevented her from comprehending the deep firmness of principle which existed in his heart, and from foreseeing the means that principle would take to combat love as soon as ever the progress of the insidious enemy was discovered. The proposal that she had made to him had produced upon the mind of St. Real an effect the most directly opposite to that which she had intended. The character of the Duke of Mayenne St. Real could not but esteem: there was a dignity, a generosity, a frankness about it, which, together with his splendid talents, commanded no small admiration; and had St. Real been convinced that his opposition to his king, that his bold rebellion, that even his connexion with a party, factious, turbulent, and depraved, originated in motives of patriotism and virtue, his views of the League might have been modified by his opinion of the leader, and his ultimate conduct determined by the judgment he might form in regard to whether that leader's efforts would, or would not, be ultimately beneficial to his country. In the course of that night, however, he had heard and seen enough to convince him that the passion of Mayenne was ambition, and that his object was his own aggrandizement; and the only hold, therefore, that the League could have had upon St. Real would have been virtue, honour, and patriotism, in the whole, considered as a party.

The question, therefore, with the young Marquis had now become, whether the League did, or did not, possess such qualities. At the Jacobins, on the preceding night, however, he had witnessed the means employed by those who were considered the holiest men amongst them to obtain ends which he could not doubt were treacherous and bloody: that very night it had been calmly proposed to him, as a bribe to attach him to the party of the League, to betray his cousin's confidence, and to gratify his own passions at the expense of his honour and integrity. In his examination of the city during the day, he had seen the high and the noble demeaning themselves to court popularity by fawning on persons they despised--an irrefragable proof that their own designs were base; he had seen the good and the just in the filthy and unsparing hands of villains and plunderers; and he had seen those who professed to be the ministers of a God of peace armed to promote a civil war and to shed the blood of their fellow-creatures!

What then could be the result, he asked himself, when a leader, whose principle was ambition, took upon him to guide a fierce and lawless multitude, composed of nobles whose motive was selfishness, of priests whose spirit was fanaticism, and of a rabble whose objects were licentiousness, bloodshed, and plunder? The answer was not difficult; and, as he turned and mounted the staircase, amidst the crowd of lacqueys and attendants who stared at his thoughtful and abstracted demeanour without his noticing their presence, he determined to proceed to the royal camp as early as might be on the following morning, doubting not that, whatever might be the vices and the follies it presented to his sight, he should there find the path which led to his country's welfare, and, he trusted, also to his own peace of mind.

Passing the doors of the saloons, he proceeded to that part of the house in which was situated the apartments that had been assigned to him; and, sending for his master of the horse--a common officer at that time, in the houses of the principal French nobility--he directed him to have everything prepared to quit Paris by daybreak on the following morning. The earliness of the hour which he thus appointed was not dictated by any apprehension that Mayenne would endeavour to impede his departure; but, his resolution being taken, and his opinion fixed by the most favourable view that could be afforded him of the party of the League itself, he wished to avoid, as far as possible, anything like solicitation; and he likewise desired neither to explain his feelings, nor reason upon his motives, in the conduct he was about to pursue regarding Eugenie de Menancourt.

His sensations, indeed, upon the subject were so painful in themselves, that St. Real did not wish either to speak of or to dwell upon them. Arguing, with the usual simplicity of his nature, that, where our wishes and our duties are at variance, it is better to employ our thoughts in performing the duties, than to give them up to the hard task of combating the wishes--in which combat they are but too often defeated--he prepared to occupy all the energies of his mind in the attempt to serve his country, and to benefit to the utmost of his power the party he had determined to espouse, leaving his cousin to pursue his suit towards Eugenie de Menancourt as best he might, but endeavouring to serve him therein by pointing his efforts to nobler objects than had hitherto employed them, and by taking care that all he did should be placed in a fairer light than that in which the levity and somewhat vain indifference of d'Aubin had hitherto permitted his own actions to appear.

Poor St. Real, however, did not know how hard is the task--how painful, how continual is the struggle, to turn the thoughts of a feeling and affectionate heart from the objects of its first attachment, and to occupy, even in the busiest scenes and most stirring actions wherein other men find employment for their whole soul, a mind to which love has given its direction elsewhere. His first experience of what he was but too long to undergo, was made when he lay down to rest, on the night of which we have just spoken.

He thought to sleep, to taste the same refreshing, undisturbed slumbers which were so rarely absent from his pillow; but, alas! alas! how changed were all his sensations. The burning thirst for thoughts to which he would not give way--the consciousness that he was resigning for ever that which would have made his happiness through life--anxieties, which he dared not probe, regarding the happiness of her he loved--self-reproaches, slight, indeed, but bitter, because they were the first he had ever had occasion to address to his own heart--and doubts respecting the conduct and vows of his cousin, which he now saw with eyes sharpened by love--all planted his pillow thick with thorns; and he tossed in feverish restlessness upon his uneasy couch, while slumber and all its wholesome balms were far away.

The sounds of music and of laughing, which to his saddened heart rang like the revelry of fiends, came in bursts up to his windows; and the roll of carriages, the trampling of horses, the shouts of torch-bearers, and the murmuring hum of a thousand less vociferous tongues, poured irritatingly upon his ear, and set sleep at defiance. Gradually, however, those sounds died away, and that space of time which the citizens of the masterless metropolis called a day, and set apart for the transaction of a certain portion of intrigue and faction, levity, sensuality, and bloodshed, came to an end. The bell of the neighbouring church, unheard during many an hour of turbulence and noise, struck two, and the whole world around sank into silence, if not into repose. Still, however, sleep came not to the eyes of St. Real; and he lay and counted the moments till a new class of sounds were heard, announcing that the sons of toil were up and busy in the task of preparing luxuries for the sons of idleness and dissipation. At length, a faint rosy light was seen to glimmer through the open window, the indistinct forms of the massive furniture began to stand out from the gray darkness, and St. Real started up more weary and fatigued with that one night of restless anxiety than he would have felt after weeks of watching in the tented field.

The first task, after dressing himself, was to sit down, and, with the writing materials that stood at hand, to indite a brief note to the Duke of Mayenne, apologizing for not waiting to make a more formal leave-taking. He did not, it is true, announce in distinct terms his determination of joining his arms to the other supporters of the royal cause, because he felt it was within the bounds of possibility that circumstances might yet change his purpose; though, as he left the matter still open, he thought that bad must be the scene presented by the camp of the Henrys indeed, if it could make him prefer the craft, the treachery, and the baseness he had beheld in Paris. In this respect, while expressing his high opinion of the Duke himself, he did not scruple to use language and to display sentiments which had already brought many a venerable and respected head low, amongst the factions and anarchy of the day; and, having said enough to show which way his feelings at that moment led him, he descended to the court, and, mounting his horse, which, with his train, stood prepared for departure, he bade adieu to the Hotel de Guise.

The streets of Paris now presented a very different scene from that which they afforded in either the full life of the risen day, or in the dregs of the evening. Few were the persons to be seen walking slowly along in the fresh, clear, unpolluted light of the early morning; and the long irregular perspective of the antique streets might be seen unencumbered by the many gaudy vehicles which obstructed the sight at a later hour. As St. Real rode on towards the suburbs, one or two patrols of horse, returning from their night watch beyond the walls, passed him with tired faces and soiled arms; but, although the numbers that composed his train were sufficient to have justified some inquiry, yet such was the confused organization of the garrison of Paris, and of the army of the League in general, that no one asked his errand, and he passed on uninterrupted to the gates.

Here, however, he was detained for some minutes, while the drowsy commander of the guard examined his pass and safe-conduct: and some suspicious glances were given to the apparel of his followers, who wore neither the black cross, nor the scarf of the followers of the League. At the end of about a quarter of an hour, however, he was suffered to proceed; and, as the position of the royal armies was not distinctly known to him, he directed his course towards Meudon, at which place it was certain that a part, at least, of the Huguenot force had shown itself the day before. Greater watchfulness was now apparent on the part of the League; and St. Real was challenged and stopped five or six times within half a mile of the gates of Paris. At length, a wide green meadow by the banks of the Seine presented itself; and at the angle of this meadow and the road stood a solitary sentinel, covered with his cuirass, his *salade* or iron cap, and steel plates to defend the thighs. In one hand he carried his long musket, while with the other he held his coil of match, smouldering slowly, between the finger and thumb, and only requiring to be blown to prepare it for immediate action. In the ground, just one pace before him, was planted the iron-shod stake, which, supporting a sort of two-pronged fork, afforded a rest for his long and unwieldy weapon in case of his being called upon to make use of it against any advancing enemy. Painted in front of his iron cuirass appeared the black cross of the League; and there could be no doubt that this was the extreme outpost of the garrison of Paris. It would seem, however, that he had no order to oppose the passage of persons coming from the side of the city; for, although he gazed attentively at the young Marquis and his party as they passed, he asked no questions; and St. Real advanced along the road skirting the meadow, towards an extensive building that he saw at the distance of a quarter of a mile before him, and which bore every sign of being, what it really was, a religious house belonging to some order of friars.

Scarcely had he passed half the distance between the sentinel of the League and the gate of the monastery, when a considerable body of horsemen drew out from behind some trees at the farther extremity of the field, and galloped towards the travellers with their lances down in somewhat menacing array. St. Real immediately halted his men, and waited calmly for the approach of the strangers, who advanced at full speed almost till the parties met, without choosing to notice the peaceable demeanour of the young lord and his attendants. The moment after, however, they came to a halt; and two or three, riding forward before the rest, demanded "*Qui vive?*" apparently not half satisfied with the appearance of St. Real and his attendants. The white scarfs borne by the leaders of this impetuous party sufficiently indicated to what army they belonged; and, replying "*Vive le Roi!*" St. Real produced the pass he had received from Henry III.

"No game for us, this!" exclaimed he who seemed to be their chief, as he read the authentic letters of safe-conduct placed before his eyes. "Good faith, Sir Marquis of St. Real, we thought that Monsieur de Mayenne had roused himself from his bed full four hours before his ordinary time, and was sending out parties to take us by surprise, thinking that we were as laggard and sleepy-headed as himself. However, we will, if you please, form your escort to the next post, and beyond that you will find your way easily to the king."

St. Real signified his assent, and, thus guarded, proceeded onward towards Meudon, conversing, as he went, with the leaders of the Huguenot party--for the strangers were followers of the King of Navarre--and gaining from them some knowledge of the real state and position of the royal armies. On the side of the two kings he found a much greater degree of activity and military caution; and, notwithstanding the presence of the party he had first encountered, he was not suffered to pass the second outpost without a strict examination of his letters of safe-conduct, and was afterwards escorted from post to post by a small body of men-at-arms, until he had proceeded beyond the quarters of the King of Navarre, and had fully entered those of Henry III. of France, who had taken up his abode, by this time, at St. Cloud. Here, again, the discipline seemed more relaxed; and St. Real was suffered to advance without any further question, till, at the entrance of the neat little village of St. Cloud, he perceived a group of persons gathered together round the door of a house, from which, the moment after, issued forth his cousin the Count d'Aubin, booted and armed, as if prepared to mount a horse that was held ready by a groom before the house.

"The lost one found!" exclaimed D'Aubin, embracing his cousin as soon as they met; "the lost one found! Why, St. Real, I had even now my foot in the stirrup to set out once more for Paris, in search of your fair person. But how has all this happened? Let me hear all; for you have had to do with the shrewdest heads in France; and his Highness of Mayenne, with his fair sisters of Montpensier and Guise, are well worth studying, if it be but to lay out a map of human cunning, in order to find our way through its tortuous roads in future."

As St. Real returned the warm embrace of his cousin, there were sensations in his bosom that he had never felt before. It was not that any feeling of rivalry had diminished his affection for Philip d'Aubin, even by a feather's weight; but it was that, notwithstanding every wish to serve his cousin and promote his suit, he had unintentionally cast in his way a greater obstacle than ever; and, although conscious of his own virtue and integrity, he felt as if he had wronged him. With St. Real the predominant feelings were not, as with the rest of mankind, concealed or distorted with laborious care, but on the contrary were always the first to find utterance. "Oh! I will give you all that history hereafter; but I have something of more importance to communicate." Thus saying, he entered the house with his cousin, who led the way to some apartments apparently appropriated to himself, and demanded, laughing, "What now, Huon? what now? You rustic nobles see things in the capital with magnifying glasses, and think many matters of deep consequence, which to us, who see them every day, are, of course, every day affairs."

"I trust you may think as lightly of it as you seem to expect," replied St. Real: "but the matter is this--last night I saw Mademoiselle de Menancourt."

"Ha!" exclaimed D'Aubin, instantly roused to attention; "what of her--where did you see her?"

"I saw her at the Hotel de Guise," replied St. Real; "supped with her there, and was near her afterwards, at the great entertainment given, as I suppose, to the partisans of the League."

"Indeed!" exclaimed D'Aubin somewhat moodily; "and what saw you then? Who fluttered round her? Who was favoured in their suit of the great heiress? To which of his partisans does Mayenne propose to give her hand? Tell me all you saw!"

"I saw much," replied St. Real. "I had an opportunity of speaking with her alone, and was near her the whole evening; so that----"

"Ay! doubtless, doubtless!" replied his cousin; "and were the favoured knight, beyond a doubt; and, probably, sweet Madame de Montpensier encouraged your suit, and Mayenne offered you her hand, if you would join the League----"

He paused; and St. Real was silent for a few moments, somewhat astonished at the accuracy with which his cousin--partly in the random venturing of passion and ill-humour, partly from a shrewd knowledge of the actors in the great drama going on at Paris--hit upon the facts as they had occurred. At length, the Marquis seeing impatience flashing up in his cousin's eye, replied, "You are right, Philip; such an offer was made me!"

"By the Lord! I thought so!" exclaimed D'Aubin. "On my honour, this is right merry and good! and fair Eugenie de Menancourt, as timid as a young fawn, and as gentle as a turtle dove, may do more good service to the armies of the League than a whole regiment of reitters, or half-a-dozen hot nobles of Provence! Why, the devil incarnate seize upon the man! he offered her to me in the morning, if I would join the League, and to you in the evening on the same conditions; and now, doubtless, Huon, if you choose to turn your horses' heads back to Paris, and call in your troops from Senlis, put on a black scarf, and sign the blessed Union, you may to-morrow have the hand of the sweet heiress of Maine, and become a distinguished leader of the hypocritical League. Ha! what say you to violating your cousin's confidence, and gallantly carrying away his promised bride? On my honour and soul, it were a worthy commencement, and would rank you high amongst us libertines of the court and the capital."

"You are angry, Philip," replied St. Real, calmly, though somewhat sorrowfully; "you are angry, Philip, and without cause. Such is not the commencement that I intend to make, nor has it ever entered into my thoughts to do so."

"But what said Eugenie?" interrupted D'Aubin, fixing his keen eyes upon him; "what said Eugenie to all this fine arrangement? Doubtless it pleased her well!"

"She said nothing to it," replied St. Real, "because she never heard it; and, in regard to what you would insinuate of myself, my being here in order to serve the King in arms, is a sufficient reply, I should think."

"And are you here for that purpose?" demanded D'Aubin, softening his tone. "Have you positively decided on joining the royal forces?"

"Positively," replied St. Real, "if I find nothing here which would render the King's service perfectly insupportable."

"Then get ye gone to the court as fast as possible, Huon," exclaimed D'Aubin, relapsing into the usual levity of tone which was fashionable at that time, even in speaking of the most serious subjects; "get thee gone to the court, and see all the vices and horrors it contains; for, till you have done so, I shall not know what you consider supportable or not. Yet, stay, Huon," he added, more generous feelings for a moment resuming their sway, "I doubt you not, my cousin--I know your nature, St. Real, too well to doubt you; so let not your determination be influenced by me. I would trust you as fully with Eugenie in Paris, as if thousands of miles, or hostile armies, or wide-flowing seas, separated you from her."

"You might!" replied St. Real; "but, in the present case, my purpose is fixed. With the private vices of Henry III. or the vices of his court either, I have nothing to do, at least, as far as regards my public actions; and, if I see no reason to believe that my joining the League is absolutely necessary for the salvation of my country, my allegiance to my King is my first public duty, after the service of my native land. Yet, hear me a word more, in regard to Eugenie----"

"Hark, what a noise!" exclaimed D'Aubin, turning towards a window that looked into the street. "Those dogs of Huguenots are always quarrelling with us cats of Catholics, and the distance between Meudon and St. Cloud cannot keep us asunder. Look, Huon, look! they will come to blows presently! See that fellow in the white scarf, how he is laying down the law and the Gospel with the bony finger of his right on the broad hard palm of his left. If he were the renegade, voluptuous, fiery Luther himself, or the keen, fierce, bloodthirsty Calvin, he could not argue the matter more eagerly. Now there, I warrant ye, goes the demonstration of the superiority of the *prêche* over the *messe*--the refutation of transubstantiation, and an utter condemnation of poor purgatory!"

St. Real had followed unwillingly to the window, wondering not a little--although his own ear had been caught by the turbulent sounds in the streets--at the light volatility of his cousin, who could so easily break off a conversation in which he had already shown such heat, and which St. Real himself felt but too deeply to be one of painful interest, in order to gaze upon a squabble between some rude soldiers. The scene which presented itself, however, soon obtained a stronger hold of his attention: it was evidently, as D'Aubin had divined, a quarrel between a small party of the Huguenot soldiers, who, serving under Henry of Navarre, had been quartered in the neighbouring town of Meudon, and a body of the Catholics, forming part of the army of Henry III. who seemed not at all disposed to show much hospitality in the streets of St. Cloud to their allies with the white scarfs. According to the usual course of such occurrences, two persons were more distinguished than the rest by vehemence of manner, loudness of tone, and fierceness of look; but behind the principal speaker on the part of the Protestants stood another of the same party, gifted with that dark and ominous look of silent determination which betokens, in general, a man more disposed to deeds than words. As the argument was evidently getting higher and higher, and the dispute was apparently reaching that point where strong blows are brought in corroboration of vigorous assertions, St. Real proposed to his cousin to interpose with that authority which their rank conferred, and which the number of their retainers, who were standing by enjoying the scene, enabled them to render effectual. D'Aubin agreed to the propriety of this proceeding; but he still continued to gaze out, more amused than affected by what he saw, till at length the more quiet personage, whom we have described as belonging to the Huguenot party, stretched forth a long arm from behind his more voluble comrade, and cut short a very vehement and vigorous tirade on the part of the Catholic soldier, by dealing him a blow on the side of the head that instantly stretched him on the bosom of his mother earth.

Swords and daggers were drawn on all sides in a moment; and St. Real, waiting for no further question, sprang down the stairs, followed by his cousin; and, calling upon the attendants to aid him, he interposed between the contending parties, thrusting his powerful form between the two principal combatants, and casting them asunder like two pugnacious curs unwilling to be separated. In the struggle, however, and ere D'Aubin and the attendants could come to his assistance and enforce order, St. Real had received a slight cut upon the face, which speedily stained his collar in blood; and his clothes suffered equally from dust and dirt, and the profaning fingers of more than one unclean hand. At length the tumult was appeased; and D'Aubin, after treating the contending parties to a witty harangue in praise of peace, turned away with St. Real, saying, "Well, well, Huon, now that you have had enough of fighting for your morning's meal, get you gone to the King, or he will be out for the day. He is not at the chateau, but in that house with the large garden--you can hardly see it as we stand; but, by the number of people I see gathering in that direction, I should suppose he was now about to set out. So hasten on, and you will find me here at your return."

"My visit to the King may well wait a few hours," replied St Real; "and I would fain, Philip, conclude with you a conversation which can never be renewed between us without pain. I have got much to tell you. But stay!" he exclaimed suddenly, as his eye fell upon the figure of a Dominican monk, who was slowly proceeding up the road, and had just passed the spot where he himself stood in conversation with his cousin; "but stay! I think I know that friar, and, if so, I must to the King with all speed!"

Thus speaking, and without waiting for any reply, he made a sign to his attendants to follow, and hurried on, after the Jacobin, on foot. The monk was proceeding at a calm quiet pace, with his eyes fixed upon the ground; and St. Real was by his side in a moment. One glance showed him the dull heavy features of Brother Clement, who had tenanted the chamber to his own in the convent of the Jacobins; and the voices and the jugglery he had seen played off upon the wretched fanatic, as well as the effect which the whole had produced upon the object of those artifices, instantly came up before St. Real's mind, and made him hesitate whether he should not question him in regard to his errand at St. Cloud. The next moment, however, a gentleman, in whom St. Real could easily recognise a high officer of the law--as, in those days, every class and profession had its appropriate garb--came up, followed by some other people carrying papers, and, stopping the friar, as a person whom he knew, held a brief conversation with him, and then walked slowly on by his side towards the dwelling of the King. St. Real, after a moment's consideration, paused, and beckoning to the dwarf Bartholo, from whose knowledge of Paris and its inhabitants he had already derived much information, inquired the name of the personage now walking forward with the monk.

"His name is La Guesle," replied the dwarf, drily: "he is the king's *Procureur Général*."

Such information was sufficient to remove from the mind of St. Real some part at least of the apprehensions which he had entertained; but, nevertheless, there was a lingering suspicion that the Jacobin's intentions were not all righteous, which made him resolve to inform the king at once of what he had seen in Paris, and put him upon his guard against the machinations of his most insidious enemies. With this view, as he saw that the *Procureur Général* and his companion were proceeding exactly in the same direction as himself, he hurried his pace, and passed them. Making his way onward through the various groups of soldiers, courtiers, and officers, that were scattered thickly through the streets of their temporary residence, enjoying the fine sunshine of the early summer morning, he hastened forward towards the spot to which his cousin had directed him as the abode of the king, inquiring as he went which was the exact house amongst the many splendid buildings that St. Cloud then contained.

At length the abode of one Hieronimo de Gondi was pointed out to him; and, entering the court, the walls of which had concealed from his sight a crowd of guards and attendants at that time constantly waiting upon the sovereign, he proceeded to the great entrance, and mounted the steps which led to the first hall. Here his name and business were instantly demanded, and his reply transmitted through various mouths to the chambers above. While detained below for the king's answer to his demand of an audience, he was ushered into a side room, where some of the superior officers of the court were whiling away their daily hours of attendance. Some were playing with dice, and some at chess; but in all there was a fearful effeminacy in dress and demeanour, which made St. Real shrink from the soft and womanly things with which he was for the moment brought in contact. He was not destined, however, to remain long amongst them; for the next moment a page--fair and soft, and smooth-spoken, with jewels in his ears, and as much satin and lace upon his slashed doublet of sky-blue silk as would furnish forth a lady on a court birthday--glided into the room, and besought the Marquis of St. Real to follow him to the presence of the king.

Ascending the broad flight of steps which led to the principal apartments above, St. Real first passed through the chamber of the Gascon guards, the same unscrupulous body which had served the monarch so remorselessly in the assassination of the ambitious but heroic Duke of Guise. Their harsh and war-worn features, shaggy beards, and affectedly rough demeanour, offered a strange contrast to the soft and silken aspect of the rest of the court: but St. Real was soon introduced to a new, but not less sickening scene of luxurious effeminacy. Passing through an ante-chamber, in which lounged a number of creatures such as he had seen below, he was led into the audience-room prepared for the king. Faint rose-coloured velvet formed the hangings of the walls, a number of green silk couches were placed round the room, and the whole air was so burdened with manifold perfumes, that St. Real, disgusted with all he beheld, felt actually sick at the compound odour that assailed him as soon as he entered. A number of personages stood round, dressed in all the gaudy colours of the rainbow, and each without the slightest spot or stain to be seen upon his glossy vestments. In the midst of them all sat a man habited, like themselves, with all the scrupulous care that folly can waste upon personal appearance. His hands and his face were as white and as delicate as the satin lining of his cloak, except where on his cheeks appeared a faint delicate colour, like the hectic blush of a consumptive girl, but which, in him, was probably rather the effect of paint than of disease. He was speaking when St. Real entered: but it was none of his lords, or minions, as they were then called, who was so honoured at that moment by the effeminate Henry III. On his lap he held a beautiful worked basket, lined with faint blue satin, and containing no less than four small dogs, neither of which exceeded in size a well-fed miller's rat; and to one of these--his favourite pets and constant companions--he was addressing some tender reproaches for the crime of having scrambled over the back of one of the others, in its unceremonious attempts to escape from the delicate dwelling, which it would willingly have exchanged for a wooden box, and some clean hay.

St. Real's bold step in the room, the sound of his heavy boot and jingling spurs, instantly caught the king's attention; and, looking up from his basket of dogs, he gazed over the person of the young noble, with a glance first of surprise, and then, apparently, of horror and disgust. The silken watchers of the king's countenance instantly caught its expression, and divined the cause.

"Good God, sir!" exclaimed one, interposing between St. Real and the king, as if he feared that the young noble were about to assassinate the monarch; "good God, sir! is it possible that any one should present himself before his Majesty in such a plight? Retire, for Heaven's sake! you had better retire!"

St. Real laid his hand upon the attendant's breast to push him back out of his way; but the minion shrank back from the touch of the same stout doe-skin glove with which the young Marquis had parted the contending soldiers in the street, as if a dagger had been at his bosom.

"I would not have intruded upon your Majesty," said St. Real, "in a garb stained with blood as this is, had I not had something to communicate which I thought of immediate importance----"

"Whatever you have to communicate, sir," interrupted the king, frowning, "must be told when you have changed your dress: I will hear nothing at the risk of being suffocated. The blood has nothing to do with the matter! I have seen more blood, and shed more blood, than you ever have, or ever will, perhaps; but you bring in with you a whirlwind of dust, enough to choke up the lungs of any Christian king upon the face of the earth. Make no reply, sir," he continued, waving his hand; "make no reply, but leave the room; and when you have changed your dress, and appear in habiliments more befitting this place, I will hear what you have to communicate, but not before."

"As your Majesty pleases," replied St. Real; "but still, let me warn you of one thing at least----"

"Of nothing!" exclaimed the king. "Why, the very percussion of your breath shakes the dust from your cloak, till the whole air is dim. Away with him! away with him! Nevers, Joyeuse, Epernon, rid me of the sight of him! But gently, gently! Do not shake the dust off him: 'tis bad enough to be obliged to ride along the high roads, once every day, without having the high roads brought into our own audience-chamber."

There was a determination in the look and demeanour of the young Marquis of St. Real which augured something in his nature not pleasant to lay hands upon; and, consequently, the courtiers of the contemptible monarch took care not to enforce his commands with any rudeness. Nor was it necessary; for St. Real, finding that any farther attempt, at that moment, to communicate to the king the apprehensions he entertained from what he had seen in Paris, would be vain, retreated from the royal presence without farther question, resolving immediately to inform his cousin D'Aubin, and beg him to convey the bare intelligence of danger to the monarch, while he himself changed his dress, and prepared to give more full and minute information.

Rejoining his attendants in the court, and looking eagerly round, as he quitted the royal residence, in order to ascertain whether the monk were still in sight, St. Real turned his steps back towards the house where he had found D'Aubin on his arrival at St. Cloud. It was not, indeed, that he could feel particularly interested in the fate of the monarch whom he had just seen, or that he thought the death of such a degraded being would be, at any other period, much to be regretted in France; but the young lord, acting upon general principles which accidental circumstances never greatly modified, felt it his bounden duty to prevent, if possible, a meditated crime; and, even had it not been so, would have been extremely desirous of preserving the life of the reigning sovereign, at a moment when political and religious factions, personal enmities, and contending interests, convulsed the realm, and required no new brand of discord to bring down sorrows, desolation, and ruin, upon the people, the country, and the state.

Whichever way St. Real turned his eyes, however, various groups of persons loitering about, without any apparent object, interrupted his view ere it could penetrate many yards. Amongst them the figure of the Jacobin was not to be seen; and, mounting his horse, which had been led after him, he proceeded as fast as possible to the dwelling in which his cousin had taken up his quarters.

He found D'Aubin surrounded by a large party of the gay nobility of Paris; and levity and merriment had so completely taken possession of every one present, that St. Real could obtain no attention for the serious matter he had to communicate. Even his cousin himself, whom he knew to be full of strong and fiery passions, and whom he had seen that very morning moved by no light emotions, appeared now to have given himself up entirely to the idlest spirit of gaiety; so that the only effect produced by the tale which the young nobleman had to tell was loud laughter at the repulse he had met with from the monarch's presence, and advice to suffer Henry to deal with his friend the friar as best he might.

Somewhat offended, and still more grieved, at his cousin's conduct, St. Real quitted him, promising to rejoin him in the course of the day; and, betaking himself to the small rooms, which were the only ones he could find unoccupied in either of the two *auberges* that St. Cloud at that time boasted, he hastily put off his riding-suit, removed the traces of travel and contention from his person, and then, dressed more in accordance with the courtly foppery of a great capital than the simplicity which he had expected to find in a camp, he returned to the temporary dwelling of the king, bent upon executing his own right purposes, whoever might laugh or sneer. Henry had by this time, it would seem, considered the impolicy of alienating so powerful a subject, at a moment when the throne so much needed support; and St. Real found a page waiting for him in the vestibule, charged, on his return, to deliver a sort of half apology for the treatment he had met with, and to conduct him immediately to the royal presence.

Led through the same rooms, St. Real entered the audience-chamber, which was still tenanted by the same personages, with the exception of the king himself, whose voice was heard in a cabinet beyond. The page, however, instantly proceeded to the door, and throwing it open, announced St. Real's return.

"We will speak with him presently," replied Henry, aloud: but the sight which met St. Real's eyes through the open door made him once more cast away all ceremony, notwithstanding his rebuke he had received in the morning. On the right of the monarch stood La Guesle, the *Procureur Général*, while at the king's feet knelt the very Jacobin friar whom St. Real had seen in conversation with that officer about half an hour before. The monk seemed in the act of presenting a letter; but though that action, and his whole demeanour, appeared perfectly pacific, yet St. Real was convinced, from his previous knowledge, that the ultimate designs of the Jacobin must be evil; and striding across the audience-hall with the purpose of interposing, he had nearly reached the door of the cabinet, when one of the nobles in attendance stopped him for an instant, attempting to explain to him that the King would summon him when he thought fit.

"Of course, of course!" replied St. Real, "but the King is in danger. See, see!" And at the same moment the Dominican, as he knelt, lifted his arm and struck the monarch, what appeared to be merely a blow of his clenched hand.

The King staggered back, however, exclaiming, "He has killed me!" And drawing from his side the long sharp knife which the Jacobin had left in the wound, he struck the assassin on the head as he was endeavouring to rise. Almost at the same time, La Guesle, drawing; his sword, passed it through the monk's body; and the nobleman, who had so ill-timedly stopped the advance of St. Real, sprang forward, crying, "The Monk has killed his Majesty;" and while the murderer was already falling under the blows of the King and La Guesle, drove his dagger into his throat and put a period to his existence. The other officers in attendance rushed into the cabinet in tumult and fury, and with an indecent excess of rage, cast the dead body of the Jacobin out of the window into the court.

There is no describing the terror, confusion, and despair, into which the large body of courtiers, interested deeply in the life of their master, were thrown by the event that had just occurred; but Henry himself, at that awful moment, recalled all the courage and self-possession for which he had been distinguished in his early years, and showed himself far more tranquil and undisturbed than any of the party.

"Send for a surgeon," he said, sitting down and pressing one hand upon the wound, while with the other he waved back those who were crowding round him. "La Guesle, you have done wrong to kill the wretch. We might have learned who were his instigators; but let the room be cleared. Monsieur de St. Real, I thought to have spoken with you, but it is impossible now. You said you had something to communicate; but if I recover, it must be told hereafter; if I die, it must be told to my successor."

"God forbid your Majesty should die at this moment," replied St. Real, whose intended communication was now rendered useless. "I trust that your wound will not prove serious."

"I trust not," replied the King; "but no one can say what, or how soon, may be the termination. Although I am inclined to think that the wound is not dangerous, yet in this body there may be but half an hour of life. Therefore remember, lords and gentlemen of France here present, that, should death be the result of this morning's bad work, Henry of Navarre is your lawful king! From the moment that my lips cease to breathe he is your king according to every principle of right and justice: the fundamental laws of the French monarchy make him so, and no power on earth can absolve you of your duty towards him. I only raise my voice to point out to my subjects what will be their duty when I am dead. Remember that this is my last injunction: but here come the surgeons; and now, once more, I say, let the room be cleared."

The monarch's orders were instantly obeyed, and the cabinet, in which he had received his wound, was accordingly abandoned by all but the surgeons and his immediate personal attendants. The whole party, however, lingered in the audience chamber, and in the ante-room adjoining, breaking into separate groups, and each speaking low, but eagerly, on the event that had occurred, and the consequences likely to ensue. As St. Real was not personally known to any one present, he was, of course, thrown out of all these small circles, and was proceeding through the rooms, in order to join his attendants and make his escape from the bustle, confusion, and tumult which were beginning to spread rapidly through the royal household, when a stout, plainly-dressed, middle-aged man, whom he had not particularly noticed in the crowd, laid his hand upon his arm, saying, "I think I heard your name mentioned as Monsieur de St. Real."

"The same," replied St. Real, bowing. "What are your commands?"

"My name is De Sancy," replied the other: "an old acquaintance of your father's. I would speak a word with you, but not here." Thus saying, he led St. Real on till they reached the court, where all was in the same state of confusion which reigned above--the gates closed, and no one suffered to go out. At the appearance of Monsieur de Sancy, however, the guards presented arms, and the porter threw open the *grille* for him and his companion to pass. A word, on his part, obtained the same facility for his own immediate followers, and for those of St. Real; and walking on foot down the road, while their horses followed, De Sancy spoke briefly to his young companion of what had occurred.

"The king will die," he said. "I see it in his countenance; and France will be thrown into a state of greater turbulence than ever. There is but one way to save her, Monsieur de St. Real; and, if you inherit your father's heart and principles, you will not hesitate to join me in following it."

"May I ask you," demanded St. Real, "what is the way to which you allude?"

"I mean," replied De Sancy, "boldness, decision, preparation, on the part of the friends of good order. You will see, Monsieur de St. Real, that as soon as the king is dead, the bonds which keep all these forces together will be suddenly dissolved. The greater part of the leaders will think all ties of honesty, loyalty, and patriotism at an end; and almost all will set themselves up for sale to the highest bidder, while many will join that party for which they have already a hankering. I heard, some time ago, that you were expected here, and I learned that you have a considerable body of troops lying near Senlis. Now tell me, supposing that the king were dead, in what light would you look upon Henry, King of Navarre?"

"As the legitimate successor to the crown," answered St. Real, "and as my rightful sovereign!"

"Then would you be as well contented to fight against the League under a Huguenot sovereign," demanded De Sancy, "as under the Catholic monarch, who has just met with such a fitting reward for his love of priests and friars?"

"A thousand times better," replied St. Real, "if that sovereign be Henry of Navarre, my father's friend and my own--honest and noble, if ever man was, and loving his country and his people better than himself."

"If such, then, be your opinions, Monsieur de St. Real," replied De Sancy, laying his hand familiarly on his shoulder--"if such be your opinions, without a word more let us mount our horses, and ride over together to Meudon, to bear to the Bearnois, as they call him, the first tidings of all that has happened here, and to promise him our unbought support in case of need. I bring with me nearly three thousand sturdy Swiss; and you, I hear, near a thousand hardy Frenchmen. What say you? shall we go?"

Great emergencies make short oratory. "With all my heart," replied St. Real, who, however brief had been the explanation, understood De Sancy's views and objects as well as if he had spoken a volume; "with all my heart!" he replied, "and we will ride quick."

Their horses were beckoned up; each cavalier sprang into the saddle; and, after a few words of direction and command to some of their attendants on either part, they galloped off towards Meudon as fast as they could go.

CHAPTER XVI

Neither St. Real nor his companion spoke much as they advanced towards Meudon. The rapid pace at which they proceeded, and the still more rapid thoughts that were passing in the mind of each, left little room for conversation. Each, however, seemed so instinctively to appreciate the character of the other, that the few words which did occasionally pass between them conveyed far more than much longer communication might have accomplished between persons whose ideas flowed in a less direct and straightforward channel. So rapidly did their horses bear them forward indeed, that but a few minutes elapsed ere they beheld the pleasant little upland supporting the village in which the witty but licentious Rabelais poured forth the biting and sarcastic torrent of satire that, however ill understood by after ages, has rendered his name immortal; and in which also he exercised all those clerical functions that were far less adapted to the character of his mind.

Coming from the side of St. Cloud, and bearing about his person those conventional signs which were understood to indicate an officer of the royalist party, Monsieur de Sancy, accompanied by his young companion, was permitted to go forward, with scarcely any interruption almost to the gates of the old chateau in which Henry of Navarre had fixed his head-quarters. Here, however, they were challenged by the sentinels; but, giving the word, they passed on, and meeting with an inferior officer attached to the prince, inquired if he had yet gone forth.

"More than an hour," was the reply; "but he may certainly be found with the advance guard at the *Pré aux Clercs.*"

Without farther question, and somewhat mortified at the loss of time, De Sancy and St. Real turned their horses' heads, and at some risk galloped down the steep descent; nor pulled a bridle rein till they reached the large open plain called the *Pré aux Clercs*, which at this time offered a singular and not unpicturesque exhibition. From the spot where the road which they followed entered the plain, the country lay flat and unvaried to the very suburbs of the city of Paris, which rose behind, forming a dense background of grey buildings, towering up one beyond another in the misty light of a summer's day. The open ground between was not exactly covered with multitudes, but was living with a hundred groups of gay and glittering cavaliers; while two strong bodies of infantry, and a squadron of horse, covered the several roads which led from that part of Paris to Meudon and St. Cloud. The groups of horsemen of which we have spoken, armed at all points, and, in general, bearing the old knightly lance--some decorated with the colours of the League, some displaying those of the Catholic Royalists, and some carrying the white scarfs and sword-knots of the Huguenots-- were seen, now wheeling about the plain, endeavouring to gain the vantage ground of a party of opponents; now standing still, waiting in firm ranks the attack of a body of the enemy; now hurled in impetuous charge against the foe, and mingling in brief but desperate struggle; with the armour, and the pennons, and the scarfs, and the rich caparisons, glancing in and out of the clouds of dust that covered them. Every now and then, also, when any of the Leaguers advanced too near, the arquebusiers, who covered the roads, would keep up upon them a rolling fire from their levelled pieces; and occasionally some of the batteries erected for the defence of the suburbs would pour forth flame and thunder upon the position of the Huguenot infantry, though with but little effect.

About a hundred yards in advance of the foot, upon one of the few slight rises which the plain afforded, appeared a group, consisting of about twenty horsemen, principally distinguished by the Huguenot scarf, who took no further part in the skirmishes which were going on than by every now and then detaching a messenger from their body, apparently to bear directions or commands to other parts of the field. At the head of this group, armed at all points except the head, appeared Henry, King of Navarre, with his fine, but strong-marked features, full of animation and excitement from the scene before him. St. Real was the first who remarked his position; and, pointing it out to Monsieur de Sancy, paused only till they had ordered their attendants to remain near the body of infantry, and then spurred on with his companion to the spot where the monarch was watching the progress of the morning's skirmish--an amusement of which he rarely deprived his soldiery. Turning round as they came up, he welcomed St. Real with a look of surprise and satisfaction, and greeted De Sancy with a smile.

"This is unexpected and gladsome, my good young friend," he said, grasping St. Real's hand. "I heard you were in Paris; and, though your cousin declared you would certainly visit us ere you decided, yet, good faith! I thought the cunning of the League would be too much for you."

"It was, I believe, too much for themselves, your Majesty," replied St. Real; "for I am not only here, but purpose to remain. We have, however, something of more importance to tell your Majesty, if you will give us your ear for one moment."

"Instantly," replied the king; and then turning to some of those behind him, he pointed with his leading-staff to one of the groups of skirmishers, exclaiming, "Some one ride in there, and bring out Rosny! The lad is mad with sorrow for the loss of his wife. Ventre Saint Gris! 'Tis a strange thing that what would make one man mad for joy, should make another man mad for grief! He will get himself killed now, in order to go to heaven after his wife; while there are many men who would almost to the other place, to get out of the way of theirs. But ride in, ride in, and bring him out--tell him I want him! Now, St. Real! now, Monsieur de Sancy! I am for you!"

Thus speaking, he rode on twenty or thirty paces in advance of his attendants, and looked first to St. Real, and then to De Sancy, as if requiring them to give him their tidings. The latter then spoke: "We have to communicate to your Majesty," he said, "an event that has occurred at St. Cloud, and which may be productive of great and sorrowful results--which pray God avert!"

"Amen!" cried Henry; "but what is it, what is it?"

"This, my lord," replied de Sancy. "About an hour ago, while Monsieur de St. Real and myself were both in the audience-chamber of his Majesty, the king was wounded severely by a Dominican friar, and I have many fears that the result will be fatal."

Henry made no reply, but gazed upon Monsieur de Sancy's face with a look of anxiety and horror. "This is ruin indeed!" he exclaimed--"to be killed at the very moment that our united arms had so nearly seated him securely on the throne! This is ruin indeed!"

"I trust not, your Majesty," replied St. Real. "First, the king is not yet dead, and may recover; and next, even should he die, you, my lord, have not only a righteous cause to support you, but a more fair renown. You would then be as much king of France as he is now, and many a subject who serves him unwillingly will draw his sword with joy for you."

"At all events, my lord," said De Sancy, "whatever may be the conduct of others, and whatever may be the result of this most lamentable affair, your Majesty will find that two at least of the French nobles, without consulting or considering any other interest but that of their country, will be ready, should fate place the crown of France upon your head, to serve your Majesty with their whole heart and soul. I, for my part, engage at once to bring over the Swiss to your Majesty's service; and, if I have understood him right, Monsieur de St. Real here present will immediately move his troops from Senlis to your support."

"Without a moment's hesitation," added St. Real; "and if I have hitherto even entertained a scruple in regard to joining the royal forces, that scruple would not exist after your Majesty's accession to the throne."

"Thank you, thank you, my friends!" exclaimed Henry, "this is noble! This is generous! But still let us hope that the calamity will be averted, which, by the death of the king, would cast amongst us a fresh ball of discord, when so many already exist. Still it is necessary for me to be prepared; but while I speed to St. Cloud, in order to learn, as far as possible, what is proceeding there, let me beg you, my friends, to converse over the matter with those you can trust, and ascertain upon whom I may rely--who are likely to be doubtful friends, and who will prove open enemies."

St. Real and his companion promised obedience; and the king, after speaking a few moments with some of the gentlemen of his train, turned his horse's head towards St. Cloud, and galloped off. De Sancy and St. Real returned more leisurely, conversing over the event that had occurred, and its probable results.

"You, Monsieur de Sancy, and the King of Navarre also, seem to apprehend much more danger from the death of the king," said St. Real, "than I can conceive likely to accrue. Far be it from me to speak evil of a man who, even now, may be dying; yet who can doubt that in virtues as a man, and in high qualities as a sovereign, the monarch who has just left us is as superior to him who now reigns in France as light is to darkness? As a military leader, too, his renown is justly among the first in Europe; and with the sole command of the army, which is now divided, the affection of all that is noble and good in the land, and the warm co-operation of many of those who have held aloof from the present sovereign, he would surely be able to accomplish far more towards reducing the land to a state of tranquillity and subordination, than a king who is not only hated but despised."

De Sancy shook his head, with a somewhat melancholy smile, at calculations made upon grounds so very different from the motives which actuated the generality of men in the disorganized land wherein they lived.

"If every one were Monsieur de St. Real," he answered, "if every one--I do not mean in France, but even in this camp and army--were actuated by the same pure and patriotic feelings as yourself, your calculations would be undoubtedly right, and the extinction of the line of Valois would be the signal for tranquillity and happiness to resume their place in our distracted land. But the men that we see around us are divided into many classes, and actuated by many motives. The Huguenots have among them one principle of action--I mean religious fanaticism. But, taking all the rest of the united armies, I suppose there are not ten men of rank amongst us who have any general principle whatsover."

"You give a sad picture of our countrymen, Monsieur de Sancy," replied St. Real; "but if your view be correct, how happen such discordant elements to have adhered so long?"

"From causes as numerous," replied De Sancy, "as the men themselves. Some have adhered to the king out of gratitude for favours conferred, and from a knowledge that their fortune, almost their very existence itself, depended upon that monarch. Such are the minions, the favourites, the priests. Others again, of a nobler nature, have remained attached to the same party equally from gratitude for favours conferred, but without entertaining any further hopes from, or being bound by any tie of interest to, the king. Such is the Duke of Epernon, and several more. Others, again, serve the monarch because their own dignity and power are connected by various ties to his. Such are the princes of the blood. An immense number follow him only because, seeing the country split into factions, and knowing that they must attach themselves to some party, they judge that they can obtain most from the court; and, at all events, can sell themselves to the League hereafter, in case they find their first expectations disappointed. Many, too, have some individual object in view, which they may obtain from the king, but could not obtain from the League; and many serve the monarch from personal hatred to some one in the opposite camp. Monsieur de St. Real, I could go on for an hour, and yet leave half the motives unreckoned by which men of different parties are actuated in every civil strife. All these motives are at work amongst us; and patriotism, depend upon it, comes in for but a very small share, when there are so many other greedy passions to divide with her the hearts of the multitude."

St. Real was silent for a few moments, and thoughtful too; for in the picture of the manifold hues and shades of human baseness thus presented to his sight, there was something very painful to a mind accustomed to view the world in a brighter light. After having considered for a short time, however, letting his mind roam to more general thoughts, he returned to the immediate matter of their conversation. "I am sorry to hear," he said, "that such is the composition of an army from which I had hoped better things. But tell me, Monsieur de Sancy, will not the same motives which have hitherto bound them to the present king bind them also to his successor?"

"By no means," replied De Sancy. "In the first place, the difference of religion will be a great objection to many, and an excellent pretext to more. A thousand to one all the zealous Catholics will abandon the heretic monarch at once. Those who personally love him will seek to make him change his religion; those who love him not will leave him without any question. All who are already doubtful will seize this favourable opportunity of going over to the League. All who are serving upon interested motives will demand place, preferment, or promise, as the price of their future assistance. Of these--and I am sorry to say that at least one half of the royal camp is composed of such--of these there will be a general market--a buying and selling, as in the halls of Paris; and if the king cannot outbid the League, they will go over together."

"Well, let them go," cried St. Real. "By Heaven! Monsieur de Sancy, I hold that we shall be better without such false and doubtful allies. Our swords will strike more firmly, our confidence in ourselves and in each other will be redoubled, when the army is purified from such a nest of mercenary villains."

"Ah! my young friend," replied De Sancy, "you may make a good soldier; but you are not yet fit for a politician in this bad world of ours. Call them by some softer name, too, than mercenary villains," he added, with a laugh; "for, till you see the event, you do not know whom you may find amongst them."

St. Real was silent; for his mind was not without some shade of doubt as to what would be the conduct of his own cousin in the event of the king's death breaking asunder all those ties which, for the time, united the incoherent parts of the royalist army together. However much St. Real might love the Count d'Aubin, and however much he might strive to conceal from himself the faults and failings which disfigured his character, he could not help experiencing a vague internal conviction that his actions were more the effect of impulse than of principle, and that there was not sufficient firmness in his character to restrain him from following where his passions or his interests led him, if to the path which he thus chose no very signal disgrace was attached in the eyes of the world.

He was silent then, and a few minutes more brought them back to St. Cloud, which exhibited all the usual marks of a small place in which some great event has happened. The eager faces; the gliding up and down of important-looking persons; the whispering groups at every corner, and at every house-door; the loud-tongued politicians, demonstrating to their little assemblage of hearers the events that were to follow, or the events that were past; and here and there the mercenary soldier, sauntering indifferently through the streets, and caring not who died, or who survived, provided that his pay was sure, and that the blessed trade of war was not brought to an untimely end.

Monsieur de Sancy and St. Real drew up their horses at the first group of respectable persons they met with, and demanded news of the king. The reply was favourable: "the monarch was better," the people said; "the surgeons apprehended no evil; and the consequences of the crime had fallen upon the head of him who perpetrated it."

After receiving this answer, St. Real and De Sancy separated, each well pleased with the other, and promising mutually to meet again before night, whatever might be the result of the events which had brought them first together.

St. Real then directed his course up the road towards the small *auberge*, in which he had hired the only apartments that on his first arrival were to be found vacant in the village, and at which he had left a part of his attendants to prepare for his return. The door of the inn, like that of every other house in the place, was surrounded by its own little group, discussing the events of the time; and as St. Real approached, he distinguished amongst the crowd his dwarf page Bartholo, together with the handsome Italian boy, who had been left in his service by Henry of Navarre. The young marquis-- whose mind was not of that indifferent cast which looks with philosophical coolness upon the dangers or discomforts of every person except its own particular proprietor--had been not a little anxious for the fate of the fair delicate youth amidst the troubles and perils of the capital and its environs, and was in no slight degree rejoiced to see him in safety in a spot where he could afford him protection.

Leonard de Monte sprang forward as soon as he beheld his lord, and welcomed him on his arrival, with all that peculiar grace which we have before had occasion to notice in his demeanour. There was something in his manner that expressed a willingness to serve and to obey; but, at the same time, it appeared to be the willingness of a free and generous mind to perform that which depended solely upon its own volition. There was a dignity withal in his tone and demeanour, that made his obedience seem a condescension rather than a duty; and yet, as we have said, it was all so cheerfully done, that St. Real, although he felt more as if he were speaking to a friend or a younger brother, than to one who was bound to obey, nevertheless did not feel the difference disagreeable, but rather looked with more interest upon a person whose demeanour was so superior to that of others in his station.

"I have had some fears for you, my good boy," said St. Real, "since I heard that you had come hither to seek me."

"Oh, never fear for me, sir!" replied the youth, speaking with that confidence in his own fortune, which is one of the many happy deceits whereby the human heart beguiles itself to forget the weariness, and the difficulties, and the dangers of the long and perilous path of life; "oh, never fear for me, sir! In my short day, I have passed through so many scenes, where others have found every sort of danger and tribulation, without receiving so much as a scratch of my hand, that I begin to believe myself enchanted against peril: besides, I had the two stout fellows you gave me to accompany me from Maine; and if I had met with any danger, I should have left them to fight it out, and have slipped away, finding safety under cover of my littleness."

"Well, well, we must not try your fortune too far, my good Leonard," replied the young noble. "But come hither with me, Bartholo, seek me wherewithal to write; and bid Martin and Paul hold themselves ready to set out in half an hour to Senlis. Have you seen the Count d'Aubin?"

"I saw him not half an hour ago," replied Leonard de Monte, ere the dwarf could answer. "He was riding forth with a gay company to the *Pré aux Clercs*."

"That is unfortunate!" observed St. Real; "I would fain have spoken with him. But hark! there is the drum beating to arms, and the clarions sounding a march! See what that may mean, Leonard."

The boy sped away quickly; and during his absence St. Real proceeded to his own apartments, and wrote to the officer whom he had left in command of his troops near Senlis, directing him, in as few words as possible, to advance without loss of time to the distance of half a march from the royal army. Ere he had concluded, Leonard de Monte returned, and, in reply to St. Real's eager question of what news, informed him, that an order had just been given out to put the royal forces under arms, as it was supposed that those who had instigated the attempt at assassination, not knowing that it had failed, would endeavour to take advantage of the confusion they expected to follow its success amongst the royalists.

"A wise precaution!" said St. Real--"a wise precaution, marking that Henry of Navarre is in the camp, even if one did not know it from other circumstances. Now, tell me, Leonard," he continued, after having sealed and despatched his letter, "how long have you been here?"

"I reached Paris some five days since," replied the boy, "and waited two days there, in hopes of your coming; but, finding that you did not arrive, I grew anxious, knowing that there are wily men and unscrupulous of all parties in these places. Then, when you did not appear the third day, I set off hither to see whether you had been delayed against your will at the king's quarters; and ever since then I have been coming and going between the camp and the city of Paris, till I learned this morning that you were here."

"But were you never stopped at the outposts?" demanded St. Real; "your pass extended only to the capital?"

"Oh, no!" replied the boy, in a gay tone; "I passed and repassed as often as I liked, and will do it again whensoever it pleases me. I have the secret of making myself invisible; and they must be sharper eyes than either those of the League or of the Huguenots that will spy me out to stop me as I go."

"Indeed!" said St. Real: "that were a secret worth knowing."

"Easy to learn, but not so easy to practise," answered the boy. "I had first to consider the sentry as I came up to him; then, if I found him a Huguenot Gascon, to stop a quarter of an hour to listen to all the great exploits he had performed at Montcontour, Jarnac, or any other place; then--seeming to believe the whole--to tell him as great a lie as any that he told me, vowing that I was the truant son of some Huguenot lord, going back to hear Du Plessis Mornay preach against the Pope of Rome; and thus might I pass by without farther question. If, on the contrary, it were a royalist, I vowed I was King Henry's new page, and talked about Monsieur de Biron, and the good Duke of Epernon. If it were a Swiss, I boldly said, 'What is your price?' put the crowns in his hands, and walked on. And when I came back to the sentinels of the League, I had but to throw this toy over my shoulders," he continued, drawing a black-and-green scarf from the bosom of his vest, which, according to the custom of those days, was made very large and full, and often served the purpose of a pocket--"I had only to throw this toy over my shoulders, and swear by the holy mass that I had gone out to kill the king, and would have done it, too, if I had not, by mischance, trod on the toes of one of his Polish puppies, and been turned out of the ante-room for that grave offence."

St. Real laughed. "You are a brave boy," he said, "and seem to know these people thoroughly--perhaps better than I do."

"Perhaps I may," replied the youth: "but still, call me not a brave boy, for I am not; on the contrary, I am as arrant a coward as ever lived; so, if you intend to take me with you into a pitched battle, or even a skirmish, or so much as the siege of a town, you are very much mistaken, for I shall certainly lag behind."

"You jest," said St. Real, smiling; "for, though you are too young to be led into battles, or to sieges either, yet you are one of those whereof, some day, men may make good soldiers."

"Not I," answered the boy, seriously, and with a sigh; "not I, my lord!--I have a vow against it. Faith, I think that heretic Du Plessis Mornay has converted even me; and I hold, that for hundreds of honest men to shed each other's blood, for the sake of making their favourite sit in a great ivory chair, wear a gilt cap with a tassel, and call himself king, is not only a folly, but a madness, and not only a madness, but a crime. Be not offended, my lord," he added, seeing a slight cloud come over St. Real's brow, as he listened to doctrines very different from those which his own bold and chivalrous heart entertained; "be not offended, nor doubt me either; for you may well rest sure that, should danger threaten you, or misfortune overtake you, when I am your follower, this heart--though not so bold as a falcon's--would find courage for the time; this hand--though not so strong as a giant's--should do its best to defend or aid you."

"I believe you in that, at least, my good Leonard," replied St. Real; "yet, nevertheless, I have always held that life is valueless without honour, and that the drops of our heart's best blood can never be weighed against the service of our country, our king, or our friend. However, you are not my sworn soldier, so I shall not try you; and, to speak of matters whereon we shall better agree, tell me--for, amongst all your wanderings, you must have heard--how go men's opinions upon the events that are taking place here?"

"Opinions!" cried the youth. "They go, my lord, as the waves of the sea. Looked at from a distance, and at first sight, they seem innumerable, and all distinct one from the other; but when one examines a little more closely, they are found to be nothing but one great flow of the same things, following the first that comes forward and dashes upon the shore. I know not well what the word *opinion* used to mean in the days of old, but now, I know it means the portrait of every man's selfishness, painted as he likes it to appear. One man has a strong desire to be governor of Dijon, and he represents it under the form of a sincere admiration of the Catholic faith; another wishes to be made marechal of France, and he displays his wish under a full approbation of the murder of the Guises."

"It is wonderful," said St. Real, with a smile, "how soon, in the camp and in the court, the wisdom of the brow of sixty years finds its way down to the curly head of sixteen! Do you know, Leonard, I have just heard this morning from Monsieur de Sancy the same fine sarcastic character of the good folks around me that you have given me now?"

"Then you have heard the truth from two people in one day," replied the boy gravely. "It is worth marking with white chalk! and, though you think that I ape the sententiousness of wiser persons than myself, you will find, that one who has lived amongst these scenes from his earliest years knows the characters that appear in the mystery as well as one of themselves. At all events, my lord, hope not to find Spartan virtues even in your dearest friend; or, if he do possess such jewels as patriotism, and firmness, and integrity, happy--thrice and fully happy, is he in this place; for nothing is so saleable here as virtue and a tolerably good reputation."

"Spartan virtue in my dearest friend!" said St. Real, repeating the words on which the youth had laid the strongest emphasis. "What mean you by that, Leonard? Tell me, are you frank and honest? If so, you have some meaning! Now, make it a plain one!"

The boy coloured a good deal, and, for a moment, seemed struggling between two emotions; but at length he replied, "I am frank and honest, sir, and I will make my meaning plain, feeling sure that you will not let my candour hurt me. When I spoke as I did speak, I thought of your noble cousin; for it is the common report of camp and city, that a large dower, and a lady's unwilling hand, will soon convert the Count d'Aubin from a bold Royalist to a zealous Leaguer."

It was now St. Real's turn to feel troubled, and the blood irrepressibly mounted to his cheek. "I trust that the camp and the city are both mistaken," he replied, at length; "and that Philip d'Aubin, if he do change his party, which may, perchance, happen, will have nobler motives to assign than any selfish advantages. One thing, however, is certain, no lady's *unwilling* hand can be the object, for no man will or can force her inclination."

The boy shrugged his shoulders. "These are times, sir," he replied, "when men can do anything; but, nevertheless----"

Ere he could finish his sentence, the door of the little saloon in which he stood was thrown quickly open; and, as so often occurs, the very object of the conversation which had just passed appeared, and put an end to any farther observations. The boy, indeed, coloured deeply, and glided out of the room; but St. Real, whose consciousness of upright purpose and integrity of heart had restored his calmness and confidence in himself, turned to greet his cousin kindly, and prepared to speak with him upon the great events of the day, avoiding, as far as possible, those subjects which might renew any painful feelings between them. "I heard that you had gone to the *Prés aux Clercs*," he said, looking at his cousin's dusty garb; "but you are not armed, I see."

"Oh, that matters not!" answered D'Aubin; "it is as well sometimes to show these gentlemen of the League that, in a velvet pourpoint and silken hose, we can overthrow their best cavaliers, clothed from head to heel in good hard iron. I had not time to arm, and therefore ran two lances in my jerkin, having promised to give a course to Duverne and Maubeuge. So the king is wounded, they say! You have heard of it, of course. Should he die now, Huon--should he die, 'twould make a great difference in men's fates."

"I do not see why or how," replied St. Real; and then--not remarking that his cousin, whose very speech had been rambling and unconnected, suffered his mind to wander inattentive to what any one else said--went on to give all his reasons for thinking that the death of Henry III. should make no earthly change in the conduct of any honourable man hitherto attached to the royal cause.

"Huon!" interrupted D'Aubin, at length, "I have been thinking over what passed between us this morning, and I have come to crave a boon of you. Your safe-conduct from Mayenne is not yet near its end; and I would fain have you make one more journey to Paris. As I said before, I would trust you with aught on earth, such is my confidence in your honour; and you have great influence with Eugenie de Menancourt. She esteems and respects you, which is a very different thing from love, you know; no woman loves a man that she respects----"

"Nay, nay, nay, Philip!" said St. Real, somewhat sickened with his cousin's conduct, and yet pained to remark the evident anxiety and distress which D'Aubin strove in vain to cover under a tone, half jest, half earnest. "Nay, nay, Philip! speak not thus of those who form more than one half of man's happiness or misery--speak not thus if you would ever win the love of those whose love is worth possessing."

"Pshaw, Huon! you know them not!" replied the Count. "Respect and esteem may be the foundation of man's love for woman, but not of woman's love for man. Fear, jealousy, revenge, scorn, even hate itself, are nearer roads to woman's love than respect and esteem. You may disappoint her wishes, contradict her opinions, insult her understanding, pain her heart, ay, even cross her caprices! and yet win her love, if you will but pique her vanity. But a truce to such dissertations. Mark me, Huon! I think you love me, and wish me well; and I tell you sincerely, it imports much and deeply to my peace and comfort, that Eugenie de Menancourt should yield me a willing consent."

"Not, I trust, from any pecuniary consideration," said St. Real, who entertained some vague suspicions that his cousin had outstepped even his princely revenues in the gay and thoughtless course he had pursued for many a year. "If so, speak at once, Philip, for you know the extent of my resources; and you likewise know, I trust, that those resources are your own, when you choose to command them."

"No, no, Huon!" replied the Count, while his brow and cheek grew as red as fire. "No, no! I thank you for your kindness, good cousin; but there are many causes which make it as necessary to me as life, that Eugenie de Menancourt should become my wife. Why, think," he continued, raising his tone, "I should become the talk and the pity of all Paris!--the laughing-stock of every friend I have!"

St. Real bent down his eyes without reply, merely muttering to himself the word, "Friend!" while his cousin went on. "What I wish then, Huon, is this, that you would return to Paris, and seeing Eugenie, represent to her that my claim to her hand in consequence of her father's promise is indubitable; that I would sooner part with life than resign that claim; and that, in order to atone for aught I may have done to offend her, and to remove whatever objections she may have, I will change my course of living, cast from me those faults that appear so much blacker in her eyes than in those of our fair dames in the capital, and live a life as pure and holy as any nun was ever reputed to do, if she will promise at the end of a certain period to fulfil her father's engagement towards me. Will you do this for me, Huon, and exert all your eloquence?"

"Philip, it would be in vain," replied St. Real; "last night, I said all that I could say in your behalf--I promised even more for you than I well knew that you would perform--on my life, on my honour, Philip, I urged all that could be urged in your exculpation and in your favour; but she remained firm; and nothing I could say made any change in her replies. Your conduct, she said, had produced its natural effect; that effect was not to be effaced. Her father's promise was conditional; and, free from any engagement herself, she was resolved, she said, never to give her hand to one who had not sought her affection, and did not----"

St. Real hesitated, but his cousin finished the sentence boldly for him. "And did not possess her esteem, or deserve her love, or something of that kind," he said; "all that she told me before! It is but the ringing of the same chime! But by Heavens! it shall go hard if I do not find means to ring that chime backwards! Yet, listen, St. Real; yesterday, you were not empowered by me to say anything, and therefore she might doubt. I now empower you on my part to vow constancy, and promise amendment, and so forth. Will you undertake it?--will you go?"

"No, Philip, no," replied St. Real, in a tone of firm determination, "I will not; I love Eugenie de Menancourt too well myself, to cheat her with promises made in so light a tone as that. Nay, frown not on me, Philip d'Aubin, for you shall hear more, that you may never say your cousin deceived you. I refuse to go back to Eugenie to plead your cause, not alone because I believe it to be both a bad and a hopeless one, but, because I feel that it would be dangerous to my own peace; and might make me unhappy without serving you."

"Ho, ho!" cried D'Aubin, his brow darkening, "is such the case? Then I see somewhat more clearly how all this may end!"

"I trust you do," replied St. Real; "I trust from my conduct through life, and from my conduct now, that you may plainly see what will be that conduct still."

D'Aubin's lip curled into a cold, unpleasant smile; but his brow did not relax, and he answered, "What your conduct may be, like all future things, must be left to fate; but I shall certainly take means to ensure myself against what it seems it might be. I give you good evening, Huon, for I find it time to bestir myself! Farewell!"

So saying, he turned upon his heel, and left the apartment. At the foot of the stairs he paused for a moment to speak a few eager words with the dwarf Bartholo, and then springing on his horse galloped back to his own abode.

CHAPTER XVII

Leaving St. Real to meditate over the effects which his candour and honesty had produced, and to strengthen himself in his integrity against the bitterness of undeserved suspicion and reproach, we must follow the Count d'Aubin to his dwelling, and be his companion for the next few hours. Springing from his charger, he threw the reins to one of his attendants, ordered fresh horses to be saddled in the stable, a change of dress to be instantly brought him, and eagerly demanded if no packet had arrived from Paris. The answer was in the negative; but still the count proceeded to change his dress, apparelling himself with no small care and splendour, brushing the dust from his dark curling locks, and adding the fine essences that were then held a part even of the simplest toilet. Ere he had done, there was a sharp knock at the door of his chamber, and the next moment the dwarf Bartholo stole in, bearing a packet in his hand.

"I saw the messenger straying about the town," he said, "and knowing you would want this, I hastened to bring it hither."

"You see into my thoughts, and anticipate my wishes, good Bartholo," replied D'Aubin, breaking open the packet, and running his eye over the words of a regular safe-conduct from the Duke of Mayenne. "It is all right," he added, "though they limit me to four and twenty hours; but say, have you aught to tell me, Bartholo; for the day wears, and I am ready to set out. There seems matter in that face of thine. Speak, man! speak boldly. We know each other well."

"Your lordship is kind," replied the dwarf, with one of his sardonic grins. "I would fain give your lordship a piece of advice; but knowing from sweet experience how advice is relished in this wise world, I wish to know whether you have any appetite for it?"

"Yes, yes; speak boldly," replied D'Aubin; "I am as hungry for good advice as a famished wolf, and I am inclined to believe thee, just now, seeing that the hint you gave me not long since concerning my simple-seeming cousin has proved but too true. He would act in all honour as yet, it seems; but we all know with what tiny footsteps love begins the course, that he determines, ere the end, to stride over like a giant. Not that I think," he added, giving a glance to the mirror, and marking there as handsome features as ever that crowning invention of personal vanity reflected to the self-satisfied eyes of man--though the countenance he beheld might be somewhat worn with the strife of passions, it is true--"not that I think that, were it come to rivalry, I should have to fear the result. But I would fain put it beyond all chances; so speak your advice, good Bartholo. If it suit me, I will take it; and if not--why it is but empty air."

"Ay, ay," replied the dwarf, "empty air, and dust and ashes! Those few words are the history of the whole world--man's fame, and wisdom, and wit, and eloquence, and power, and strength, and beauty--empty air, and dust and ashes, are the whole!--so that brings me to my tidings, and to my advice;" he continued, resuming his ordinary tone. "You have heard of the king's wound, my lord. Now, do not you be one of the fools who deceive themselves, and think he will recover! Take my word for it, he will die!"

"Nay; but the surgeons say," replied D'Aubin, "that he is already far better, and give many shrewd reasons to show that he is nearly well."

"Let them give what reasons they will," answered the dwarf, "do not you believe them. Why, my good lord, do you think that your fair friend, the Duchess of Montpensier, or any of the holy and devout men of the Catholic union, are such fools in grain as to trust to a simple bit of smooth innocent iron to do the work of their hatred, while they have our dearly beloved Rene Armandi at hand, to smear the edge and the point with some of his blessed contrivances for shortening pain and making the work sure? No, no! my lord. Not more than two days ago, I was hanging about the gate of that very Jacobin convent from which this foul monk came forth, and I saw three people arrive to lay their heads together with the very reverend and respectable Father Prior, whose meeting told its own tale, whereof this morning's butchery is but the comment. First came Armandi the poisoner, next came the Duchess of Montpensier, and then came Wolfstrom the rogue; so be you sure, my lord, that the king will die; and this very night make your bargain so firm that no one will dare to break it. To-night," he added, his lips curling with more cynical bitterness than ever, "to-night you may dispose of your assistance and co-operation at what rate you like; but if you wait till tomorrow, your merchandise will fall a hundred per cent., for the market will be overstocked."

The manner in which the dwarf put his counsels was certainly not the most agreeable; but D'Aubin was accustomed to his bitterness, and was willing enough to cull wholesome advice for the direction of his own plans and purposes from amongst the gall and wormwood wherewith good Bartholo seldom failed to savour his discourse. "I believe thou art right, Bartholo," he replied; "and as I am determined sooner to lose life itself than to be foiled, and made a laughing-stock and held up to the scorn of all my companions by this fair-faced country-girl, I must even make the most of my time, and bind Mayenne to his promises by ties that he cannot shake off. Thanks, then, good Bartholo, for your advice; I will be back before dawn to-morrow, and will reward you better than by thanks. In the meantime, keep a wary eye on all that is going forward here; and, both for ancient love, and for future advancement, bring me, as often as may be, a hint of other men's doings. And now, fare thee well--away to thy lord, lest he miss thee. But hark I there are the horses, and I go."

Thus saying, he threw on his hat and plume, cast a wrapping cloak round his shoulders to keep his apparel as much as possible from the dust; and, springing down the stairs, mounted his horse, which stood saddled at the door. Bartholo watched him, as making a sign for his usual train of attendants to follow, he struck his spurs into his charger's flank, and galloped away at full speed towards Paris. A grim smile hung upon the dwarf's lips as he saw him depart, and muttering--"Ay, there he goes! to seek an unwilling bride, and for pure vanity to marry, neither loving nor beloved: but it matters not--my end is gained!"--he turned back towards the abode of St. Real.

In the mean time, D'Aubin galloped on hastily, giving the word as he passed any of the posts of the royal army, till at length, having got beyond the precincts of his own camp, he was challenged by the outmost sentinel of the League. Occupied with other thoughts, and giving way to the vehement impatience of his nature, the Count spurred on without reply; and the man, presenting his matchlock, fired without further ceremony. The ball whistled past D'Aubin's head; but, merely shaking his clenched hand at the sentinel, he pursued his rapid way, till at length he was encountered by a body of Mayenne's horse, who again challenged him, and obliged him to display his pass. More than once, ere he was permitted to enter the town, the same ceremony was observed; and, what between one delay and another, the evening sky grew deep purple, and then faded into grey, as he rode along, at a more cautious pace, through the streets of the capital.

Directing his course by the shortest way, he passed through many of the narrow gloomy lanes of the Faubourg, and, crossing one of the bridges which joined the island in the middle of the Seine to the shore, he plunged in amongst that dingy accumulation of tall, dark, small-windowed houses, which lie behind the great cathedral of Notre Dame. In these streets, at the hour of which we speak, the twilight, which would have still been seen in the open country, existed not; and all was darkness, except where, here and there, citizens returning from their shops to their dwelling-houses, or persons of a higher class going on some expedition of pleasure or business, were seen finding their way along, preceded by a lantern or a torch; and also where, before the hotel of some of the old nobles of the court, who still lingered in that quarter, were to be seen a few torches fixed in sockets at the door. It was to none of these more lordly dwellings, however, that D'Aubin took his way; but, at a door which stood open in a tall, unlighted, gloomy-looking house; he sprang to the ground, and after giving his servants directions to take up their temporary abode in an inn, where he should find them in case of necessity, and some money wherewithal to provide themselves their evening meal, he entered the house, followed by his page and one armed attendant, and began mounting, in utter darkness, the long, steep, narrow stair.

At the second story D'Aubin stopped, and by the little light that found its way from a lamp through a small lattice upon the staircase, he struck several hard blows with the hilt of his dagger against a massive unshapely oaken door, which stood on one side of the landing-place. Immediately after, a sound was heard within, and, the door opening, the Count was admitted, shading his eyes from the sudden glare of light, into a small ante-room or vestibule, where, stretched on benches or settles, were ten or eleven stout attendants, together with one of those large sort of vehicles which we are accustomed to call sedan-chairs, wherein the ladies of Paris were very much accustomed, at that time, to go from house to house, and one of which we have already described.

The person who opened the door was a trim-looking serving-man, dressed somewhat in the garb of an inferior burgher of the town; and, conducted by this personage, D'Aubin was led on, leaving his groom behind him, but followed by the page. The next chamber into which he was led presented a different aspect, being a small octagon room, with the ceiling of black oak exquisitely carved, the walls beautifully painted and gilt, and the furniture as rich and elegant as the art and taste of that day could produce.

Here D'Aubin was met by no less a personage than Armandi the perfumer, who, bowing low and reverently, welcomed him to his house, and then led him on through several chambers, each more tastefully decorated than the other, into one where eastern luxury itself was outdone, and where Madame de Montpensier was waiting the guest she had invited there to supper. Strange as it may seem that the highest and noblest in such a capital as Paris should abandon their own convenient and splendid dwellings, to make these little parties at the houses of inferior, and often of very base and dishonourable persons, yet the custom was not restricted to this period of French history, but even in the succeeding reigns the monarch himself was frequently known thus to indulge; and the custom, which was begun probably with political views, or for the sake of a temporary relaxation from the fetters of state, was found to be too convenient for a debauched court to be readily abandoned.

"True to your appointment, most noble Count," said the Duchess, in a light tone. "I augur from your punctuality, that all goes well and happily with the heretics and tyrants beyond the walls, so that they can spare the services of so gallant a cavalier as the Count d'Aubin."

"The fact is, most beautiful Lady Catherine," replied D'Aubin, whose plan was already fixed, "that their majesties are waiting till the day after to-morrow, ere they begin serious operations against the city; for, first, with that brilliant forgetfulness which characterises great men, they did not remember till yesterday that fifteen hundred cannon-balls are hardly enough to begin a regular bombardment; and, secondly, they wished that my worthy cousin should bring up his troops on the side of St. Denis, in order to straiten you a little in your diet, as they are resolved, absolutely, to try whether your stomachs are not like that of the ostrich, and capable of digesting mere iron in default of other food. They must therefore wait a day to give time for casting bullets and marching men."

D'Aubin spoke with so much of his ordinary levity, that he left Madame de Montpensier still doubtful whether he spoke in earnest or in jest--whether he was saying what was really the case, or from some particular motive was endeavouring to deceive her.

"You seem in a mood for revelations to-night," she said. "Thank you for your warning, Monsieur d'Aubin, we shall be upon our guard; but whether the two kings will thank you for telling us, remains to be proved."

"I care very little whether they thank me or not," replied D'Aubin; "besides, what I have said can do you no good, and them no harm, otherwise I should not have told it. You are here in a net, fair lady; and you must employ some other means to get yourself free than those you have hitherto employed, or depend upon it, the fisherman will put in his hand and take you."

"He may find that he has a shark in the net," replied Madame de Montpensier, "and be glad enough to let it escape ere it devour him."

"Well, we shall see," replied D'Aubin--"we shall see. But oh! by the Lord, I had nearly forgot to compliment your Highness on your exploits of this morning. Has none of the Dominican come back to you yet?

"None of the Dominican!" exclaimed Madame de Montpensier, with evident astonishment--"none of the Dominican! What do you mean, D'Aubin?"

"I simply mean," replied the Count, "that by this time I thought your Highness might at least have got a leg, or an arm, or a foot, or a little finger of your martyr, to make a relic of; for it could scarcely be more than two o'clock when he was torn to pieces by the four horses. No, it could not be more than two; for as soon as ever he attempted to stab the king, La Guesle ran his sword through him, and, almost immediately after, casting him out of the window, they tied him to the horses' heels, and tore him to pieces, in the little square down by the end of the bridge."

"*Attempted* to kill the king!" said Madame de Montpensier, but ill concealing, in her desire to hear more, her previous knowledge of the act that had been perpetrated--"attempted! Then he *did not* kill him."

"Oh, no," replied D'Aubin, gaily, and purposely affecting to laugh at her disappointment. "You do not think Henry is such a fool as to let himself be killed by a bungling Dominican. You should have sent our friend in the next room there, Armandi, or some other skilful, delicate, dexterous personage. Besides, dear lady, when you and Armandi and good father Bourgoin were consulting together, surely three such shrewd heads as yours might have fallen upon some better and more politic plan of getting rid of a bad king than that of trusting the execution of the act to an ignorant, clumsy, timid friar. Good faith! I should have thought that you might have even acted Judith yourself, and have delivered the land of our worthy Holofernes of St. Cloud with your own hand."

Madame de Montpensier turned pale, and red, and pale again; and there was a quivering of her fine lip, and a flashing of her proud dark eye, which showed D'Aubin at length that he was urging her too far. As soon as he perceived it, he dropped the sarcastic irony which he had been using; and drawing nearer to her, he took her fair, soft, jewelled hand in his, and raised it to his lips. "Forgive me," he said, "for teasing you. I love not Henry of Valois more than you do--as you well know; and though I will not say that I regret your attempt has failed, yet I do believe that all knowledge of the share you had in it rests with me alone, and, believe me, my lips are and shall ever be sealed by this kiss upon this hand--except towards yourself."

Madame de Montpensier gazed on him in no small surprise. "You assume things, sir," she said with some hesitation, "which you have no right to assume."

"Nay, nay," replied D'Aubin, "say not a word, dear lady. I know the whole as well as if I had been one of your triumvirate at the Jacobins the day before yesterday, all the means employed, the vision of the angel, and all----"

"Either some one has betrayed me, or you deal in magic, D'Aubin!" cried the Duchess.

D'Aubin smiled to see her consternation; for although, by combining the information he had received from St. Real with the hints that had been given him by the dwarf, and adding thereunto his own knowledge of the parties, he had been able to form a very correct guess at the truth--and although he knew the effect which vague hints of greater knowledge than one possesses, supported by one or two distinct facts, will produce upon a mind loaded with a heavy secret and apprehensive of discovery, yet he had hardly calculated upon so completely deceiving such a shrewd intriguer as Madame de Montpensier, in regard to the extent of his information. "No one has betrayed you," he replied; "nor do I deal in magic; but I have far greater means of knowing things that pass both in the city and in the camp than you suppose. What I have said just now I said but to tease you; and, indeed, fair lady, you deserve somewhat worse at my hands."

"Wherefore, wherefore? How so?" demanded Madame de Montpensier; "how have I offended you, D'Aubin?"

"Why, I do think," replied D'Aubin, "that considering all the old friendships which had existed between us, it should not have been you who attempted to mar my fortunes, and thwart my purposes. Did you not only last night propose to my cousin St. Real to bestow on him the hand of my promised bride?"

"I did," replied Madame de Montpensier, boldly, recovering in a moment all her composure--"I did, and I will tell you why I did so, Philip d'Aubin. I saw, by your conversation of the day before, that you had irretrievably attached yourself to the party of the tyrant; and I consider the interests of our cause far before any private interests or friendships. I am resolved, and so I know also is Mayenne, that the hand of Mademoiselle de Menancourt shall never be given to any but a member of the union; and it was therefore that I offered her hand to your cousin, if he would bring his forces to our side."

"Ah! but, lady," replied D'Aubin, "how could you venture on such an offer, when your own brother, the very morning before, had made the same to me, and left me a certain time to deliberate and act?"

"Nay, of that I know nothing," replied Madame de Montpensier. "Had I been aware of that, of course I should have acted differently."

"But if you and your brother will play at cross purposes," said D'Aubin, "what surety is there that the promises of either will be kept? And observe the consequences of this sort of dealing! My cousin at once determined to join the forces of the king, told me the story, and thus well-nigh changed all my views and purposes, unsettled my designs, and nearly determined me to take an oath of perpetual service to the kings."

"Nay, nay," replied the Duchess, giving him her hand, "but join us at this moment of our need, and Eugenie shall be yours."

"Ay," said D'Aubin; "but I must have some better security than mere promises."

"Surely you do not doubt me," said Madame de Montpensier, "when I most solemnly declare----"

"Declare nothing, dear lady," answered D'Aubin; "I doubt nobody, but my resolution is taken. The hand of Eugenie de Menancourt must be promised to me this night, under the hand and seal of his Highness of Mayenne, as lieutenant-general of the kingdom; or when I return to the camp to-morrow, I pledge myself, in the most solemn terms, to serve the Kings of France and Navarre, till there is no such thing as a Holy League and Union in France. And more, I assure you most solemnly, that I will instantly send an order unto Maine to cut down remorselessly every acre of my old forests, in order to raise another regiment for the service of the state. Now, mark me, lady!--mark me well! In doing this, I know what I am doing; for, if you cannot obtain this written promise for me, it will be evident your brother does not intend that the hand of Eugenie should be mine, and I have no other means to obtain it, but the capture of Paris and the destruction of the League. It will be therefore well worth my while to sacrifice everything to swell the ranks of the royal forces, in order to insure success."

"Well, well, say no more, say no more," replied Madame de Montpensier; "the promise you shall have, if I have any influence with Mayenne; and besides, you say he voluntarily made it himself, and therefore he will not hesitate to write it. But tell me what are the terms in which this promise is to be couched--you mean him to promise you her hand, if she herself consents?"

"No, no," replied D'Aubin; "I will leave no hold for after tampering and intrigue by any party. But," seeing a cloud come over the brow of Madame de Montpensier at his intemperate words, "I mean not any offence to you, dear lady. Others may tamper--there are others may intrigue, and may delay her consent and our union so long that my views in favour of the League itself may be overthrown. The moment that the hand of Eugenie is mine, I will raise for the service of the Duke all the retainers of the house of Menancourt who are now either lying idle, or swelling the ranks of the royalists. What I demand then is, that your brother--acting as lieutenant-general of the kingdom, as well as calling himself so, and consequently considering himself as the lawful guardian of all wards of the crown--shall promise me, without other condition than that in three days I subscribe the Union and join my forces to his, the hand of Eugenie de Menancourt, which was promised to me by her own father."

Madame de Montpensier mused for a moment; and then rising, she replied, "It shall be done, D'Aubin; it shall be done. The world--which Mayenne fears more than he will acknowledge--can say nothing against this act, for it is but a ratification of her father's promise by him who now stands in her father's place. Here," she cried aloud, ringing a small silver bell that stood on the table before her, and which was instantly answered by the appearance of Armandi, "bring me ink and paper, René. You shall write down the promise as you would have it, D'Aubin, and I will get my brother to sign it before you go; but make haste, for every moment I expect Wolfstrom to make our third at supper."

"I, too, must be speedy," replied D'Aubin; "for I must be back in the camp long before dawn, lest there be any tampering with my troops. They are all fresh, and new-arrived, so that I can do with them what I will at present; but there is many a shrewd head both amongst the Huguenots and royalists, and, not being too sure of my attachment, they may think to make sure of my soldiers."

With his swift and gliding step Armandi soon re-appeared, bearing the writing materials which had been demanded, and D'Aubin proceeded to put down the brief promise which he required from Mayenne; but scarcely had he finished, when the leader of the reitters made his appearance, and seemed somewhat surprised at the grave and business-like faces by which he was received.

"What is the hour, sir Albert?" demanded Madame de Montpensier. "Has it yet struck nine?"

"The light, or rather the darkness, says that it is nearer ten," replied the German; "and I heard the nine o'clock bell near an hour ago."

"Then I shall not find Mayenne till eleven," replied the Duchess. "His clock-work habits have, at all events, the advantage of letting one know when and where he is to be met with. Come, Armandi, is the table ready? We may as well fill the moments with something more real than poor thought."

In a moment Armandi re-appeared, and with soft and courtly words informed the Duchess that the best refreshments which his poor house and inferior artists could prepare waited her gracious presence. Catherine of Guise and her two companions followed where he led; and, proceeding into another small cabinet, they found a table covered with what might well have merited the name of *cates divine*, if ever anything can be so called which is destined to pamper the most animal propensity of our nature.

Placing himself beside the Duchess's chair--while his own lacqueys and the pages of the guests served and carved the dishes, and poured out the wine--Armandi, in his low, sweet tone, mingled in the conversation, descanted upon the merits of the various kinds of food, and read one of those lectures upon the mysterious art of cookery which persons addicted to the pleasures of the table are always well pleased to hear during their meals--stimulating their appetite for the good things before them, by exciting their *eating imagination* with pictures of unseen delicacies.

The exquisite fare, however, which was placed before them, the choice and delicious wines that flowed amongst them like water, and even the culinary eloquence of Armandi, did not seem capable of rousing either Madame de Montpensier or D'Aubin from the thoughtful seriousness into which their preceding conversation had thrown them. Albert of Wolfstrom, indeed, ate and drank, and enjoyed to the uttermost, and showed his white teeth in many a grin at the thoughts of all the rare ragouts and savoury sauces which the perfumer described; but his companions were grave and abstinent, and when the dessert was placed upon the table the Duchess rose.

"I leave you, gentlemen," she said, "for half an hour, trusting you can amuse yourselves, at least for that time, without a woman's presence. D'Aubin," she added, turning to the Count, and marking a certain degree of stern anxiety upon his brow--"D'Aubin, it shall be done!"

Thus saying she quitted them; and Wolfstrom looked to D'Aubin with inquiring eyes, as if for information regarding what was passing. But D'Aubin's countenance replied nothing; and the German, filling high a glass with sparkling Burgundy, exclaimed, "Come, come, Count, think no more of your mysteries with the lovely Duchess! Let us have the dice, and pass her half hour's absence pleasantly."

"With all my heart," replied D'Aubin; and there shot through his own bosom one of those strange dreams of superstition which are felt even in the present time, but which were much more common then. "I have cast my last great stake already," he thought; "but the dice will soon show me whether fortune favours me to-night or not!"

The dice were brought, a small table placed beside them, and Wolfstrom and D'Aubin shook the accursed boxes, and cast throw after throw. Fortune, however, *did* favour D'Aubin: he won invariably; and though the sums for which they played at that time were too small to make the gain or loss a matter of any consequence, yet the fancy which had taken possession of him made him rejoice more at the winning of a few hundred crowns than if he had acquired a fortune. His lip smiled, his eye sparkled, his cheek glowed; and though the time of Madame de Montpensier's absence was nearly double that which she had anticipated, D'Aubin found it not tedious, even under expectation.

At length she returned; and, without a word, laid down a paper on the table before the Count. D'Aubin ran his eye over the promise he had himself drawn up; and there assuredly, at the bottom of the page, stood Mayenne's name in his own handwriting, together with the broad seal of his arms.

What arguments she had used, what reasons she had assigned, what motives she had called into action, to obtain that signature, the Duchess did not tell, but gazed for a moment with a look of triumph upon the Count; and then, as her eye caught the dice upon the table, she turned with an air of gay indifference to Wolfstrom, demanding--"Well, sir Albert! have you won the Royalist's gold!"

"Good faith, no!" cried the German, throwing the dice into a water-jar of rock-crystal that stood upon the supper-table; "those little demons have played me false, and he has won six hundred of as good crowns of the League as ever were squeezed from a heretic Huguenot."

"Well, well!" replied Madame de Montpensier, "if the dice forsake you, turn again to the wine, Sir Albert; there is a resource for you in all time of trouble. Fill me yon Venice glass too; and you, D'Aubin, give me that sweet manchet--for, to tell the truth, the thoughts of this encounter I was about to undergo in your behalf, sir Count, kept me from supper."

D'Aubin gracefully spoke his thanks, taking care, however, to veil, in the circumlocutory ornaments employed in that day, all direct allusion to the nature of the service for which he expressed his gratitude. The conversation became gay and animated for half an hour; roamed to a thousand indifferent subjects, touching each with a momentary light--like a sunbeam breaking through the clouds of a windy autumn day, and skipping from point to point in the landscape as the vapours are hurried on before the gale--and then, drooping for a moment, paused as if to breathe the wits of the gay little coterie. Madame de Montpensier took advantage of that minute to rise and depart; and D'Aubin, bidding his male companion "Good night," proceeded to call together his attendants and return to the camp.

A more strict watch was kept in the night than in the day; and, what between one halt and another, the dawn was beginning to purple the eastern verge of the sky, when the Count arrived at the spot where his troops were quartered. As he was dismounting from his horse, however, some one whispered a word in his ear; and, springing again at once into the saddle, he turned his horse's head, and galloped on to his lodgings at St. Cloud.

CHAPTER XVIII

While such was the conduct of the Count d'Aubin, St. Real, whom he had left hurt, agitated, and gloomy, continued to pace his little chamber, giving way to many a melancholy thought. The more he yielded to reflection, the more he examined the state of his own heart, the more deeply and bitterly he felt that the deceit he had practised upon himself did not date from a late period, but had been of long existence. He remembered the pleasure he had felt in the society of Eugenie de Menancourt from his earliest days, in the sweet reciprocation of simple and innocent feelings, in the mutual communication of thoughts and sensations peculiar to the retired state of life in which they then passed their days. He remembered how much pain he had felt when her father, taking part in the troubles of the time, had removed for a short period from his neighbourhood; and he remembered how gladly he had heard that the hand of Eugenie de Menancourt had been promised to his cousin the young Count d'Aubin, inasmuch as that engagement was destined to bring her back to the vicinity of his father's chateau. He had calculated, simply enough, upon always regarding her as a beloved sister; and as he never for a moment having dreamed of any other feeling towards her during his early days, the idea certainly never presented itself after he was informed of an arrangement which he was taught to look upon as a positive engagement towards his cousin. When she did return to Maine, he greeted her with what he fancied brotherly affection; and though when he beheld his cousin apparently neglecting her, to pay devoted attention to the gay and sparkling beauties of the royal court, he felt a degree of anger and indignation on Eugenie's account, which made him devote himself entirely to her, he would have considered those feelings--had he thought of the matter in such a light at all--as the surest proofs that his inmost sensations towards Eugenie de Menancourt were merely those of a relation, inasmuch as, instead of feeling jealous of the attentions his cousin paid her, he was angry that those attentions were not more. Now, however, he knew the whole--he saw that the love he had felt had been early conceived, and secretly nourished; and the insight that he gained into his own feelings showed him that those feelings could never change, but would last in all their intensity to cause his misery through life.

While these thoughts passed in his mind, the time flew quickly by; and the meal which his principal attendants took care should be placed before him, was served and taken away almost untouched. Shortly afterwards, Monsieur de Sancy visited him; and St. Real, whose mind was not one to yield where it could resist, endeavoured to enter vigorously into everything that could distract his attention from himself, spoke again and again of all the probable consequences of the events that were occurring, and endeavoured to gain a clear and distinct knowledge of the characters, purposes, and power of the various nobles forming the royalist party.

For the time the attempt succeeded, and his mind found some relief from the memory of personal sorrows; but the moment that Monsieur de Sancy left him, his thoughts returned to himself as bitterly as ever. As evening fell, he fancied that music might soothe his mind or distract his attention; and sending for his page, Leonard de Monte, he asked, "Did you not once tell me, Leonard, that you could sing, and play upon the lute? I am somewhat sad just now, my boy, and would fain hear a little music to while away unpleasant ideas."

The boy smiled with a peculiar expression, and replied. "Music!--I will sing, if you like--that is to say, if I can find a lute; but music which will soothe care, and refresh the mind fatigued of business, calm the turbulent thoughts of ambition, or soften the feverish pangs of sickness, is no antidote against sorrow, and is, they say 'the food of love.'"

"Well, well," replied St. Real, "let me hear your instrument and your voice; I must have amusement of some kind, for this night wears heavily."

"I have not my own lute here," replied the boy, "but the dwarf will soon find one, I warrant;" and, going out, he returned in a few moments followed by Bartholo, carrying one of those guitars with eleven strings which were the principal musical instruments then in vogue. The boy struck his hand across the chords, and then pushed it from him to the dwarf, exclaiming angrily, "Take it from me, and tune it. Why give me a thing all discord, like that?"

"May it please you," replied the dwarf, with a look of humble deference, which did not escape St. Real's eyes, and which he had never seen assumed towards himself, "I did not know that it had been out of tune, or I should not have failed----"

"Well, well, take it away," replied the boy; and, remaining seated on the spot where he had placed himself to sing, he leaned with his elbow on the arm of the chair, and his head upon his hand, and the dark shining locks of his black hair falling in linked curls over his clear beautiful brow and small graceful fingers. He seemed to be thinking over the song he was about to sing. At least, so St. Real read his attitude. But the tone in which the youth had spoken to the dwarf, and that in which the dwarf replied, had struck and surprised their common master, and he was about to disturb the page's reverie, by making some inquiries in regard to his previous history, when Bartholo again returned with the lute. The boy took it, and running his fingers through the strings, scarcely seeming to know what note he struck, produced, nevertheless, a wild plaintive wandering melody, which nothing but the most exquisite skill and knowledge of the instrument could have brought forth.

"There are few songs," he said, looking up in St. Real's face, "that are good to soothe sorrow; but I will sing you one of the battle-songs of my own unhappy land, in which liberty begat anarchy, and anarchy strife, and strife weakness, till foreign tyrants made a prey of nations who knew not that military and political power are the children of internal union and civil order--a land which, from sea to sea, has been one vast battle-field for ages past."

He paused, and seemed to give a moment of sad thought to the sorrows of his native country; then suddenly dashing his hand over the chords, he made them ring with a loud and peculiar air, so marked and measured that one could almost fancy one heard the regular footfalls of marching men, mingled with the sounding of the trumpet, and the beating of the drum. Then joining his clear melodious voice, he sung of the dreams of glory and of patriotism wherewith the soldier on his way warms his heart to battle, and conceals from his own eyes the dark and bloody nature of the deed itself. Then again the chords of the instrument, with a quicker movement, and more discordant sounds, imitated the clang and clash of charging hosts; and the deep and frequent tones of the bass might be supposed to express the roar of the artillery, while still between came the notes of the clarion, and sounds that resembled the distant beating of the drum. At the same time the voice of the youth, in few but striking words, and, as it were, with brief snatches of song, called up the images more forcibly, and aided imagination in supplying all that the scope of the lute could not afford. Gradually, however, as he sung, the louder sounds were omitted; the imitation of the trumpet changed from the notes of the charge to those of the retreat; the strings seemed to rustle under his touch, as if from the hasty rush of flying multitudes; and then, with a sudden change of time, the music altered to a sweet and plaintive strain of wailing, while his voice took up the song of mourning for the dead.

Till that moment St. Real had no idea of all that music can produce. He had heard sweet songs, and what were then considered fine compositions; but this was something totally different; this was a painting addressed not to the eye, but to the ear; and that not with words which with laborious minuteness, describe insignificant parts, without conveying effectually grand impressions; but with sounds which, rousing fancy's greatest powers at once, called up all the splendid pageantry of imagination to complete for the mind's eye the grand pictures that those tones suggested. The boy, too, as he sung, looked like one inspired; his eyes flashed and glittered; his voice rose and fell with every touch of feeling which his song expressed; and his hand seemed now playing amidst the strings, as if in childish sport; now sweeping them with all the fire and power of some mighty master of song; but ever with such perfect ease and grace, that it seemed a gift rather than an accomplishment. When his voice had ceased, St. Real sat rapt for one moment by all the feelings which the music had inspired; and then, gazing upon the youth, he said, "You are an extraordinary boy, and I must one day have your history, Leonard."

The youth shook his head; but then after a short pause added, abruptly, "Perhaps you may, perhaps you may--but now while the lute is in tune, I will sing you another song--a song about love;" and without waiting for reply, he struck the chords, and began, with a measure and a tone so different, as for a time to seem almost tame and insignificant, when compared with the wild and thrilling energy of the former music. But as he went on, there was a touching and melancholy pathos in the words and in the air which went direct to St. Real's heart, rousing feelings which he would fain have lulled to sleep, and overwhelming him with deeper melancholy than ever. So sad, so sorrowful did it make him,--so completely did it master him and take possession of his imagination, that he could have given way even to tears, if there had been no eye to see him so unmanned.

The boy was still going on; but St. Real waved his hand, exclaiming, "Hush, hush! no more! It is too much for me!"

The boy looked up with a smile, saying,

"He that will not find

Ease when he may,

Leaves all joy behind

For ever and a day.

"Yet let him wither

His own hopes at will,

So that no other

Blossoms he kill."

St. Real started, somewhat surprised. "You seem to know," he said, "more of me and mine than I fancied. I must hear what you do know, Leonard, and how you know it, before you quit me."

"Nay, nay, my good lord," replied the boy, still smiling, "look not so suspicious. Does it need a very shrewd guess to discover, or to fancy, when a gallant cavalier, like yourself, falls into sadness suddenly, as if he had caught some infectious disease, and then looks more dark and gloomy still, when one sings a simple song to him about love, and beautiful eyes--does it need a very shrewd guess to fancy that after all, that same passion of love is at the bottom of the mystery?"

"But you spoke but now," replied St. Real, "as if you knew more than that, and made allusions that you could not have made unless you had known more."

"Faith then, my lord," replied the boy, "the man who compounded the old proverb I repeated, must have had a mighty skill in divination, to see what was likely to go on in your lordship's heart some hundred years after he himself had lived, and that it would serve a page at his need instead of a better answer--but yet the proverb is a good one," he continued, rambling on. "Good faith! I hold that no man has a right to make a woman love him, and then leave her for any whimsy whatsoever. I do not know much about these things, it is true, but I think that it is dishonourable."

"But suppose," replied St. Real, "that honour has some other claim upon him which calls him in a different way--what should he do then?"

"Why, methinks he should become an apothecary!" replied the boy; and then added, seeing St. Real's brow slightly contract, "what I mean is, my lord, that he should take the very nicest scales that conscience can supply to weigh out medicines for hurt honour, if he have got himself into such a scrape that honour must be injured either way. Or he may do the matter differently, and weigh in those nice scales which is the heaviest sin,-- to break a lady's heart; to leave her unhappy and cheerless through the long days of life; to doom her to wed one that she does not love, or perhaps hates; to have her reproaches and her sorrow to answer for at his dying day; or, on the other hand, to violate what he may think a claim upon his honour, which very likely priests and prelates, and saints and martyrs, and his own heart too, in the calm after-day of life, may tell him was no claim at all."

"And do you tell me that you speak thus from mere guess?" demanded St. Real. "No, no, my boy! You have some other knowledge; and you must give me an answer how it was obtained."

"Indeed, my lord," answered the youth, starting up and laughing "I am tired, sleepy, and thirsty, with looking for you all the morning, and singing you two songs at night. So, by your leave, I will e'en go to bed and sleep; and I dare say before to-morrow morning I shall be able to make an answer, for I have not one ready made; and even if my wit should run low, I will away by cock-crow to the nearest *fripier*, and buy me an answer second-hand. One often finds one as good as new that has served twenty people before;" and seeing St. Real about to speak again with a serious brow, he ended with a gay laugh, and darted out of the room.

A momentary feeling of anger passed through St. Real's breast, and he half rose in his chair, determined to call the boy back and make him explain distinctly what was the meaning of the allusions he had made, how he had obtained his information, and to what length it extended. Brief reflection, however, caused him to pause and change his purpose; thinking that it would be better to take time to regulate his own thoughts, and command his own feelings, ere he questioned his page upon subjects so likely to awaken and expose deep emotions in himself. Casting himself back into his seat again, he revolved all that had just passed; and his mind, reverting to everything that was painful and distressing in his situation, fell into one of those sad and melancholy dreams which must have visited almost every one at some time of life, when the bright and brilliant prospects of youth are suddenly obscured by the dark and lowering clouds which precede the first storms of life.

However painful may be this mode of mind,--however desirous we may be of escaping from it,--however sensibly we may feel that the only relief we can hope is to be found in activity, occupation, and resistance; yet there is a benumbing influence in that peculiar state of grief and disappointment, which, like the fabled fascination of the serpent in regard to the birds it seeks to devour, prevents us from employing the only means of delivering ourselves. St. Real knew as well as any one, that the occupation of his thoughts upon other subjects was the only relief he could hope for; but still he lingered on from hour to hour, no sooner attempting to turn his mind to other things, than falling back again into the same desponding memories of all that he cast away when he resigned the hope of ever seeing Eugenie de Menancourt again. Ere he was aware of it--for deep grief, like intense happiness, "takes no note of time"--the grey daylight of the early summer dawn began to pour through the open window. All had been long quiet in the town, the inns and cabarets had long been closed, and not a sound had for some time stirred in the *auberge* where he had taken up his quarters. But at length his reverie was broken by the distant sound of horses' feet; and, rising from his seat, he almost mechanically proceeded to the window, and gazed out up and down the road. At first no one was visible, except a small group of guards at the gates of the Maison de Gondi, in which King Henry III. had fixed hie abode, and though they were apparently speaking together, the tones they used were so low that not even the murmur of their voices reached St. Real's ear through the still, calm silence of the early morning. The next moment, however, the sound of coming horse became suddenly more distinct, as, turning the corner of the road from Meudon, a party of five cavaliers galloped into the village. St. Real fixed his eyes upon them as they advanced, and instantly recognised in their leader Henry of Navarre.

The guards at the gate of the Maison de Gondi seemed, from the bustle created amongst them, not only to see the party, but to recognise the cousin of their monarch. The tidings of his arrival appeared to be passed on into the court; and the moment after, the soldiers and officers of the Scottish guard came pouring forth without any symptoms of their usual discipline and orderly demeanour. The King of Navarre perceived their approach; and nearly opposite to the window at which St. Real stood drew up his horse, which hitherto had proceeded at full gallop. Several of the officers of the guard instantly rushed forward, and cast themselves upon one knee at the stirrup of the monarch, exclaiming, "Oh, sire! you are our king and our master!" and, at the same moment, one or two voices from the crowd pronounced, for the first time, the often repeated words, "Vive Henry Quatre!"

The king sprang to the ground, affected even to tears, exclaiming in a tone of unfeigned regret, "Alas, alas! is he then really dead?" Walking rapidly forward, he proceeded towards the royal headquarters, and entered the Maison de Gondi; and the news of Henry III.'s death proceeded rapidly through the town. Every house began soon to pour forth its inhabitants; and ere the sun was well risen, all was bustle, and agitation, and confusion.

Although a feeling of reverence for that fearful thing, death, and the awe which an event of such magnitude might well inspire, repressed much of the noise which otherwise would have been heard: and though the eager consultations and busy rumours were carried on in no louder tone than a whisper, still it was evident, from every symptom displayed by the multitudes which now thronged the streets of St. Cloud, that the ties which linked society together were broken, that the foundations were shaken, and that not only the fabric of the royal army, but even of the French monarchy itself, was wavering as if to fall.

After gazing out for a few minutes upon the scene below, with the feelings of a mere spectator, St. Real remembered that he himself had a part to act; and as the *auberge*, in common with all the other houses of the town, was by this time roused, he called for his attendants, and despatched a messenger to his cousin, intimating his wish to speak with him immediately. Then casting on his cloak, he went forth into the street; and entering into conversation with some of the inferior officers of the troops, he tried to gain some insight into the various feelings and motives by which the lower ranks of the royal army were actuated; and, wherever he found it possible, endeavoured to give a bias to the wavering and undetermined in favour of that conduct which could alone save the monarchy and the country.

To every one whom he addressed St. Real was a stranger; and though his dress was such as became his station, yet his rank and character being unknown, it was not at all improbable that he would have met with insolence, if not violence, had there not been in his whole demeanour that mingling of frankness and dignity, of sincerity and of grace, which went far, not only to win and to persuade, but to command attention and respect. While he was thus engaged, the attendant whom he had despatched to his cousin returned, and informed him that the Count d'Aubin had gone up to the royal quarters; and, almost at the same moment, a hand was laid upon his arm, and turning round, he beheld Monsieur de Sancy.

"A moment's conversation with you, Monsieur de St. Real," he said, leading the way towards the *auberge*. St. Real instantly followed, and on entering, conducted the old officer to his own apartments.

"Is your mind the same as when last I saw you?" demanded De Sancy, as soon as the door was shut.

"Undoubtedly," replied St. Real; "you cannot suppose I would change."

"One can never tell," replied De Sancy, smiling; "you will find this morning that more than fifty have changed since the same hour last night; and, to speak plainly, Monsieur de St. Real, your own cousin amongst the number. However, let us ourselves lose no time. The leaders are flocking up to the quarters of the late king, and many, I fear, will be the differences we shall find. Nevertheless, I hope that we shall still be able to make up a good party on our side, and perhaps we may shame a great many more to join us by taking a bold position ourselves, and letting the others see that they are not only contemptible, but weak. Will you come, for every moment is of consequence?"

"Instantly!" replied St. Real. "D'Aubin is there already."

"Then there will be mischief going on," said De Sancy; "for I have very sure information that your cousin has decidedly chosen his part. I do not fear to say to you, Monsieur de St. Real, that he is wrong, and that he knows it; and when such is the case, it is natural that a man should endeavour to persuade as many others to act in the same way as possible, in order that, at all events, he may shelter his own conduct from the odium of singularity."

"Very often, too," replied St. Real, as they walked on, "when a man is determined upon a thing, and does not clearly know whether he is right or wrong, he strives to satisfy himself that he is right, by bringing over as many more to his own side as possible. This I believe to be D'Aubin's case; for his opinions on any points are never very fixed, and many is the time that I have heard him defend both sides of a question with equal skill."

"Vanity, vanity, all that!" replied De Sancy, "and a most unhappy vanity too; for it has cheated many a man out of his honour and integrity, out of his own self-respect, out of the world's esteem--ay, and even out of his hopes of heaven. But at all events, as apostates, whether religious or political, are the most vehement against the creeds they abandon, so we may feel sure that Monsieur d'Aubin, and all those who have cast off their loyalty, will have many a furious argument in store against the cause which they are quitting. Let us be prepared then to assert in words, as well as deeds, the ancient loyalty of the French nobility."

"Of course, to the best of our abilities," said St. Real; "but my voice can have small weight. Who is that going in?" he added, just as they reached the gates of the Hotel de Gondi, the court of which was filled with guards and attendants--"I mean that stout, hard-featured man, who walks forward with as consequential a step as if the throne were his."

"By my honour, if it be not his to take," replied De Sancy, "it may be his to give; for if he act heartily with the king, there is little fear of the result. If he go over to the League, the clouds, which are dark enough already, will grow deeper still over our heads. It is Armand de Gontaut, Marechal de Biron. He is stopping to speak with the officer on guard. I will see if I can learn his determination; for he is so much in the hearts of the soldiers, that one half the army will fall off if he fail us."

Thus saying, De Sancy advanced; and, with an air of some deference, saluted Biron, who in return shook him warmly by the hand. He failed, however, in his object of gaining any insight into the purposes of the old soldier, though his questions were dexterously put. Whether at that moment the Marshal had not yet determined upon any precise line of conduct, or whether he hoped to gain greater advantages by concealing his own views, he evaded De Sancy's enquiries; and then said abruptly, "A great number of our friends are assembled already in the lower hall to talk over all these affairs. If you are going to them, I will walk in with you."

De Sancy replied that they were about to join the rest; and Biron, after running his eyes with a glance of some attention and pleasure over the fine and soldier-like person of St. Real, asked his companion in a low voice who he was. De Sancy replied in the same tone; and the Marshal rejoined in a louder voice, "Indeed, indeed!--I knew his father too--I knew him well, in the time of my uncle, you know. Monsieur de St. Real, I am glad to see you here, and I hope----" But here their conversation was interrupted by an officer requiring them to give up their swords, a ceremony which the two commanders seemed prepared for, and with which St. Real, of course, complied without opposition. De Biron then again turned towards St. Real, as if to conclude his sentence; but ere he could speak, a young man, whom St. Real had remarked with the King of Navarre as he rode into town that morning, came up, and after shaking hands with Monsieur de Sancy, drew Biron aside, whispered a word in his ear, and then passed on. The Marshal smiled, and from this slight indication De Sancy drew a favourable augury, saying to St. Real, ere the other rejoined them, "I think from that smile all will go well. That young gentleman is Rosny, an especial friend and adherent of his present Majesty."

By this time they had nearly reached the chamber in which the nobles of France, with the body of their late monarch lying in a room not very distant, and their lawful sovereign seated in the apartment directly above them, were deliberating what use they should make of the power which a foul and unjustifiable act of their common enemy had thrown into their hands. The table at which they were placed was nearly full, and Marshal Biron, with De Sancy and St. Real, placed themselves in a group at the end next to the door; while the Duke of Longueville, who was speaking when they entered, went on. He was a young man of a handsome and prepossessing appearance; but his manner was timid, and his elocution hesitating and difficult. He did not seem so much to want ideas as words, and appeared even to want words more from not having any confidence in himself, than from any other cause. He expressed shortly and confusedly the determination of himself, and of the little knot of princes and gentlemen by whom he was surrounded, to acknowledge the title of Henry IV. to throne of France, and to serve him with their whole souls, if he would renounce the Protestant heresy, and reconcile himself to the church of Rome. If he refused to do so, the Duke continued, it would be for the gentlemen, in whose name he spoke, to consider whether they would not beg leave to retire from his service.

Apparently not knowing how to wind up his speech, he was deviating into one of those long and unmeaning tirades with which unskilful orators often attempt to let themselves drop by degrees, when he was suddenly interrupted by the Duke of Epernon, who said, somewhat sharply, "In your offers of service, my lord Duke, I beg you to omit my name. I have much to do on my own lands, and have borne arms long enough."

"I will beg you to except me also," said the Count d'Aubin, who was sitting near the Duke of Longueville, and rose to speak as soon as he saw that Epernon had concluded. "I will not serve Henry King of Navarre, and I trust that my reasons are good ones. As a Catholic, I should think it treachery to my faith were I to attempt to establish a heretic monarch upon the throne of this realm. Therefore, if the king remains attached to the Huguenots, notwithstanding the eloquence of Monsieur de Longueville, I cannot remain in his army; and if he be suddenly converted by the arguments of my lord Duke, my faith in the miracle will be too small to assure me that it will last. For myself, gentlemen, I see no choice. If the king remain unchanged, he is a heretic; were he to change suddenly, he would be a hypocrite; and in neither case can I draw my sword in his behalf."

There was something sneering and bitter in the tone of the Count d'Aubin, which, though it made the Duke of Longueville, and others of the undecided party, hate him, and inclined them more than before to the service of Henry IV. yet rendered others, even better disposed towards the monarch, afraid to answer; and, for a moment there was a pause. Seeing that no one spoke, however, St. Real took a step forward to the table, and, without the slightest degree of hesitation, addressed the assembly, while his name passed from mouth to mouth, and many an enquiring ear was turned to hear what one of the simple St. Reals would say, after the speech of the sarcastic Count d'Aubin.

"Gentlemen of France," he said, "my opinion, in many respects, coincides with that of my cousin who has just spoken." D'Aubin, De Sancy, and Biron, looked at him and each other in astonishment. "My opinion," he repeated, "in many respects coincides with his; but, as is very often the case with us, my conduct will be the direct reverse. I think as he does, that to ask his Majesty to change his religion on a sudden change of fortune, were to ask him to become a hypocrite; and I should as soon think of requiring him to do so, in order to gain my services, as he would think of requiring me to abandon my faith to merit his favour. Let us be too just to do the one, and we may feel sure that he is too just to do the other. The claims of his majesty, King Henry IV. are known to us all. As the lineal descendant of St. Louis, he is king of this realm of France, unless some of his acts have been so black as to render him incapable of reigning. Now what have his acts throughout life been up to this day, but noble, generous, chivalrous, worthy to lead a nation of brave hearts upon the path of honour? And shall we attempt to pry into his conscience? Shall we demand that, by a sudden abjuration of his long-cherished belief, he should stain that honour which he has ever held so pure and spotless? The worst that the most zealous Catholic can apprehend--and none is more zealous than I am--is that a Protestant monarch should interfere with our faith. Let us not set him the example by interfering with his, and take for a guarantee of his future conduct the whole of his conduct that has gone before. We have, at this moment, two claims upon us--the claims of our country and our king,--both equally powerful on the hearts of Frenchmen, and happily both in this instance leading us in the same direction. Our first duty is to put an end to the factions which have torn this unhappy land, and left her scarce a shadow of her former prosperity; to compel the rebellious to submission, and teach the ambitious to limit their expectations to their rights,--to bring back, in short, security, and peace, and union to France. This can only be done by bending all our energies to uphold the shaken throne, and with those good swords, which have never yet been drawn in an unjust quarrel, to open a way for our gallant and our rightful monarch to the seat and the power of his ancestors. This, at least, is my determination; and I trust that I shall see no one who aspires to honour during life, or glory after death, fall from his duty at a moment when the safety of his country and the throne of his king depend upon union, energy, and fidelity."

"Well spoken, on my soul," cried Gontaut de Biron. "Well spoken, on my soul! And if all here present act up to it, the monarchy is safe!"

"That at least will I," rejoined De Sancy; "for I hold that to propose any terms to his Majesty at this moment when--encompassed is we have too fatally seen, by assassins, surrounded by difficulties and dangers, and opposed by an ambitious faction--he comes unexpectedly to a perilous throne, were base and ungenerous indeed. Let those who will, join the party of the assassin; my voice and my sword are ready for Henry IV."

The speech of De Sancy was followed by one of those slight murmurs which betoken a vacillation of opinion in a popular assembly. Each man looked in the face of his neighbour; some smiled and nodded to the speaker, as if in approbation of what he had said; some frowned and bit their lips; some whispered eagerly to the persons next whom they sat; and the cheek of the Count d'Aubin, as De Sancy denominated the League "the party of the assassin," grew as red as fire, while the veins in his temple might be seen swelling out through his clear dark skin.

There was a pause for a moment; but D'Aubin recovered himself quickly, and said, "Methinks the three noble gentlemen who, not deigning to take a seat amongst us, remain standing at the foot of the table, have not come here to deliberate, but to announce their determination; and if that determination were binding upon all the princes and nobles of France, it would become us to submit and break up the council; but as that is not exactly the case, I would propose that we should continue our consultations, without yielding more than due weight to the veto of Monsieur de Biron, the pithy sentences of the noble leader of the Swiss, or to the speech of my worthy but somewhat inexperienced cousin--a speech evidently got by heart."

"It is got by heart, Philip d'Aubin," replied St. Real, opposing to the sarcastic sneer of the Count d'Aubin a look of calm and dignified reproof. "It is got by heart; for it comes from my heart, and the actions of my hand shall justify it. As to my inexperience, what you say is true,--I am somewhat inexperienced; and I would thank God for it, did I believe that experience would ever debase me to take advantage of a noble monarch's utmost need either to dictate terms which he could not comply without dishonour, or to abandon his cause for a selfish motive or a weak pretext."

D'Aubin rose angrily from his seat, and, for a moment, it did seem that everything like deliberation was to be merged in anger and contention; but De Biron and the Dukes of Longueville and Epernon interfered; and after, in some degree, restoring order, Monsieur d'Epernon addressed the French nobles, and put an end to a meeting from which no good could accrue. "Angry words, gentlemen," he said, "can do no good, and are not at all required. We are not here to determine any settled plan which is to be binding upon us all; but each is as free as before to follow his own purposes and determinations. However, as the communication of our various opinions has produced some heat, I think it better that we should conclude a discussion which seems to be fruitless. Let each of us follow his own path. For my part, though I do not draw my sword against the king, yet I cannot reconcile it to my conscience to fight the battles of an excommunicated monarch against my brethren of the faith."

Thus saying, he rose; and beckoning one or two of those on whom he could rely, into one corner of the hall, he entered into conversation with them; while the same conduct was followed by various other persons in different parts of the room.

St. Real and his companions, however, did not remain long to witness this scene; for Marshal Biron laid his hand upon the arm of the young noble, saying, "Come, Monsieur de St. Real; come, De Sancy! Let us to the king. It is easy to see that he will need the consolation and support of all that are faithful to him." Thus saying, he quitted the chamber, followed by those to whom he spoke, and two or three others; and, speaking a few words with one of the attendants, he was led on to a large upper hall, where Henry IV. waited the result of the deliberations which he was well aware were taking place around him; the nature of which he knew, and the termination of which he feared, but which he had no power to stop or to control.

Almost alone, with only two attendants of an inferior class stationed at the door, he was walking up and down the room in evident agitation. The moment he saw De Biron, however, he stopped, and gazed for a moment anxiously in his face; but the Marshal advanced at once, and throwing himself at the king's feet, kissed respectfully the hand that he held out to him. Henry instantly took him in his arms, exclaiming, "Rise, rise, Biron! Tell me what tidings you bear?" And at the same time he extended his hand to St. Real and De Sancy, who knelt and pressed it to their lips.

"The tidings I bear your Majesty from below," replied De Biron, "are, I am afraid, not very satisfactory. Several, I fear, will fall off from your Majesty, and several will be but lukewarm friends."

"That I expect," replied the king; "but if you, Biron, stand fast by me, on your shoulder will I lean, and defy all the factions in France to shake me."

"Thanks, sire, thanks!" replied De Biron, in his usual blunt tone. "Of my fidelity and attachment your Majesty need have no doubt; and I think," he added, "I think I can answer for the greater part of the troops."

"Then we are safe!" cried the king. "Then we are safe! What with my own forces, and those that you can bring me, Biron, the Swiss under Monsieur de Sancy here, and the fresh troops of Maine promised me by my young friend St. Real, I will not fear anything, even though D'Aumont and his division go over to the enemy."

"I do not think he will, sire," replied Biron. "He is not the most active of soldiers, but he is an honest and true-hearted man. De Rosny told me but now that he was going to him, and I doubt not but, at the first word, he will come to join your Majesty; but it might have been better to have directed Rosny to speak with his officers, and bring them over too, for D'Aumont will never think of it; and besides--"

"He has not the whole hearts of his soldiers, like Biron," added the king. "I thought of it, my friend, I thought of it, and begged De Rosny to see what could be done. But who have we here? Oh! our cousins of Longueville and Nevers; and Monsieur d'O, too, whom we hope speedily to replace in his government of Paris, which has been ill-governed enough certainly since he left it."

As he spoke, a large body of French nobles, headed by the persons whom he mentioned, entered the hall; and Monsieur de Biron and the others who were with the king, forming a semicircle on either hand, the gentlemen who had just arrived advanced, and one by one knelt and kissed the monarch's hand. There was, however, a degree of gloom and coldness in their countenances, which betokened no hearty wishes for the welfare of him who had so suddenly been placed upon the throne. When they had all saluted the king, Monsieur D'O, the titular governor of Paris, advanced a step before the rest, and addressed the monarch in the name of all. His tone was respectful, and his words well chosen; but after proceeding to offer some faint congratulations to the king on his accession to the throne, he stated that the fact of his Majesty's adherence to the tenets of the Huguenots pained and embarrassed many who were his faithful subjects and sincere well-wishers; and then he proceeded boldly and unceremoniously to propose that the monarch should reconcile himself to the Church of Rome, and receive absolution for his past heresies, holding out but a half-concealed threat, that if he did not comply with this sudden proposal, the great body of the French nobles and princes of the blood would be obliged to withdraw from the royal army.

Henry heard him patiently and calmly; though for a moment, while he was making his somewhat extraordinary request, one of those gay and brilliant smiles, with which his countenance was so familiar on ordinary occasions, passed over the king's lip and chequered the gravity of his attention. "My noble cousins and gentlemen," he said in reply, "I confess myself not a little astonished to find that you, who are so strongly attached to your religion, should think me so little attached to mine. It is true my attachment is more a matter of habit than perhaps of reason; for, living as I have lived in the tented field, and spending the greater part of my time between the council chamber and the battle plain, I have had no opportunity of hearing discussed the merit of those questions which unhappily divide the one church from the other. Nevertheless, I should think myself base, and--what is more to the purpose on the present occasion--you also would think me base, if for any worldly advantage I, unconvinced, were to sacrifice the religion in which I have been brought up. That, gentlemen, is impossible. But still I am not so foolish as to say that I will never abandon what is called the Reformed Faith; for, on the contrary, I will zealously and diligently investigate the merits of the arguments on both sides; and, if my conscience will allow me, will take those steps which I well know would be pleasing to the great majority of my subjects. Nevertheless, this must be the work of conviction, not of interest; and I tell you candidly, that I must have, at least, six months to hear, and ponder, and judge, ere I can give you any determinate answer as to what my ultimate conduct in these respects will be. In the meanwhile, believe me, I love you all as my children, and will serve and protect you as such to the utmost of my power; and should there be any one amongst you who has the heart to leave his king at the moment his king most needs his service, let him go in peace, and not be afraid, for I will serve him still, as far as may be, even against his will."

When the king ceased, there were one or two amongst the group of nobles who looked as if they would fain have added something to the speech of their orator; and it was evident the noble and dignified manner in which Henry treated their absurd proposal was not without effect upon any. Like all other bodies of men, however, there were those amongst them destined to lead, and those only fitted to follow; and the latter did not venture to act without the approbation of the former. Bowing in silence then, the whole party retired, and were immediately succeeded by the Baron de Rosny, afterwards famous as the Duke of Sully, who approached with the Marechal d'Aumont. The latter at once, and with graceful zeal in words and manner, tendered his faith and homage to the king, and assured him that the officers under his command would present themselves within an hour to swear allegiance to their new monarch. He again was succeeded by another, in whom St. Real instantly recognised the Duke d'Epernon, though he had changed his garb within the last hour, and now appeared in deep mourning.

The keen eye of Henry IV. at once read his purpose in the countenance of the Duke; and, preventing him from kneeling, he said, "Pause, my cousin, and think what you are about to do. We will excuse your bending the knee to-day, if it be not to be bent tomorrow."

Though fantastic, and even effeminate in appearance, D'Epernon was brave even to rashness, and by no means destitute of that calm and dignified presence of mind which approaches near to greatness. Gravely taking half a step back, he persisted in bending his knee, and kissed the king's hand, replying, "My lord the king! your majesty's right to the throne of France and to the homage of your subjects is incontestable; and deeply do I regret that any circumstances, religious or political, should lessen that zeal which the nobles of France are so willing to display in behalf of their kings. But, to avoid all subjects which it would be painful for your majesty to hear and for me to speak, I come to crave leave to retire for a time to my own lands, which have much need of their lord's presence. I am weary of warfare, sire, somewhat anxious for repose, and my poor peasantry require protection and assistance."

"Well, cousin of Epernon," replied the monarch, "if you be really disposed to imitate the great Roman and hold the plough, my service shall not detain you; but let me trust that you are not about to reverse the scriptural prophecy, and turn the ploughshare into a sword in favour of new friends."

"I need no sword, sire," replied the duke, "but that which I lately proved beside your majesty at Tours; and be assured that if it be not drawn in your service, it shall not be unsheathed against you."

"Well, well!" said the king, with a sigh, "so be it, if it must be so. Fare you well, fair cousin of Epernon! and may the harvest you are going to reap have fewer thorns than that which is before me, I fear!"

The duke bowed and withdrew; and Henry, turning to those who surrounded him, proceeded with a sigh, "Let them go, gentlemen of France, let them go," he said; "better a few firm friends, than a discontented multitude. On you I repose my whole hopes; but we must lose no time. My confidence in your judgment and in your affection is unlimited; and therefore I send you forth amongst the mingled crowd of friends and enemies which surrounds me in the camp, with no other direction or command than this. Do the best you can for your king and for your country. Rejoin me here again in the evening, to let me know what has been done; by that time we shall have learned what troops remain with us, and shall be able to determine upon our future conduct."

All the king's immediate attendants now took their leave and withdrew. Biron and D'Aumont proceeded instantly to their several quarters. De Sancy set off to insure that there was no tampering with the Swiss under his command; and St. Real, returning to his lodging, called his attendants about him, and ordering a certain number to mount with speed, prepared to go in person, in order to bring up more rapidly the troops he had left near Senlis. In the hurry and agitation of the last few hours, his personal situation had been forgotten; but as he was just about to mount his horse, the appearance of his page, Leonard de Monte, recalled to his mind both the events of the preceding evening and his own determination of questioning the boy upon that knowledge of his inmost thoughts which Leonard seemed by some means to have obtained. He had no time, however, at the moment to pursue such a purpose, and after commanding him to remain at the *auberge* till he returned, he inquired if the boy knew where the Count d'Aubin's forces were quartered.

"They lie under the hill at the back of the park," replied the youth. "Shall I show you the way?"

"Quick! get a horse, then, and come," said St. Real.

"I will run by your side, and be there ere a horse could be saddled," said the page. St. Real assented; and proceeding in the direction which had been pointed out, he rode on, determined to make one last effort to recall his cousin from a path which he firmly believed would lead to dishonour.

When they had mounted the little hill, however, underneath which, as the page had said, the Count d'Aubin's troops had been quartered, nothing was to be seen in the meadow where their tents had lately stood but one or two carts of the country, in which a small party of soldiers were busily stowing the canvass dwellings wherein they had lately made their abode, together with the spare arms and baggage of the larger body of troops just gone.

As St. Real halted and gazed, the sound of a clarion at a little distance struck his ear, and made him turn his eyes to the opposite slope. Over the brow of the hill, upon the road which led towards Paris, appeared horse and foot filing away with their arms glittering in the summer sun; and the distance was not sufficiently great to prevent St. Real from recognising the retainers of the house of Aubin, joined to another body apparently little inferior in number. The step thus taken by his cousin was too decided to admit a hope of change; and bidding the boy, who was gazing steadfastly in the same direction, return to St. Cloud, he resumed his own path, and rode on with all speed towards Senlis.

CHAPTER XIX

We must now once more change the scene, and lead the reader back into the heart of Paris, where, on the very morning which witnessed, at St. Cloud, the events we have just been describing, the Duke of Mayenne held a conference with some of his principal officers, and some of the leaders of the faction called the *Seize*. It was at an early hour, and he had already given directions for re-establishing in some degree the rule of law and justice within the city of Paris; which directions, though spoken with a tone that left no reply, were listened to by those whose power and fortunes were founded upon tumult and disorganization, with gloomy and discontented countenances.

"And now, gentlemen," continued Mayenne, turning to his own officers, "having taken measures to restore order to the city, it becomes me to adopt some means for preserving order in the camp. I have often reprobated in your presence the system of continual skirmishes and defiances which are going on in the *Pré aux Clercs*; and yet I hear that no later than yesterday evening a cartel was exchanged between Maroles and one of the adversary, called Malivaut, I think. The defiance given, I do not choose to interfere; but this once over, I will permit these things no longer: we thus lose some of our best officers and bravest soldiers, without the slightest advantage to our cause."

"They have gained us a great advantage this morning, my lord," replied the Chevalier d'Aumale, who had entered just as the Duke began to speak. "That same *coup de lance* between Maroles and Delisle Malivaut has obtained intelligence for which your highness would have given a spy ten thousand crowns had he brought it you."

"How so? how so?" demanded the Duke of Mayenne. "Crowns are not so rife in our treasury, Aumale."

"Nevertheless you would have given the sum I mention," rejoined the chevalier; "but I will tell you, my lord, how it happened. Maroles and Malivaut met as appointed, and we stood back at a hundred yards on one side, while the enemy remained under the old oak where Malivaut had armed himself. As soon as the two were mounted, and the trumpet sounded, they spurred on, and both charged their lances well: the shock was smart, and Maroles was beat flat back upon his horse's crupper. I thought he was unhorsed; but somehow it had happened that Malivaut's visor had been ill-rivetted, Maroles' lance struck it just at the second bar, drove it in, and entering between the eye and the nose, broke sharp off; leaving the iron in the wound. For a moment we did not see that he was hurt, for he sat his horse stiffly; but the next instant, as he turned to get back to the oak, his strength gave way, and he fell. Maroles instantly sprang to the ground and made him prisoner, and both parties crying truce, ran up. A glance at his face, however, showed us that death would soon take him out of our hands, and, in fact, he spoke but two sentences after. The first was, 'Give me a confessor!' The next, 'I care not to live longer, since my king has been murdered!'"

"What! what!" exclaimed Mayenne, starting and gazing steadfastly on Aumale.

"Ay, my lord, even so!" replied the chevalier. "*Murdered* was the word; and we heard from the others who stood round, that Henry of Valois died last night of a wound given him by a Jacobin the day before."

Mayenne clasped his hands; and, looking up, exclaimed, "Guise! my brother! at length thou art avenged!" And taking off the black scarf which he had worn ever since the death of his brother, the Duke of Guise, he cast it from him, adding, "So Henry of Valois is dead, the base, effeminate, soulless tyrant! But you have not told me how it happened, D'Aumale. Let me hear the particulars! Who ended the days of the last of those weak brothers? Was it one of his own creatures, unable to support any longer the daily sight of his crimes? or was it some zealot of our party, who ventured the doubtful act for a great object?"

The satisfaction which he derived from the event was so unconcealed, and his surprise at hearing the intelligence so unaffected and natural, that although those were days of suspicion, no one ventured to suspect, for a moment, that Mayenne had any previous knowledge of the intrigues which ended in the death of Henry III.

"Good faith! my lord," replied Aumale, "I can tell you no more than I have already told. The friends of Malivaut let out the secret, that the king had been stabbed by a Jacobin friar, and died of his wounds; but we could not expect them to enter into any minute particulars. I have still more good news, however, my lord. Ere I quitted the ground, a servant of the gay Count d'Aubin came up, and besought me to obtain for his master a pass for the morning, adding, that by noon, D'Aubin, with seven hundred men, horse and foot together, would be at the outposts on the side of St. Denis, with the purpose of joining the Union."

These tidings did not appear to surprise Mayenne so much as the former; but he seemed well pleased, nevertheless. "D'Aubin is better than his word," he said, "both in regard to time and numbers. He fixed three days, but I suppose the death of Henry has hurried his movements. How comes he to enter by St. Denis, though? It is leading his troops a tremendous round! There surely can be no foul play, D'Aumale! Are you sure the servant was his?"

"Quite sure, my lord," replied Aumale, "for the fellow was once my own *ecuyer de main*; and, besides, he gave a reason for taking that round. 'The Huguenot army,' he said, 'was advanced as far as Meudon, occupying both banks of the river, and the ground as far as Beauregard; D'Aubin was afraid of being stopped, and having to cut his way through, if he did not make a *detour*.'"

"Nevertheless, Aumale," replied the Duke, "let us be upon our guard. Strengthen the posts towards St. Denis, and bid Nemours take his regiment to meet and do honour to the new comers. D'Aubin I can trust, for he plays for a great stake; but he has not seven hundred men with him; and though he may very likely have brought over some other leader to our cause, yet it is as well to be prepared, and to be able to repel force by force, in case Henry of Navarre should present himself instead of Philip d'Aubin."

Measures of precautions were accordingly taken; but at the hour appointed, the Count d'Aubin and one or two inferior leaders, who had joined their forces to his, presented themselves at the outposts of the army of the League; and once having placed their troops within the limits of the garrison of Paris, so as to be out of danger, D'Aubin and his companions rode into the city, followed by merely a small train of common attendants. His reception from the Duke of Mayenne was as gracious as the circumstances had led him to expect; and the news which he bore of the doubts and differences in the royal camp not only removed from the leaders of the League every fear of attack, but suggested the hope of obtaining some striking success by assuming the offensive. Mayenne, however, though a skilful general, and a bold, decided, and courageous man, was wanting in that great quality, activity. Much time was spent in preparation; and it was not till the third day after the king's death, that it was determined to march a body, consisting of ten thousand of the best troops of the League, by a circuitous route to Meulan, and to take up a position in the rear of the king's army, thus cutting off his retreat upon either Normandy or the south, and exposing him, if he held his present camp, to be attacked at once in front and flank. The command of the force destined for this important expedition was divided between the Chevalier d'Aumale and the Count d'Aubin, whose skill, courage, and activity, were undoubted, and whose zeal in favour of the League, and against the Royalists, was likely to be the more energetic from the fact of his having just joined the one and abandoned the others. The march was ordered to commence the next morning early; but late in the evening, when Mayenne, seated alone in his cabinet, was busily preparing his last written order for the two officers in command, the Count d'Aubin was suddenly announced, at least an hour before the Duke expected him. He was instantly admitted, however, and advanced to the table at which Mayenne was sitting, with one of those smiles upon his lips, which showed that his errand had its share of bitterness. "Well, my lord," he said, "I come to save you unnecessary trouble. You may lay down the pen; for--as I thought we should be--we are too late."

"How so?" demanded the Duke of Mayenne. "We cannot be too late, if they have not bribed Saint Mark. The place could hold out a year."

"They have not bribed him," replied D'Aubin, "but they have done just as good; they have outwitted him. Yesterday, towards five o'clock, Rosny, and some others, engaged the thick-headed fool in a parley, and while they amused him with fair words, who should present himself at the bridge but the Marechal d'Aumont, as if merely to pass the water, according to convention; for St. Mark's forces have never been sufficient to defend the bridge. Well, when the troops were in the midst, they thought they might as well walk into the first open gate they saw, which happened to be that of the castle. So now Meulan is in the hands of the Huguenots; and we may save ourselves the trouble of a march which can produce no results."

"Saint Mark is a fool," said Mayenne, as calmly as if nothing vexatious had happened: "when we retake Meulan, we must put some person of better understanding in it; and at present we must change our plans. What think you, D'Aubin? will the Bearnois retreat upon Normandy and the sea coast, or will he fall back upon Maine and Touraine?"

D'Aubin paused thoughtfully--so long, indeed, that the Duke added, "Speak! speak, D'Aubin! I know no one whose foresight is more shrewd than yours. Why do you hesitate?"

"To tell the truth, my lord," replied D'Aubin, "I paused, considering how I should answer; for your interests lead me one way, and my own keenest wishes would make me go another. Did I choose in this instance to consider myself, before either country, or party, or truth, or honesty, as nine hundred and ninety-nine out of a thousand of your faithful followers would do, I should answer at once, that the Navarrese will march upon Maine; but we are all playing too great stakes at this moment for trifling, and my sincere opinion is, that Henry will fall back on Lower Normandy."

It was now Mayenne's turn to muse. "I see not how it affects you, D'Aubin, whether I am led to believe the Bearnois will turn his steps the one way or the other," he replied. "Tell me what interests have you therein more than other friends of the Catholic faith.--But first let me hear your reasons for judging that Normandy will be the direction of his march."

"For three strong reasons, my good lord," replied D'Aubin; "because the Normans are well affected towards him; because he expects succour from England; and because he is a good soldier. The first he will soon find out, if he do not know it already; the English troops must land on the Norman coast; and his knowledge of war will not suffer him to leave such advantages behind."

"And now, D'Aubin," said the Duke, after listening attentively to his reasons, "let me hear why, if you considered your own interests more than mine, you should desire me to believe that Harry of Navarre will march upon Maine and Touraine?"

"Simply, because I could then show you the best of all reasons for at once fulfilling your promise in regard to the hand of Mademoiselle de Menancourt," replied D'Aubin.

"My promise *shall* be fulfilled, Count," replied Mayenne, with some emphasis. "Fear not that Charles of Mayenne will shrink from the performance of his engagements; but you are somewhat too pressing. You cannot expect me to employ force in such a matter; and you have as yet given yourself no time to obtain, by gentleness and persuasion, that consent which the poor girl seems somewhat reluctant to grant."

D'Aubin coloured a good deal, piqued by the terms of commiseration in which Mayenne spoke of her who had so deeply wounded his vanity; but he was a great deal too wise to let his displeasure have vent on the present occasion. "My lord duke," he replied, "I should have thought your highness knew woman better. This is all caprice. During her father's life, Eugenie showed no such reluctance; and it was but some slight and unintentional offence on my part which first made her declare she would not fulfil the engagement between us. Once having said it, she makes it a matter of consistency to adhere to her purpose; though I could very well see, in our interview of yesterday, that her feelings in these respects were much altered. As long as she is suffered to make a point of vanity of her refusal, she will persist, even contrary to her own wishes; but once let her be my wife, and I will make her contented and happy, I will be answerable for it."

Mayenne shook his head, observing dryly, "Her reluctance did not seem to me much shaken when I spoke with her yesterday, Monsieur d'Aubin;

but still I do not see how this question is affected by Henry's march upon Maine."

"Were he likely to execute such a march, I would soon show you how, my lord," replied D'Aubin. "As it is, it matters little. However, the simple fact is this: the lands of Menancourt lie contiguous to my own; and did Henry of Navarre march thither, it would be absolutely necessary to your best interest that I should instantly become the husband of Eugenie, and set out for Maine, armed with power to bring all the retainers of her father in aid of the union. Full seven hundred men, trained to arms, and caring little which party they join, are lying idle in the villages and hamlets there; and if Henry reaches Le Mans before the husband of Eugenie de Menancourt, those men will be arrayed against the union instead of in favour of it. My worthy cousin of St. Real, who is much loved amongst the peasantry, is not a man to stand upon any ceremonies in serving a cause which he thinks just; and it would but little surprise me, to find the vassals of De Menancourt marching under the banners of St. Real. But as I hold it certain that the Huguenots will retire upon Normandy, the matter is not so pressing that we cannot wait a few days longer, to allow your highness's notions of delicacy full time to tire themselves out, by doubling like a pack of beagles after a woman's caprices."

There was something in the reasoning of D'Aubin which seemed to affect Mayenne much more than even the Count himself had expected. Rising from his seat, the Duke strode up and down the room for a moment or two, as if not a little embarrassed how to act; then, turning suddenly to his companion, he said--"You hold it certain, then, D'Aubin, that the Bearnois will fall back on Normandy and the sea? Hold it certain no longer!" he added, taking from a portfolio, which lay on the table at which he had been writing, an unsealed letter, and placing it in D'Aubin's hands. "Read that, D'Aubin, read that! and you will soon see that you are mistaken. There you see De Rosny himself, under the king's dictation, writes to the Count de Soissons to tell him, that if he will advance to Chateau Gontier, or even as far as Le Mans, Henry will meet him there within fifteen days. Mark, also, he lays out the line of march which they intend to pursue,--by Meulan, Mantes, Dreux, Verneuil, and Mortagne."

"May not this have been thrown out to deceive us?" demanded D'Aubin.

"No," replied Mayenne. "No; it was taken upon the person of Monsieur de Gailon last night, and they would not have risked a man of such importance with a letter which was not of the utmost consequence."

"Well, then, my lord Duke," replied D'Aubin, returning him the letter, with a calm and well satisfied smile, "I trust that all our purposes will be answered. Henry has committed a fault, of which you, of course, will take advantage."

"No immediate advantage can ensue," replied the Duke. "It was the knowledge of these facts which made me so eager to push a strong force upon Meulan; but as that fool St. Mark has suffered himself to be deceived, Henry's line of march is secure. What you say of Maine, however, is of importance, and must be thought of farther."

"By your good leave, my lord," replied D'Aubin, somewhat sharply, "methinks it needs no farther thought at all. Either you must let the retainers of Menancourt be raised and marched for the use and benefit of Henry of Navarre, calling himself King of France, or I must be the husband of the fair heiress of Maine; and before this time to-morrow night must be on my horse's back with a hundred stout cavaliers behind me, riding like the wind towards Chateau du Loir. The road by Chartres is open, and all that side of the country in our favour. In three days I shall be in Maine; and if I cannot gather together forces sufficient to make head against the Bearnois, I will at least do something to impede his march, and will join you with all the troops I can raise, wherever you give me a rendezvous."

Mayenne again walked up and down the room, knitting his brow and biting his lips with a degree of emotion which showed an evident distaste to the proposal of his companion. D'Aubin gazed upon him with not the most placable look, understanding the nature of his feelings, and not a little displeased to see a disposition to delay the fulfilment of the promise made to him; but at the same time feeling a secret triumph in his heart at the concatenation of circumstances which would compel the Duke of Mayenne, from political motives, to grant that which he, D'Aubin, thought ought to have been willingly accorded to his own merits and services.

"My lord," he cried, with a somewhat bitter laugh, after gazing upon the Duke for two or three minutes, "I am sorry to see you hesitate upon a matter in which both policy and justice should make you decide at once. Your unconditional promise has been given, that Eugenie de Menancourt shall be my bride; and circumstances have arisen, which render it as necessary to you as agreeable to me that she should become so immediately. In regard to these circumstances, I have dealt with you honestly, and have done what you know there is scarcely another follower that you have would do,--given you advice contrary to my own interest and wishes. Now, my lord----"

"Well, well!" interrupted Mayenne, "it must even be as you say, D'Aubin. There is no other resource; but remember, in wishing to find one, I am not influenced by any desire to evade a promise made to you, but solely and simply by the hope of inducing Mademoiselle de Menancourt, by persuasion, entreaty, and remonstrance, to fulfil her father's engagement, and thus spare me the pain of doing what I feel to be harsh, uncourteous, and unknightly."

"Your lordship is mighty delicate in all this," replied D'Aubin; "but I am not so much so. A little wholesome compulsion will do this proud beauty no harm. Proud I may well call her; for, proud of her wealth, her loveliness, and her rank, she thinks, it seems, that she is to be treated in a different manner from every other woman in France; and I am not sorry that, in the very fact of our marriage, that proud spirit should be a little humbled, which would certainly render her not the most yielding or obedient of wives."

Mayenne bit his lip. "I have never seen anything in her, Monsieur d'Aubin," he said, "but gentleness and sweetness. Determined she certainly is upon one point--her personal objection to yourself. What cause you have given her for such objection I know not, and shall not inquire, as my promise to yourself, and great state necessity, compel me to act in a manner which no other circumstances could excuse. Now mark me, Monsieur d'Aubin; what I intend to do is this, to yield you my whole authority to bring about your marriage with Eugenie de Menancourt to-morrow evening. There is a chapel in the house where she lives, and at a certain hour my own confessor shall be there, ready to perform the ceremony. But still remember, that I can hardly hold such a marriage to be legal, if she persists to the last in opposing it; and I must take measures to guard against doing aught that may either affect my own honour and reputation, draw upon me the censures of the church, or infringe the laws I am called upon for the time to defend and uphold. Under these circumstances, I will write down the exact terms and conditions on which I consent to what you propose. If political motives alone move you to press the marriage so hastily, what I require will be easily conceded. If otherwise, I say No! and will try no means of compulsion till all other efforts have failed."

Thus saying, Mayenne wrote down a few words on a slip of paper, and handed it to the Count d'Aubin, who gazed on it, while the shadows of many a quick passion flitted over his countenance. Thrice with a frown, he lifted his eyes to the face of Mayenne; but all that he beheld there was calm, stern determination; and, after again reading the paper, he replied, "Well, I consent, because I doubt not, my lord, that when she finds the matter inevitable, she will yield, even if not with a good grace; but if we were to set out for Chartres on the following day, it would surely be time enough for--"

"No, Monsieur d'Aubin, no;" replied Mayenne: "the plan which I have drawn out must be followed exactly. I will myself be present at the ceremony; and I require that you sign that paper to guard against misunderstanding on either side, otherwise I stir no farther in the affair. Are you contented with this arrangement?"

"Perfectly, my lord," replied D'Aubin, signing the paper with a smile. "I merely thought that, by delaying the marriage till the following morning, I and you, and your noble sister of Montpensier, might, perhaps, have more time to reason her out of her prejudices; but, as you say, it will after all be better tomorrow night, for the only danger of interruption on my journey lies in the neighbourhood of Paris, and it will be better to take our departure under cover of the darkness. As for the rest, let us but show this fair lady that it is inevitable, and I will engage that she shall soon make up her mind to it. For this purpose, my lord, let me beseech you to furnish me with a billet to her, under your own hand, telling her what we have determined, couched in what courteous terms you will, but sufficiently explicit to let her know that there is no chance of evasion."

"Perhaps you are right," said Mayenne, "perhaps you are right; but nevertheless, D'Aubin, try all gentle means. You are not one, as far as ever I have heard, to fail in persuasion, when you choose to use your eloquence against a woman's heart."

D'Aubin smiled, but replied, "Nevertheless, my lord, it goes somewhat against the grain to flatter, and to soothe, and to beseech, when one is treated with scorn, and has, at the same time, the right to command; but still, fear not; I will do my best; and, if ever woman was won with fair words and soft entreaties, Eugenie de Menancourt shall come willingly to the altar; but, to give those entreaties greater force, it will be necessary to show her, by your handwriting, that it is not from want of power that I use the gentler before the harsher means."

Mayenne took up the pen, but mused for many minutes ere he put it to the paper, and even then wrote no less than three billets before he could satisfy himself in a species of composition to which he was not accustomed. At length, abandoning all formal excuses, he contented himself with simply announcing to the unhappy Eugenie de Menancourt, that motives of importance to the state compelled him to require her without farther hesitation to fulfil her father's engagement to the Count d'Aubin; and that he had appointed the hour of nine on the succeeding evening for the celebration of her marriage.

"There!" he said, as he handed the note to D'Aubin--"There, sir Count! Seldom has my hand so unwillingly traced a few lines as to-night. But I will send my sister Catherine early in the morning to soften the matter to the poor girl; and now, farewell! for I have matters of much import to attend to."

D'Aubin took the note, and before he noticed the hint to withdraw, read it over attentively, to satisfy himself that it was such as he could wish, and then folding it up again with a triumphant smile, he uttered a few words of thanks and took his leave. Ere long, however, those feelings of triumph died away; and other sensations took their place. His pride had been wounded, his vanity insulted, and many of his worldly prospects endangered by the steadfast rejection of Eugenie de Menancourt; but his heart was not so hardened as he himself believed it to be, nor as it appeared to others, in the fierce pursuit of his object; and when he turned away from the cabinet of Mayenne, and took his path homeward, he asked himself whether after all, he should make use of the cruel power he possessed; he asked himself whether, for the sake of humbling a fair and innocent girl, and of gratifying his vanity by triumphing over her opposition, he could resist the tears, and entreaties, and reproaches of a being whom he had been accustomed to regard with tenderness, if not with love; whether he should cause the unhappiness of her whole after days, and at the same time unite himself, against her will, to a woman whose dislike would only be increased by the force that was put upon her inclinations. Even while he revolved these ideas, the memory of one that he had long--ay, that he still loved, was wakened by the other thoughts which struggled in his bosom; and although he had contemplated the deed he was about to commit a thousand times before, and fully made up his mind to it, he now shrunk with cold and chilly repugnance at the idea of placing between himself and her who possessed the only stronghold of his affections, the impassable barrier of his union with another. All these feelings leagued together, and for a time made head against his less generous purposes; but there were difficulties in retreating, which could hardly be overcome; and as he reached the house in which he had fixed his dwelling at Paris, he thought, "I will sleep over these new doubts, and decide to-morrow."

When he entered, however, he found Albert of Wolfstrom and several gay companions, waiting to sup with him, and to bid him farewell, ere he set out upon the expedition against Meulan, for which they still thought he was destined on the morrow. D'Aubin despised them all, but nevertheless he sat down with them, and drank deep. Dice succeeded to wine; and when the Count rose from table, he had no resource, but to wed Eugenie de Menancourt, or to descend more than one step in the scale of society.

CHAPTER XX

If every minute event which took place in the beginning of August, 1589, was matter of importance to the inhabitants of Paris, a thousand times more deep, intense, and thrilling than that experienced by any other person, was the interest taken by Eugenie de Menancourt in all that passed at that period. Her happiness, her misery for life, hung upon the die which other hands were destined to throw; and without the possibility of aiding herself in the slightest degree of changing the fate that awaited her, or arresting its progress for a moment, she was obliged to abide the unknown result in the power of people, whose purposes she neither knew nor could control. Every rumour, every sound, created some new sensation in her bosom. Every change, where change was constant, either raised a momentary hope, or cast her back into the depth of apprehension. The distant roar of the artillery, the march of the troops through the streets, the galloping of messengers and couriers, the military parade, even the processions of the clergy, as they proceeded from shrine to shrine, petitioning for the aid of God to support them in rebellion, and encourage them in assassination, all agitated and alarmed her, till at length, her mind fell into that state in which terror has so much the predominance, that every fresh tidings are anticipated as tidings of sorrow. The news of the death of the king, and the particulars of the manner in which that foul act was perpetrated, struck her with horror and despair, as showing to what length the men in whose hands she was placed dared to go in pursuit of the objects of their party. Scarcely, however, had she time to think over this event, when another, more deeply and personally painful to herself, banished all other feelings but anxiety for her future destiny.

One morning suddenly, the Count d'Aubin was announced, and, hardly waiting to see whether his visit were or were not acceptable, he followed the servant into her presence. The result of their meeting we have already seen in his conference with Mayenne; but either vanity or policy had induced him to distort the truth, when he had asserted that Eugenie de Menancourt had shown the slightest symptom of vacillating in her determination against him.

From his words and his manner, she had soon learned that he had joined the party of the League, and that he considered all the authority and influence of Mayenne at his command, in support of his suit towards her; and perhaps the fear of irritating him, and driving him on to use the power he possessed to the utmost, might make her more gentle in her language, and less disposed to express the reprobation and dislike she entertained towards him, than would have been the case had he persisted in his pursuit under other circumstances. But Eugenie was too noble, too candid, too sincere, to suffer him to believe, for one moment, that her feelings would ever change towards him. She was gentle, but she was firm; and D'Aubin, when he left her, was, perhaps, the more mortified to find, from her calmness, as well as determination, that she was influenced against him by no temporary pique, by no fit of passion or indignation, as he had represented the matter to others, and tried to regard it himself; but that positively and certainly, he who had thought that her heart was at his command whenever he chose to demand it, had never caused it to beat one pulse more rapidly; that he had never been loved, and was now contemned and disliked.

Although during his stay he had employed persuasion and entreaty, and all the arts that none knew better how to use than himself, there had still been in his tone that consciousness of power and authority which alarmed Eugenie for the result; and with a trembling hand she wrote a few words to the fair Beatrice of Ferrara, beseeching her to come to her aid, determined as she was to risk any thing in order to escape from her present situation. Fate, however, ever overrules our best efforts; and, as if disdaining to cast away the greater exertions of its almighty power to thwart our petty schemes, contents itself with throwing some trifling stumbling-block in our way-- some idle, insignificant trifle, over which our pigmy plans fall prostrate in their course. The servant whom Eugenie had charged with the delivery of her note returned, and brought her word that Beatrice had gone out on horseback to witness the movements of the Royalist army in their retreat, an amusement worthy of her bold and fearless spirit. The lady's attendants, however, had informed him, the servant said, that she would be back long before nightfall; and Eugenie waited and counted the anxious moments till the daylight waned, and the shadows of evening fell over the earth.

"Beatrice must soon be here now," she thought; but moment after moment, and hour after hour, went by, without the appearance of her she waited for. At length, giving up hope for that night, and wearied with wearing expectation, Eugenie retired to rest; but it was rest broken by fears and anxieties; and early on the succeeding morning she was up, and watching eagerly for the coming of her friend, whose bold counsels and skilful aid might, she trusted, give her courage to undertake, and power to execute, some plan for her own deliverance.

Watching from the large projecting window we have mentioned, she was not long before she beheld one of the carved and gilded equipages of the day turn into the court-yard of her own dwelling, and in a few minutes after the door of the saloon was opened to give admission to a visitor. But the countenance that presented itself was that of Madame de Montpensier, not of Beatrice of Ferrara; and the heart of Eugenie de Menancourt sunk at an occurence, which though not unusual, she felt in the present instance could bode her no good.

The conversation which now took place may easily be divined, from the conference between Mayenne and the Count d'Aubin. We shall therefore not repeat it here, it being sufficient to say, that when about an hour afterwards, D'Aubin himself entered the saloon, he found Madame de Montpensier rising to depart, and Eugenie de Menancourt, with her face buried in her hands, weeping in hopeless bitterness of heart.

Lifting her shoulders with an emphatic shrug, Madame de Montpensier quitted the room in silence, and D'Aubin stood for a moment gazing upon the fair unhappy girl whom his ungenerous pursuit had reduced to such a state, with a variety of passions warring in his breast, in a manner which it would be difficult to describe. After a brief pause, Eugenie withdrew her hands from her face and turned her tearful eyes upon him. As she looked, a sort of involuntary shudder passed over her frame, and she again pressed her hands upon her eyes for one moment; then, rising from her chair, she advanced direct to where he stood, and cast herself upon her knees at his feet.

"Philip d'Aubin," she said, "you were once generous and kind of heart:- -nay, nay, hear me!" she continued, as he endeavoured to raise her. "Hear me, I beseech you; for my happiness or misery--perhaps my life or death-- depend upon this moment."

"Mademoiselle de Menancourt," replied D'Aubin, "I can hear nothing, I can attend to nothing, while you there remain in a posture unbecoming to us both--for you to assume and for me to suffer. Rise, I entreat you!"

"No, no!" she replied, clasping her hands earnestly. "I will not, I cannot rise till you have heard me. Have I not used every other means? have I not employed every other form of entreaty without avail? and I now kneel at your feet to beseech you to spare yourself and me misery interminable. I have told you, and with bitter regret have I been obliged to tell you, that I cannot love you as woman should love her husband; and I did not resolve to tell you so till I had struggled with my own heart,--till I had combated all my own feelings,--in order, if possible, to fulfil what had been a wish of my father. I struggled, I combated in vain, Monsieur d'Aubin; for the more I did so, the more I found that my peace of mind required me to take a decided part,--that honour and justice towards you required me to tell you that I could not, that I would not, be your wife. Why, why persecute me thus, Monsieur d'Aubin?" she continued; "you do not love me--you have never loved me; and, under such circumstances, how can you expect me to love you? Why not turn to any of those who will not only consider themselves as honoured by your suit, but who, much better suited than I am to your views, your habits, and your feelings, have it in their power to return your affection, and to meet you, as I doubt not you deserve to be met, with love for love?"

"You mistake me altogether, Eugenie," said D'Aubin, raising her almost forcibly, and leading her back to her seat; "I do love you; and I trust that, though you doubt your own feelings at present, you will find it not so difficult, when you are my wife, to feel towards me in such a manner as to be happy yourself and to render me so."

"Do not deceive yourself, Monsieur d'Aubin!" exclaimed Eugenie. "I do not doubt my own feelings! I am but too sure of them! I do not love you, I cannot love you, any more than you love me; and if you persist in your pursuit, you do it warned of what are my sentiments towards you, and assured that those sentiments will but become more repugnant, in proportion to the degree of constraint used towards me."

"Nay, nay," replied D'Aubin, willing as far as possible to use gentle means, and try those powers of persuasion which he believed himself, not unjustly, to possess; "nay, nay, dear Eugenie, you do me wrong altogether; believe me, I do love you sincerely. I know that I have acted foolishly, wrongly towards you; I know that, prompted by vanity, and the gay and roving disposition of youth, flattered and courted, idle, perhaps, conceited, I appeared to neglect and undervalue the jewel that was offered to me in the hand of Eugenie de Menancourt. But, believe me, dear Eugenie, that it was not that I failed to esteem that jewel at its full and highest price; it was but that foolishly I thought it my own beyond all risk. Consider in what school I had been brought up,--consider the lightness and fickleness of all by whom I was surrounded; forgive me the errors and the follies that are past away for ever, and give me an opportunity of proving to you that they are deeply regretted, and will never be renewed. My whole life, my whole thoughts, my whole endeavours, shall be devoted to wipe out the evil impression which a few acts of folly have left upon your mind; and surely the unceasing devotion and tenderness of one who will never forget that he wronged you, and that you forgave him, will be sufficient to atone for errors which proceeded more from idle levity than from evil purpose."

"Monsieur d'Aubin," said Eugenie, sadly, "I accuse you of nothing, I blame you for nothing. What might have been my feelings towards you, had your conduct been different towards me, I cannot tell--I cannot even guess: but you greatly deceive yourself if you think that my sentiments towards you originate in anger, or mortified vanity, or wounded pride. I must be candid with you to the very utmost, and tell you that I never felt towards you anything which could enable your conduct to others to inflict one pang upon me. I have never loved you, Monsieur d'Aubin, and the only effect of your behaviour has been to teach me that I never can love you."

"You have inflicted upon me that mortifying reiteration, somewhat often," replied D'Aubin; "and perhaps I am not wrong when I ask, whether the want of love towards your promised husband in the past and the present, has not originated in love for another?"

Eugenie's cheek crimsoned to a hue deeper than the rose; and something between confusion and indignation kept her silent. D'Aubin drew his own conclusions; but, strange to say, though those conclusions were as bitter as well might be, they only added fire to the fierceness of his pursuit. His cheek, however, reddened also; but it was with the struggle of anger, and interest, pride and vanity; and he went on: "I see I am right, Mademoiselle de Menancourt, and am sorry to see it. Nevertheless, my confidence in you is such, that I entertain not the slightest doubt, that however unwisely you may have entertained such feelings hitherto, you will crush them with wise precaution, and bury them in speedy oblivion, when you become my wife. Nor am I inclined to resign my hopes of teaching you to change all such opinions by my own conduct, and of bringing you to love me, when your duty shall be engaged to second all my efforts."

Eugenie saw that her fate was determined, as far as the Count d'Aubin had power to govern it. She saw that with him entreaties would be ineffectual, and tears of no avail. Nothing then remained but resolution; and although she knew not what protection the law of her native land held out to one under her circumstances, and was too well aware that in the city where she was detained, popular violence had broken through all the restraints of society; yet she determined that no weakness or want of energy on her own part should favour the oppression to which she was subjected. As soon as she perceived that the humble supplications to which she had descended fell as vainly upon the ear of the Count d'Aubin as the song of the charmer upon the deaf adder, her whole manner changed; and, assuming the same look of unconquerable determination which he had put on towards her, she replied, "My duty, Sir Count d'Aubin, will never either second or prompt any efforts on my part to feel differently towards you than I do now; for I never will be, and never can be, your wife. The arm of power may drag me to the altar, and a mockery of religious service may be read between us; but there, as here, my voice shall steadfastly pronounce the same refusal; the ring, with which you think to wed me, shall be trampled under my feet; no contract shall ever be signed by me; and as long as I have strength to lift my voice, I will appeal against the tyranny which oppresses me. Moreover, let me warn you, that every step that you take forward in this brutal and ungentlemanly course will but increase those feelings which you have this day striven in vain to remove, till indifference becomes dislike, and dislike grows into detestation."

"You will think better of this, Eugenie," said D'Aubin, surprised and struck by energy and vehemence, such as he had never witnessed in her before. "We are destined to be united, and be assured that nothing can make a change in this arrangement. Let us not meet, then, at enmity. You will think better of this."

"Never," replied Eugenie, "never! You have roused a spirit in my bosom, Count d'Aubin, that you knew not existed there--that I knew not myself till this hour. But I feel that it will bear me through everything; and I tell you boldly, and at once, that I would infinitely rather die, were death within my choice, this moment, than be the wife of Philip d'Aubin."

D'Aubin bit his lip, and casting his eyes upon the ground, paused for a moment in deep thought, his resolutions and purposes shaken by what he had heard, and his mind once more undecided. "Tell me," he said at length, "tell me, Mademoiselle de Menancourt, if by my application to the Duke of Mayenne the ceremony of our marriage this night, which I see has been announced to you by the Duchess de Montpensier, can be put off to some later period, will you give me the hope, that after a certain time, during which my conduct towards yourself, and towards the world, shall be in every respect irreproachable, I may obtain your hand, without doing that violence to your feelings, which it seems would be the consequence of our present union?"

Eugenie turned deadly pale, under the emotion that she felt. The words of the Count d'Aubin offered her the prospect of a temporary relief--offered the means of obtaining invaluable time, during which a thousand changes of circumstances might take place to free her from the difficulties and dangers that surrounded her; but she asked herself, how was this to be bought? By deceit, by the first deceit she had ever been guilty of in life; and though many a casuist might argue, and argue perhaps justly, that she had a right to oppose the unjustifiable means employed against her, by any method in her power to use, the heart of Eugenie de Menancourt was not one that could admit such reasoning in regard to honesty and truth. She would not have bought her life by deceit; and though perhaps in the present instance she might feel that more than life itself was at stake, she would not sacrifice her own good opinion even for that.

"No, Monsieur d'Aubin," she replied, after a long and agitated pause--"No!--I will not deceive you. No time can change my opinion or determination. I never can be your wife. If you will desist from your present pursuit--if you will recollect the former generosity of your sentiments--if you will consider your own honour, and my peace of mind, and set me free from this persecution, you will merit and obtain my deepest gratitude, my thanks, and my admiration; but, Philip d'Aubin, you never can have more."

"Then you seal your own fate, Eugenie de Menancourt," replied D'Aubin, "and things must take their course, as already arranged. Yet think not that this arrangement has been planned solely to gratify me. Other and more important interests are involved therein, and you will see by this note from the Duke of Mayenne, that motives of state necessity compel both him and me to abridge that ceremonious delicacy which otherwise would have been extended towards you."

Eugenie took the paper, and tried to read it over; but agitation and apprehension caused the letters to dance before her eyes, and she only gathered the general import, and saw that as far as Mayenne and the Count d'Aubin had power, her fate was sealed indeed. Although her resolution remained in full force, and her mind was as unconquered as ever, she felt that her bodily powers were failing her; and fearful that Aubin should see how much she was overcome, as well as anxious for a few hours of uninterrupted thought, she waved her hand for him to leave her.

"Not one word more?" he said, advancing as if to take her hand. "Not one word more?"

"No," replied Eugenie, shrinking back from him with involuntary horror. "No, I have nothing more to say."

D'Aubin turned on his heel, mortified to the very heart by the personal dislike which he marked with the keen eyes of wounded vanity: and without another word, left Eugenie to solitude, and to feelings very nearly akin to despair.

CHAPTER XXI

A long summer's day was over, and nothing remained of its splendour but a fading tint of purple in the deep blue sky; while Venus and the moon came hand in hand together above the trees, as if to divide between their bright but gentle rule the tranquil kingdom of the night. The royal camp no longer sounded with the clang of arms or the tramp of marching men; the man[oe]uvres for the day were over; and the soldiery, quartered in the village of St. Cloud itself, had left the streets vacant, while they sought consolation after all the labours and exertions of the morning, in the gay evening meal and often replenished flask. The body of the dead king lay--almost forgotten, by those who had fed upon his bounty and encouraged his vices,--in the house where the hand of the assassin had struck him; and lights were just beginning to twinkle in the windows of the old chateau where the new monarch had fixed his abode the night after his accession to the tottering throne of France.

Such was the state of St. Cloud, when, on the third evening after the death of Henry III. a party of horsemen paused at the gates of this park, and, dismounting there, advanced towards the old palace on foot. The guards at the gates saluted as the cavaliers passed; and Henry IV. who walked a step before the rest, mused as he proceeded, leading the way with a slow step, and sometimes gazing up thoughtfully at the blue twilight sky, sometimes fixing his eyes upon the gravel of the path, absorbed in deep and silent reverie. At length, turning to those who accompanied him, he said, "Our arrangements, I think, are all now complete, and we may begin our march to-morrow. I have to thank you, Rosny, for Meulan; and you, St. Real, for as fine a body of men as ever a loyal heart brought to the aid of a poor king. D'Aumont has, I suppose, already marched to see what friends he can raise for us in the east; but I much fear that our messenger has never reached our worthy cousin, the Count de Soissons! However, it matters not, as, by the reports from Normandy, we shall most likely change our plans. Still I could wish, De Rosny, that you would write a few lines to the Count, bidding him advance as fast as possible upon Mans, and then regulate his movements by what he hears of ours; remembering, however, that the great object is to bring me men and money as speedily as possible. Let the letter be copied six times, and I will come and sign each ere half-an-hour be over. Sent by six separate messengers, one of these letters can scarcely fail to reach him.

You, St. Real, look well to your quarters; for these Leaguers must know by this time how much our forces are diminished, and may strive for some advantage. Fare you well! Good night! Quick! up to the chateau, Rosny, and take all these others with you. I would fain have half-an-hour's quiet thought, amidst these moonlight walks, where so many of my ancestors have wandered, ere I quit them, perhaps for ever, after having been their sovereign but for a day!"

"Were it not better, your Majesty," replied De Rosny, in a low voice, "to keep a few of your attendants around you? Remember that the dagger of the assassin found your predecessor in the midst of his army and his court, and that treason has been so evident amongst those by whom we are surrounded, that we cannot tell whose hand may next be armed against his monarch's life."

"I fear not, De Rosny," replied Henry, "I fear not! If it be the will of God that I fall, the weapon will find me in the midst of guards and precautions, as easily as alone in the open field. Nor do fear the treason you seem to apprehend. Our camp has lately been like a butt of new made wine, in one general ferment, where all was troubled and unpalatable; but that very ferment, I trust, has worked it clear, and I would not be the man to fancy myself continually surrounded by secret enemies--no, not if I could thereby spin out this mortal thread for centuries beyond the length of ordinary lives! No, no! De Rosny, I fear not, and I would be alone."

The last words were spoken in a tone that left no reply; and De Rosny, beckoning to those who followed, walked on directly towards the chateau, while Henry turned into one of the lateral alleys, down which the moonlight was streaming in full effulgence. One or two of the attendants lingered for a moment, as if still unwilling to leave the king; but Henry waved his hand for them to depart, and then walked on.

There are periods in the life of every man, when so many events are crowding into the short space of a few days, when such manifold calls upon attention, and such deep and important interests for consideration load the wings of every minute as it flies, that time is wanting for the recollection, for the thought, for even the feeling, of how the mighty changes which are going on around us affect our own individual nature, and work upon our being and our fate. At those periods, to every thinking and intellectual mind, comes a thirst and a longing for even a brief space of calm reflection; and we gladly seize the very first opportunity of withdrawing our thoughts from the wearying necessity of directing our actions on the instant, and give them up for a time to that consideration of remote prospects and general feelings, which, after the energetic activity lately required of us, is comparatively a state of tranquillity and repose.

Such had been, and such was the situation of Henry IV. Since the assassination of the late king, scarcely an instant had passed without some imperious demand for immediate exertion. Mighty and deep were the interests involved; imminent and terrible were the perils that surrounded him; and the consequences of every step that his foot trod, in the rough and precipitous path before him, were not only destined to affect himself as an individual, but to carry weal or woe to thousands and tens of thousands; to change the fate of states and kingdoms, and decide the destiny of generations yet unborn. His crown and station for life, the security and fortune of his friends, the power of recompensing those who served him, the right of chastising the rebel, and of punishing the traitor; the means of restoring peace to his rent and devastated country, the weal and welfare of his whole people, hung trembling in the balance of every instant, and required the exertion of all the energies with which God had blessed his great and powerful mind for the direction of his feeling and generous heart. The exertions of those energies had not been spared by Henry IV. He had lost not a moment; he had neglected not an opportunity; he had done more than mortal frame could well endure; and had taken from the cares of empire not even the time for necessary refreshment and repose. But now that the hurricane had in some measure passed by, that the evil of the hour was accomplished, and that every means which human sagacity could devise had been taken to remedy past misfortunes, and to guard against future perils, he gave way to that longing thirst for communion with his own heart, which the heat of the great storm of difficulties and dangers he had undergone, and the fatigue of mighty exertions, had left behind. Well, well might he think of that vast, dim, misty prospect, the future! Well, well might he look around to see, if beyond the rocks, and shoals, and tempests, which surrounded him, he could perceive no calmer scene, no haven of repose, no gleam of sunshine to light him on over the dark and troubled waters around him! Well, well might he ask his own heart, if he could have courage, and energy, and perseverance sufficient, to dare all the dangers, to bear all the reverses, and again and again breast the waves which had so often dashed him back against the rocks.

Such were his thoughts, such the matter of his contemplation, as, with his eyes now bent on the ground, now raised towards the sky, he walked slowly along one of the alleys of the old park of St. Cloud. But his mind wandered far, and paused for a moment upon many of those collateral associations to which his circumstances and situation gave rise. He thought of the sorrows and cares of kingly lot, of the ingratitude and baseness of mankind, of the hollowness and heartlessness of courts, and of the selfishness and insincerity of many of those who dwelt in them. He remembered the fate of his immediate predecessor; betrayed by those whom he had favoured, driven from his capital, and almost hurled from his throne by the friend and companion of his youth,[3] opposed in arms by those whom his bounty had fed and pampered, and murdered by the representative of an order which he had loaded with benefits and degraded himself to serve. He thought of what might be his own fate; and, judging from all the signs that he saw around him, he argued, that the well of bitterness was but freshly opened for him, and that his hand held a cup of sorrow whereof he was destined to drink to the very last drop.

Then again, as he raised his eyes towards the beautiful planet which was diffusing the flood of her tranquil light over field, and plain, and wood, over armed camp and beleaguered city, as calmly and tranquilly as if nothing but peace, and virtue, and happiness dwelt beneath her beams, his mind reverted to his early days, when he had seen the same effulgent rays pour through the mighty masses of his native mountains, and stream down the lovely valleys in which he had first learned to shoot his boyish arrows at the mark, to cast the light line for the silver trout, or to pursue the swift-footed izzard over the beetling crags: and as he thought of those sweet times and happy hours, how he did long, with the deep yearnings of the disappointed heart, to be able to cast away crown and sceptre, sword and shield, the miseries of high station, the bitter wisdom of manhood, and to sport again, a boy, with the happy carelessness of other years, by the bright waters of the Gave, and amidst the lustrous valleys of Ossau, Argelez, and Pau!

By this time he had nearly reached the end of the alley, where it opened out upon a small lawn, over which, in the neglect of all things that existed during the civil wars, the grass had grown up long and rank; and he was preparing to return and bend his steps towards the chateau, when a light rustling sound amongst the trees caught his ear, and made him draw round his sword belt, till the hilt of his well-tried weapon was within easy reach of his hand.

The next moment the cause of that sound stood before him, at the distance of about ten paces; and the moon afforded quite sufficient light to show the monarch that no fresh peril was near. The form was that of a page, and the next moment Leonard de Monte advanced, and cast himself upon his knee at Henry's feet. "Ha! my friend the page!" cried the king; "I saw you yesterday, as I passed through the village, and recognised you instantly; but had no time to speak. What would you now, good youth?" and as he spoke he extended his hand towards him.

Leonard de Monte raised it to his lips, but still continued kneeling, while he replied, "I crave a boon, sire. You may remember that I once, not many moons since, led you in safety through more than one path of danger; and you promised me then, that if ever I asked you a boon consistent with your honour, you would grant it."

"And so I will, if it be possible," answered Henry; "though I have granted you one boon already without your asking it; I mean that I have kept your secret!" Leonard de Monte started up and drew a step back; but the king continued, "Did you fancy I did not recollect you? Ay! within five minutes after our first meeting: but never mind, and do not fear; speak your boon boldly, and, if it be in my power, I will not say nay; though, to tell the truth, within these three days I have granted so much that I doubt if there be anything left in all France to grant!"

"Mine will not be difficult, sire," replied the page; "it is but this, that you will give me, under your royal hand, an order addressed to all your lieutenants, officers, and seneschals, and to all persons, in short, who hold you dear, to aid and help me with the whole of their power whenever I shall call upon them; to protect me and all who are with me in case of danger, and to give me every kind of information and assistance which I may require for my personal safety."

"You ask a very high and unlimited power of command for a boy of your age!" said the king, laughing; "but I think I may trust you; and yet," he added, in a graver tone, "such authority might be abused."

The boy again advanced and once more bent his knee, "Never by me, sire!" he said; "and to think so for one moment, would be to do me foul injustice. Born in a foreign land, and my own sovereign at least, I cannot offer you allegiance; but I swear with truer intentions than many of those who have vowed faith and service to you within these three days, that I will never use the power I ask from you but for the purposes of safety. I promise it upon my word--a word that was broken; upon my honour--an honour that has never known a stain."

"You are an extraordinary being," said the king, "and I will do what you ask without a doubt; but tell me," he added with a smile, "what name shall I put in this general order? Shall it be Leonard de Monte, or a nobler name?"

"Show me that you do really know me," answered the other, in a gayer tone than he had hitherto used, "by writing the name you would fix upon me in the letter."

"Do you think I have forgotten the conferences of Niort?" demanded Henry; "no, no! I remember them well; and I recollect, too, that when I pressed Madame de Saulnes somewhat hard to tell me what I was really to expect from the court of that day, she told me to ask you, not her; for that your habits were different; you never told a falsehood, and she never told the truth!"

"But I told you nothing!" exclaimed the boy, eagerly.

"No, but you said plainly you would not!" answered the king, "and therefore I trusted you with my life when last I met you; and will trust you to the very utmost now. Come, let us go back to the castle."

As he spoke, he took the hand of the youth, who had again risen; but Leonard de Monte instantly withdrew it, saying, "Perhaps I had better send for the paper when your Majesty has had leisure to finish it."

"Good faith, you must take it now or never!" answered Henry: "but who have we here?"

"'Tis but a page I sent to seek you at the chateau, sire," replied his companion, "while I waited amongst the alleys for his return. I heard your voice, however, as you dismissed your attendants, and followed you hither."

"Ha, St. Real's dwarf, who met us in the wood!" cried the monarch, as the page Bartholo approached, "Pardie! your schemes seem to have been well and deeply laid; and yet there is a mystery which I cannot altogether fathom; though I have been accustomed to deal with those whose trade is deceit, till my eyes, I believe could well nigh penetrate the nether millstone. You must some day let me into the secret of all this."

"Perhaps I may, your Majesty," replied the youth; "that is, I may some time give you the secret of my own conduct. The secret of my present request, sire, is very soon told. I seek but to aid the oppressed, and if your Majesty will listen to the tale, it shall be told as we go along."

"Speak, speak!" replied the king; "we treat as crown to crown, you know; and I must e'en take as much or as little of your confidence as your diplomacy is pleased to offer. Speak! and if I can aid you, count upon my help."

Leonard de Monte made a sign to Bartholo to draw back; and then walking by the side of the king, with the ease of one accustomed to courts and the society of princes, proceeded to tell the tale he had mentioned, in a low voice, the tones of which scarcely reached the dwarf's ear. It was evident, however, that the king soon became interested; sometimes suddenly interrupting the soft melodious tones in which the voice spoke, to ask some rapid question, sometimes abruptly pausing to listen with greater attention, and then resuming his walk towards the chateau. When they had nearly reached the gates, the monarch again turned, exclaiming, "Marry her to St. Real!--Pardie! that was not the consummation I expected."

"And why not, sire?" demanded the boy. "Wherefore should she not be married to St. Real?"

"Why, certainly, I did not suppose you wished to marry her yourself!" replied Henry, laughing. "You are very generous, however."

"Sire, your majesty mistakes me," replied Leonard de Monte in a grave tone,--"mistakes me, my views, wishes, and purposes entirely."

"I perceive I do," replied the king, "and acknowledge you are more a mystery to me than ever. However, this is all irrelevant to the matter of deep interest which you have just told me, and to the shrewd but daring plans which you have formed. On my honour," he added, "you have a bold and generous heart, and, could we but get you to grow a little taller, would make as good a knight as ever couched a lance. But let us speak to the point. You must have my counsel and advice, for I have been somewhat famous for *coups de main* in my day;--be so good, Sir Dwarf, as to put at least a hundred times your own length between your steps and ours; we shall give you notice when we want your presence at our conference." Thus saying, the king again entered the lateral alley, in which he had first met Leonard de Monte, and dropping his voice so as to confine the sense of his words to the ears for which they were intended, he continued the conversation with rapid and eager interest. Leonard de Monte frequently joined in; and, by the time they reached the end of the walk, it seemed that their plans were fully arranged; for, wheeling suddenly round, they returned with much quicker steps towards the chateau, keeping silence also as they went, till at length, when within a hundred yards of the terrace, Henry burst into a loud laugh, exclaiming--"Ventre Saint Gris, 'twill be worth half a province so to circumvent his slow Highness of Mayenne!"

He then led the way into the palace; and, bidding the dwarf wait in the vestibule, proceeded to a small cabinet in which De Rosny, together with a secretary, was busily engaged in writing the letters before mentioned to the Count de Soissons. The grave and somewhat formal Huguenot raised his eyes with some surprise to the handsome and glittering youth who entered with the king, and to whose face and person he was totally a stranger. Henry, however, without noticing his astonishment, and seemingly entirely occupied by the thoughts to which his late conversation had given rise, led the way on into a chamber beyond, bidding the secretary bring him instantly materials for writing. Then casting himself into a chair, he wrote with a rapid hand, in the first place, the general letter, which the youth had originally demanded, and then another longer epistle, which he folded and sealed with his private signet.

"This," he said, handing the letter to Leonard de Monte, "this is to be your last resource if other means fail; and I do not think, however he may deny our authority, that our worthy cousin will neglect the warning there given him. Nevertheless, try all other means first, and forget not to give me instant information of the result; for even should the beginning be successful, it may require some pains and some power to render the end equally fortunate."

The boy, who had remained standing, took the papers; and kissing the king's hand, with many thanks, retired from his presence. Passing through the vestibule, he beckoned to the page to follow him, and, with a rapid step, proceeded to the outward gates. Then taking his way to the *auberge*, in which St. Real lodged, he entered the room in which the young marquis was seated.

St. Real beckoned him to approach, saying, "I have sent for you twice, Leonard."

"No one told me of it, sir," replied the boy, "and in fact no one could, for I was absent till within this moment. But what are your commands?"

"Come hither," said St. Real, with a smile, "and I will tell you." The page approached; and the young lord marking some sort of impatience in his countenance, for a few minutes played with his expectation as one might do with the eagerness of a child.

At length, however, he asked more gravely----

"Do you remember, on the night of the king's death, you sang me a song, and repeated me a proverb, which, together with your own words, too well applied to myself to have been spoken accidentally? You escaped me at the time; and since, I have not had an opportunity of speaking with you on the subject. But now I must not only demand to know how you have fathomed secrets which I thought confined to my own bosom; but I must also require of you to tell me who and what you are, for your language and your station are at variance, and I must have my doubts satisfied."

"Sir," replied the boy, while first a playful smile, and then a look almost approaching to sorrow, passed over his countenance, "with regard to what I know of yourself, some day I may tell you how I know it, but I cannot tell you now. In regard to what you ask concerning myself, I can give you but one answer. Did you ever hear of beings called fairies, who, for some particular motive of friendship or regard, sometimes come down to do better than mortal service to a chosen race, or a particular individual? If you have heard of such beings--and who has not?--you must know, that the very first question concerning their nature, or their fate, dissolves the spell that binds them to the person they serve, and ends their term of service. Such, sir, is the case with me. So long as you asked me no questions, I was your willing page and humble attendant. Your curiosity has dissolved the spell, and all I can do is, to bid you farewell, and to tell you, that you will never see Leonard de Monte more."

Thus saying, he again darted out of the room, leaving St. Real uncertain whether he spoke in jest or earnest. Determined, however, to know more, the young nobleman started up, and opened the door, in order to call the gay youth back, and question him farther. Bartholo the dwarf was seated in the ante-room, together with another attendant; and St. Real bade him instantly follow the page, and bring him back. The dwarf stared for a moment, as if in astonishment at the command; and then replied, that he knew not where to find Leonard, for that he had seen him enter the room from which the young lord had just come, but had not seen him return. The other attendant was in the same story, and St. Real caused the boy to be sought for in vain.

The next morning, however, a greater defection was found amongst his followers, which satisfactorily accounted to St. Real for the magical disappearance of his page on the preceding night. The dwarf Bartholo, and three of his ordinary attendants, were nowhere to be heard of; but, by this time, the tampering of the Leaguers with every class of persons in the royal camp was so great and notorious, that St. Real was not at all surprised to find that five of his followers had been induced to quit his service. The loss of Leonard de Monte, however, he felt more than he could have anticipated from the short time the youth had been in his service, and from the slightness of the duties required at his hands; but, from the first moment he had seen him, the young lord of St. Real had conceived an interest in his page which every hour had increased. During his first deep sorrow for the loss of his father, he had found the boy's attentions so soothing and well judged, his sympathy apparently so deep and true, his few words of consolation so mingling together sense and feeling, that he felt gratitude towards him as well as regard; but there was something more than all this. With all the boy's occasional boldness and daring, there was blended a softness and a gentleness, which, together with the apparent weakness of his slight frame, and a few traits of timidity, approaching to cowardice, rendered him an object of that tender care which always endears those in whose behalf it is exercised. Thus, when St. Real found that the youth had really left him, though he felt some slight degree of anger at a desertion which he was conscious he had not deserved, he experienced no small desire to know the former, and guide the future fate of Leonard de Monte.

Events, however, calling for frequent and vigorous exertion, were multiplying so rapidly round his path, that he had but little time to give to matters of more remote interest. He occasionally thought of the youth, it is true, but more often grieved over the conduct of his cousin, and never ceased to ponder, with bitterness of heart, on the fate of Eugenie de Menancourt, and on his own feelings towards her. But still every hour brought some claim upon his attention of a different kind; and in the retreat of the royal army, which began two days after his page had left him, he had scarcely time for any other sensations than the anxiety and foresight attendant upon withdrawing a small and ill-supplied body of men from the presence of a powerful adversary.

It was in the midst of the arrangements incident to such a retreat, that, at the first halting place on the march, Monsieur de Sancy came into the small room in which St. Real was seated at Mantes, exclaiming--"I have news for you, Monsieur de St. Real! Your cousin has already secured the recompense at which he aimed in quitting us. He was married last night to Mademoiselle de Menancourt, the rich heiress of Maine. I have it from one who was in Paris at the time."

St. Real made no reply; but he turned so deadly pale, that De Sancy could not but observe that something had gone amiss, and instantly strove to turn the conversation into another channel.

CHAPTER XXII

It was toward that hour in the evening, at which the rays of twilight that linger behind the rest of the lustrous retinue of day are called away from the sky, and our hemisphere is given over to the absolute rule of night--it was at that hour, too, which is more important, when the joyous denizens of the gay capital of France, after having sunned themselves through the long afternoon of a summer's day in the gardens and highways, were in those times wont to retire each to his individual home, to enjoy such dainties as the bounty of nature and the skill of his cook had prepared for the last meal of the evening. It was about nine o'clock, then, on a night in August, when, the streets of Paris being nearly deserted by every one else, a strong troop of horsemen assembled in the little square, nearly opposite to the dwelling of Eugenie de Menancourt.

The gentleman who was at their head, springing to the ground, advanced to the door; and after asking a few questions of one of the servants, entered the court. Shortly afterwards the carriage of Madame de Montpensier rolled heavily up; and that fair dame herself, with one or two ladies in her train, descended therefrom and mounted the great staircase. Then, after a pause of five minutes, the Duke of Mayenne appeared on horseback, with his habiliments somewhat dusty, as if unchanged since his return from some long expedition, and accompanied by a numerous train of officers and attendants. Dismounting from his horse, the Duke dismissed at once the principal part of his suite; only retaining two or three of the inferior attendants who remained below at the gate, while he himself, with a slow and seemingly unwilling step, entered the house.

The servant who marshalled the Duke on his way to the saloon did not seem to look upon him with the best-satisfied countenance in the world; and the faces of the three or four attendants who had been permitted to remain with the young heiress of Menancourt after their old lord's death, and who now appeared in the lobbies and ante-chambers, seemed full not only of grief, but of a sort of sullen determination, which, had their numbers been greater, might have broken out at once in a more serious manner.

Mayenne, however, marked them not, but mounted the stairs and entered the saloon; and certainly, if his heart revolted at the part he was about to act, the scene which now presented itself to his eyes was not calculated to reconcile him to the proceeding.

Standing at one of the farther windows, and looking out into the dark street, where he certainly could see nothing to engage his attention, was the Count d'Aubin, while seated at a table, on which stood two or three lighted tapers, was the unhappy Eugenie de Menancourt. Her dress was still deep mourning; and her eyes gave evident tokens of having shed late and bitter tears: but she was now calm; and fixing her gaze upon vacancy, seemed totally inattentive to the words which Madame de Montpensier and her ladies, who stood round her, were pouring upon her dull unheeding ear.

"We cannot persuade her to change her dress, Charles," said the Duchess, pointing to the mourning in which Eugenie was clothed.

"Never mind, never mind!" replied the Prince, impatiently; "why tease her more than necessary? Let her wear what dress she will!"

"Nay, Charles, but it is ominous," cried the Duchess; "pray speak to her about it."

"Mademoiselle de Menancourt," said Mayenne, in a grave but not unkind tone, "let me persuade you to change this garb, if it be but for this night. It is unusual and ungracious to go to the marriage altar in the robe of mourning, as if you were following some friend to the grave."

Eugenie had started at his voice, and now looking up she replied, "Were I going willingly to the marriage altar, my Lord Duke, I would change my garb; but what robe, but the robe of mourning, would you have me wear, when you are about to drag me to a fate, in comparison with which the grave itself were happiness. But, my Lord, you mistake me. If, as I am told, marriage must depend upon consent, and that none other is legal, my consent shall never be given to a union with the Count d'Aubin."

"I am sorry to say, Madame," replied Mayenne, "that imperative motives of state necessity compel me--"

Mayenne was suddenly interrupted; for, unperceived by himself, the few servants and retainers of the old Count de Menancourt, who had, as we have said, been suffered to remain with their young mistress, had glided into the room one after the other, and stood ranged across the door; and while the Duke was speaking, the principal officer of the unhappy girl's household, indignant at the oppression exercised towards the daughter of his beloved lord, strode forward and boldly confronted Mayenne, as if he had been his equal. "My Lord Duke," he said, "we will have none of this! Our young lady shall be free to give her hand to whom she likes; and if you drag her to the altar against her will, it shall be over our dead bodies!

Nay, frown not on me, Count d'Aubin. I have seen more stricken fields than you are years of age; and a great man when he is doing a wicked thing is less than a little one. But all I have to say is, that though we be but few, we will die sooner than see our lady ill-used. Stop him in the way, Martin," he continued, speaking to his companions as he perceived the Count d'Aubin striding towards the door. "We have them here; but two against us seven; and though, doubtless, we shall be hanged for it after, we can, by one means, make sure that Mademoiselle shall never be forced to marry a Count d'Aubin!"

Rage and fury had evidently taken possession of D'Aubin; but Mayenne, on the contrary, listened calmly and tranquilly, with a slight smile curling his lip, till the man had done speaking; then, pointing to the window, he said, "Do me the favour, Monsieur d'Aubin, to call up the guard. By the window, by the window, D'Aubin!"

"Lock the door, Martin," exclaimed the old attendant, as a comment upon Mayenne's words; "we can settle the matter here before the guard comes. Out with your swords, my men, and upon them!"

But Eugenie interposed: "No, no! my friends," she cried, rising; "no, no! blood shall never be spilt on my account. Quit the room, I beseech, I command you, and let them have their will, however iniquitous that will may be. Only remember, that whatever may be said, or whatever may be done, I do to the last protest, that I do not, and that I will not, wed the Count d'Aubin; and though they may drag me to the altar, I am not, and never shall consider myself, his wife:--leave me, I beseech you," she added, seeing some hesitation on the part of her attendants; "leave me, if you would not increase my sorrow," and sinking down into her chair, she burst once more into a flood of tears; while the attendants, still muttering and eyeing Mayenne and his companion with somewhat doubtful glances, slowly and sullenly quitted the apartment.

"Really, Monsieur d'Aubin," said Mayenne, in a low voice, "this should not go forward!"

"Your promise, my Lord Duke," replied D'Aubin, drily.

"Well, well," said Mayenne, shrugging his shoulders; and then producing a roll of parchment, he laid it on the table before Eugenie de Menancourt, whose weeping eyes were still covered with her hands, and said, "Mademoiselle de Menancourt, I am compelled by circumstances, much against my inclination, to request your signature to this contract of marriage between yourself and the Count d'Aubin."

"Never!" answered Eugenie, distinctly; "never!"

Mayenne looked towards the Count d'Aubin, who said, in a low and hurried tone, "Never mind the contract, my Lord! let us get over the ceremony in the chapel. That will be sufficient. Marriage is a sacrament, you know, and that once past, it cannot be shaken off."

Mayenne paused for a moment, as if scarcely able to master the reluctance which struggled in his bosom against the fulfilment of his promise to the Count d'Aubin. "Where is Father Herbert?" he asked at last; "Catherine, did you not bring him with you?"

"He is waiting us in the chapel by this time," replied Madame de Montpensier: "some one gave him a note just as we were in the court, and he said he would follow instantly, and join us below."

"Send down and see, Monsieur le Comte," said Mayenne: "you had better call up some of the attendants, by means of that window," he added, "for we may be troubled by these pugnacious peasants again; and, indeed, I must take care that they be looked to till this business be blown over and forgotten. You are well aware," he continued, in a low tone, speaking to D'Aubin, "that what we are doing is contrary to the law."

"I will take my share of the responsibility," replied the Count, sharply; "and for your part, my Lord, if you cannot manage a parliament which is wholly devoted to you, I am afraid you will never be able to manage a kingdom, which is more than one half devoted to another." Thus speaking, he approached the open window, and, in a few words, directed some of the persons below to come up; but almost instantly turned to Mayenne, saying, "I suppose that is your confessor just arrived--at least I hear some one inquiring for you in great haste apparently."

Almost as he spoke, the door opened, and the Chevalier d'Aumale entered the saloon, followed by a person, who was evidently to be distinguished as a priest, both by his tonsure and robe, but upon whom Mayenne and his sister gazed as a stranger. "I beg your highness's pardon for intruding," said Aumale; "but two things have occurred which called upon me to wave ceremony. After leaving you, I rode on direct to your hotel, where I found the whole world in confusion in consequence of that insolent villain, Bussy le Clerc, having caused your own confessor to be arrested by a party of his people within a hundred yards of your dwelling, upon the pretence of his favouring the Huguenots--your own confessor favouring the Huguenots!"

"I will hang that pitiful demagogue to one of the spouts in the chatelet before many weeks are over!" said Mayenne, sternly; "but why did you not follow and release the good father. Monsieur d'Aumale?" he continued.

"Because, just at that moment," answered the Chevalier, "this reverend gentleman trotted up on his mule, begging instant audience of you on urgent business from his highness the Prince of Parma."

"Indeed! indeed!" exclaimed Mayenne; "what is your business with me, reverend sir? I can but ill attend to it at this moment, unless it be important indeed."

"My business is to deliver that despatch, my son," replied the priest, placing in the hands of the Duke a sealed paper, which he instantly tore open and read.

"Most warlike and joyful news, by a most peaceful messenger!" exclaimed Mayenne. "Spain sends us a thousand men, Aumale, within three days! Most joyful news, indeed! and not the less acceptable from being conveyed to us by a minister of our holy religion."

"Glad am I to hear you say so, my noble and princely son," answered the priest; "for his Highness of Parma, when he over persuaded me to quit my little flock at Houdaincourt, because he fancied a cassoc would pass more safely with the tidings than a buff belt, did mention something about a vacant stall in the cathedral church of Cambray, and the great love and reverence of our father, the Bishop, for your Highness, and all your illustrious family."

"Well, well, your good service, father, in the cause of the faith shall not go without reward," replied Mayenne; "but you are just come in time to do us another good service. Have you any objection to read the marriage service here, and win a rich benefice for your pains?"

Eugenie had heard everything that passed, as if in a troubled dream; and when the Chevalier d'Aumale had related the arrest of the confessor, a momentary hope of reprieve had crossed her mind. The last words of Mayenne, however, and the ready assent of the priest, instantly extinguished it. The next moment it revived again, as she heard the somewhat strangely chosen missive of the Prince of Parma observe, "But the lady seems to be weeping! what is the cause of that?" and a vague purpose of beseeching him not to join in the oppression which was exercised towards her entered her thoughts. Ere she could execute such a design, however, Mayenne, in a low voice, directed the Count d'Aubin to take the priest out of the room, and explain to him, as he thought best, the circumstances of the case, promising him what reward he judged right to stop all troublesome inquiries.

As the door opened and closed, Eugenie looked fearfully around; and feeling that the last hope of moving any one to pity lay in the temporary absence of him whom she regarded as her most determined persecutor, she rose, intending to cast herself at the knees of Mayenne, and to beseech him, by all that was noble and chivalrous in his nature, to become her protector against the violence of others, rather than to join in oppressing her himself. During the last two days, however, she had undergone more mental suffering than her corporeal frame could endure. The efforts of the last few minutes had poured the drops of overflowing into the cup; and though by great exertion she staggered to the spot, where Mayenne remained standing, after speaking to the Count d'Aubin, she could not utter a word, but fell fainting at his feet. At the same moment D'Aubin returned; and there was a slight interval of confusion and uncertainty, some calling for water and essences, some proposing to bear her to her own apartment. But D'Aubin interfered. "Let us seize the present moment," he said, "to carry her to the chapel, where we can find means of restoring animation. One great difficulty will then be got over, and we can proceed with the ceremony at once."

"I have often heard," said Madame de Montpensier, "that yours is a determined nature, Monsieur d'Aubin, but I did not know how determined till to-night."

Without noticing the sneer by any reply, D'Aubin raised the senseless form of Eugenie de Menancourt in his arms, and followed by the rest, bore her down one flight of stairs to the chapel, which, as usual in many of the principal hotels of Paris at that time, was attached to the dwelling, and independent of the parochial clergy. During his short absence, the Count had taken care that his own followers and those of Mayenne should clear that part of the house of the attendants of the unhappy object of his persecution, so that, by the way, he met with neither opposition nor inquiry. The chapel was reached, and all was found prepared, with the priest standing at the altar.

The situation of Eugenie instantly called his attention, however, and he exclaimed, "I cannot go on till the lady has recovered."

"Nobody wishes you, sir priest," exclaimed D'Aubin, sharply. "Some one bring water; quick!"

This command was rendered unnecessary, however; for by this time Eugenie was beginning to regain that miserable consciousness of the evils that surrounded her, from which even temporary insensibility had been a relief. Madame de Montpensier raised her head; Mayenne, in broken and scarcely intelligible terms, endeavoured to speak a few words of comfort; and, being lifted up before the altar, the vain ceremony of her marriage with the Count d'Aubin was begun by the priest, in hurried and not very distinct tones.

Rallying all her powers for one last effort, Eugenie freed herself from the hands of those who supported her, and once more distinctly and firmly protested her dissent from the idle rite which they were performing. Again overpowered, however, she sank upon her knees, the priest went on, and ere she well knew what past, the fatal ring was upon her finger.

Snatching it off instantly, however, she cast it down upon the floor of the chapel, and again fell back fainting into the arms of Madame de Montpensier.

"See her carried back to her own apartments, poor girl!" cried Mayenne; "and do you, Catherine, stay with her awhile, and comfort her."

"Let us leave her with her own people, Charles," answered Madame de Montpensier, comprehending better than her brother the nature of the only solace that one in the situation of Eugenie de Menancourt could receive. "We are all comparatively strangers to her; and the best comfort in time of sorrow, to a woman's heart at least, is some familiar and long-remembered face. Will you call some of her own people, Monsieur le Comte d'Aubin?"

It was not, perhaps, from any unnatural hardness of heart that D'Aubin was mortified by the tone of commiseration in which both Mayenne and his sister spoke of Eugenie de Menancourt; but he felt, and could not help feeling, that their pity for the object of his persecution was a direct condemnation of himself. He believed also, and perhaps not erroneously, that Madame de Montpensier, on various accounts, experienced a degree of pleasure in rendering every particular of the scene, in which he was so principal an actor, as painful to him as possible; but he was a great deal too deeply skilled in the world's ways not to struggle to prevent those feelings and suspicions from appearing, either in an angry word, or in any attempt to make light of the sorrows he had caused. Sending for some of Eugenie's attendants, therefore, he gave her over into their hands; directing them, in a grave and earnest tone, and with the air of one who now had a right to command, to bear her up to her usual apartments slowly and gently, and use instant means to recall her to consciousness. "Perhaps, madame," he added, turning to the Duchess, "you would at least watch the applications of remedies to promote her recovery, as these good people may be more affectionate than skilful."

"I will do so with pleasure, Monsieur le Comte," replied Madame de Montpensier; "but I will retire as soon as I perceive that animation is returning; for I am sure the sight of any one who has mingled in the horrible scenes through which the unhappy girl has just passed will, for a long fill her with terror and abhorrence."

D'Aubin bit his lip, but made no reply; and Madame de Montpensier in silence followed the attendants, who bore the insensible form of their young mistress out of the chapel.

"And now, Monsieur le Comte," said Mayenne, "it must be time, I think, for you to put your foot in the stirrup, and ride to make those preparations which we spoke of yesterday."

"A few moments more, my good lord," replied D'Aubin, with a cynical smile. "Your Highness has so scrupulously fulfilled your part of the engagement, that you need be under no fear lest I should fail in mine. But ere I go, I must ask this worthy priest to give me a regular certification of my marriage with Eugenie de Menancourt, otherwise the retainers of her house may refuse to acknowledge the authority which it is so necessary for the interests of your Highness that I should be fully enabled to exercise."

"You are right," replied Mayenne, calmly. "Be so good, reverend father, to draw up the document required. The names are, Philip Count d'Aubin, and Eugenie Lady of Menancourt and of Beaumont en Maine."

In the little room which answered the purpose of a sacristy, materials for writing were soon procured, and the priest sat down to prepare the certification which was to place D'Aubin in possession of the property he had so unjustly acquired.

"You are somewhat slow, sir priest," said the haughty noble, perceiving that every now and then he paused, and seemed to think of what he should say next; "you are somewhat slow, as if you had never drawn a certificate before."

"I generally do leave it to the sacristan," replied the priest, mildly: "but that was not what made me hesitate, my son. I pondered whether I should insert that the marriage was against the lady's will;" and a sly, though half-suppressed smile played about his lips, and put D'Aubin to silence.

Mayenne however replied: "No, no, good father," he said; "make it as brief and as simple as possible. We need no comments."

The priest accordingly concluded his task; and D'Aubin taking the certificate, glanced his eye hastily over its contents, and then turning to Mayenne, he said, "Now, my lord, I make all speed to Maine, leaving my bride in your hands, and trusting to find on my return, that during my absence, you have used more eloquence in my favour, than you have thought fit to do to-night in my presence."

"I will do all that I can, Monsieur d'Aubin," replied Mayenne, with calm dignity, "to efface from her mind the impression which this night must have left, to overcome objections founded on former conduct, of which I know nothing; and to reconcile her to her fate, which she does not at all appear to consider the less bitter because it is inevitable."

Both the Count d'Aubin and the Duke of Mayenne felt that, under existing circumstances, the fewer words that passed between them the less was likely to be the diminution of their friendship. Each had in a considerable degree a hold over the other; for D'Aubin, possessing an extended right of command over the lands of Eugenie de Menancourt, was too powerful to be alienated from the League; and yet, on the other hand, retaining possession of the person of Eugenie de Menancourt, Mayenne held D'Aubin to his faction, by a bond that it would have been dangerous for him to break. D'Aubin, therefore, curbed the anger which during the whole evening had been gathering in his bosom, and merely bowing in reply to the last words of the Duke, quitted the chapel, mounted his horse, and galloped off, followed by his attendants.

"And now, my good father," said Mayenne, "return with me to the Hotel de Guise, and we will speak over this letter from the Prince of Parma, and his promise regarding the stall in Cambray."

"May it please your Highness," replied the priest, "as you are on horseback and I am on foot--for I left my mule at the door of your hotel--I will follow you with all speed, if you will leave some one to show me the way, for I cannot boast much acquaintance with the topography of this vast and labyrinth-like city."

"Well, well, so be it," replied Mayenne. "But now, I think of it, my sister, the Duchess of Montpensier--that lady, who was here just now," he added, "will bring you with her in her coach. It will hold ten with ease, and she has but four ladies with her. Wait here, and I will tell some of the attendants to let you know when she comes down."

The priest bowed his head, and Mayenne departing, left a message for his sister, and rode back to the Hotel do Guise. Not long after the carriage of Madame de Montpensier rolled into the court, and the Duchess instantly sought her brother's cabinet.

"One of your grooms told me, Charles," she said, "that I was to bring the priest with me."

"Certainly," replied the Duke. "Have you not done so?"

"No," she answered, "I have not, because I could not find him. We sought everywhere, in the chapel and the sacristy, and over all the lower part of the house; but he had evidently gone away, and left the door of the chapel open behind him."

"The foolish man has mistaken me, then," said Mayenne; "but it matters not. He will not be long in finding me out, for he has not got his reward for either of the two services he has rendered to-night; and if I may judge by his face, he is not a man to perform either the one or the other for the love of God. So we shall hear of him ere half an hour be over, depend upon it." And he turned the conversation to the distressing scene in which he had so unwillingly played a part.

In regard to the priest, however, Mayenne was mistaken. The night passed over without his appearance; and the following morning, as the Duke was making inquiries concerning him, he was interrupted by news of a different nature, in regard to which we must give some previous explanation.

CHAPTER XXIII

When Eugenie de Menancourt, slowly and painfully, returned to consciousness of life and sorrow, she found herself in the saloon in which she usually sat, and in the arms of her own women. Gazing fearfully around, she sought to discover where the forms of those who so lately surrounded her were now concealed; and as she satisfied herself that there was no one present but her own attendants, her bewildered imagination almost led her to hope, that the terrible scenes she had gone through were nothing but the phantasms of some horrible dream. Gradually, however, memory recalled every circumstance with too painful a degree of accuracy to admit of her indulging any longer in such a happy delusion; and now, unrestrained by the presence of any but those whom she knew and loved, she gave way to all the bitter sorrow that swelled her heart, and burst into a long and silent flood of tears. The tears seemed to relieve her; but the words which one of her young attendants whispered in her ear tended more than all to afford consolation, and to revive almost extinguished hope.

"Do not weep so bitterly, lady, do not weep so bitterly," said the girl. "He is gone, and may not return for months!"

"Who is gone?" exclaimed Eugenie, starting up, and hurriedly wiping the tears from her eyes, that she might gaze the more intently upon the speaker. "Who is gone? Who may not return for months?"

"The Count d'Aubin, lady," replied the girl. "Madame de Montpensier bade me tell you so, and gave me this note to be delivered to you, when you were well enough to read it."

"Give it to me--give it to me now," cried Eugenie; and tearing it open, she held it to the light, gazing with eager eyes upon the contents. It was very brief, but almost every word spoke comfort, for they went to inform her that the Count d'Aubin, on business of importance, had been obliged to set off for Maine; that the period of his return was not decided, but that it certainly could not take place before the end of the month, while it might be delayed longer; and though the conclusion of the letter went to say, that both the Duke of Mayenne and Madame de Montpensier trusted that, ere the Count's return, Mademoiselle de Menancourt would have made up her mind to receive him as her husband, and to sign the formal contract of marriage, yet the intelligence of his absence was a reprieve; and imagination fondly clinging to the uncertainty of the future, at once renewed hope in her bosom.

With hope came back the spirit of exertion which had been crushed beneath despair. Dropping the note upon the table, as the lightning progress of thought ran on in an instant from one object to another, she clasped her hands, exclaiming, "Where, where! can Beatrice of Ferrara be? She must be ill, or she would have come to me, I am sure."

"Shall we send, and see, lady?" demanded one of the women.

"Yes, yes! do so," replied Eugenie, "and leave me alone for half an hour; I would fain think--I would fain consider what is best to be done! I am better, indeed I am better now," she added, seeing the women look at her with some hesitation. "Stay in the ante-room, and I will call, if I want you."

The women obeyed; and Eugenie, leaning on the table, covered her eyes with her hands, and remained endeavouring to reduce, to some definite and feasible plan, the vague hopes of relief which she had again conceived. But the effects of the agitation she had suffered still remained, and she found it impossible to fix her thoughts upon the future, so perseveringly did they wander back to the past.

In this state, she had continued about five or ten minutes, when the sound of creaking hinges made her raise her eyes. The door which led into the ante-room was shut, as well as that which gave egress, at once, upon the staircase; but on the other side of the room there was another door, which communicated with an unoccupied part of the house, looking into a back street which led away towards the Faubourg St. Antoine; and when Eugenie turned her eyes in that direction, she started up with surprise, and some degree of alarm, on perceiving it gently and slowly drawn back. Remembering, however, that her attendants were in the ante-room, she paused, to see what would be the result, suppressing the exclamation which had nearly burst from her lips.

The sight that the open door presented, when farther drawn back, was certainly one which in no degree diminished her surprise, but at the same time added nothing to her alarm; for the person who opened it was alone; nor was he one whose appearance was calculated to inspire terror. It was the figure of a youth, apparently not more than fifteen years of age, that now presented itself, carrying a lamp in one hand, and unclosing the door with the other. His dress was of the gay and splendid costume of the court of Henry III. and from under his high-crowned beaver, and its manifold ostrich feathers, the bright and glossy curls of his coal-black hair fell round as handsome a face as ever was beheld. A large cloak was wrapped about his arm, and riding-boots pushed down to the ankles, as was then customary, seemed to indicate that he either came from or was bound upon a journey; and as Eugenie gazed upon him, she concluded at once that he was some page attached to the Count d'Aubin, who, sent with some message or letter ere his lord's departure, had either by accident or design passed by that part of the dwelling which was for the time out of use. As soon as this conviction struck her, she rose to call in her women, but the youth held up his hand with a gesture which was easily interpreted into an entreaty to be silent; and Eugenie again paused, saying in a low tone, "What do you seek here, sir? Do not advance, or I must call my servants!"

The youth, however, did still advance, but with an air of deprecation and gentleness, that took away all fear; and when, within a step, he placed the lamp on the table, and bent one knee to the ground, Eugenie gazed upon him with doubt and astonishment; but a confused and uncertain hope began to take possession of her mind, as the boy raised her hand to his lips, and then, as he glided his arms round her waist, and, with the jetty curls of his hair mingling with her light-brown locks, kissed her tenderly on either cheek, the fair girl's face dropped upon her new companion's shoulder, and with a flood of tears she exclaimed, "Oh! Beatrice, Beatrice! why did you not come sooner?"

"I did come sooner," replied Beatrice of Ferrara--or Leonard de Monte, as the reader will,--"I did come sooner, my dear Eugenie. I did come sooner! and have been in these apartments all the evening, directing everything that has passed in all this sad scene, though those who were actors therein knew nothing of the prompter. I could not come to console you, my Eugenie, nor to give you one word of comfort and assurance, lest I should be discovered by all the spies and messengers who were going to and fro about this house during the whole of yesterday; but I arranged the only means of saving you, and, making my way into the house by the back street, watched till I saw my plan executed, and then came to bear you away to a place of greater security."

"But, alas, alas! your plan has failed," replied Eugenie. "The fatal ring has been upon my finger."

"Fear not! fear not!" replied Beatrice, with a smile. "That ring binds you to nothing, Eugenie. Such a marriage is lawful in no land under the sun; and I took care that there should be plenty of witnesses to prove, hereafter, that your consent was refused to the last."

"I know," replied Eugenie, "I know that such a marriage cannot be legal; and I would sooner die than ever render it so. But still, Beatrice, still a ceremony has taken place; and though I will not be his wife, yet I can never, never feel myself free again!"

"Yes, yes, you can," replied Beatrice, with one of her gay smiles; "yes, you can be free as ever to give this fair hand to any one in the wide world you choose."

Eugenie shook her head; but Beatrice drew her arms closer around her, saying, "Well, well, you little infidel, if you will not believe me without farther proof, hear the secret of it all--but I dare not speak it aloud, lest the very spirits of the air should catch it, ere the poor man get back to the Huguenot camp; for they would burn him alive in the Place de Greve, if they caught him; and the two thousand pistoles which bribed him to the adventure would be but cold comfort in the midst of the flames;" and putting her lips close to Eugenie's ear, she whispered one or two words in a tone so low, that Mademoiselle de Menancourt herself might rather be said to divine their meaning than to hear them distinctly. That she understood them fully, however, was evident; for the light of joy instantly broke over her countenance; and clasping her hands together, while she raised her eyes towards heaven, she exclaimed, "Then I am saved indeed!"

At that moment, the door from the ante-room suddenly opened, and Beatrice started up from the position in which she had remained ever since her first entrance into the room, while Eugenie turned a terrified glance towards the door. It was only one of her women, however, who entered; and, contrary to her mistress's expectations, she evinced no surprise at the sight of Beatrice of Ferrara, disguised in the manner we have described.

"She knows it all, Eugenie," said Beatrice, "for it was by her means I obtained admission."

"I suppose, madam," said the waiting-woman, with a smile, "that I need scarcely tell you that Jean Baptiste has returned, with the news that Mademoiselle de Ferrara is still absent from home, and is not expected for many days."

"But why did you not tell me, Caroline," demanded Eugenie, "that she was here? It would have saved me many a miserable moment. If I had known that she was in this house, I should never have lost hope that all would go right."

"But it was impossible to tell you, lady," replied the waiting-woman; "for the Duchess de Montpensier sent us all away; and after she was gone, I could not say what I knew, because your other women were with you."

"Well, well," said Beatrice, "we have matters of more importance to think of now, Eugenie: we will keep all explanations for an aftertime, when you and I, in some little cottage, far away from these scenes of strife, want conversation to pass away the hours till the storm has worked itself out, and the sky is once more clear. And now, sweet sister of my heart, call up all your courage, summon all your resolution, for we must lose no time, but make the best of our way out of this hateful city. Ere to-morrow morning be two hours' old, Mayenne will have discovered that he has been cheated; and though Philip d'Aubin be by that time beyond recall, his Highness the lieutenant-general, and the Holy League, even if they find not out all the windings of our plot, will take such measures for your security, that all after efforts will be vain."

"Oh! I will do anything! I will fly anywhere!" replied Eugenie. "I have courage, I have resolution for any effort. The worst that can befall me is death; and I would rather die a thousand times than be the bride of Philip d'Aubin."

Beatrice smiled, half sorrowfully, half playfully. "He is not reputed, my fair Eugenie," she said, "to be so very hateful, as you seem to think."

Eugenie blushed deeply, pained to believe that her undisguised abhorrence of the Count d'Aubin might have wounded the feelings of one whom she loved so much as Beatrice of Ferrara--one who, she well knew, was not indifferent to the man whom she herself so deeply detested. "I mean not to say that he is so hateful in himself, Beatrice," she replied; "but has not he given me good reason to hate him? Perhaps I might have loved him, too, if--"

"If you had not loved another," interrupted Beatrice, with a smile. "But we have not time for all that either," she added; "and will talk of it, too, another day. At this moment we have other things on hand. You, my good Caroline, bring your mistress some refreshments quickly; but take care that no one else enters while you are gone."

"Indeed, Beatrice, I need no refreshment," said Eugenie, rising. "Joy at my deliverance, and hope for the future, will give me strength and support to go any length of way; and I am ready, quite ready, to set out directly."

Beatrice smiled. "I will command to-day," she said; "Caroline, do as I bid you! Alas, my poor Eugenie, you have much to do, ere you can set out, for the danger lies at our threshold; and when once I have led you twenty yards in safety from the door of this house, I shall think the battle half won at least."

"What, then, is it that you fear?" demanded Eugenie, eagerly.

"Delay, above all things!" answered Beatrice; "for though, I trust, our plot has been too well laid to be discovered immediately, yet there is always danger where there is anything concealed. First, then, Eugenie, you must change your dress, and take such a one as will most completely disguise you, should you be sought for more speedily than we suppose."

"I know not where to find any dress but my own," replied Eugenie. "What dress would you have me to take, Beatrice?--Though, now I think of it," she added suddenly; "one of my maids has her own country costume with her,--a white petticoat, and a red open gown above it, with----"

"Impossible! impossible!" exclaimed Beatrice. "It would betray you at once. Remember, my dear Eugenie, that I go with you; and though in the streets of Paris they might but think that the gay page was deceiving the country girl with a tale of love, that would not do beyond the gates. I once thought of a nun's dress for you, which would do very well in the city also; but one must care for other things than those of the mere present; and recollect that if I, dressed as a bold youth, and you, dressed as a pretty nun, were seen getting into either coach or litter together, we should have the ecclesiastical officers at our heels. No, no, Eugenie! we must have some dress for you which will neither attract attention in the city, nor beyond the walls; which will tell its own tale, and, by sparing all inquiries, conceal our sex and character without an effort."

"Oh, not a man's dress!" exclaimed Eugenie, imploringly.

"None other, indeed!" answered Beatrice, smiling; "but knowing the timid shyness of that heart which pretends to be so bold, I have chosen one for you, Eugenie, which will hide your person as effectually as the fullest robe that ever woman wore, which will accord with a smooth cheek and a demure look, and which will yet admit of your travelling in company with a bold page. Come and see! for I have brought it here along with me."

Thus saying, Beatrice of Ferrara took her hand, and led her through the same passage by which she herself had entered, to a room wherein she had lain concealed during the time that the other apartments were occupied by the party assembled for that sad bridal. There, on one of the old oaken chairs, lay the robes of a young abbé in complete costume; not such as that costume appeared in after years, when the gradual blending of the dress of different orders permitted the aspirants to ecclesiastical stations to assume habiliments only distinguished from those of the laity by colour; but full, ample, and flowing, and offering to Eugenie that modest concealment for her fair form, to which even she, under existing circumstances, could not object. Deeply sensible of the kind and delicate appreciation of all her feelings, which Beatrice--whose wilder and more daring nature scoffed at such scruples in her own instance--had displayed in this choice of her disguise, Eugenie was eagerly thanking her for all her consideration; but her friend cut her short, to hasten her new and unusual toilet, taking care, however, as indeed she had hitherto done, to avoid, even by any eager hurry, alarming her more timid companion in the outset of their perilous undertaking.

The dress, chosen by an experienced eye, fitted admirably in every respect, with the exception of the shoes, which were far too large for Eugenie's small feet. The robe, however, was sufficiently long to conceal this defect, in a great degree; and, when all was complete, Beatrice gazed over the changed appearance of her fair friend with a smile of gay satisfaction.

"Well, Eugenie," she exclaimed, "certainly you are the prettiest little abbé that ever was seen; but, nevertheless, you will do admirably. Only remember not to uncover your head, for your ringlets will betray you. See how I manage mine! I can pull off my hat without fear; cannot you do the same? Only cut off those two lower curls at the side; they will grow again in a month."

"I will cut them off altogether, with all my heart," answered Eugenie. But her friend assured her that such a sacrifice of her bright locks was not necessary; and showing her how she herself contrived to conceal in one mass her own profusion of dark hair, she soon put that of Mademoiselle de Menancourt into the same form, but still bade her uncover her head as little as possible, lest the want of all tonsure should call attention, and betray her disguise.

"And now, Eugenie, take some refreshment," said Beatrice; "meat to give you strength,--for you may have far to walk ere morning--and wine to give you courage; for, after all, I doubt the resolution of that little heart; and depend upon it, that the only sure means of carrying through a great undertaking is to begin boldly, and go on without stopping. But I hear your girl, Caroline, in the other room; she had better bring the refreshments in here, lest we should be interrupted."

Beatrice, accordingly, called the maid in; and not small was the girl's astonishment to behold the transformation that had taken place in the person of her mistress during her short absence. Beatrice, however, suffered no exclamations; and while Eugenie, whose appetite had not been increased by all the events of the night, took what refreshment she could, her friend proceeded to give directions to the *suivante* concerning the course that was to be pursued after her mistress's departure.

"In case any one returns to the house to-night," she said, "seeking the priest, all you have to reply is, that you know nothing about him, and that your mistress is in her own chamber in deep grief. I do not think, however, that any one will come; and, in that case, by eight o'clock to-morrow--for

Mayenne does not rise before--go yourself to Madame de Montpensier, and with a grave and serious face ask to see your mistress, adding, before she can answer you that you have brought her such apparel as she may stand in need of for the morning. Mind, you must not move a muscle of your face! She will instantly be all astonishment, and ask if you are mad; then tell her that, about this hour to-night, a gay page and a young abbé came here saying, that they brought a letter from her Highness, and took your mistress away with them, as if to the Hotel de Guise, to which place you were directed to bring various things the next morning. Will not that do Eugenie?" she continued, turning to her friend, "and am I not fit to be a general of reitters?"

Eugenie smiled, but replied, "Suppose they do not believe her, Beatrice, and send to examine the other servants?"

"Oh! I am prepared for all that," replied Beatrice. "As soon as ever we are gone, send the women to bed, good Caroline, and dispatch the greater part of the men upon different errands: you can direct two of them to my house, bidding them wait till my return. One you can send to the Count d'Aubin's, to inquire whether he has really set out for Maine; and while these are gone, explain yourself to those whom you can best trust amongst the others, telling them simply, that if any inquiries are made, they have merely to keep to the same story about the abbé and the page which you are going to tell."

"But suppose we are asked to describe the abbé and the page, lady, what are we to do then?" demanded the woman.

"Why, describe them, to be sure," replied Beatrice. "Here we are, take an exact picture of us. You cannot do better; and if you say, that your mistress went away in our company, you will but say the truth. Now I bethink me, you may as well add, that you think you have seen the page somewhere before, and rather believe that he is in the service of the Count d'Aubin-- which is true too, Eugenie, when all things are wisely considered, though we are serving him against his will. But now, my pretty abbé--I shall call you Eugene for the future--we must lose no more time. Run down, Caroline, and see that the door at the foot of the back stairs is open, and give a glance round the court-yard, to make sure that it is clear."

The girl, with a ready promptitude in man[oe]uvring, for which French *soubrettes* are not unjustly famed, required no farther explanations, having that internal consciousness of great resources of intrigue, which rendered her quite confident of being able to make up a new story, or to mend the old one for the occasion, in case anything in Beatrice's plan went wrong. Tripping away then through the unused apartments, to the back staircase that led out into the court, she descended to the bottom, and gently unclosing the door, to the extent of about a hand's breadth, closed it again as quietly, and returned to the two ladies with the unpleasant tidings, that all the male attendants belonging to the house were standing under the arch of the *porte-cochère*, apparently talking over the events of the evening.

"Get ye down then, Caroline, to the *maître de hôtel*," cried Beatrice; "bid him express your mistress's thanks to the honest fellows for their attachment; and tell him, in her name, to call them into some room, where their voices will not be heard by the spies of the League, and to give them each a bottle of the best Burgundy, to drink to their lady's health and deliverance, and confusion to her enemies and persecutors."

With a smile at the lady's readiness and resources, the *soubrette* ran off to obey; and in a few minutes returned with the better news, that all the men were safely housed, with bottles before them which would occupy them for some time. Beatrice then drew Eugenie's arm through her own, and led the way towards the staircase, followed by the *suivante*, for the purpose of closing the doors behind them.

Eugenie felt that her happiness for life was at stake; that she was taking the only means to save herself from oppression, persecution, and, in all probability, ultimate misery. She felt that the object was worth any exertion; that if ever she displayed energy, resolution, and courage, this was the moment in which they were all most needed: and yet it were vain to say, that her heart did not palpitate; that her knees did not shake; and that her trembling hand did not feel like a piece of ice, even in the midst of a hot and sultry night of August.

Beatrice perceived her agitation; and, though her own firm heart did not share in her friend's terrors, she felt for her deeply, and endeavoured to support her by every means in her power. "Fear not, dear Eugenie!" she said, "fear not! Be assured that ere I came hither, I took every means to ensure success; and that we shall not pass along two hundred yards of the way without finding some one stationed by me to aid and protect us in case of need. I have spared neither gold nor thought, Eugenie; and, in this world, gold, and thought, and courage, will do everything; so there wants nothing but the courage, my fair friend, and that you must try to have."

"I will! I will!" whispered Eugenie in return. "But, indeed, Beatrice, I cannot but find it terrible to go out thus alone into the streets of a strange, turbulent, vicious city, in the dress of a different sex, and with no one but another girl to guide and protect me!"

"Not terrible at all," replied Beatrice. "It is but what many a gay light heart would do for a jest, and many a base heart for a worse purpose. It is only on account of the great stake we are playing for, that you feel terrified, Eugenie; but that, on the contrary, should give you courage."

By this time they had reached the top of the back staircase, the narrowness of which obliged them to descend one by one. Beatrice, holding the lamp, led the way, and Eugenie followed. At the bottom of the stairs, the fair Italian, telling the maid who accompanied them that she must find her way back in the dark, blew out the light, and gently unclosed the door. The moment she did so, the summer air rushed in; and though it was as soft and warm as the breath of southern spring, it felt chill to Eugenie's cheek, while the rolling sound of carriage-wheels, in some distant street, made her shrink back upon the maid as if she were already detected. Beatrice glanced her eye quickly around the court, and seeing that it was vacant, took Eugenie's hand to lead her on. The maid, at the same time, feeling sure that her mistress would gain more courage as soon as all means of retreat were cut off, kissed her affectionately on either cheek, by way of leave-taking, and gently supported her forward till she was actually in the court, then suddenly closed the door; and Eugenie heard the lock turn within. For a moment her heart sunk; but making a great effort, and recalling the image of the Count d'Aubin, she hurried forward with Beatrice across the court to a small door which opened into the back street.

When one is in haste there is always some impediment. The door was locked, and though the key was in it, it fell out of Beatrice's hand as she attempted to turn it, and rattled on the pavement. Some moments passed ere it could be found again, during which time Eugenie's courage waned fast. At length, however, the key was recovered, and placed in the lock, but ere the door was opened, some one rang the bell at the front gate. Eugenie felt as if her fate was sealed, and clung to the doorway for support. Luckily, however, no servant loves to obey the summons of a bell; and Eugenie's attendants, happy in their Burgundy, resolved that the visitor should ring again. Ere that occurred, Beatrice, with a steady hand, had turned the lock, the door opened; and springing through after her friend, Eugenie de Menancourt stood in the streets of Paris.

CHAPTER XXIV

Taking Eugenie by the arm to give some support to her tottering frame, Beatrice hurried on, and they reached the end of the street in safety. As they were turning into another, however, a man who was walking slowly on the other side of the way paused to mark them in their advance towards him, and seemingly attracted by a certain degree of agitation as well as haste in their demeanour, crossed over and accosted them:--

"What now, my young rovers!" he exclaimed. "Whither away so fast? Some intrigue, I warrant!"

"What is it to you?" demanded Beatrice, turning towards him fiercely, while she still hurried on, holding up the trembling form of her timid friend. "If no one meddles with your intrigues, meddle you with no one's either."

"What is it to me!" cried the stranger. "Do you not perceive that I am the captain of the quarter? and I doubt you have been about some notorious evil, by your haste and this young lad's trembling;" and, as he spoke, he laid a somewhat rude grasp upon Eugenie's arm.

"By the blessed Union, and the holy catholic faith!" exclaimed Beatrice, in a tone that made the man start back, "if you hold his arm another moment, I will drive my dagger into you, twice as far as Saint Jacques Clement did the other day into the tyrant at St. Cloud;" and, without hesitation, she drew the weapon out of its sheath, and brought the gleaming blade so near the man's breast that he dropped Eugenie's arm, and laid his hand upon his sword.

Bursting into a loud laugh, Beatrice taunted him with his fright; and putting up her dagger, hurried on, diverting the stranger's attention by raillery, till at the corner of another street, Eugenie saw her raise her two fingers in the moonlight, and the next moment a man sprang out from a gateway on the dark side of the way; and running forward as fast as possible, as if intending to pass them, he rushed full against their undesired companion, and laid him prostrate in the gutter in the middle of the street. Then taking the first word of quarrel, he stopped and turned to abuse the fallen man for not getting out of his way, while Beatrice and her companion hurried on, and were soon at a distance from the scene of strife.

"Matthew managed that well!" exclaimed Beatrice, when she thought herself at a sufficient distance to pause and take breath; "I must promote that fellow to some better office for his skill."

"Then that was one of your own people?" said Eugenie, with her confidence in the success of their endeavour somewhat strengthened by every new proof of the foresight and precaution which her fair companion had used to ensure support. "But what if the captain of the quarter calls up the guard, and takes him into custody?"

"Captain of the quarter!" she exclaimed, with a laugh, "and did you believe that? Do you not know that, in these times, every one assumes what name he pleases? Captain of the quarter, indeed! Rather some *filou* or some *escroc*, who seeing two youths fresh from an idle scrape, as he thought, fancied he could lay a tribute on their purse as the price of his silence and departure."

Still hurrying on, Beatrice of Ferrara led the way through a number of streets towards the gates of the city; but, warned by their late adventure, she no longer proceeded at such a rapid pace. Assuming, on the contrary, somewhat of a swagger in her air, yet still holding Eugenie firm by the arm, she walked along, displaying no bad imitation of the vastly important demeanour of some noble page, who, just liberated from his mother's careful eye, overlays the inexperienced timidity of youth with affected self-confidence.

More than once quitting the quieter and less frequented streets, Beatrice was obliged to lead the way into others, through which the human tide that rarely ebbs entirely in the city of Paris, was still flowing on, though the hour was approaching to midnight. Eugenie's heart beat quick at every fresh group that they encountered, and many a pang crossed her bosom, and many an unseen blush passed over her cheek, at some of the scenes that she thus for the first time witnessed in the streets of the metropolis. Twice as they walked along, Beatrice paused for a moment to speak a single word to persons who seemed to be common passengers, and Eugenie, whose timid glance was frequently cast behind, remarked that the men to whom her companion spoke turned and followed at the distance of a few paces. At length, as they approached the extremity of the Faubourg St. Germain, Beatrice whispered in her ear, "It will be impossible to pass the gates at this hour of the night, and, therefore, we must take shelter till the morning begins to dawn in a place of refuge which I have prepared."

Eugenie expressed her willingness to do anything her companion thought fit; and in a few moments Beatrice stopped opposite to a small house in the suburb, and pushing the door which was open, led the way in. All was darkness within; and Eugenie, though she had the most perfect confidence in her friend, felt her terror increased at the aspect of the place. Taking her hand, however, Beatrice led her on, up a narrow staircase, and through a still narrower passage, to a door at which she knocked for admittance. It was instantly opened, and the next moment Eugenie found herself in a neat, plainly furnished room, where two of Beatrice's women, whom she had frequently seen before, stood ready to receive them. The moment they had entered, Beatrice cast her arms round her; and kissing her tenderly, exclaimed, "Now, my sweet friend, I trust we are safe; to-morrow morning, I think, we shall be able to pass the gates without obstruction, and the rest of our expedition will be easy."

"Thank God!" cried Eugenie, sinking down into her seat. "Thank God! and next to him, Beatrice, I have to thank you!"

"Spare your thanks to me, Eugenie," cried her companion, "till we have reached the end of our journey. I will then try to hear them with patience. But now, I dare say, you will think it strange that I have not taken you to my own house, instead of bringing you here. But I have three sufficient reasons for not doing so. First, because on many accounts they might suspect you of flying to me; secondly, because we are here much nearer to the gate, and, thirdly, for a reason, Eugenie, that you would scarcely suspect, which is, that I did not choose any of the gossiping fraternity should say they had seen two gay-looking youths enter the house of Beatrice of Ferrara at night, and remain there till morning shone. So you see, Eugenie, that I, even I, am not without fears of scandal; I who have not scrupled, when my purpose served, to go disguised as I am now, and live disguised in the house of a strange man. Ay, Eugenie I do not look so horrified, for I was as safe there as in my own chamber. I was surrounded by own attendants, whom I had contrived by one means or another to force into his service. He was too simple and unsuspicious to suspect me, and even had he discovered me, was too noble-minded to have misused his advantage."

"You do not mean," exclaimed Eugenie, "you do not mean surely the----"

"Not the Count d'Aubin!" exclaimed Beatrice, with a blush that spread like lightning over her cheek, and forehead, and temples; "not the Count d'Aubin! I would not have trusted myself within his gates in this guise for millions of kingdoms. No, not to have obtained a century of the brightest happiness that ever yet shone upon the path of mortal!"

"I did not mean him," replied Eugenie, smiling; "I meant the Marquis of St. Real."

"Then you have divined more shrewdly than I thought you would," replied Beatrice. "But I will tell you all that story another time," she added, quitting suddenly a subject on which she evidently wished to speak, but did not know well how to proceed. "What was I saying? Oh! that I feared to have two gay-looking youths seen to enter my house at this hour; but the fact is, Eugenie, I have found that by caution and propriety, and determination in certain things, I have acquired, as it were, a right prescriptive to be as wild, and as daring, and as unhesitating as I like in all others,--but now, my fair friend, let us think of the present moment. You have four good hours to rest yourself ere we set out. In yonder room you will find a bed; and one of my girls shall sit by you, while you lie down to repose, if you are afraid of sleeping in a strange apartment. Yet stay, I must have those delicate shoes of yours; for ere we set out to-morrow, we shall need a pair more conformable to your dress, and must send a model to my own shoemaker, who perhaps may have some that will fit. He is accustomed to my whims; and will not mind being roused out of his bed to serve me. In the meantime, I must change my dress and hasten away; for I am determined to show myself, if but for an hour, at the fete given to-night by old Madame de Gondi, so as to turn away all suspicion from the right direction. I will be back long ere it be time to set out to-morrow."

Exhausted with all she had gone through, grief, terror, mental exertion, and corporeal fatigue, Eugenie de Menancourt gladly availed herself of the opportunity of repose. Casting off her upper robe, but without undressing herself farther, she lay down to rest. She did not refuse, however, the attendance of one of Beatrice's women; for danger and terror, instead of losing their effect on her mind by custom, had only rendered her more timid and apprehensive.

For more than an hour, agitation prevented Eugenie from sleeping; but towards two o'clock weariness prevailed, and she sunk into profound slumber. It seemed scarcely a moment, however, ere she was roused by some one touching her arm; and she found Beatrice standing beside her, while the grey light that found its way into the room through the open window showed that she had slept longer than she imagined.

"It is time for us to depart, Eugenie," said her friend, "and unwillingly I must break your short repose; but I see the market carts coming in; showing both that the gates are open, and that the siege of Paris is not only raised in name but in reality. We must make the best of our time, Eugenie; for in five hours more your absence may be discovered."

Eugenie de Menancourt needed no admonitions to haste. Her dress was soon resumed, her shoes tried on and found to fit tolerably, her hair re-arranged so as to conceal its length; and once more taking Beatrice's arm, she proceeded down the narrow staircase to the door of the house, where, stretched upon some benches in the passage, lay two or three men in different costumes, who instantly started upon their feet as the two maskers approached.

"Do not come out," said Beatrice, stopping to speak with them, "but look forth from the side window where you can see the gate. If I hold up my handkerchief, run up to help us; and, good faith, you must even risk a hard blow or two, should need be; but if you see Andrew join us, or if I do not hold up my handkerchief, be sure that all is safe, and return home with the women."

The men bowed and made way; and Eugenie, accompanying her companion through the doorway, found herself once more in the street in the cool, clear light of the early morning. During the former part of her flight, she had thought the very darkness increased her terror; but now as she walked on, with faltering steps, in an unwonted garb, and fancying that every passing eye must penetrate her disguise, she would have given worlds for night once more to afford her the covering of its dull obscurity.

The gate lay at the distance of not more than a hundred yards before them; and Beatrice whispering, "Do not be surprised or alarmed at anything you see or hear, for I expect a confederate here," led the way with a quick step.

Not to be alarmed, however, was out of Eugenie's power; for even the great interests she had at stake, though they prompted to exertion, were without effect in giving birth to courage: nor was the sight of the gate at that moment calculated to remove her fears, for although the siege was, as Beatrice said, absolutely at an end, and the royal army already many leagues from Paris, yet sentinels were to be seen in every direction, and a number of the fierce-looking soldiers of the League still hung about the gates, some examining the market carts as they entered the city, some jesting with the countrywomen who accompanied them.

Beatrice advanced boldly, however, her confidence and presence of mind appearing to increase as the dangers became more imminent, and gliding between two carts which stood in the archway, she was leading Eugenie on, when the *lanceprisade* of the guard darted out of the gate-house, and caught her by the arm.

"Ha, ha! my young truant," he exclaimed, "whither away so fast? none passes here without question: this is not the door of a church, young man!"

Beatrice shook off the man's hold without showing the slightest symptom of alarm or agitation; and ever ready with a reply, she answered, "Not the door of a church! Is it the door of a Huguenot *prêche* then? and are you a *maheutre* minister? Come, come! what do you stop us for? They told me that the Bearnois and his beasts were gone, and that we could go out in safety and see where the Huguenots roasted their apples."

"You have more malice in your heads than that, my good youths, I have a notion," replied the soldier. "We must have your names at least. Give us your name, my good boy."

"Mine is Monseigneur le Duc du Petit Chatelet," replied Beatrice, laughing; "so put that down in your book."

The soldier shook his finger at her good-humouredly enough. "You are a wild one," he said, "and will break many a country wench's heart, I'll warrant you, ere you be done with it. But what is your name, my pretty little abbé, that stand there holding by the cart and blushing like a girl of fifteen?"

Eugenie hesitated, and blushed a thousand times more deeply than before; but Beatrice instantly came to her aid, exclaiming, "Do not tell him your real name, silly boy; have you not wit to make one? What has he to do with your real name? Monsieur le Soldat, or better still, Monsieur le Lanceprisade, this gentleman here present is called L'Abbé des Ponts et Chaussees,--so put that down in your book also!"

"Very well, I will," replied the man; "but before I let you go farther, I must know whether these are your real names or not, and I think we have one within there who can tell us."

Eugenie's heart sunk, and even Beatrice's confidence seemed a little shaken, while the soldier, turning to some of his companions, exclaimed, "send out the old man there, and we shall soon see if he recognises these two pretty youths!"

The moment after, an elderly man, dressed much in the costume of a major-domo belonging to some old family of distinction, came forth from the gate-house and approached them, holding up his hands and eyes, as if in horror and astonishment. Eugenie looked to Beatrice, to see what was to come next; but a suppressed smile upon the countenance of her fair friend re-assured her, although the words that accompanied that smile tended to a contrary effect. "We are caught now, Eugene," she exclaimed aloud, "we are caught now, that is clear!"

At the same time the old man advanced, crying, in a lamentable tone, "Ah! young gentlemen, young gentlemen! how could you play such a trick? There's my Lord the Marquis been storming like mad, and your lady-mother crying her eyes out, ever since you left the chateau. We thought you must have fallen into the hands of the Huguenots, and there has been nothing but fear and anxiety through the whole household. You, Monsieur Leonard, your father said he could understand your running away, for you are always in mischief, but how you could persuade Monsieur l'Abbé here to accompany you, he could not understand!"

"I am sure if my father be in such a rage," replied Beatrice, in the tone of a spoilt boy, caught in some trick more outrageous than ordinary, "I am sure if my father be in such a rage, I shall not go back till he is cool again; and so you may go and tell him, good Master Joachim!"

"Oh, let us go! let us go!" said Eugenie in a low tone; and now comprehending her companion's scheme, but anxious to bring the scene to an end as speedily as possible, "Oh, let us go! it is useless to delay."

"That is right! Monsieur l'Abbé, that is right!" cried the old man; "but you need be under no fear of your father either, Master Leonard, for good Father Philip has made him promise that nothing shall be said if you do but come home quietly. There is the carriage, as you see, standing ready, with Jean the lackey, and nothing shall be said I promise you; but if you will not go peaceably, of your own will, I must make you go whether you will or not, and these good gentlemen of the guard will help me."

"Ay, that we will," cried the lanceprisade. "Two young truants! If ye were not two such pretty boys, I should feel tempted to make your backs so well acquainted with the staff of my halbert, that you would jump into the carriage fast enough, I will answer for it!"

"We will not give thee the trouble, most redoubtable hero," answered Beatrice, in a mocking tone. "But, as we must go, there is a crown for you and your pot companions to drink to the health of the Duc du Petit Chatelet and the Abbé des Ponts et Chaussees."

The man laughed and took the money; and Beatrice, with the same gay and swaggering air, marched forward through the gate, followed by Eugenie; while the old man came after; the lanceprisade of the guard taking care to whisper in his ear, with a knowing look ere he went, "You had better look sharp to them, or that young chap will give you the slip yet; he is as full of mischief as a loaded cannon."

"Ay! ay! I will look to them," said the old man, with a solemn shake of the head; "I will look to them, sir Lanceprisade, and many thanks for your kind help and assistance in taking them."

Thus saying, he followed Beatrice to the side of the carriage or rather *chaise-roulante*, and having assisted her and Eugenie in, took his seat in one of the boots. The lackey, who had waited with the carriage, now closed the leathern curtain, which served the purpose of a door, and then springing up beside the driver, who sat ready in his seat, gave the signal for putting the whole in motion. The short whip cracked, the two strong horses darted forward, and, after drawing to its full extension the complication of ropes, leather straps, and iron rings, which formed the harness, started the heavy carriage from the spot where it rested in the full force of its *vis inertiæ*; and in a moment, Eugenie, with a heart palpitating with joy, felt herself rolling away from the gates of Paris, over roads which were rough, indeed, with the recent passage of waggons and artillery, but every step of which seemed to her hopes to conduct to safety and to peace.

For her part, Beatrice cast herself back in the carriage; her lightness, her gaiety, her air of daring passed away; and for some minutes she remained with her hands clasped over her eyes, as if exhausted with all the exertion she had made. When she looked up, she was still grave, and there was a languor about her which spoke plainly that all the ease, and the courage, and the unconcernedness which she had displayed through the difficult scenes just passed, had been, in fact, the triumph of a ready and determined mind over the weakness of a frame as delicate as that of the most timid of her sex.

"We are safe, Eugenie!" she said, "we are safe! and now give me credit. Have I not played my part well? But it has almost been too much for me. When by myself I can go through anything, but I was alarmed and agitated for you; I feared not only lest you would be overtaken, but lest you should sink under the trial. But now I trust you are safe, dear Eugenie, for these horses go fast. We have nearly five hours before us ere Mayenne will be up; ere he will be well awake, and his eyes rubbed, and his boots pulled on, we shall have an hour more; then to discover the whole, to think which way we are gone, and to cross-examine your servants, will bring him to dinner time: the poor man must eat, you know; and what with other business, and the time required to give orders, and mount horsemen, and consult with his sister, the day will be done, so that we may well calculate upon its being to-morrow morning ere any one sets out to seek us. Therefore, my Eugenie, with God's help, you are safe!"

"Thanks! thanks, Beatrice! A thousand thanks, my sister, my more than sister!" cried Eugenie. "Well, indeed, as you say, and skillfully have you played your part. But you would say I have not played mine badly either, if you knew all that I have suffered, especially when we were stopped at the gate. If you had told me, however, that you had got such a comedy ready for our deliverance, I should have been better prepared."

"But I knew no more than yourself," replied Beatrice, "what was to come next; I had only time after your letter reached me to take general measures. Luckily I had a number of my own people around me without the walls of Paris. I bade Joachim have a carriage and horses prepared this morning, and to hang about as near as possible, telling whatever story he thought fit, if questioned. Thus, when the soldier spoke to me, I took great care not to say a word that could contradict my confederate's story, whatever it was; but kept to general nonsense, which could signify nothing under any circumstances. As to the comedy which you talk of, between Joachim and myself, it was like one of those mysteries which people play in the convents, where the names of the different characters, and some general idea of the story, is all that is given, and the actors fill up the speeches as they think best at the time. But my good major-domo played his part admirably too, and shall not have reason to repent of it when we come to speak of rewards."

"And, now, whither are we going?" demanded Eugenie; "for this does not seem to me to be the road towards Maine."

"The road towards Maine!" exclaimed Beatrice--"why, my dear, simple girl, that would be going into the lion's den, indeed. They will seek you there in the first instance, and we must give time to let their search be fully over ere we think of going near to Maine. At present we are following, as fast as ever we can, the march of the king's army, and I hope to pass the rear-guard to-night."

"But may not that be dangerous?" demanded Eugenie. "We have no pass from them; and if any of the parties of soldiers meet us, we may be taken and discovered, and perhaps maltreated."

"No fear of that," answered Beatrice; and then added, with a smile that called the warm blood up into Eugenie's cheek, "we can send for the Marquis of St. Real, you know, Eugenie. But, no, no! Do not be afraid of that, or anything else. I have orders and safe-conducts in the king's own hand. In short, Eugenie, I do not think that there is one thing, which can tend to your safety, that has been forgotten by Beatrice of Ferrara."

CHAPTER XXV

The night was dull and rainy; a thick shroud of clouds was drawn over the sky, so that the summer moon could not look down with any of her sweet smiles upon her wandering companion through the blue fields of space; and the air was loaded with a foggy dampness, through which fell a few drops, increased every now and then to a momentary shower, heavy, but brief. The valley of the Seine was dark and gloomy, and the night was so obscure, that nothing met the eye of the coachman who drove the carriage containing Beatrice of Ferrara and her fair friend, except the glistening of the river as it wound along not far from the road, and the dull and somewhat indistinct line of the highway itself, which, bad and sandy at all times, was now, as we have already said, channelled and cut up by the passage of heavy carts and still heavier artillery.

The second day after their flight from Paris was now drawing to its close. Beatrice, from hearing that some of the troops of the League had been hovering about in the neighbourhood of the Pont de l'Arche, had kept quiet during the latter part of the day, in a farm-house, where they had sought refreshment at noon, for themselves and horses, and was now proceeding as rapidly as possible on the high road, believing that the parties of the Union would not expose themselves to the sudden and brilliant strokes of so active a commander as Henri Quatre, by following his march too closely during the night. Eugenie, on her part, though habit and distance from her immediate persecutors had removed part of the load from her mind, was still agitated by many a fear; and her terrors were not a little increased by proceeding in the darkness over a road, the roughness of which, and the jolts thereby occasioned, precluded all possibility of conversation. Beatrice could but speak a word of comfort every now and then, which Eugenie could scarcely hear, as the carriage ground its way through the sand, or rattled over the large uneven stones. Thus had the two fair girls proceeded for nearly two hours, in the darkness, when a cry of, "Who goes there? Stand! Give the word!" brought the carriage to a sudden stop, and roused all Eugenie's fears again to the highest pitch. The lackey, who sat beside the coachman, jumped down, and went on to speak with the soldier who had challenged him; and old Joachim, who sat in the leathern projection at the side not unaptly called the boot, got out, and went on also.

"Oh! Beatrice, what is this?" cried Eugenie, drawing nearer to her friend in her increasing terror.

"Call me Leonard," replied Beatrice, in a gay tone; "call me Leonard! till I have got off my boy's clothes at least. What is this, do you ask, little timid fawn. Why nothing but the outpost of King Henry. They will let us pass in a minute."

At that moment Joachim returned, and approached the side of the carriage next to Beatrice, saying, "This is his Majesty's outpost, sir, commanded by the Marquis of St. Real; and they demand to examine who are in the carriage before they let it pass."

"Oh, he will know me directly!" whispered Eugenie to her fair companion; "I would not have him see me in this garb, Beatrice, for the world!"

"He will not examine the carriage himself, sweet girl," replied her companion in the same low tone; "he will know nothing about it. Some of his ancients or lieutenants have their orders for the night, of course."

"But we cannot go much farther to-night," rejoined Eugenie; "and we shall be to-morrow in the midst of his troops. Oh, Beatrice, do not! If I should be found there, the people would say I had followed him."

"What can we do?" asked her companion with a smile, which the darkness concealed from the eyes of Eugenie. "Joachim, show the sentry the king's pass; but ask if there be not a road somewhere hereabout which leads to the little town of Heudbouville. If there be, direct the coachman thither; for we love not to sleep within the outposts of an army, lest the enemy should treat us to an *alerte*. Gain us the good sentinel's bitter contempt, Joachim, by telling him that we are two cowardly boys, who hold the fire-eating soldiers of the League in great terror."

"We have passed the road to Heudbouville some hundred yards or so," replied the attendant: "but we can easily turn the carriage here, for there is more room than ordinary;" and having satisfied the outpost that no evil was intended by the denizens of the carriage, Joachim, the coachman, and the lackey, performed the difficult feat of making the ill-constructed vehicle revolve upon its axis, and brought the horses' heads back again on the way to Paris. The road to the little village which Beatrice had mentioned was soon found, and for about an hour the carriage rolled on, without any further obstruction than was given by stones and ruts, which threatened to scatter the wheels of the luckless *chaise-roulante* to the four winds of heaven, in some of the manifold jolts to which it was subjected; but at length the coachman came to a halt, and seemed consulting with the lackey beside him, who in turn put back his head to speak to Joachim in the boot.

"What is the matter, Joachim?" demanded Beatrice, perceiving that some impediment had occurred, and trusting more to her own skill and presence of mind than to the readiness of her attendants, although they were selected expressly for their shrewdness and promptitude. "What is the matter? Why does the coachman stop?"

Ere Joachim could reply, however, there was the sound of galloping horse, and the next moment the carriage was surrounded by a number of cavaliers, whose polished arms, as they rode up with a loud "*Qui vive?*" caught and reflected the little light that still existed in the air.

"*Vive le diable!*" replied Joachim, who was a great deal too wise to answer seriously till he had ascertained to what party the interrogators belonged; "*Vive le diable!* why do you stop two young gentlemen, going to the schools, on the highway? We are neither soldiers nor robbers, nor anything else that you have aught to do with."

"Well answered, Joachim!" muttered Beatrice, as she leaned forward to examine the persons of the horsemen nearest her; but the darkness was too complete to suffer the faces of any of them to be distinguishable, or to allow the colours which they wore t" be seen. Beatrice, however, caught a glance of the peculiar cross of the house of Lorraine upon one of the cuirasses, as the fiery horse of the rider pranced by the side of the carriage; and she instantly interposed, exclaiming, "Speak to me a moment, Monseigneur! I am the young Baron de Bigny, son of the Marquis de Bigny at Amiens, and am going with my brother here, the Abbé de Bigny, to La Fleche. I do not know whether you are of the party of the king or of the Holy League and Union; but I am sure you will not stop two youths like us, but let us pass quietly."

"But this is not the right way from Amiens to La Fleche, my good youth," replied the officer. "How came you thus thirty miles out of your road?"

"We came here to get out of the way of the Huguenots," replied Beatrice; who had now gained a better sight of the cross of Lorraine, which was to be found alone on the side of the League. "We had nearly fallen into their hands an hour ago; and--but perhaps you are one of that party too, Monseigneur; if so, I beg your pardon with all--"

"No, no, I am no *maheutre*," replied the officer; "but, do you know, my good youth, it would not surprise me if you were. Methinks I should know the voice of Auguste de Bigny, seeing I am his first cousin; and so, without more ado, I shall march you up to the village, to see who you really are, for I am very sure you are not the person for whom you give yourself out. Come, coachman, drive on, and we will give you an escort which you did not expect, I rather fancy."

"I went a step too far," whispered Beatrice to Eugenie; "but do not fear, dear Eugenie, I will manage matters yet.--Many thanks, many thanks, Sir Cavalier," she continued aloud. "Drive on as he bids you, Jean Baptiste. I shall soon amuse all the companions of Monsieur Francois de Bigny by the history of his adventures in the well at Houdlaincourt. How he went to make love to the miller's daughter; and the miller and his men caught him, and put him in a sack, and let him three times down into the well, maugre his high rank and gallant bearing, and brought him up, all white and dripping, like a dumpling out of the pot. Ha, ha! Monsieur Francois de Bigny, how will you like that story told to the *gens d'armes* over their wine?--I never take the name of any one I do not know," she said in a low voice to Eugenie, while the officer paused irresolute, and spoke a few words to Joachim and the coachman. "There is many a good tale to be told against that noble cavalier, which I had from Adela de Bigny, his cousin, and which he will not much relish; and I doubt not he will send us on to escape laughter; for though he may have found out that I am not his young cousin Auguste, he must see that I know all his history."

What would have been the result of Beatrice's expedient cannot be told; for at the very moment that Monsieur de Bigny was speaking to the coachman, and inquiring apparently whether the person who knew so much of his adventure was or was not really his young cousin, there appeared, upon what seemed--as far as the darkness suffered it to be discovered,--a sloping field upon the right of the road, a multitude of small lights in a line of about two hundred yards long.

"Down, down, in the bottom of the carriage!" cried Beatrice, who appeared to comprehend at once what those small sparks of fire meant; and she instantly crouched down below the seats, dragging Eugenie after her: "the king's troops are upon them."

As she spoke, a bright flash ran along in the same direction as the lights, and then the loud rattle of musketry, while three or four balls passed through the upper part of the carriage. Eugenie felt as if she were about to faint; but the moment after there was the sound of charging horse, and the whole space round the carriage became full of strife and confusion. Little could be seen, except when every now and then the flash of a pistol showed, for an instant apart of that strange and exciting scene, a night skirmish; and it was only by the sounds of blows and shots growing fainter and more faint around, that Beatrice perceived the Leaguers had been beaten and driven up the road by the royal forces. "Is any one of our people hurt?" she cried at length, raising herself, and looking out. "Eugenie, you have not suffered? Take courage, dear friend. Joachim, Joachim, where are you--where are the men?"

"Here, madam!" replied Joachim, creeping out from below the carriage. "We ensconced ourselves here as soon as we saw the matches blown on the hill--but what we shall do now, I do not know, for one of the horses is killed."

"That is unfortunate, indeed!" replied Beatrice; "but see, they are fighting in the village;" and she pointed on to a spot where repeated flashes of musketry might be seen gleaming between the dark masses of the houses and other buildings in what seemed a small town. "Henry Quatre is there himself," she said. "This is one of his daring enterprises--to dislodge the League from his flank as he advances upon Rouen, I dare say; but at all events we must wait till the matter is settled one way or another. If he be forced to retreat, we must retreat with him, Eugenie. If he drive out the Leaguers, the road will be clear before us. Take heart! take heart, Eugenie!-- why I thought I was a terrible coward till I saw you."

For about ten minutes possession of the village seemed to be severely contested; but at the end of that time the firing ceased; the trumpets might then be heard blowing a recall; and at the end of half an hour the sound of a body of horse coming at an easy pace down the road was distinguished at the spot where Beatrice and her trembling friend had remained.

"Ask the commander of the party to stop and speak with me, Joachim," cried Beatrice; "run on and meet them. Tell them how we were stopped by the League, and save me explanations."

The man did as he was directed, and the moment after, a cavalier rode up to the side of the carriage, saying, "your servant says you wish to speak with me, young gentleman. I command this party. What want you with me? One of your horses is shot, I see; but, good faith, I can give you no other; for Ventre Saint Gris! I want more than I have got of my own."

"On my word, your Majesty must find me one, nevertheless!" answered Beatrice, boldly. "If you have not forgot Beaumont en Maine, you will understand that though an ass served my turn then, I must have a horse now!"

"Pardie, my friend the page!" cried Henry. "Then you have accomplished your bold undertaking."

"True, sire, I have," replied Beatrice, "as far as getting away from Paris; but I had nearly lost all, by my own fault, this very moment, and fallen into the hands of the League. I attempted what I thought a *coup de maître*, and was well nigh taken in my own trap."

"The same misfortune has just befallen the League," replied Henry; "they thought to get upon my flank, and take possession of Louviers, but we have taught them that we do not slumber on such occasions. However, my brave page, you run great risks in going forward on the road where you now are. We have driven them out of the village, but they will rally not far behind, for it was too dark to pursue them far."

"Then we will turn round," replied Beatrice; "and, escorted by kings and princes, make the best of our way through your Majesty's host, till we can sleep in peace a couple of leagues beyond your outposts."

"The best plan you can follow," replied the king; "we will not ask you even to pause and refresh yourselves, lest the morals of two such simple boys should get corrupted by the license of our camp. Though here is the Marquis of St. Real, within a hundred yards of us, would doubtless be willing to receive one or both of you into his quarters."

Eugenie instinctively shrunk back farther into the corner of the carriage, and the king proceeded; "But we must get you a horse, at all events. Colonel James, send up some of your arquebusiers to that farm-house upon the hill, and see whether in the stables thereof you can find a horse. As your fire has killed one of the beasts which were dragging these two young gentlemen, it is but fit you should take the trouble of providing them with another."

The king waited to know if his embassy were successful; and after having seen the soldiers return with a strong cart horse, which was instantly harnessed to the carriage, in the place of the dead one, he gave orders for a party of troopers to escort the young wanderers as far as the Pont de l'Arche; and then, taking his leave, rode on towards his camp.

When the carriage was once more in motion, Eugenie breathed again; but still, at every place where it stopped her terrors were renewed, and she gazed out, with alarm and anxiety, upon the dark figures of the soldiery, who watched with unsleeping vigilance in the camp of the warrior monarch, till, at the Pont de l'Arche, which was the advanced post of the king's army, the horse they had obtained was exchanged for another, and they rolled on more smoothly towards the little hamlet of St. Ouen. The fears of Eugenie de Menancourt were during those moments of a very varied kind; for with her terrors so strongly roused as they had been, she found it impossible to submit them entirely to the influence of reason; and yet, strange to say, the thing she dreaded most, after immediate personal danger was over, was to meet and be known by the man whom she now felt, she loved more than any other being upon earth. She shrunk from the thought of seeing St. Real in the garb that she had assumed to escape from the persecution of his cousin,--she shrunk even from the thought of seeing him, now that a ceremony, however vain, illegal, and compulsory, had taken place between her and any other; and though she felt, even to pain, how much she detested the Count d'Aubin, and how much she loved St. Real, yet it seemed to her as if she had wronged her love for him in not dying sooner than suffering even the shadow of an engagement to pass between herself and another. Thus, it was not till they had passed the extreme outpost of the royal camp, and were rolling along in the quiet darkness of the night, that she breathed at ease, free from the constant expectation of seeing the Marquis of St. Real gallop up to the side of the carriage, and recognise her under her disguise.

At the little village of St. Ouen all the world was sound asleep; and manifold were the strokes of sword hilts upon the door of the *auberge*, many the shouts up to the unlistening windows, before the inmates could be roused to comprehend that there were strangers on the road demanding admission. At length, the hostess, half dressed, and scarcely half awake, came scolding down the stairs, extremely angry that anyone should travel at such unseemly hours; and on her steps soon followed her husband, a big burly Norman, but shrewd withal, and sufficiently sensible of his own interests to smother all expression of annoyance, and give his guests the best welcome that he could.

Early the next morning, the carriage was again in motion, but not before some of the light troops of the matutinal monarch of France were upon the road, and Eugenie was more than once alarmed by their gazing boldly into the vehicle when the curtains were undrawn, and by talking to the driver and the servants when the carriage was closed. These parties, however, as they marched but slowly, and the carriage went fast, were soon passed, and the rest of the journey proceeded as peaceably as any journey could do in those disturbed and unhappy days. Beatrice of Ferrara, after the experiment at Heudbouville, did not suffer herself again to be drawn from the route which she had laid out at first for her fair friend, but advanced as rapidly as possible towards the sea-side, seeing security only in the hope of Henry's army still interposing between them and the League, and thus preventing all search for Eugenie de Menancourt in the direction which she had really followed.

"At all events, dear Eugenie," she said, as they approached Dieppe, "here, upon the sea-coast, you will always have an opportunity of escape to England, should need be; and I will take care that our friend King Henry shall furnish you with such letters to the queen of those bold islanders, as to ensure you protection and assistance. For my part, you know, Eugenie, after a week or fortnight's rest, I must leave you, if you can do without me. My destiny, dear girl, has to be fulfilled, and I must back to Paris by a different road, both to hide my having aught to do with your successful flight, and to watch the progress of all on which my ultimate fate depends."

"Would to Heaven," said Eugenie de Menancourt, "that I could have such a happy and saving influence on your fate, Beatrice, as you have had on mine! But I am destined only to be a burden to you, and to rely upon you for everything, without knowing or comprehending the past or the present, as far as it regards you, without understanding your means, your wishes, or your purposes."

"I will tell you all, dear Eugenie, I will tell you all," replied Beatrice of Ferrara; "and then, as my daring rashness was necessary to give vigour to your timid nature, your gentle counsel may now perhaps tend to moderate and restrain my bold, wild schemes. But wait till we come to a resting-place, and then in some sweet quiet cottage in green Normandy, with the soft autumn sun shining upon our door, I will rest beside you for a short time, and drawing you a picture of my wayward fate, will see whether we cannot find means to give it a brighter colouring and a happier hue."

So spake Beatrice of Ferrara; but ere we go on to look into the picture to which she alluded, we must beg the reader to pause for a few minutes, upon some of those dull details, which in books calling themselves historical romances serve the mind as bad post-houses on a much-travelled road-- places where, after scampering on for many a league in pursuit of pleasure, the little traveller is obliged to stop, kicking his heels in impatient irritation till the horses are brought out, the harness prepared, the postilion has got into his boots, the lash is put on his whip, and, in short, all is made ready for carrying on that same little eager traveller, the human mind, once more upon his way.

Giving up, then, heroes and heroines, knights and ladies, we must even follow the progress of that lumbering and uninteresting machine called an army, and pause for a while to consider its clumsy and crocodile-like movements. We have already seen that on the day preceding Eugenie de Menancourt's escape from Paris, the camp of the besieging Royalists had broken up; and that the gay and chivalrous Henry Quatre led his meagre and somewhat ill-furnished host down the bright and laughing banks of the Seine, in such a direction that, should need be, he could either march across Normandy, and fall back upon Touraine, or advance at once to the sea-coast, and cover the disembarkation of his English allies.

We have followed him some way on his march; but it would appear, that inasmuch as the Royalists had been rather improvident of their supplies, and had been found, during the life of Henry III. somewhat unwilling to pay for the good things of this life, with which, at first, the peasantry had been very willing to furnish them, a want of provisions, both eatable and potable, had made its appearance in the camps of St. Cloud and Meudon. The jaws of the Royalists had got unaccustomed to maceration, and their lips to the taste of sweet things; so that as they took their way through the pleasant little towns and villages of Poissy, Triel, Meulan, Mantes, and sweet Fontenay, they lived very nearly at free quarters amongst the inhabitants, taking care to make the fat of the land through which they now passed, compensate for the meagreness of the diet they had so long endured. Nevertheless, as the king and his followers paid where they could, promised where they could not pay, and never took toll of rosy lips, except where there was a smile upon them, the people of the country in general gave them a better character when they were gone than might have been expected; and declared, that, after all, the Huguenots were not so bad as they were called.

In the meantime, as we have already shown, to diversify these employments, a little interlude of fighting did now and then take place; a town was now and then besieged and taken; and Henry IV. made arrangements for giving the inhabitants of the loyal city of Rouen an entertainment, which brings down the walls of a city more by the double-bass of the cannon than by the shrill sound of the trumpet. Pausing a sufficient time before the walls of that town to give and receive various proofs of amity, which left his own host diminished by several hundred men, and the garrison of the town less by perhaps double that number, the king received news, which made him judge that the situation of his army might be improved by a very rapid change of air; and consequently without longer hesitation or delay, he struck his tents, left success to follow, and at once led his troops to the sea-side.

Divining, however, that his enemies would anticipate with great satisfaction the moment for driving his scanty forces into the sea, he seemed resolved to disappoint them, if admirable dispositions could effect that purpose; and choosing for his troops the strongest position which he could discover, with their backs to the element and their faces inland, he ranged them along the side of a fair and beautiful hill, on the ridge of which still stands all which Time has left of the old and interesting castle of Arques.

Leaving the king and his men, however, thus posted for that battle which covered with immortal renown the monarch and his little host, we must turn for a moment to Paris, in order to investigate what proceedings had taken place in the capital, and what were the tidings which caused the monarch so suddenly to strike the tents he had pitched before Rouen.

CHAPTER XXVI

The morning after Eugenie's departure, no small surprise was expressed in the Hotel de Guise at the non-appearance of the priest, who had not only performed the marriage ceremony for the Count d'Aubin, but also rendered the much more important service of communicating to Mayenne the approach of aid from the Duke of Parma. While Mayenne, in his usual slow and deliberate manner, discussed the fact with his sister, and, shrugging his shoulders, declared that if the good father did not choose to come for his reward, he could not help it, the thought crossed his mind that he had not yet seen his own confessor, who had been carried off by the myrmidons of Bussy le Clerc; and although he doubted not that the Chevalier d'Aumale had before this time set the good priest at liberty, he determined to inquire farther: a vague suspicion for the first time crossing his mind that all was not right in regard to the transactions of the preceding evening.

By this time the hand of the dial pointed to the hour of nine; and Eugenie's maid Caroline, who, in order to give as much time to her mistress as possible, had ventured to prolong the period at the end of which she had been directed to present herself at the Hotel de Guise, was even now at the door inquiring for the Duchess of Montpensier. Her message was brought to that lady as she sat by her brother; and although she comprehended not one word thereof, she saw that it in some manner bore upon the point they were discussing, and ordered the girl to be brought into the room.

"He says that Mademoiselle de Menancourt's tire-woman has brought some apparel for her mistress," she repeated, turning to her brother after the attendant who made the announcement had left the room; "what can this mean, Charles?"

"I know not, Kate," he replied with a doubtful smile; "but when the girl comes, make her repeat her message," appearing perfectly unconcerned.

Before he could add more, the tire-woman was in the saloon; and playing her part with a natural talent which none but a French *soubrette* ever possessed, she approached towards Madame de Montpensier, and with a low and reverent courtesy, and a look of the most perfect simplicity, said, "I have brought all the things, your Highness, that my mistress thought she would require; but in regard to the filigree girdle, as I told her last night, I have not seen it for these two months. It was given into charge to Laure, who was sent away when my old lord died." And she went on into a long story, solely the invention of her own brain for the occasion; but which was so circumstantial and minute, and delivered with so much apparent earnestness and sincerity, that Mayenne looked at Madame de Montpensier, and Madame de Montpensier looked at Mayenne, with eyes in which bewilderment and surprise were then plainly visible.

"And pray what made you think that your mistress was here at all?" demanded the Duchess, at length cutting across the thread of the girl's story, which bade fair otherwise to be interminable.

It was now the maid's turn to be surprised, and most skilfully did she represent the passion of astonishment; standing before Madame de Montpensier in silence, and looking at her without one trace of comprehension in her eyes. "Pray what did your Highness say?" she asked at length; "I did not understand you."

"She demanded what made you think your mistress was here at all?" repeated Mayenne, in a harsh voice.

"Lord bless me, sir! Your Highness! Dear me! What made me think my mistress was here?" cried the girl, with an affectation of wonder and doubt and affright that was perfectly admirable. "Did not her Highness send her own carriage for her last night, with a young abbé and a page, and a billet sealed with green wax?"

The story, as it had been prepared by Beatrice of Ferrara, now came out at full, and the whole Hotel de Guise was soon in agitation and confusion:- -Madame de Montpensier alternately laughing and frowning, Mayenne striding up and down the room, and vowing that if it were the Count d'Aubin who had served him such a trick, he would find means to make him rue it; and the maid Caroline weeping as bitterly as if she had lost a lover or a gold necklace, and wringing her hands for her poor mistress with all the phrase and circumstance of sorrow.

In the midst of this scene the Chevalier d'Aumale appeared, informing Mayenne that Bussy le Clerc denied all knowledge of his chaplain, and that the guards at the Bastile were in the same story. Ere Mayenne, however, could include Bussy le Clerc in his denunciations of vengeance against the Count d'Aubin, the confusion of the whole was rendered more confused by the apparition of the confessor himself, who exculpated the demagogue by declaring that he had never been in the Bastille, but, on the contrary, had been carried away by persons he knew not, who, at a certain point, had put him into a carriage, and blindfolded him. They had then lodged him for the night in a small room with nothing but a bed, a crucifix, and a missal.

Here, in mortal terror, he had watched and prayed, till the grey of the dawn, when, being again blindfolded, he was led out through a great many streets and turnings, of whose name and nature of which he had not the slightest conception, and at length finding himself free from the hands of those who had held him, he uncovered his eyes, and perceived that he was standing in the midst of the Pont Neuf, by the side of a blind man who was singing detestable melodies to the discordant accompaniment of that most ancient instrument the hurdy-gurdy. Tired, frightened, and bewildered, he had made the best of his way home, without attempting to seek for his ravishers; and after sleeping till he had incurred a penance for forgetting his matins, he had come to add his mite of confusion to that which already existed in the hall of his patron.

His tribute, however, small as it was, aided to perplex the ideas of Mayenne far more than ever. Ere he made his appearance, it had been the natural conclusion of the lieutenant-general and of his sister, that the carrying off of Eugenie de Menancourt had been the work of the Count d'Aubin; and the absence of the confessor had been considered entirely as a thing apart. No sooner, however, were his adventures related, than they instantly connected themselves in the minds of all with the non-appearance of the priest, who had performed the ceremony, and with the absence of Eugenie; and the shrewd intellects of Mayenne and Madame de Montpensier, thus put upon the right track, seemed likely soon to discover no small portion of the truth. Eugenie's tire-woman was again strictly examined, and though she acquitted herself to a wonder, suspicion was roused. "Think you, Kate," demanded Mayenne, "that shrewd plotter, Beatrice of Ferrara, has a hand in this? There was some talk of love--ay! and even of marriage--between her and D'Aubin in the old Queen's time."

"No, no!" replied the Duchess, "that has all gone by, and she now despises him, as every woman of common sense must do. Besides, I saw her at old Madame de Gondi's fete last night at one o'clock! You had better question the other attendants of De Menancourt. You may gain more tidings there."

Mayenne accordingly determined to proceed instantly to Eugenie's dwelling, in order to interrogate the rest of her servants; and he commanded, in a stern and threatening tone, that the girl Caroline should be detained till he returned. As the door was thrown open, however, to give him exit to the court, a gentleman was introduced as the captain of the lansquenets, sent to his aid by the Duke of Parma; and all Mayenne's conclusions were once more deranged, by finding that the intelligence brought him by the priest was genuine.

How Beatrice of Ferrara had obtained that intelligence Mayenne never discovered; but true the news certainly was, and most important were the results to the cause of the League; for what between the auxiliary force which thus joined him, and reinforcements brought in by Bassompierre, Nemours, and Balagny, the army in Paris was soon so strong as not only to justify but to bespeak bold and energetic measures. Mayenne instantly prepared to take the field against the royal army; and ere Henry IV. had been three days before Rouen, the forces of the League were in full march to give him battle. Before he left Paris, however, the Duke used every means not only to discover the retreat of Eugenie, but to ascertain the cause and the manner of her flight. In regard to the first, he was baffled at every point; and so skilful had been the arrangements of Beatrice, that in respect to the second he returned to the conclusion, after long and repeated investigations, that to the Count d'Aubin was to be attributed an act which, under such circumstances, he looked upon as a base breach of faith, approaching to a personal insult. The tidings, therefore, that Eugenie had disappeared from the capital, and was nowhere to be heard of, were conveyed to D'Aubin by a reproachful letter from the Duke of Mayenne; and mad with anger and disappointment, the Count, on his part, gave his mind up to the belief that Mayenne was deceiving him, threw himself on his horse, and travelled with frantic rapidity, till he reached Paris. There finding that the army of the League was already on its march, he followed with all speed, overtook Mayenne at Gournay, and a somewhat vehement altercation was the consequence.

Mayenne, however, could not afford to quarrel with a person of so much importance to his cause; and acting with wisdom and moderation, an explanation soon ensued, which cleared either party in the opinion of the other. As D'Aubin, however, giving way to the natural impetuosity of his disposition, had not waited to put the troops in motion which he had collected in Maine, he returned thither after one day's rest, while Mayenne marched forwards towards Dieppe.

Accompanied by some of the first officers in France, and supported by an overwhelming force, it seemed that the great leader of the League was about to drive the handful of men which opposed him, and their heroic monarch, into that sea which was already bearing to their aid the expected succour from England. Strongly posted, however, and powerful both in courage and in right, Henry IV. calmly awaited the attack of his adversary; and, after several preliminary movements, the day of Arques dawned heavy and dull, without a breath of air to stir the trees or to dispel the autumn fog that obscured the scene of that memorable fight.

It were tedious here to tell all the minute particulars of the glorious day, when, attacked at all points, and assailed in all manners, not only by the arms of the enemy, but by the treason or folly of part of his own troops, Henry IV. defended the hill of Arques against forces more than six times the number of his own.

Every one has heard how, when monarch and soldiers were alike wearied out with sustaining through a long day the unceasing attacks of infinitely superior numbers, when scarcely a horse could bear his rider to the charge, and scarcely a hand could wield a sword, the little band of Royalists beheld the powerful and yet untouched cavalry of the League wheeling round upon their flank, while a light wind springing up tended to clear the air, and showed to both armies the insignificance of the one and the tremendous advantages of the other. But in stricken fields, as in the daily strife of life, the event which seems destined to seal our misfortunes is often but the harbinger of unexpected success. The wind, it is true, rose higher, and rolling the sea-fog, in heavy clouds, away down the valley of Arques, left the few gallant defenders of that long-contested hill exposed, in all their need, to the eyes of the mighty host that swept round them in dreadful array; but, at the same time, the full sunshine poured upon the advancing squadrons of the League as they came on to the charge, and those upon the hill, for the first time during the day, could distinguish clearly the separate masses of friends and foes. The cannon of the castle of Arques opened at once, with tremendous effect, upon the cavalry of Mayenne; the first ranks were swept down as they advanced; the second rolled over their dying comrades; the horses, mad with pain and terror, broke through the ranks behind; and the charge of a few hundred men, at that critical moment, put all the gallant array into irremediable flight. Mayenne saw that the day was not for him; and withdrawing his masses in slow and soldierly order, he retreated for several miles, and left the field of Arques to the glory of Henry IV.

CHAPTER XXVII

It was in a cottage by the sea-side--a mere hut, belonging in former times to a fisherman--that Eugenie de Menancourt sat one autumn day beside Beatrice of Ferrara watching the clouds of mist roll over the waters, as the exhalations which night had left behind struggled with a light wind and a still powerful sun for place upon the bosom of the ocean. It was a mere hut, as we have said, but there was something picturesque in its position, seated halfway up, halfway down a sand-cliff to the east of Dieppe, with a projecting shoulder of the rock sheltering it from the winds of the Atlantic, and a few trees and shrubs--stunted in size and not very luxuriant in foliage, it is true, but still green and fresh--keeping it company in the warm nook where it was placed. It is not impossible that the very picturesque beauty of its situation might be the reason why it had been selected by one who had more poetry in her heart and soul than half the poets of the land in which she lived. But, at the same time, there was another motive which she would have assigned if she had been asked, and which was, that the shore beneath formed a little bay in which the waves seldom broke boisterously, but even in very stormy weather seemed to play there in innocent sport, while their parent sea was all in trouble and contention without, as we may have seen the children of a warrior playing in peace by their cottage-door while their father was urging the bloody strife upon the battle plain. In this sheltered bay lay a small vessel, and on the beach were two or three boats, while up above upon the cliff were several more cottages, from which to that we have described a winding and somewhat difficult path led down the face of the crag. Although the cottage had not contained more than ten days its two fair tenants, who had now resumed their appropriate dress, yet they had contrived to ornament it with a very different sort of taste from that which was displayed by any of the neighbouring dwellers on the shore: for Beatrice had her full share of that knowledge and love of what is beautiful in art or nature which was then general in her native land; and although she had daily talked of returning soon to Paris to play her appointed part upon that busy scene, yet she had lingered with a fond clinging to the peaceful moments she spent there, musing away her time upon the ever-varying sea-shore, or decorating the cottage she had hired for Eugenie with somewhat whimsical care. As if her journey to Paris had been a duty, for the neglect of which she owed an apology to her own heart, she often spoke of the difficulties and dangers of reaching the capital when two hostile armies were interposed: but difficulties or dangers had rarely stopped Beatrice of Ferrara when she willed to go in any direction upon earth; and, perhaps, the real reason of her delay might be, that Philip d'Aubin was not in the metropolis, and that she knew it.

As we have said, however, beside her Eugenie de Menancourt; upon an autumn day, little more than a fortnight after we last left them. Their eyes were bent upon the sea-fogs rolling along over the bosom of the waters below, and contending in vain against a rising wind, which every now and then swept them away, and showed to old Ocean the blue eyes of Heaven looking upon his slumbering waves, when the curtain of the mist was withdrawn by the soft hand of the morning air.

"See, Eugenie! see!" cried Beatrice of Ferrara, as, with their arms twined in each other, they gazed forth upon the changing scene; "see how the soft and downy masses of fog roll dark above the sea, and how, every now and then, a scanty gleam of light breaks in, and gilds the moving vapour and the waves below! Do you know, dear Eugenie, that the bosom of that sea seems to me like my own fate, wrapped up, as it has been for many years, in clouds and gloom, with every now and then a gleam of brightness breaking through, for a brief moment, and obscured again almost as soon as given. Do you know, dear girl, I could stand and gaze upon that sea, and, with all the superstition of the ancient days, I could play the augur to my own heart, and read my after-lot in the changes that come over the bosom of the water."

"Well, let me read it!" cried Eugenie: "see, see, Beatrice, what a long bright gleam is coming now!"

"Ay! but the clouds roll up behind," replied her friend.

"Yes, but beyond them again all is clear and bright," rejoined Eugenie, as the sun and the wind gained the mastery, and the last wreaths of mist were swept away, leaving nothing but a thin filmy veil upon the expanse of sea. "See, Beatrice, how bright it looks!"

"And, on the other hand, gaze on the dark cloud of the past," replied Beatrice, with a smile which was not without its share of hopefulness; "and as you, dear Eugenie, have read me my coming lot, and would fain make me believe that it is to be so bright, I will tell you shortly, very shortly, the history of the past; that you may judge how much cause I have to augur well of the approaching hours from my experience of those gone. I cannot dwell long upon such painful things, but I will speak them briefly."

Sitting down together, and still gazing out upon the golden sea, Beatrice began her tale; and as she told it in as few words as it could well be told, so shall it be repeated here.

"I was born amongst the lovely Euganean hills," she said, "where nature has compressed into one small space all that is beautiful and all that is grand; mountain and valley, stream and lake, profuse abundance, vegetation and cultivation, an atmosphere of magic light, and an air of balm. My father was the sovereign prince of----, but that matters not; though we were of the house of Ferrara, which has given sovereigns to many another land, and has allied its princes to the highest upon earth. My father's dominions were small, but they were rich and beautiful; and he himself, born of a warlike race, kept well with the sword those territories which, doubtless, the sword had first acquired. He, when the sovereigns of Ferrara were closely allied to the house of France, visited this court; and wedded, more for her beauty than her wealth, and more for her virtues than her beauty, the heiress of a noble house, whose lands lie not far from your own in Maine. He carried her to Italy, where they ever after lived; his rights to his lady's lands in France being still respected by the sovereigns of this country, though the management of them was somewhat neglected by those in whom he trusted. Still, however, those lands were rich, and made no small addition to the revenues of an Italian prince. His favourite residence was amongst the Euganean hills; and there, where he had collected everything that was beautiful to the eye, or pleasant to the ear, where the wise and the good, the poet and the sculptor, the painter and the musician, ever found a home, I, his first-born child, saw the light, now some four-and-twenty years ago. About four years after, a brother was born, and, in his birth, my mother died; but though my father never wedded again, but buried his heart in the tomb of her he had loved, yet we were well, carefully, fondly nurtured, both by our surviving parent himself, and by an uncle, who, high in the church of Rome, looked on both my brother and myself as if we had been children of his own. Abandoning the paths of ambition for our sake, he left the ancient capital of empires for our peaceful castle in the Euganean hills; and there, while my father was often absent fulfilling the duties of a prince or a soldier, he devoted himself to the cultivation of our young minds, and to the strengthening of our young hearts against the sorrows and the temptations of the world. He was, he is, one man out of a multitude. But, Eugenie, we had another uncle, who, through life, had followed a different path, and who was destined to act a different part. He was bred a soldier, and lent his sword, and the troops he had contrived to raise, to any one who held out to him the prospect of wealth or aggrandisement. His expeditions, fortunate to others,--for he was brave and skilful,--were not fortunate to himself; for the artful and deceitful men he served generally contrived to withhold from him his promised reward. From my father he always met kindness and protection; and often did my parent support his cause, and avenge his quarrels, to the detriment of his own best interests. How that uncle acted in return, you shall hear. His heart was corrupted by dealing with the base, and he became base himself, from believing that all others were so.

"My uncle Albert, the Cardinal, saw more deeply into his heart than my father; and I remember well that it was when speaking of his brother, my other uncle, that he took pains to impress upon my mind a truth that struck me as a child, and which I have never forgotten. 'True virtue,' he said, 'comes out the brighter for shining amidst vice. It is only those who feel themselves weak that fear the contagion of corruption. We may hate evil, and not willingly mingle with those who practise it; but, if forced to do so, my child, we shall only hate it the more if we be really virtuous at heart. Meaner stones derive a lustre from that which lies beneath them: we set the diamond upon black, and it shines by its own light.' My father died, Eugenie; and the manner of his death was not altogether without suspicion; but as, in his territories, it was a doubtful question, whether the coronet, where there were male and female children, descended to the eldest of either sex, or was the portion of the first-born son, my uncle Ferdinand came hastily to settle the succession; and, to prevent all dispute, he took the inheritance unto himself. For fear of greater evils to us, and greater crimes to his brother, my other uncle, Albert, sent my young brother and myself, with speed and secrecy, to the court of France. I was then but thirteen years of age, and my brother nine, and with us were some attached dependants, who had either followed my mother to Italy, or had dwelt long in my father's house. My brother instantly received my mother's inheritance in France, burdened only with a small portion for myself; but, to better my fallen fortunes, the late Queen-mother, Catherine of Medicis, received me as one of her women, and, to do her but right, showed me, through life, unvarying tenderness. I will not offend your ears, Eugenie, by telling all that I saw in that corrupt court; but I had three great safeguards, dear friend--a heart naturally not easily moved; firm principles of truth and virtue, implanted in my earliest years; and one faithful woman, who had nursed my mother and myself, and who to vestal purity of heart added a daring courage, which strengthened her to do what she judged right in defiance of all dangers, and would speak truth to the highest of God's creatures upon earth. Yet I must not take credit to myself for any great powers of resistance. I do not say that there were not many who sought me, some in marriage, and some with lighter vows; but so deep and thorough was the contempt I felt for the vain and idle butterflies of that vicious court, that my scorn extended to the whole sex, and I fancied

I should never give one thought to any man in the whole world. You know, Eugenie, and I know too well, how much I was mistaken. At length came one who sought my love as others had not sought it. Four years, or more, have since passed, my friend, and those years have changed him not for the better. There was a freshness of young feeling about him then, that is now gone, and it was that which first won a way to my heart. I now found that, if my heart had been difficult to move, when once it was moved, like a rock broken by some earthquake from the Alps, it was likely to bear all away before it. Oh, how I loved him, Eugenie! and when, after having, I own, made him sigh for many a month, to prove his love for me, I at length let him know that I did not feel towards him as towards the rest of men, and that he might, at some distant time, hope for the hand of Beatrice of Ferrara, the relief, alas! was greater to my heart than his. Then came the change over him, Eugenie. I believe he had injured his fortune with those hateful dice; the hope of obtaining your hand was held out to him; ambition and interest called him loudly to pursue that prospect; for I was poor, comparatively, and had no hope of better fortunes; and I heard that he was offering his vows to Eugenie de Menancourt. I resolved to see with my own eyes if this was true; and as the queen was then about to undertake one of her gay and politic progresses through Maine, I joined her, with my young brother; for my faithful nurse was by that time dead, and I did not choose to dwell in that court alone. You remember well, Eugenie, those days, and how my truant lover seemed chained, like a slave, to my bridle-rein. My pride was satisfied, if my heart was not, and I returned to Paris. He remained some months behind, and when he came, I found that he was changed indeed. He fled my society, and yet he seemed struggling with himself; full of passion and tenderness when we met, his words were wild and strange: he plunged deep into the vices of the court; and, though I saw and knew he loved me still, yet I resolved, by appearing to despise his conduct, and to forget himself, to recall him, if possible to better deeds. I went down to the dwelling of my brother in Maine, and there, roaming wildly over the country, I soon heard enough to show me that, notwithstanding all his large possessions, the Count d'Aubin was struggling vainly with the consequences of his own follies. There was then a contagious disease raging here in France, and my brother caught it, and died. His possessions fell to me. I had it now in my power to raise up again him I loved, and to sweep his embarrassments away; and it became my favourite dream to reclaim him from all evil, to lead him back to virtue and to right, to restore him to honour and to station, and to make him owe to me at once peace of mind and ease of fortune. For the last two years I have laboured for this object, Eugenie, by many a different means. I have been thwarted by accident, and by his own perversity; but I cling the more tenaciously to those hopes, the weaker becomes the foundation on which they rest. Sad and sorry I am to say he has weakened it more and more every hour; but yet, Eugenie, I hope. I have had him watched, Eugenie, not that I might know his weaknesses, for to those I have ever shut my ears, but in order to seize the moment, if ever the moment should come, for snatching him from his follies or from his evil fate. To himself I have pretended to hate and despise him, the better to conceal my views, and also to make him feel my kindness the more when my time comes. Sometimes I think, however, that he suspects me; and a dwarf page, who has been attached to me from my childhood, and whom, in other days, I gave to him to be his cupbearer, he sent away, a year or more ago, to his cousin St. Real. I had directed that page to give me notice of all that passed in Philip d'Aubin's household; but the tidings he gave were scanty, even while he was there, and as soon as he was gone, I formed a bold resolution, which I executed boldly. Shortly after you had come to Paris with your father, and I had contrived to gain your love and confidence, you may remember that Philip d'Aubin went down to Maine; and I did hope, that, in companionship with so noble a heart as his cousin St. Real, and under the eye of the good old Marquis, who was then living, his better feelings might expand, like flowers in the sunshine; and I resolved, at any risk, to go down thither and watch him myself; for I knew that men, to whom he owed large sums, were pressing him hard, and that, had it not been for these sad wars, his estates would long ago have suffered from their claims. I thought that the moment might come when the full and tender generosity, which is so often to be found in woman's heart, might have room to act, that I might save him from the consequences of his own faults, and thus, perhaps, save him from those faults themselves. I contrived, by means of the dwarf, to force several of my own servants into the household of St. Real; and I was following down rapidly myself, to try whether I could not, for a time, obtain admission there also, when messengers from my uncle Albert, telling me of the death of Ferdinand, the usurper of my little state, conveying to me considerable treasure, and beseeching me to return, and take possession of territories which were now universally acknowledged as my own, reached me at Orleans, and brought me back to Paris.

"As soon as I had dispatched them back with other letters, begging my uncle to rule in my stead till my return, I pursued my plan; but D'Aubin had, in the meantime, returned to Paris, and had thence again been summoned to the sick bed of his uncle of St. Real. Of this I knew nothing, however; and, after manifold risks and difficulties, owing, perhaps, to the negligence, perhaps to the malice, of the dwarf Bartholo, I accomplished my object, and found myself established as a page in the house of the lords of St. Real. I had determined, in any great difficulty, to apply at once to the old Marquis, and tell him all my history and all my views; but I found him dying, and soon saw that I must withdraw from the household into which I had thus intruded, or risk detection, and, perhaps, ill repute. To guard my name at home, however, I caused my women to give out that I was ill of the fever; and they played their part with skill. Day by day, however, my disguise produced more and more pain to myself; for I had but hourly proofs of how completely D'Aubin had given himself up to the vices and follies of his comrades of the court; and I determined, soon after St. Real and his cousin reached Paris, to cast that disguise off at once. The wealth which I had now at command in that venal city, and in these venal times, procured me every sort of facility in coming and going between Paris and St. Cloud; and I believe that, for one half the sum which I possessed unknown within the town, I could have procured regular passes for the two kings and all their troops to march quietly in and take possession of the capital. Thus, as soon as I had notice of the last sad and daring means which Philip d'Aubin was about to employ against you, my Eugenie,--the most base and profligate step of any he had yet taken,--I cast myself at the king's feet, who owed me some gratitude for a former service; told him your situation, my own plan for saving you, and besought him to give me his assistance. He did so in a generous manner, and even furnished me with intelligence to give Mayenne from the Prince of Parma, which is certain to mislead and puzzle the Duke regarding all our plans. Learning from an attendant, whom I still have in D'Aubin's service, that the Count had bound himself to set out on the very evening of his marriage for Maine, I conceived the Duke of Mayenne's plans at once; all his views; all his policy. I set every engine to work to gain information. I had his chaplain seized and carried away; I induced a wild drunken Huguenot soldier, not without talents, but without religion or principle, to enact the priest, and brought him to the Hotel de Guise at the moment that a priest was wanted. I took care that your refusal should be witnessed by so many, that, even had the person who performed the ceremony been what he seemed, the whole would have been illegal; but I also ensured that proof of the man's condition, and of all the other facts, should be lodged in the hands of the king, so as to render you free as air. And now, dear Eugenie, here we are, safe and at liberty, with a bark to bear you to England, if the king should lose the approaching battle; and, doubtless, you wonder that, with all I have seen, and with all I know, I can for one moment think again of Philip d'Aubin. Such is the voice of reason, Eugenie, and the voice of sense; but there is another voice in my heart, which drowns them all, and fills my mind with excuses for his conduct--vain and light, indeed, as the changing clouds upon the sky, I know; but still those clouds cast shadows, which alter the aspect of everything whereon they fall; and so, to my weak eyes, the excuses found by love cast an obscuring shade upon his actions, which will not suffer me to see them as I should if the full sun of unbiassed judgment shone upon them. I will make one more effort, dear Eugenie--I will essay one more trial; I will find the means of serving him deeply and truly; and if he be then ungrateful, I can cast him off--and die."

"Oh, not so, Beatrice!" replied Eugenie; "make every effort; try every means; but, even if all should fail, talk not of dying, but seek happiness in some other shape."

"In vain, Eugenie! in vain!" replied Beatrice, "all the feelings of my heart are engaged in this one effort. If it fail, there will be nothing else left for me on earth. The body may live, Eugenie--it perhaps may linger on some few years; but the heart and the soul are dead. Still, let us hope better things, dear friend; you have read me a happy fate in those passing clouds and the sunshine that followed, and I will trust----"

As she spoke, an attendant hurried in. "They are flying, madam!" he said; "they are flying!"

"Who?" demanded Beatrice, eagerly, "who are flying?"

"Mayenne's horse, madam," replied the man: "do you not hear the cannon? They have been fighting at Arques for these four hours."

"Send out! send out to see!" cried Beatrice. "On this battle may depend our future fate, dear Eugenie."

In less than an hour the news of Mayenne's defeat was borne to Beatrice and Eugenie; and the servant who brought it added, that he had seen the king and Monsieur de St. Real both quite safe, and directing the operations which followed up the victory.

"Thank God for this, also!" replied Beatrice. "This battle will secure the western provinces to the king; and now, dear Eugenie, ere I wend my way back to Paris, we will journey together to Maine, where, between my lands and yours, there lies a spot secluded and calm, and surrounded by people attached both to you and to me. Mayenne must fall back on Picardy; the king will march on Paris; and Maine will offer a safer asylum than even this which we possess at present."

The political anticipations of Beatrice of Ferrara were not far wrong: scarcely had the day of Arques been won, when the English succour disembarked at Dieppe. Henry effected his junction with the Duke of Longueville and the Count of Soisson, the former of whom had been detached to levy troops; and then resuming the offensive, he marched in search of Mayenne, and attempted to provoke him to another battle.

Retreating upon Picardy, however, Mayenne avoided the large force which was now opposed to him; and, by a number of skilful operations, both military and political, repaired the disadvantages incurred by the lost field of Arques. Anxious to withdraw him from a province into which, from the disaffection of many of the larger towns, the royal forces could not with safety follow him, Henry marched direct upon Paris, and, taking several unimportant places by the way, attacked and carried the suburbs of the capital itself, to the horror and dismay of the Leaguers. The scheme was perfectly successful. Mayenne, in terror lest the metropolis should be lost, spurred with all speed to Paris, leaving his army to follow as they might. The forces of the Royalists was not sufficiently numerous to invest the city entirely; and the troops of Mayenne following from Picardy soon placed such a number of men within the walls as to set farther attack at defiance.

Withdrawing from a useless enterprise, Henry retreated upon Mont l'Hery, and then turned upon Etampes; taking a number of towns under the very eyes of the League, the leaders of which seemed little disposed to risk the chances of another battle. Thus passed the winter, and a considerable part of the spring. The town of Le Mans, it is true, made some resistance to the royal arms, but at length yielded; and thence directing expeditions towards different parts of the country, the gallant monarch recovered a great part of the rich provinces towards the centre of France. Almost all Maine and a considerable part of Normandy were now subject to the king; and, amongst the rest, the lands of Eugenie de Menancourt were, for a time, occupied by the royal troops. The tenantry, however, and the vassals, had been generally called into the field, by the Count d'Aubin, who had by this time joined Mayenne in Paris; and the changing events of the war soon obliged the monarch to withdraw his troops from that part of Maine, and advance to new victories and more important conquests.

Shortly before Easter, Henry IV. had laid siege to Dreux, in Normandy; and Mayenne having taken the castle of Vincennes, Poissi, and several other places, endeavoured to reduce Meulan. The demonstrations of the royal army, however, showed a purpose of compelling him to raise the siege; and having been joined by fresh levies from various parts of France, and considerable reinforcements from the low countries, he determined to risk another battle; and for the purpose of choosing his own ground put his army in motion. Nonancourt had fallen before the arms of Henry IV. and the siege of Dreux was rapidly advancing; when news reached the royal camp of various unexpected movements on the part of the army of the League. First came tidings that five thousand infantry had passed the bridge of Mantes; then came reports of large forces of cavalry having been seen in march on both sides of the Seine; and, lastly, intelligence was brought to the king that the foragers of the Duke of Mayenne had appeared in the neighbourhood of Dammartin.

Calling his principal officers to council, Henry informed them of the tidings he had received, and then at once made his own comment; and announced his determination thus:--"From these facts, my friends, it is evident that our good cousin of Mayenne is seeking us; and therefore I propose instantly to raise the siege of Dreux."

The members of the council looked in each other's faces, with glances of surprise at such an unexpected proposal from one who was not, in general, easily turned from his enterprises. Henry for a moment suffered their astonishment to continue, and then added, with a smile; "You seem surprised, my friends; but I have no scruple in regard to abandoning a siege when it is for the purpose of fighting a battle. What say you, my gallant St. Real; will you strike for Henry IV. as bravely here as you did at Arques?"

"With all my heart, sire!" replied St. Real; and this is one of the few instances on record of a council in which there existed no difference of opinion.

CHAPTER XXVIII

Willingly we turn once more from the dull, dry page of history--that uninteresting record which no one reads in these days, and probably never will again, unless by some unforeseen accident the world should grow wiser and better--to the more entertaining and instructive accidents and adventures of the individual characters, which, with somewhat less skill than that of a Philidore, we have been moving about upon the little chess-board before us. It is always the most skilful game, we are told, to begin with the pawns, of which we are well aware, though we somewhat deviated from that rule in the commencement; but now that we have got our pieces scattered about in different directions, and have just been obliged to make the king abandon his attack upon the castle, we must even have recourse to pieces which we have found very useful in many a previous game, and play this chapter out with the knights.

The evening was cold and still; for the ordinary winds of March had not yet begun to blow, although that month was well advanced; and the dull heavy clouds that hung over the world might descend in rain, or might still assert the rule of winter, and come down in a fall of snow. The sky, therefore, looked chill and comfortless to the eyes of a considerable body of the army of the League, as it moved along the heavy and channelled roads in the neighbourhood of Evreux; and to say sooth, the aspect of the earth itself was but little more cheering than that of the heaven which canopied it. Days of trouble had impoverished the land, and the cold season which had just passed had left the earth brown and rugged; while the woods, that swept over every favourable slope, presented nothing but a tangled mass of dull grey branches, diversified alone by a few patches of crisp yellow leaves, that adhered, with all the tenacity of old attachment, to the stems which were soon to cast them off for the greener and gayer children of the spring. Thinly peopled, too, was then the land; and though here and there a village church raised its tower against the evening sky, or a cottage appeared upon the upland, in many instances the bell had long ceased to sound from amidst the scenes that war had visited; very often the light of the cottage was found extinguished, and the fire of the once warm hearth gone out for ever. The hamlets were few, and generally gathered round some castle, which afforded the inhabitants refuge or protection in time of need; and solitary but inhabited cottages, if met with at all, were but mere huts, in which dwelt the lowest and most miserable of the population, upon whom war itself could inflict nothing worse than existence.

In short, the whole scene was cold and desolate; and its effect upon the mind of one of the leaders, who conducted the detachment we have mentioned, was such as it was naturally calculated to produce. He had ridden on, at about the distance of half a mile from the head of the mingled masses of cavalry and infantry which were under his command; and, accompanied by one companion, and several attendants, advanced silently upon the rude road, which, winding along the side of an easy hill, displayed a wide extent of dull grey slopes, slightly tinted here and there with a faint and melancholy hue of green, till a dark and gloomy wood, at several leagues' distance, cut sharp upon the leaden sky, and closed the cheerless prospect. Although the eye of Philip d'Aubin, for such was the horseman we have spoken of, roved far and wide over the uninviting face of the country, it was clear that he looked not upon it as a general reconnoitring the land through which he passed, with the keen glance of strategic inquiry; but rather that he seemed to regard it with the look of one whose heart--not wholly dead to nobler feelings than those which armed him in civil strife upon a bad and unjustifiable cause--grieved for the state of ruin in which his native land was plunged, although his own evil passions aided to produce the desolation that he lamented.

The other who rode beside him, Albert of Wolfstrom, drew his cloak round him, and, as he gazed upon the bleak and desolate landscape, thought of nothing but himself. Mercenary by nature and by habit, he scarcely knew what it is to have a country; and--like many others who believe themselves to be citizens of the world--in truth and in reality, his own individual selfishness was his world, his country, and his home. D'Aubin knew the nature of the man too well to suffer the slightest hint of what was passing in his own bosom to escape his lips; well aware that his companion could not understand his feelings, and that, setting aside even the mercenary leader's own particular philosophy, there was cant of many kinds to be brought forward against the sensations which forced themselves upon him; for where was yet the unholy cause which did not inscribe upon its banners the names of virtue, religion, patriotism, and honour?

"It is a chilly night," he said, as he remarked the action of his companion; "it is a chilly night, Wolfstrom!"

"Ay, and a dreary prospect," answered his companion. "Which, think you, my noble Count, shall we have to warm our blood tonight with; raising the wine cup, shaking the dice, or hard blows upon bright steel?"

"With wine, if anything," replied D'Aubin; "Mayenne is not one fond of night encounters and sudden surprises; and if he have not fought the king's force to-day, which is not likely, he will let another sun rise ere he strike a blow. As for dice, you know, I have abjured them."

"Ay do I, to my sorrow," answered Wolfstrom; "for we have not had one merry night since we began our march; but, by my life, it is a dreary prospect. I trust that all the centre of this good land is not so bare and wasted. I have been so long in Picardy, where things wear a better aspect, that I expected not this sad scene in Normandy."

D'Aubin turned upon him an inquiring eye, not understanding, for a moment, what curious combination could have excited in the bosom of the adventurer anything like feelings of regret for the devastation of any land on earth. "You are compassionate, Wolfstrom!" he said: "France indeed has suffered terrible evils; and Normandy, lately, more than all; for here has been the hottest fire of war during the last four months."

"And pray has not Maine suffered as much?" demanded Wolfstrom in a quiet tone.

D'Aubin laughed aloud: "By the Lord!" he exclaimed, "I thought thy heart had grown mighty tender over the woes of France, most worthy and considerate Wolfstrom; forgetting, that in the *hypothèque*,[4] which I gave thee over my lands in Maine, on account of that accursed throw of the dice, thou hast acquired a certain tender and generous interest in my unhappy country, through the only channel by which thy heart can be reached,--but rest satisfied! The war would be sweeping and desolating indeed, which would leave the lands of Aubin unable to pay the pitiful interest of thy pitiful debt; and besides, I shall soon be able to discharge the whole, and load thee with that sort of moveable ore, which is better suited to thy purposes and thy nature than any claim upon the soil."

"You mean when your marriage can be completed with Mademoiselle de Menancourt," replied Wolfstrom, not unwilling to retort some of the bitterness of Aubin's speech upon himself. "By my faith, Sir Count, if it wait till then, it will wait long enough apparently; for your fond and affectionate bride seems to conceal herself from your longing arms with wonderful skill and perseverance."

D'Aubin bit his lip, and paused for several minutes ere he replied; but wrath he felt was vain in regard to circumstances far too well known to admit the possibility of concealment, however much it might sting him to find them a subject of common conversation to every mercenary follower of the camp. It cost him an effort, indeed, to smother all the angry feelings at his heart; but that effort over, he replied in a tone of calmness that disappointed

Wolfstrom's malice: "She does, indeed, conceal herself skilfully," he said; "and in truth, I little thought that so slight an offence as I gave her would so deeply wound woman's jealous love, or I should have taken greater care to please; but as soon as this battle is over, and these provinces cleared, I will bend my whole thoughts and efforts to the search; and when once I have found her, a few words of apology, and a few vows of eternal love and fidelity, will set the whole to rights again."

"I heard that you tried all that before," replied Wolfstrom, dryly; "and the good, free-spoken Parisians seems to think, that it was love for one cousin made her run away from the other so eagerly; at least, so Madame de Montpensier, and the Duchess of Guise, and young La Tremblaye, and several others, fancied."

"It is false as hell!" cried D'Aubin; "and those who say it, and those who repeat it, lie."

"I trust it is false," answered Wolfstrom, calmly; "and will not take up the hard word you have used just now, Monsieur d'Aubin, till the battle is over, and our personal affairs are in a little better order. After that, however, I shall have to inquire how far the word lie was applied to my share in the story. At present, let me say, that my repeating unpalatable rumours to you was but an act of kindness, intended to direct your mind towards a particular point. Even supposing that nothing like love exists between your cousin and this fair fugitive, every one knows that he used to regard her as a brother might a sister; and it is a common supposition that she has fled to his protection, and is concealed by his assistance."

"Nonsense, nonsense, Wolfstrom!" replied D'Aubin, musing a little while he spoke. "It is all nonsense, depend upon it; and as to the word lie, I applied it alone, of course, to those who spread such reports maliciously--not to you. Eugenie, wherever she has fled, has too deep a sense of female modesty to put herself under the protection of any idle boy, like my cousin of St. Real."

"Pardie! call him not an idle boy!" cried Wolfstrom. "Call him rather a stout soldier, and skilful commander; for such has he proved himself in all these last affairs; and the very best in either camp may now and then take a lesson from him."

"Pshaw!" said D'Aubin. "You are credulous, Wolfstrom! The followers of the Bearnois take care to vaunt their great officers and skilful soldiers, in order to make up, by the fears of their adversaries, for their own want of strength. Do not let us be such gulls as to believe them; and only let us so far reckon on their power, as to take every means of employing our own to the best advantage. Do not you spare your men, Wolfstrom; for one of these great battles lost might place the whole of France in the power of the Bearnois."

"I shall neither spare my men nor my person, as I am bound in honour," answered Wolfstrom; "but it matters little to me whether France falls under the power of the Bearnois or not. The term for which I took arms will soon be expired; and I can always find employment for my sword, thanks to the Protestants and Catholics here and in other lands."

"True," replied D'Aubin; "but you may find my lands confiscated to the crown for treason and rebellion some fine day, if the Bearnois wins the day of us ultimately; and then what becomes of your *hypothèque?*"

"That consideration shall make me give a good stroke or two more, my dear friend," replied the German coolly; "but I seldom find means wanting to repay myself; and, methinks, if the Bearnois does beat us completely, and declares himself your heir, I shall still contrive to skin his inheritance before I go."

D'Aubin made no reply, and for some time the two commanders rode on in silence; the German leader probably calculating upon the best means of skinning, as he termed it, other men's inheritance, and the Count d'Aubin, on his part, revolving bitterly all that had just passed in a conversation which presented so very few agreeable points for the mind to rest on. What his companion had said in regard to Eugenie and St. Real, he had repelled only the more angrily because it was confirmed by suspicions existing previously in his own mind; for such is the nature of the human heart, to combat on the lips of others the self-same feelings that we experience with terror within us. To that point of their conversation, therefore, did he most earnestly turn his thoughts; and bitter and angry were the sensations which he now felt towards a being whom he had once loved, but who had since committed the unforgiveable offence of holding firm to virtue and to honour where D'Aubin's own grasp had given way. Gradually as he nourished and pampered the doubts and suspicions within him, the emotions of his mind communicated themselves to his features and to his frame; and suddenly remembering himself, as he was spurring on his horse under the impulse of his irritated feelings, he affected to see some object in the distant plain, and asked his companion whether he did not perceive a light in the eastern part of the landscape.

Wolfstrom answered in the negative; and the conversation between them was renewed, but took a different turn, touching chiefly upon the chances of a battle on the following day, the respective forces of the Royalists and Leaguers, and the probability of success on either part.

"We should soon know how the strife will end, if we were in my country," said Wolfstrom; "at least, we might easily find persons to tell us."

"How so?" demanded D'Aubin. "I hear that our holy Father the Pope, although friendly to our cause, predicts that the day will go against us."

"Ay, but in Germany," replied Wolfstrom, "we should find those who pretend to know as much as his holiness, and do know a great deal more. Have you never heard, that in the Odenwald, when a war is about to begin, the Wild Huntsman goes out with all his dogs, and that, on the tops of our mountains, on many a stormy night, the spirits of the rivers and the floods hold their meetings, and reveal dark secrets of coming events to those who have the courage to go and consult them?"

"No, indeed, Wolfstrom," answered D'Aubin, "I never did hear all that; and I can but say, that I think those spirits must be very foolish spirits to haunt Germany at all, when there is many a warmer and a fairer land would be very willing to receive them; and still more foolish to go up to the tops of mountains on a stormy night! No, no, Wolfstrom; I am no believer in spirits, or ghosts, or phantasms, or necromancers, or any sort of portents, except the wonders to be effected by strong wits and strong arms."

"Say many a warmer land, if you will," replied Wolfstrom, angry at D'Aubin's sneer at his native country. "Say many a warmer land, if you will, but not many a fairer; for the whole earth does not contain a fairer than Germany. Why, everything that stream, and mountain, and forest, rich plain, and sweeping upland, can do to make a land lovely is to be found in Germany: but as you have not seen it, you cannot judge; and as to your disbelief in portents, you, as every other incredulous doubter, will some day be convinced."

"Never!" answered D'Aubin, with a laugh: "but now, good Sir Albert, as night is falling, and we shall not reach St. Andre before midnight, I think we had better fall back to our men, and throw out some scouts. Not that I fear surprise; for as Mayenne is between us and the enemy, it would be strange to meet with a foe before we rejoin our friends. 'Tis as well, however, always to hold one's self prepared."

The views of the leader of the reitters perfectly coincided in this cautious doctrine; and D'Aubin and his companion, slackening their pace, suffered the head of their corps to come up with them. Arrangements were then made for a night march; and the sun went down ere they had proceeded far, bursting forth for a moment as he touched the edge of the horizon, and dyeing the heavy clouds that rolled around him with a dull and misty red. The clock struck nine as the Count and his forces entered the little village of Gross[oe]uvre; and the leaders, riding forward to the old chateau, were welcomed with kindness and hospitality by the ancestors of my poor friend, the gallant and chivalrous De Vitermont, one of the noble and generous hearts of France, who, after having shed his blood, and lost health and comfort in defence of his country, could still hold out the hand of friendship and affection to those who had smitten him so severely, but who were enemies no more.

So good was the wine, so hospitable the hearth at which he sat, that Albert of Wolfstrom, with the true love of a soldier of fortune for comfortable quarters, would fain have delayed the farther march till morning, alleging that the horses and men were both fatigued, and could just as well proceed an hour or two before daylight as at that late hour of the night. D'Aubin, however, would not hear of delay; well knowing of how much importance it is to bring troops fresh into the field, rather than wearied with a long march. Determined, therefore, that whatever rest the soldiers obtained should be as near the expected field of battle as possible, at eleven o'clock he caused the trumpets to sound; and shortly after the troops were once more on their march towards the small town of Ivry, at which place the Duke of Mayenne was now ascertained to be. A circuitous route, however, was necessarily followed through the great plain which lies between Pacy and St. Andre, as the latter place was understood to be occupied by the forces of the king. Sure guides had been obtained, indeed, at Gross[oe]uvre, and much were they needed, for the night was as dark as the mouth of Acheron; and not a ray found its way through the black covering of clouds to mark the road from the fields amongst which it wound. The air was calm and still; and no sound was to be heard except the occasional howling of the wolves, which were then frequent, and are not now uncommon, in the many woods which diversify that part of the country. Instead of bringing additional chilliness to the atmosphere, however, the night had become warm, and was growing more and more sultry as it advanced; and every now and then the wind, as if struggling to rise against some oppressive burden in the sky, came with a momentary gust of hot breath, which instantly fell again, and all was still.

"It will turn to rain!" said D'Aubin, speaking to Wolfstrom, who rode beside him; "it has grown too hot for snow."

"No, no, noble Sir!" replied the old man who walked beside D'Aubin's bridle-rein, to show him the way; "that which you feel is the hot breath of the battle coming up! They will fight to-morrow, that is certain! When I served with the Great Duke, we never felt a night like this, without being sure that there would be bloody work the next morning, whether we expected it before or not."

"Indeed!" said D'Aubin; but as he spoke, a slight momentary flash played along the verge of the far sky, showing, for the brief instant that it lasted, the plain and the woods around, and then leaving all blank and dark once more.

"Ay, that's always the way," said the old man; "the spirits of the two armies are trying to-night which will have the victory to-morrow. We shall hear more of it soon."

Several minutes, however, elapsed without his prophecy being verified; and D'Aubin began to fancy, that what he had at first supposed to be a flash of lightning had proceeded from the discharge of some distant gun, the report of which had escaped his ear; when again a broad blaze illumined the sky, and a clap of thunder, resembling the discharge of a whole park of artillery, echoed and re-echoed through the air. Then came another pause; but the moment after appeared a spectacle which--if it had not been seen by the unimaginative Sully, and the keen and inquiring eyes of D'Avila the historian, as well as those of every other person then awake in either host,-- might well have passed for a superstitious fable. The sky became suddenly in a blaze with flickering lightning, which scarcely left it for a moment in darkness; while in the midst appeared forms of fire, like those of mounted horsemen and charging squadrons. Shifting, advancing, wheeling, now meeting in impetuous shock, now mingled in the confusion of the *mêlée*, now broken and scattered, now fleeing, now rallied, the aerial combatants acted in the clouds the fierce drama of a hard-contested field of battle before the eyes of the astonished soldiers. For some minutes an uncommanded halt took place; the soldiers gazed upon the blazing sky with eyes of wonder and terror; several of the horses started from the ranks, and were only brought back by skill and strength; and then stood with foaming hides and distended nostrils, straining their eyes, with their riders, on the bright but fearful phenomenon above them. Still that strange warfare in the sky seemed to go on, while the thunder rolled around in one incessant peal; and gradually shaking off the first effects of terror, the soldiery began to take an interest in the scene, worked up their imaginations to the belief that the combat was real. So complete at length was the illusion, that when the phantom army appeared defeated by their adversaries, and the forms that composed it were driven over the sky in confusion, the trumpeter of the horsemen of Aubin instinctively put his clarion to his lips, and blew a rally. The Count took advantage of the incident to give the word to march; and turning to Albert of Wolfstrom, as he spurred on his horse, exclaimed, "In truth, in truth, this is very strange!"

The troops followed their commander in some disarray; but ere they reached the edge of the upland the pageant had passed away, and all was darkness, except when an occasional flash of lightning broke for an instant across the sky.[5]

CHAPTER XXIX

The morning of the fourteenth of March broke through a sky filled with scattered clouds, the light fragments of the past-by storm, which, borne away by a quick soft wind, hurried shadowy over the laughing sunshine of the early day, like the momentary woes and cares of infancy. After a night of watchfulness and inquietude, the soldiers of Henry IV. rose not the less full of hope and courage, for all they had endured. Marching out from the villages in which they had been quartered, they advanced to a position which the king had chosen some time before, and which his army had occupied the greater part of the preceding day, in expectation of being attacked by the forces of Mayenne, whose army had been in sight during the whole afternoon.

Some apprehension had been entertained in the Royalist camp during the night, lest the enemy should have retired across the Eure, to avoid a combat which bade fair to decide the fate of France; but the first dawn of the morning effaced this fear, by showing the outposts of Mayenne, still occupying the edge of the gentle slope which terminated the plain towards Monçeaux and La Neuvillette. The main body of the Leaguers had, indeed, withdrawn to a little from the position they had occupied on the preceding day; but this movement had only taken place in order that they might pass the inclement night which followed in the shelter afforded by the villages towards Ivry; and ere the monarch had been long on his ground, the heavy masses of cavalry and infantry which supported Mayenne were seen congregating on the upland, considerably increased in number by reinforcements which had arrived during the night, and early in the morning.

Some small bodies also had joined the forces of the king; and although the rolls of the League presented at least double the number of names which the list of Henry's followers could display, yet upon the part of the Royalists there was that undoubting, confident resolution, which so often commands success, joined to that cautious energy which insures it against almost every chance.

Towards ten o'clock, the position of the royal army was taken up, the squadrons of cavalry formed along the whole line, and the infantry disposed in masses between the small bodies of the horse. On the right appeared the squadron of the Marechal d'Aumont, with several infantry regiments; towards the centre were the cannon, few in number, but well placed, and directed by officers of skill and activity; and on the left was the squadron of the king himself, with the reserve of the Marechal de Biron. The appearance of the royal host offered nothing very brilliant; for every leader amongst the Royalists had been so long expelled from the gay capital, and so many of them had suffered in fortune by their attachment to the monarch, that steel-- cold grey steel--was the only ornament that the ranks of Henry IV. presented. The king himself appeared amongst his troops without that surcoat of arms which was borne even by the poorest gentleman on the other side; but in order that he might be known and distinguished in the *mêlée*, a large white plume of feathers rose above his casque, and a similar mark was placed in the head of his battle charger. It was thus he appeared in the front of the squadron he particularly commanded, when the young Marquis of St. Real and several other gentlemen rode up, and sought permission to fight near the person of his Majesty.

"No, no, St. Real," replied the king; "you will be required at the head of your own troops."

"I can perfectly trust my lieutenant, sire," replied St. Real. "If you will grant me my request, I will answer for his conducting the troops as well as I could myself."

"No, St. Real, no!" answered the monarch, again smiling gaily upon him; "I must not have all my best officers in one place. I am vain enough to think that my own hand is here a host, and I must have my gallant friends posted where they may do as much. Besides, I have other work for you. Here is my noble Rosny, who has brought me up James's arquebusiers from Passy: I wish you to join them to your force, and hold yourself as the commander of my own especial reserve. If you see my squadron broken, come to my aid,--but not otherwise, mind. You won glory enough at Arques, St. Real, and you must let us have our share here. But stay; were you not in the room last night when Schomberg came to ask for his men's pay, and I spoke somewhat harshly to him in reply?"

"I was, sire," replied St. Real, bowing his head gravely; for he had thought at the time, that the king had treated the veteran unkindly.

"Well, then, come with me!" said Henry: "you witnessed the fault, you must witness the reparation." Thus saying, he rode along the line, followed by St. Real and about twenty other horsemen, sometimes pausing to gaze upon the swarming host of Mayenne, which, crowning the opposite slope, was making every disposition for immediate battle; sometimes turning towards his own army to address the heads of the squadrons he passed, or the gentlemen who accompanied him. "Ha! there is the white standard and black *fleurs de lis* of the Guises!" he exclaimed, speaking to St. Real. "Our good cousin of Mayenne must be in person on the field already. 'Tis a wonder he is so soon up! How mild the day is, De Givry! Well! you and your brave fellows, I see, run no risk of overheating yourselves before the battle; for, by my faith, we have none of us much over-clothing besides cold steel. Ah! Monsieur de Brigneux, you have a good view of the enemy, and will not lose sight of them till they have tasted the quality of your steel, I'll warrant. They must be two to one, Vignoles! I am sure I hope they are; for I would not have to defeat a less force for one half of Burgundy. They tell me our friends from Picardy are within two miles; but faith, I shall not wait till they come up, lest we should have too many to share our glory. Ha! here we are, St. Real; do me the favour of putting your foot to the ground with me."

St. Real instantly flung his rein to an attendant, and followed the king on foot to the head of a regiment, where sat a strong elderly man, whose countenance--the features of which were bland and mild--wore a stern and sullen air, and whose cheek, showing here and there the red lines of florid health, was now, nevertheless, pale in its general hue. He dismounted from his horse as the monarch approached, and rendered him a military salute with the same grave sternness which had marked his aspect ere the king came up. Henry, however, instantly laid his hand upon his arm in silence and led him back--for he had advanced a few steps--to the head of his regiment; and then, when every soldier in the ranks could hear, he said,--"Colonel Schomberg, we are now on what will soon be a field of battle, and it is very possible that I may remain upon it. I gave you hard words last night; and it is not fair that I should carry out of the world with me the honour of a brave gentleman like you. I come, therefore, to recall what I said, and publicly to declare, that I hold you for as good a man, and as gallant a soldier, as at this time lives." Thus saying, he took the veteran in his mailed arms, and pressed him to his bosom, while the warm tears streamed down the rough cheek of the old soldier.

"Ah, sire!" cried Schomberg; "in restoring me the honour which your words took from me, you now take from me life, for I should be unworthy if I did not cast it away in your service; and if I had a thousand, I should wish to pour them forth at the feet of such a king."

"No, no!" said Henry, again embracing him; "spend your blood, Schomberg, as I will mine, when there is need of it; but still keep it as long as you can, for the service of your master. And now, my friends, we will all do our duty. St. Real, my friend, to your post! Schomberg, farewell! Monsieur de Vicq, have the kindness to tell the Baron de Biron to advance the squadrons on the right for about two hundred paces; for I see the front of the enemy begin to shake, and the battle must be no longer delayed than sufficient to enable us to get the sun and wind behind us, otherwise we shall be blinded with the smoke and glare."

Henry now rode back to his squadron; and St. Real returned to the head of his own forces, which had by this time been reinforced, according to the king's command, by James's horse arquebusiers. Here the young leader, now well accustomed to scenes of battle and victory, fixed his eyes upon the squadron of the king; and though anxious, with all the fire of a chivalrous heart, to take an active share in the coming contest, he yet determined to observe to the letter the orders he had received; well knowing that they had been dictated by experience and skill, such as he had not the vanity to believe he himself possessed. Although the thought of danger or the thrill of fear never crossed his bosom for a moment, yet the countenance of St. Real was grave and sad. No man felt more for the suffering people of his native country, no one regretted more deeply every fresh act of the great tragedy which day after day deluged France with blood; but at the present moment, it must be owned, St. Real's feelings were personal. He thought of Eugenie de Menancourt; and his heart sunk, when, contemplating the loss of the present battle, he suffered imagination to dwell on all to which she might be exposed if the League were triumphant. Her real situation he knew not, nor had he more than a vague idea of the circumstances that attended her flight from Paris, for nought but rumours of the event had reached him during his long service with the royal army. But on that very morning he had learned from a trumpet, who had brought him an insulting defiance from his cousin D'Aubin, that the vassals of Menancourt were now led by the Count; that Eugenie was still a fugitive from her home; and that it was generally supposed amongst the Leaguers she had sought refuge with him. These tidings, at least, taught him to believe that she was unprotected in the wide world with which she was so little fitted to cope; and the letter of his cousin showed him that misery and violence waited her, if fortune favoured the arms of those who had already oppressed her.

Such thoughts called a pang into his bosom, and a cloud upon his brow; but feeling that even his individual exertion might aid in winning a field on which so much was staked, he sternly bent his thoughts to the events immediately before him, and watched, as we have said, the squadron of the king with steadfast and eager attention. Scarcely had the monarch rejoined that squadron, when the army was put in motion; and taking its left as a centre, wheeled a little, so as to gain the advantage of the sun and wind. When this was completed, the troops again halted in a position decidedly better than the former ground; and the next moment, a horseman, riding from the side of the king, galloped at full speed to the artillery. Only four cannon and two culverines were on the ground upon the side of Henry IV; but they instantly opened against the enemy, and were recharged and fired with such rapidity, that ere Mayenne could bring his guns to bear, those of the Royalists had nine times poured death and confusion into the midst of his ranks. The squadrons of the League could be seen to shake and waver under that terrible fire; and horseman after horseman, parting from the spot where Mayenne and his officers were placed, galloped up to the tardy cannoneers, as if to hasten them in the execution of their duty. An ill-directed volley at length followed; and at the same moment the light cavalry of the League advanced to charge the left of the Royalists. They were met, however, half way, by the impetuous D'Aumont; whose squadron, passing through them like a thunderbolt, turned and charged them again. The battle then became general; troop after squadron was hurried into the fight; the smoke rolled in heavy masses over the plain; and one of the dense clouds thereof, sweeping between the troops of St. Real and the squadron of the king, for several minutes prevented the young noble from seeing aught but indistinct forms of dark whirling masses, now lost, now appearing again in the white wreaths of vapour. Anxious to fulfil his charge exactly, he led his squadron a few yards in advance; and at the same moment the smoke clearing away, allowed him to perceive the principal mass of the enemy, in which appeared the standard, or cornet, as it was called, of the Duke of Mayenne, in the very act of charging the small square of cavalry headed by the king.

Wheeling the horse arquebusiers which had been joined to the troops of St. Real, upon the flank of the advancing column, the English officer who commanded them poured a volley into the ranks of the Leaguers, which shook them severely; but still they came on at a thundering pace, numbering nearly two thousand men; and the handful of gallant gentlemen who surrounded the monarch were soon lost to the sight. The heart of St. Real beat quick for his king; but the moment after, the dark and struggling mass of Leaguers seemed rent by some mighty power within. It reeled, it wavered; the clash of arms grew louder and louder, and the flashing of pistols and the shouts of the combatants were more distinctly heard where St. Real sat. The next moment forth burst the unbroken squadron of the king, and wheeling rapidly, the white plume pressed onward against the very front of the repulsed enemy.

At that instant, however, Count Egmont, the brave but unworthy son of a noble and patriotic father, cast himself in the way of the horsemen of the League, who were in the very act of turning their bridles to fly; rallied them with words of fire and indignation, and brought them back in fury to the charge. Already somewhat disarrayed by the fierceness of the combat, the king's squadron was broken in every part; and though the white plume was still seen towering over the thickest of the strife, St. Real felt that he had abstained enough, and led on his squadron to the support of the monarch. In the very act of charging, however, he observed a strong body of horse draw out from behind a little wood, called *La Haye des Prés*, on the left of the army of the League, and bear directly down upon him. A moment's glance showed him the arms of Aubin and Menancourt; and the next instant he beheld his cousin giving the order to charge. St. Real instantly halted, so as not to expose his flank; and the troops of his cousin galloped furiously towards him, till they were within the distance of a hundred yards, when some hesitation was seen in their ranks.

"Thank God!" thought St. Real; "his heart is touched, and he will seek some other foe."

But the next moment this hope was done away, and the hesitation was otherwise explained. The forces of Aubin approached still nearer, but at a slower pace; and at length the whole of the horsemen levied on the lands of Menancourt halted short.

"Charge!" cried D'Aubin, with a gesture of furious indignation. "Traitors, do you refuse to charge?" And galloping across the front, he struck the headmost horseman of that troop a blow with his clenched gauntlet that made him reel in the saddle. The man instantly recovered himself, and shouting "For St. Real! for St Real! Vive Henri Quatre!" galloped forward, followed by all the rest of the vassals of Menancourt, who ranged themselves in good order by the troops of the young Marquis.

The forces composed of D'Aubin's own followers, small in proportion, had halted in some disarray while their leader had crossed them to chastise the refractory trooper; and they now found themselves suddenly opposed to a body of more than double their own number. D'Aubin himself, it would seem, was taken by surprise, although it was evident that the defection of the retainers of De Menancourt was a premeditated act, and although he had long remarked a coolness in their service, and a disposition to quarrel with his own followers. He paused then in doubt, glaring with eyes of rage and hatred over the powerful squadron before him. Then whispering a word to his lieutenant, he rode two or three yards forward, and shaking his clenched fist, exclaimed, "St. Real, you are a traitor, and have practised on my troops; but I will meet you yet, and force you to give me reason." Thus saying, he turned his horse and rejoined his troops, who were already slowly, and in better order than before, withdrawing from the perilous position in which they stood.

St. Real hesitated for a moment as to whether he should overwhelm them, as he felt he could, by a single charge of his powerful squadron; and duty struggled for a moment with the kindlier feelings of his heart: but turning his head, a glance towards the king's division saved him from farther hesitation, by showing him the reitters of the League pouring down upon the monarch, in support of the force under Mayenne; and he immediately wheeled his troops, and met, in full charge, the superior body thus offered. Although the heavier horses and armour of his own men-at-arms enabled them to break the first rush of the German horse, the superior numbers of the latter for a time prevailed, and the squadron of St. Real was borne back upon that of the king. The ranks, however, on all parts, were by this time broken; and, perhaps, never was a more complete exemplification of the word *mêlée* than the centre of the field of Ivry at that moment. Man to man, and hand to hand, the fight was now continued. The lance had fallen quite into disuse amongst the royal forces before this period; the sword, the pistol, and the mace decided all; and so mingled and perplexed were friends and foes, that more than one man-at-arms was struck down by others fighting on the same part. The sounds of the cannon still pealed from other parts of the plain; and, together with the shouts, the pistol shots, the discharges of musketry, and clash of steel, rendered the words of the loudest voices unintelligible, even when vociferating words of command to any handfuls of men that still held together; while from time to time a cloud of smoke rolled in amongst the combatants, hiding everything else from their eyes, except the little group of horsemen fighting around them. In the midst of the enemy's troopers, and only accompanied by two or three of his most devoted followers, St. Real's personal strength, skill, and valour, wrought over again the deeds of chivalrous times. The reitters fell back before the sweep of his tremendous sword; and plunging his strong battle-horse in amongst them, he dealt death and terror around; while his own soldiers began once more to gather and to form by twos and threes behind him. At the moment when about a third of his squadron had rallied, through the rolling smoke, he caught a glimpse of the white plume dancing still in the midst of a dark group of horsemen, while a hundred weapons, waving around it, seemed aimed at that life on which hung the destinies of France.

Without pausing even to think, St. Real spurred towards the king: the reitters closed in behind him; and the next moment his path was crossed by the man of all others whom he least desired to encounter--his cousin.

"Out of the way, Philip d'Aubin!" he cried, heated with the strife of the moment; "out of the way! By the soul of my father, you will urge me too far!"

D'Aubin probably heard not what he said; at least his reply was too indistinct to convey any definite meaning to the ear of St. Real, though the furious gesture by which it was accompanied spoke for itself. The Count spurred on upon his cousin; and St. Real, with his beaver up, paused to see whether one in whose veins flowed the same blood as in his own, would really raise the hand against his life. He himself, however, was, as we have said, heated with the combat; and when he saw D'Aubin gallop on, with the point of his heavy sword aimed directly at his face, he lost patience, and spurred forward to meet him. Dropping his sword, however, by the thong that attached it to his wrist, he seized the mace, which, according to the old customs cherished by his family, he carried at his saddle bow; and, parrying the weapon of his kindred adversary wherever it attempted to strike him, he made the mass of iron play round his head like a willow wand--without, however, returning one blow of all the many that were aimed against him.

"Leave me, D'Aubin!" he exclaimed at length, as they wheeled their horses close together, and he perceived that his cousin was bleeding from several wounds he had previously received: "leave me, I say; you are wounded, and no match for me.--Leave me, or you will provoke me too far!"

D'Aubin felt, however, that his cousin used not either his strength or his skill against him; and his pride was more hurt to be spared than it would have been to be vanquished. He replied nothing but "Traitor!" and snatching a pistol from his saddle, levelled it at St. Real's head. But the Marquis had marked the movement of his hand towards the holster; and exclaiming, "Take that then, to cure your folly!" he struck him full on the casque a blow that he intended to be slight, but which drove in the steel, and laid him prostrate on the plain.

St. Real paused for an instant, to see whether the ill-fated D'Aubin would rise; but a cry of "*Au Roi! au Roi!*" struck his ear; and turning, he perceived the Baron de Rosny, covered with wounds, pointing to a spot where the white plume of Henry Quatre was still floating in the midst of the foe. It still floated; but nevertheless there was about it that uncertain wavering, that staggering rise and fall, which showed St. Real at once that his sovereign was hard pressed by the multitude that surrounded him. Every other thought was instantly cast aside before the feeling of superior duty; and calling to some of his troopers who were near to follow, he galloped on, and cleft his way like a thunderbolt into the press around the king. Ere he could reach him, however, a loud shout echoed from the midst of the crowd, and the white plume disappeared. Two sweeps of St. Real's sword dealt death to the reitters that lay in his path; and the next moment he reached the spot where Henry was struggling up from the carcass of his gallant charger, who had fallen dead beneath him, after receiving a multitude of wounds.

The young cavalier instantly sprang to the ground, exclaiming, "Mount my horse, sire!" and held the stirrup while the monarch sprang into the saddle. At the same moment a pistol shot struck him on the casque, and made him reel, but it did not penetrate the well-tried steel; and, looking round, he saw that in the brief space of time which had elapsed since he came up, the spot on which they stood had become comparatively clear, with none but one or two of his own and the king's attendants very near, while on the slope of the hill appeared a confused mass of the enemy, with their backs to the field of battle, and their faces towards the Eure.

The next instant his own ecuyer led him forward a horse, while the king, exclaiming, "They fly, St. Real, they fly! Mount and follow with what men you can collect!" struck his spurs into the charger's side, and galloped on to gain the horsemen who were in the act of pursuing the fugitives. St. Real hastened to obey, and springing on the charger's back, in a moment gathered together about fifty of his own troopers, and spurred after the king. As he reached the top of the slope, the whole field of battle lay open before his eyes; and a strange and confused, but not unpicturesque, sight it was. Three dark masses of the Leaguers and their pursuers were seen hurrying over the distant country towards the river; while, as the broken clouds were borne rapidly over the sky by a quick wind, the different groups of Royalists and fugitives, dashing on in fury after each other, were at one moment covered with deep shadow which hid all the several parts; at another, exposed, with the sunshine picking out in bright relief each individual horseman as he scoured across the upland. On the other side lay the plain where that fierce and bloody fight had taken place, covered with knots of fugitives, prisoners, wounded and dead, with the artillery playing upon a village in which the Leaguers were making a last effort; and the clouds of smoke still rolling solemnly over the field, after the fierce flash was gone, like heavy remorse following the eager act of angry passion. Small bodies of the Royalists too were seen, dispersing any group of the Leaguers who attempted to reassemble, and taking those prisoners whose horses were incapable of bearing them away; while the reserve under Marshal Biron, dark and heavy, hung upon the opposite slope, advancing slowly like a lurid thundercloud, borne along by the slow breath of the summer wind.

Near the same spot whence St. Real took a hurried glance over the field, the king himself had stopped for the same purpose; and the moment after he turned back. "St. Real," he said, as he came near the young noble, "the battle might be lost yet! Do you see the Walloons have still possession of the village?--and that strong body of Swiss there on the left still holds a good position. Come with me; we must make sure of the victory ere we urge too far the pursuit." Thus saying, he rode back at full speed towards the spot where his own squadron had been originally placed.

Lost sight of in the *mêlée*, his long absence had caused it to be very generally believed that the king was dead; and his approach was greeted by long and reiterated cries of "*Vive le Roy!*" from a number of his chief officers, who were engaged in rallying and reforming the squadrons which had been broken in the beginning of the battle. "Thanks, gentlemen, thanks!" cried Henry, taking off his casque. "Look to those Swiss, Monsieur de Biron: they may give us some trouble yet."

"Shall I send the infantry of the right wing to break them?" demanded the Baron de Biron.

"No," said Henry, thoughtfully; "no! the Swiss have always been good friends to the crown of France: nor would I shed the blood of any fellow-creature, could it be helped. Some one take a white flag, and offer them their lives if they lay down their arms and submit quietly. Beseech them to spare more bloodshed--for they must fall if they resist."

The Swiss, however, were too wise to protract resistance when resistance was vain. The offer of the victorious monarch was gladly accepted; the last of Mayenne's army that kept the field, laid down their arms. Henry then gave instant orders for a speedy and vigorous pursuit of the fugitives: and thus ended the battle of Ivry.

On the field where it had been fought, and on the spot where he himself had contended hand to hand with his cousin, St. Real caused diligent search to be made for Philip d'Aubin, superintending the examination himself, and gazing anxiously upon every corpse that was raised, until it became clear that the Count had not remained upon the field of battle. It was late in the evening ere this task was over; but when at length, after much useless labour, taken in order to leave not a painful doubt behind, St. Real was at length convinced, he returned to his quarters with a lightened heart and a thankful spirit.

CHAPTER XXX

We must now turn to the Count d'Aubin; but ere we inquire what became of him after he fell under his cousin's hand on the field of Ivry, it may be as well to relate some of the events which intervened between his night march from Gross[oe]uvres and his encounter with St. Real. On reaching the quarters of the Duke of Mayenne, he found that prince, whom he had not seen for some weeks, still up, notwithstanding the lateness of the hour; and he was immediately admitted to his presence. Mayenne was in high spirits, and full of confidence in regard to what would be the result of the approaching battle; and, after some conversation respecting the military arrangements about to be made, the Duke handed D'Aubin a small strip of parchment, asking him if he knew the hand-writing which it displayed.

"If the Duke of Mayenne," the writing went to express, "desires to recover a prize which not long ago escaped both his hands and those of the Count d'Aubin, he will detach a small force of cavalry to sweep the valley of the higher Eure between Courville and La Coupe."

"Know it!" cried D'Aubin, "know that hand! I know it well! It is that of my cousin St. Real's dwarf Bartholo. By the Lord! then Albert of Wolfstrom was not so wrong in his suspicions; and, with your highness's leave, after to-morrow's business be over, we will take counsel how this fair fugitive may best be recovered. I know that part of the country well; the St. Reals have a chace in the valley, and it is wild, wooded, and difficult for the movements of troops. But after the battle we shall have the whole country clear before us; and, if I be not sadly disappointed, ere to-morrow is at an end, I will make my fair and simple-seeming cousin pay for his perfidy towards me."

"In that, act as you think best," replied Mayenne; "and after the battle we will find means to recover the runaway, let the ground she has taken for her refuge be as wild as it will: and now, D'Aubin, farewell for the present. I will not bid so good a knight as you do his *devoir* to-morrow."

D'Aubin slept little during the night, and he was up betimes on the following morning; for a heart full of bitterness and anger chased slumber away. One of the first in the field, after sending a defiance to his cousin by a trumpet, he rode over the ground and narrowly observed the position of the king, as the small army of Royalists advanced from Fourcainville and the other villages where they had passed the night; but as he rode along, he perceived that four or five strange horsemen followed him about, as if watching his movements; and, on inquiry, found that they had joined his troop as volunteers since his arrival in the camp of the League. He took no farther notice of them at the time, and full of other thoughts, fierce, bitter, and engrossing, forgot what he had observed, till in the midst of the battle he was abandoned by the troops of Menancourt; and doubting not that they had been seduced by the pretended volunteers, he turned a vengeful and searching glance towards the rear, where they had been stationed; but to his surprise, the strangers closed up in line as soon as the others had gone over to the Royalists, without showing the slightest disposition to join them. D'Aubin then, as we have previously related, retreated, intending to unite his diminished force to some of the larger squadrons; when, perceiving that the reitters under Albert of Wolfstrom had followed Mayenne in his charge against the division of the king, and that the gallant chivalry of Henry Quatre were still maintaining an equal field against the more numerous forces of the League, he also poured his troops into the *mêlée*, in the hope of deciding the contest. Scarcely had he done so, however, when he heard the war-cry of the St. Reals, and caught a momentary glance of his cousin's person, as the dark and rolling cloud of battle broke away for a moment from before his eyes.

Maddened by fancied injuries, but still more by a feeling of inferiority and a consciousness of wrong, he strove to cleave his way through the press, in order to try, against one whose powers his pride undervalued, that skill and courage which had been so often successful against others. He succeeded, as we have seen, in at length meeting St. Real; but not till he had received several slight wounds--without which, indeed, he would have been no match for his more powerful and equally skilful cousin, but which tended to render him still more unequal to the encounter that he sought. Baffled in the combat by St. Real's skill, that vanity, which through life had led him forward from evil to evil, urged him on with redoubled force; and when he saw, without the power of parrying it, the descending blow which struck him from his horse, he groaned, in bitterness of spirit, not from the fear of death, but from disappointed hate. That blow, though light when compared with what St. Real's arm might have dealt, drove down his casque upon his head, split the rivets of the gorget, and laid him without sense or feeling upon the plain.

Scarcely had he fallen, when one of those fell monsters who frequent fields of battle to plunder the dying and the dead, attracted by his splendid surcoat, stooped over him, and, unbuckling the plastron, felt his heart beat. To make sure of no interruption from a reviving man, the human vulture struck him a stroke with his dagger. The wound he inflicted was but slight, and his arm was raised for a more effectual blow, when the sweep of a long sword, taking him in the back of the neck, severed his head from his body, and stretched him across the prostrate form he had been intent to plunder. The person who thus interposed to save D'Aubin was no other than one of the five volunteers who had joined his corps, and who, keeping close together through the *mêlée*, without striking a stroke except in self-defence, had followed, as fast as circumstances permitted, wherever the count had turned his steps. The press round the spot where St. Real and his cousin had encountered, had delayed them for some moments; but still they came up in time to rescue D'Aubin from the dagger of the assassin. The tide of battle had now somewhat rolled on; the ground around was clear; and springing from their horses, the strangers raised the senseless body of the wounded man in their arms, lifted him on a horse, and taking every precaution in order to bear him safely and easily, turned their steps with all speed from the field. Although confused bodies of the Leaguers and the Royalists were by this time mixed all over the plain, the men who bore D'Aubin wound their way amongst the contending squadrons with skill and presence of mind, and soon were behind the woods which skirted the plain to the right. The musketry was no longer heard, the sound of the cannon was faint; and pausing for a moment, they undid and cast away the Count's armour, and bound up his still bleeding wounds. Then, once more bearing him amidst them, they hurried from the field, taking the road towards Chartres.

When Philip d'Aubin, after a long period of sickness, during which insensibility and delirium had filled up the place of thought and understanding, at length recovered a clear perception of his own condition and of external things, he found himself lying, reduced to a state of infant weakness, on a soft and easy bed, in a chamber which was strange to his eye. Rich arras covered the walls; the hangings of the couch were of velvet and gold; and through the open casement at the end of the room breathed in the air of spring, sweet with the perfume of jasmine and of violets. Mingled with that scent, however, was a faint odour of incense; and on the left of the bed stood a priest in his robes, with two or three of the inferior clergy; at the foot were men in the dress then reserved for the followers of the healing art; while on the right stood two or three women, and a page.

For a moment these things swam indistinctly before the eye of the sick man; but the next instant, one particular object attracted all his attention. It was as lovely a form as ever man beheld, advanced before the rest, and kneeling by his bedside, with her face hidden in the rich coverings of the bed, and her dark black hair broken from the large gold pin that ought to have confined it, and falling in masses of bright dishevelled curls over her neck. The convulsive grasp with which she held the bedclothes, the deep sobs that shook her frame, the scared and anxious glances of the attendants, the solemn aspect of the priests, the sacred vessels for the communion and extreme unction, the extended cross held up before his eyes--all showed Philip d'Aubin that those who surrounded him supposed him to be dying; and that what he beheld was the last solemn ceremonies, and the last bitter tears, which attend the passing of the living to the dead. All eyes, but those which were hidden to conceal the burning drops that filled them, were fixed upon his countenance; and as his eyelids were raised, the priest, believing it the last effort of life, lifted his hands, saying in a solemn tone, "*Accipe, Domine*"--but as the eye wandered round the group, and the light of life and meaning beamed faintly up in the lamp that had seemed extinguished, the old man paused and stooped eagerly forward.

D'Aubin would have given a world to speak, but his tongue refused its office; and all that he could do was to turn a feeble glance of inquiry to the countenance that gazed upon him. The priest, without speaking, beckoned forward the physician, who laid his hand upon the patient's pulse, and then whispered eagerly a word in the ear of an attendant. A cup was instantly brought forward and held to the sick man's lips; a few drops of wine moistened his tongue. With difficulty and pain he swallowed the draught, and the unwonted effort made his heart flutter like that of a dying bird; but soon the beating became more regular; thick drops of perspiration stood upon his brow; he tried again to speak; his lips moved for a moment without a sound; but the next instant he succeeded better, and the name of "Beatrice!" murmured on his lips.

Hitherto there had not been a sound in the chamber, but the struggling sobs of the beautiful girl who knelt by the bedside, and the stealthy step of the attendant who brought the cup; but that one word, "Beatrice," spoken by a voice that had been so long unheard, struck the ear for which it was intended. Loosing her hold of the bedclothes, she lifted her streaming eyes, saw the change that had taken place, gazed for an instant with all the lingering incredulity of apprehension, and then, seeing that it was true-- quite true--Beatrice of Ferrara started on her feet, and ere any one could save her, fell back senseless on the floor. With as little noise and confusion as possible, she was carried from the chamber; and every means that the science of the day suggested, were employed to complete the recovery of the Count d'Aubin. The physician, however, who attended him, was a disciple of the great Esculapius, Nature; and therefore, slowly but progressively, the patient regained a degree of strength. All conversation was forbidden, and everything that might agitate him was carefully removed from his sight. No one visited his chamber for several days but the attendants necessary to watch over him, and the physician who directed their movements; and when, at the end of three days, the first returning struggles of D'Aubin's impatient spirit would not be controlled, and he would speak in spite of all injunctions to the contrary, the physician continued to sit beside him all day, in order to ensure that the subjects permitted contained nothing which would retard his recovery by agitating his mind. Beatrice of Ferrara had never entered his chamber since the day when, believing him to be in the agonies of death, she had cast off all reserve, and given way to that passionate burst of grief, which revealed to all around the secret of her heart's inmost shrine. Feeble as he had been at that moment, D'Aubin had not failed to mark and understand the whole; but in sickness, and with death at our right hand, we feel such things in a manner different from that in which they affect us in the high glow of insolent health, and all the vanity of life and expectation. D'Aubin felt touched and grateful for the love he saw; and when he asked for "The lady!" it was in a tone of reverence and softness, unmingled with a touch of the vain lightness which characterised the society in which they lived.

"If he meant the Princess," the physician said, "she was well--quite well."

D'Aubin replied, that he meant Mademoiselle de Ferrara whom he had seen in the room when he first recovered from the long stupor in which he had lain.

"Not many months ago," replied the physician, "Mademoiselle de Ferrara, as you call her, became, by her uncle's and her brother's death, Princess of Legnagno; but, as I said, she is well--quite well."

The Count mused for a moment; but after a while he besought the physician, in earnest terms, to obtain for him once more an interview, however short, with the lady in whose dwelling he lay. The good man, however, who had marked all that passed before, would not hear of it; and it was only on the following day, when he found that Aubin's impatience of contradiction was likely to injure him more than any other agitation he could undergo--he consented to bear his request to the ear of Beatrice. With her he found more difficulty than he had expected. She hesitated to bestow that care and attention upon the wounded man, now that he was recovering, which she had lavished on him without reserve when he had appeared dying. Her answer to his entreaty was cold and backward; and it was not till the physician brought her word that her reply had so much grieved the Count that his health suffered, that she consented once more to visit his chamber.

With a pale cheek, and with a timid step, Beatrice again approached the couch where D'Aubin, still as feeble as a child, anxiously awaited her coming. Her dark bright eyes stole a momentary glance at his worn countenance, and then fell again to the ground: for the feelings that were within her bosom--the knowledge that her love could no more be concealed, yet the wish to hide it--the compassion for D'Aubin's present state, which prevented her from covering her real sensations with the garb of coldness and disdain--and the doubt and the fear that even yet the chastening rod of suffering might not have had its due effect on him she loved,--all rendered it impossible for her to play the bold and careless part she had hitherto acted, yet left it difficult to choose another.

Seating herself by his bedside, while the physician stood gazing from the window, she strove to speak; but, for the first time in her life, her ready wit failed her; and ere she could call it back, D'Aubin himself broke the silence, and relieved her. "Beatrice!" he said in a low tone, "how much have I to thank you for! how much deep gratitude do I owe you!"

"Not so, Monsieur d'Aubin," she replied, without looking at him: "I have done but a common act of charity, in tending one so badly hurt as you were."

"Beatrice, dear Beatrice!" he replied, "use not cold words towards me; for believe me, that of all the medicaments which the leeches have applied to bring me back to life and strength, the sight of Beatrice, when I woke from that cold and deathlike trance, was the best cordial to my heart."

She looked up, and there was something like tears in her bright eyes; but all she could answer was, "Indeed, D'Aubin? Indeed?"

"Indeed, Beatrice! and in truth!" replied D'Aubin; "and ever since that hour the sight has been present to my eyes. I have remembered it--I have fed upon it; and believe me, that it has not only tended to heal the wounds of this weak frame, but has done much to cure the diseases of my still weaker heart and mind. Beatrice, my beloved, I have done you wrong. Wild, vain, and heedless, I have acted ill, and have cast away my own happiness through idleness and folly. That time is past: forgive me, Beatrice; and believe me, D'Aubin is changed."

"I hope it may be so, Monsieur d'Aubin," replied the fair Italian, more composedly--"I hope it maybe so; for though the past has given pain to many of your noblest friends, still Beatrice of Ferrara never yet gave up the hope that all might be amended. But now I leave you for to-day, because such conversation is not fitted to your present feeble state."

"Nay, nay, stay yet awhile, Beatrice," he cried, holding her hand, which he had taken, and gazing on her lovely features as if he would have impressed every line on his memory so deeply that remembrance might become a picture rather than that vague shadowy phantasmagoria which at best it is. Beatrice, however, disengaged her hand, and saying, "I will come again to-morrow; I must not be profuse of my presence, D'Aubin, lest you cease to value it;" she glided away and left him.

Eagerly did Philip d'Aubin watch for her coming; and day after day, so long as he continued unable to rise, did Beatrice accompany the physician back to his chamber, after the man of healing had made his morning's report touching his patient's health. Still fearful of yielding to all she felt, and with an intuitive knowledge of that subtle thing--the heart of man--Beatrice would fain have put a strong restraint upon her words and actions, and struggled against each of those little signs of deep and passionate love into which every day's conversation was prone to betray her. But who is there with a heart so obedient, and with a demeanour so completely under the rule and government of the mind, as to avoid every tender word, or smile of affection, or look of love, under a daily intercourse with one so dear as he was unto her? Besides, too, he was recovering from wounds, and had but by a miracle escaped death; and there is something sadly traitorous to all strong resolutions in watching the coming back of health--the reviving colour, the brightening eye, the expanding look; and in hearing the round tone of life's full breath take place of the low trembling voice of sickness. At first, as Beatrice entered his chamber, she would smile with a look of arch gaiety, to see the anxiety with which he turned to ascertain if it were her step he heard; but as day passed by on day, that smile lost all but the signs of gladness, and Beatrice might be seen watching for the hour of the visit, as well as her wounded lover. One day only was that visit not made; and that was the first on which D'Aubin rose from a couch whereon he had passed nearly six weeks in danger and anguish. It was not coquetry that made her refrain; it was not the least abatement of her love; but a feeling which she strove not to explain, even to herself, and which it would be impossible to explain to others. Be it what it may that moved her, she passed that day in prayer.

D'Aubin had been warned of her purpose not to come, and important business was the cause that Beatrice assigned for her absence; but the day having lost its usual occupations, neither the anxiety for her coming, nor the remembrance of her visit, affording matter for reflection, the thoughts of Philip d'Aubin turned to other things. Had he been one of those stern moralists who examine with microscopic exactness all their feelings, try every idea in the fine balance of equity, and search out all the lurking motives of the heart, D'Aubin might have started to discover how much he was recovered, by finding out how much his thoughts were flowing back into old channels. There were fancies crossed his mind, there were ideas presented themselves to his imagination, at which he recoiled; and he was still so feeble, his convalescence was still so far unconfirmed, that he blamed himself for the recurrence of thoughts that, still smarting as he was under the lash of suffering and the correction of adversity, he looked upon as base and ungenerous. He hastened, then, to banish all such ideas, and tried to look with horror and disgust those past vices and follies which had been once his pride. But the surest sign that our faults still cling to us, is the necessity of an effort to banish them from our thoughts. So long as he had been really ill, D'Aubin had hated his errors without an effort; but he was now convalescent, and they began to play around his imagination as familiar things.

The next morning broke in floods of splendour, bearing in a golden day of May; and as soon as his attendants would permit him, D'Aubin rose, and, supported by the physician, walked feebly forth into the garden of the chateau, where many a flower was opening its young bosom to the sweet breath of the spring air, and the warm beams of the genial sun. Under the spreading branches of an old tree, which, standing by the castle wall, cast its scarce unfolded leaves over the garden, some seats were placed; and there sat Beatrice with several of her women, busily employed at their everlasting embroidery: but ever and anon the eye of the lady turned to the low postern door; and when she at length beheld the expected sight, a smile, bright and beautiful as the morning, beamed upon her lip, accompanied by as warm a blush as ever touched with crimson the timid cheek of love.

Hours went on, and days, working with their usual power to the change of all things: but, oh! how differently does the mighty artist, Time, labour on the world of subjects ever beneath his hands. Who would dream that the same handiwork gave expansion to the bursting bud, and shrivelled up the withering leaf of winter; or at the same moment cast the pale violet dying on the green lap of spring, and called forth the rose to bind the temples of the lusty year? Yet as different, as strangely different, were the changes which he worked in Beatrice of Ferrara and in Philip d'Aubin; and those changes must be told and dwelt on separately.

Beatrice gave herself up to hope, that bright deluder, whose skilful, unseen diplomacy outwits, with scarcely an effort, the whole cabinet of reason. Fondly, idly, she gave herself up to hope; and the triumph of the magician was the more powerful, inasmuch as she had nobler allies than the mere selfishness with which she usually works her ends. Beatrice's hope was--not solely that the period of anxiety and pain for herself was past--

that the long-sought, dear-bought, well-earned happiness was before her--that the intense and burning love, which none but a nature passionate and ardent as her own could feel, was returned with full and answering passion; but she hoped, that he whom she loved, taught by severe affliction, had learned to know and value virtue--had become nobler, wiser, better, under the chastisement of sickness. The biting disdain which she had assumed towards him, when, in the insolence of unchecked prosperity and vigorous health, he had dared to speak the same language of love to her that he held towards others--the scorn, the defiance, with which she then treated him--had not survived the sight of a man, whose vices even had not estranged her heart, lying wounded, senseless, and apparently dying, before her eyes: and now, as day after day went by, and she was permitted to trace the bright progress of returning health on the face of him she loved; as a thousand new interests and tender feelings sprang up under the little cares and anxieties of his convalescence; as with the mild and gentle words of yet unconfirmed health, he spoke vaguely, but not the less ardently, of hopes and wishes, and feelings in common, the reserve which she afterwards assumed, as a light armour against slight perils, was cast away piece by piece; and she loved even to sit alone, and dream of him and happiness.

Such was the work of Time with Beatrice of Ferrara; with Philip d'Aubin it was different. He saw Beatrice in all her beauty, and in all her excellence, it is true, and he loved her better than any other upon earth; and yet, as health returned, came back the thoughts that he had known in health--the vanity, the pride, the levity. The heart of man can love as deeply and as fondly as that of woman; and who denies it such capability, libels it most foully; but the heart of man or woman either, worn by the touch of follies and of vices, soon loses its power to love: the temple is profaned, and the god will no longer dwell therein. Women, less called upon to pass amidst the foul and polluting things of earth, keep the heart's bright garment longer in its lustre--that lustre which, like the bloom upon the unplucked fruit, is lost at every touch; and this is why so few men are found to love with woman's intensity; because they have staked the fortune of the heart upon petty throws, and lost it piece by piece. So was it with Philip d'Aubin: he could not love as Beatrice of Ferrara loved; he could not feel as she could feel; and yet he loved her as much as he loved anything, but other thoughts shared that love; and when he remembered Eugenie de Menancourt, his unstable mind wavered under contending doubts and purposes. The tie between himself and her could easily be broken, he well knew, if both parties sought its dissolution; but he knew too, that she would seek its dissolution with an eagerness that roused every evil spirit in his heart in the cause of mortified vanity. He fancied to himself her triumph; he fancied the scoffs, and the sneers, and the jests of all that knew him; he pictured the smiles that would hang upon the lip of many whom he had scorned in his day of pride and success; and he crowned the whole by representing to the eye of imagination, her who had disdained his vows and rejected his hand, united to him who had supplanted him in love, and overthrown him in battle. And yet he loved Beatrice of Ferrara deeply, passionately; and while, at times, he revolved the means of triumphing over Eugenie, and casting back the pre-imagined scoff in the teeth of the world whose slave he had made himself, at others he longed to fly with the fair Italian girl, whose love and devotion were of so firm a quality; and, dying to his follies, his vices, and his native land, to live in some far country in peace, and love, and forgetfulness.

Such were often his meditations as health and strength slowly returned; and the increasing success attending the arms of Henry IV. which reached his ear in vague rumours, rendered the better course even the more immediately politic. It was thus one evening he had sat listening to the lute and voice of Beatrice, and thinking that ever to have that voice and lute to soothe the moments of gloom, and that lovely being to be the star of a domestic home, were, in truth, a lot that princes might envy, when the careful physician warned him away from the garden where they had been sitting, and through which the evening air was beginning to blow somewhat cool and sharp. D'Aubin lingered a moment; but Beatrice, with gentle urgency, enforced the old man's authority; and retiring to his chamber, the Count continued to gaze out, in solitude, on the spot where his fair companion and her women still sat. He heard the door of his apartments open, but he heeded not; so fixed was his attention upon the beautiful line of Beatrice's reclining figure, as--leaning back till the flowers of the jasmine behind her mingled with her jetty hair, and with her hand resting still upon the lute-- she gazed up at a bright passing cloud, that, tinted with the hope-like hues of the setting sun, was floating fast overhead.

"My lord Count!" said a low voice near him, "I have risked all to come to you for a moment, and to glad my eyes with the sight of your restored health."

D'Aubin turned in some surprise, and beheld the small form of Bartholo, his cousin's dwarf page. That form, indeed, seemed even more shrunk and small than ever; and on the usually sallow cheek of the dwarf there was a red and fiery glow that was not that of health; but nevertheless his voice was calm and strong, and his bright large eyes full of meaning and intelligence.

"Ha, Bartholo!" cried D'Aubin; "art thou here? Right glad am I to see thee: but how doest thou risk aught in thus coming to see me? Thou art safe here!"

"You know not, sir, that I have left your cousin long," replied the dwarf, "and am now with my first mistress; the only one who has ever had a real right to call me servant. But she wills not that I should come hither. It was only because the other page was sick that I was brought here to-day; and I tremble lest the time of departing comes, and she should miss me; for she has the eye of a lynx, and would instantly divine that I was here, against her express command."

"Why, how now, man of mysteries?" cried D'Aubin. "The hour of her departure! Does she not sleep in the castle to-night?"

"Never, sir! never!" replied the page. "Since three days after you began to mend, she has never passed one night within these walls. But I have not time to explain more mysteries, and only came to see you well, and perhaps, if I had a moment, to give you some counsel that were not ungrateful to your ear."

"Oh, you have time, plenty of time!" cried D'Aubin. "Lo, there she sits, and she is running over the strings of her lute in another air, though we cannot hear it here; but we can see when she rises; beautiful creature! One could gaze on her for ever! What is it you would say?"

"I would ask," replied the page, "if his Highness of Mayenne ever showed you some information he received concerning one whom you thought no less fair than the fair thing before you?"

"Yes, yes, he showed it to me!" answered D'Aubin. "But know you, Bartholo, that since we met, my mind has undergone a revolution. Like you, my little friend, I have changed my service also; and, as you said, am now with my first mistress, the only one who ever had a real right to call me servant."

The cheek of the dwarf turned pale; and he replied, "I thought, indeed, that you might be her servant, as we use that word in Italy: her servant *par amours*; and yet might like to wed the other too, if it were but to set your foot for ever upon all the gay jests and ribald laughter that are going on in the capital and the camp at your expense. But if you are set on marrying the fair Princess, Heaven forbid that I should stay you from such a righteous purpose!"

D'Aubin paused in thought for several moments, while the dwarf alternately glanced his eye to the changing countenance of the Count, and to the garden in which Beatrice still sat. "You speak strange words, Bartholo!" said D'Aubin at length: "I, with all the world, have deemed her as pure as the falling snow, ere it touches earth."

"And so she is," cried the dwarf, eagerly; "and so she is, I do believe. But yet, Monsieur d'Aubin, she loves--loves with that passion which makes such steps as we speak of easy. Besides, we in Italy are accustomed to look upon the marriage tie as a form much less binding than that which love twines for itself--a mere form indeed; and she, who worships the spirit of constancy, abhors all idle forms. But I speak too boldly, noble sir; and yet I seek to serve you. I have heard that Sir Albert of Wolfstrom, too, has betaken himself to your estates of Aubin, and--but I must fly!--see, she is rising!"

"Stay, stay a moment!" cried the Count; "she is not yet prepared to go forth, and I have much to ask you. Tell me, where is the Lady of Menancourt, and how may I best find her?"

"I dare not stay, sir!" replied the dwarf. "As soon as she enters, she will ask for me; but I will find another opportunity soon, of telling you more. In the mean time, fear not, sir, to press your advantage; for you know not passion's force with those upon whose birth a brighter sun has shone. Remember, I never gave you false information or wrong advice."

"Good faith, no!" said D'Aubin; "but she is coming in! Farewell, and return if you can to-morrow, my good Bartholo."

Without further reply, the page glided out of the room; and while D'Aubin, gazing upon Beatrice as she advanced towards the house, pondered over all the poisonous words that had just been dropped into his ear, Bartholo glided down the small and narrow staircases that led to a far part of the building, laughing with a bitter laugh as he went, and murmuring something of a goodly scheme well spoiled.

CHAPTER XXXI

D'Aubin passed a restless and unquiet night; and the next morning his pale countenance and languid look re-awakened in the bosom of Beatrice of Ferrara all those apprehensions and anxieties which are treacherous internal allies of the ambitious tyrant love. From that day, however, the conduct of Philip d'Aubin underwent a change, slight, indeed, to appearance, but yet of no small import. His demeanour grew softer, tenderer, more solicitous towards his fair companion; his conversation was all of love. From every bright thing in external nature, from the stores of history, or the pages of imagination, he drew matter for comparing, and illustrating, and typifying the ardent passion of the heart. Beatrice listened, pleased, and joined in, and felt that she was beloved; and spoke her own warm feelings boldly, so long as the words were general. Her eyes, and the varying colour of her cheek, told all the rest: and much would they discuss the evil and the good of strong and fiery passion; and to their hearts' content they proved that it was aught but a fault, a capability in a bright spirit, a proof of superior energy of heart and mind. But then Beatrice said it must be ruled and governed by ties and principles as strong and energetic as itself; and D'Aubin, though he did not venture to dissent, went on in the praise of intense and vehement love without restriction, and brought forth a thousand examples in which that passion, in what he called nobler and more generous times, had been carried to a height unknown in their own age. Still, on every point where he and Beatrice might differ, he touched the subject lightly, and then left it; pointing still, by many an endearing name and soft caress, the object and application of all his bland eloquence. Beatrice hoped and believed, and was happy; and now that her bosom was at rest--that the conflict of hope, and fear, and passion, which had ceaselessly agitated her during the last four years, was at an end, and her heart reposed in peace on the conviction of being loved, and the prospect of future happiness, her demeanour grew milder, softer, tenderer; it lost the wild and eager fire which it had acquired, and fell back into all that was sweet, and womanly, and gentle. The days passed on, too, in peace; for D'Aubin asked no questions upon the many matters which might have called up subjects painful to either; and Beatrice, ere she spoke of the past, wished all those things completed which would put an irrevocable seal upon the happiness of the present. Then she thought that addressing her husband and her lover both in one, she could tell him that all he had done amiss was forgiven; that he had been ever loved, even in his errors; and that her eye had been ever watchful, her hand ever stretched out, to snatch him from the consequences of his faults, and to lead him away from those faults themselves.

At length, on one bright and sunshiny morning in June, when the clear lustre of health had fully returned into D'Aubin's eye, and his step was as firm as it had been four months before, the lovers sat together in a wood near the chateau, passing away, under the shadow of the old trees, the hot hours of summer noon. She scarcely knew why, but with a lingering touch of timidity, to which she yielded willingly, without trying to scrutinise it, Beatrice had ever, in her interviews with D'Aubin, kept some of her women round her; and although, feeling that there was much to be said between them which were better said without witnesses, she had day after day determined to dispense with their presence, still there they sat at a little distance, plying the busy needle on the object which served to occupy their discreet eyes. Their presence was no great restraint, it is true, but still D'Aubin found it burthensome; and, resolved to hesitate no longer in his purposes, he besought Beatrice to send the women away. With a blushing cheek, and somewhat of an agitated tone, Beatrice complied; and then, turning away her head, played idly with the flowers that gemmed the grass on which they sat.

D'Aubin paused and hesitated, even at that moment, if he should go on; but his determination soon returned, and gliding his arm round her waist, while with his right hand he took hers unresistingly, he said, "Beatrice, dear Beatrice, do we not love one another?"

Beatrice replied nothing; but the trembling of her whole frame was a sufficient answer; and D'Aubin went on. "Hear me, Beatrice, and believe me, when I say that I love you with my whole heart and soul, with the deepest, the truest, the most lasting affection; that I love you better than anything on earth; and that for you I am ready to abandon friends, and country, and station altogether."

He paused, and Beatrice replied in a low voice, "But, thank God! no such sacrifice is necessary, D'Aubin."

"If it be, I am ready to make it," pursued the Count, in a voice to which deep and sincere passion lent all its earnestness; "if it be, I am ready to make it. Oh, Beatrice, you know not how I love you! but I must be loved with the like affection, not with the cold and formal love of fashion and society--

idols to which I have only bowed because I found no better godhead. Now I have found a power above,--now I know that, however I have erred, I have loved you ever, and you alone; that without you the earth would be one vast piece of desolation to my eyes. Wherever you are, is henceforth my country; wherever you dwell, is henceforth my home; for you I will sacrifice everything, for you I will regret nothing. Tell me, Beatrice, is your love for me the same?"

"Can you doubt it, Philip?" she replied, "can you doubt it?"

"Then I am happy," he cried, pressing her to his bosom; "the vain ties, the idle ceremonies of the world may bind together cold and careless hands, and indifferent and unimpassioned bosoms, but between your heart and mine, Beatrice, there will be a dearer, a nobler, a more lasting tie, and we will have no other!"

Beatrice disengaged herself from his arms. "What do you mean, D'Aubin?" she cried: but then pausing, she added, "but I forgot; you fancy yourself bound to another by one of those bonds of society which cannot be broken: but you are mistaken; your supposed marriage with Eugenie de Menancourt is null. The ceremony was vain, the seeming priest was none, and I have papers here to prove that he was but a soldier in the army of the Huguenots."

"Glad am I to hear it," cried D'Aubin, again throwing his arms around her; "yet listen to me, Beatrice; is the same idle ceremony necessary between you and me? Do you doubt my love, Beatrice? will your constancy faint unless upheld by an idle form? Is your love so weak, that, when I am ready to resign all, even to my country, for you, you will not make the sacrifice even of a mere name for me?"

Beatrice turned, as he held her in his arms; and for an instant gazed in his face, with a look of wondering inquiry, as if--even acquainted with the world and all its ways as she was--the base, ungrateful wickedness of his purpose were too much for her belief. At length, convinced that her ears had not deceived her, and satisfied, from the soft, entreating expression he assumed, that his proposal was the result of calm, deliberate forethought--no idle jest, no capricious trial of her heart--she burst from him like a young eagle from a net which had been spread for larks; and, standing in all the majesty of indignant beauty on the spot where she had lately sat, she gazed upon him with flashing eyes, and a quivering lip, while the fingers of her right hand felt along her girdle for the dagger, which, according to a common custom of the day, usually hung there. But it had been forgotten; and it might be lucky for the Count d'Aubin that it was so.

For a moment anger and surprise, and bitter indignation seemed to take away all words; but ere D'Aubin could speak again, she had recovered herself. "Out of my sight, viper!" she cried; "base, ungrateful, perfidious snake! Oh God! Oh God! never let woman, henceforth and for ever, love man again. Let her trample upon that black thing, his heart, and sport with his torture, and deceive his love, and betray his confidence, till he know not where to find faith or truth in all the world; for, the moment that he believes her true, or kind, or gentle, or affectionate, he turns a serpent which would sting her, and poison for her the life, the feelings, the happiness, she is ever ready to devote to him. Out of my sight, traitor, I say! Why linger you here?"

"Hear me! hear me, Beatrice!" cried D'Aubin, rising and attempting to take her hand. "Hear me! I meant not to offend you! I am no traitor. I meant but----"

"No traitor!" cried Beatrice. "Is he no traitor, that, received with friendship and hospitality into the heart of a fortress in time of war, treated with confidence and love, saved from death, cherished, protected, befriended, strives to corrupt the garrison and betray the leader, to ruin the defences, and destroy the walls? Out on thee, man! Out on thee! I would not be the base, ungenerous, contemptible thing thou art, for all the power of a Cæsar!"

D'Aubin saw he had deceived himself; and at the same moment that he perceived that he had risked the love of Beatrice for ever, he felt most strongly what an inestimable jewel that love was. "Hear me--but hear me, Beatrice!" he said. "Have I not said that I am ready to sacrifice everything for you? I make no exception to that sacrifice; not a pride, not a vanity, not a prejudice do I wish excepted. I will sacrifice all! Be mine on any terms. I did but think that Beatrice was more liberal, more unprejudiced, than our idle crowd of courtly dames, who insist upon a ceremonious vow that they break, one and all, most unceremoniously, rather than that private compact which binds the heart."

"Say no more, Sir--say no more," cried Beatrice. "Those last words are quite enough, if all the rest of your conduct were insufficient. There is hope in every man who can yet believe in purity; but he whose vice is so confirmed, that he does not credit the existence of virtue, is irreclaimable. So you did but think," she continued, while her cheek again glowed, and her eye flashed--"you did but think, that Beatrice of Ferrara was too liberal, too unprejudiced, to hold her honour as a jewel, without which life is darkness and bitterness. You did but think, that, because to save, to reclaim, to elevate a man she fancied not wholly lost, she braved opinion, and, strong in her own righteousness, set the world's maxims at defiance. You did but think that she had forgotten the line between virtue and prejudice, in her mad love for Philip d'Aubin, and would soon, for his sake, trample upon the one, as she had spurned the other? But, sir, you were mistaken; and you will now quit for ever her you have insulted."

D'Aubin had nothing in the shape of reason to reply, but he had much in the shape of love; and with a heart full of passion, and shame, and regret, he failed not to plead for forgiveness with vehemence and eloquence. Forgetting pride and all its train, he cast himself at her feet; he held her hand when she sought to go; and he poured forth, from the deep feelings in his heart, all those ardent and fiery words which well might move and win. At first Beatrice strove to stay him, and to disengage her hand; but when she found that his vehemence would be heard, she stood and listened, but with that calm and cold demeanour, which ere long brought his eloquence to an end. Then withdrawing her hand and her robe from his grasp, she said, in a low and agitated, but determined tone, which, full of deep feeling but strong resolution, was much more striking than the words of passion which had at first broken from her lips, "Rise, Monsieur d'Aubin! and as I have heard you, now hear me! When first you talked of love to me, I knew you to be young, and light, and foolish; but I thought that I discovered, underneath the follies of youth and gaiety, deeper feelings, better aspirations, and a nobler soul. I then saw you flutter round many another woman, and I heard of vices into which I did not inquire; for, in your language and your manner towards me, there was much that gave me better hopes, and I strove to reclaim you by gentleness and kindness. Deeper offences succeeded; and it became me, though love loses hope but slowly, to assume a demeanour towards you, which might at once tend to awaken you, and do justice to myself. The weakness of a woman's heart taught me to believe, that, on one occasion I had carried severity too far, and I reproached myself for having hurried you on in evil. I soon had an opportunity of mending that. In a battle, where I had good assurance that your party would fail, I caused you to be followed by some faithful and skilful men, who had orders to rescue you at any moment of extreme need. They brought you wounded, and apparently dying, to my dwelling, and like a sister I tended you night and day, till all hope was lost; and then I wept for you as no sister could have wept. Against all calculation you recovered; saw how deep, how strong, was my love towards you; taught me to give full scope to that love, by pretending reformation and virtue: and now you have ended all, by proving to me that kindness, like the spring sun upon a torpid snake, but re-awakens your venom with your strength; that you look upon the love of woman but as the means of injuring her; that kind deeds and services but hire you to ingratitude; and that, though you may be capable of passion, you are incapable of love! Thus convinced, sir, I bid you quit me, and for ever. No time, no circumstances, will change my resolution of banishing you from my thoughts for ever; for Beatrice of Ferrara would sooner die than wed one whom she has at length learned so thoroughly to despise, could he offer a kingly crown."

D'Aubin rose in silent bitterness, and half turned away; but ere he went he again paused, as if to speak, and a few indistinct words trembled on his tongue. Beatrice, however, stopped him, and with an air of calm, stern dignity, exclaimed, "No more, Monsieur d'Aubin, I will hear no more; it is time, sir, that you should quit one whom you have so basely insulted. Your horse is in the stable, your health is restored; my servants will guide and guard you on your way, should you need protection; but never let your step cross the threshold of Beatrice of Ferrara again, as never again shall your image enter her mind."

"Your commands shall be obeyed, Lady," replied D'Aubin, proudly; "and as to protection, I need none. Fare you well, madam, with thanks for the kindness you showed me at first; and with silence--if so it must be--for the harshness you now show; and yet I could wish to be heard."

"Not a word more!" replied Beatrice. "Sir, I bid you farewell! Laura! Annette! Where are those girls? Annette, I say!" and turning from him, she hastened on in the direction which her maids had taken when she sent them from her. They were at no great distance; and bidding them follow her, Beatrice with a rapid step retrod her way towards the chateau. Firmly, and apparently unshaken by what had passed, but with her dark bright eyes bent upon the ground, the beautiful girl entered the gates of the house; hurried along its many passages to the chamber in which, during the first period of D'Aubin's illness, she had been accustomed to repose; and opening the door, advanced towards a chair. But the energy of her great effort did not last till she reached it; her brain reeled, her steps wavered, and she sunk upon the floor, insensible and silent, ere her attendants could catch her in their arms. That innate faculty which teaches women to divine, as by intuition, the secrets of their fellow woman's hearts, held the girls who had followed Beatrice quite silent and noiseless, as they did all in their power to recall her to herself. There was no bustle, no outcry, no running hither and thither for assistance; but with quiet and persevering assiduity they tended her, till at length she opened her eyes and gazed languidly round the chamber. Then came some broken sobs, and then a flood of tears; and then, wiping away the drops that gemmed her long dark eyelashes, Beatrice of Ferrara once more shook off the bonds of woman's weakness, and was herself again.

"Be silent on what has past, Annette," she said; "Laura, I know I can trust you. I would fain learn whether the chateau is free of all guests; I long to be alone in my own house again. Fly, Annette, and see."

The girl sped away, and soon returned, saying, "The count mounted his horse, lady, and rode away some twenty minutes since."

"Did he?" said Beatrice--"did he?" and she fell into a deep fit of thought.

CHAPTER XXXII

So long as there was a human eye upon her, Beatrice of Ferrara governed the mingled and passionate feelings that struggled with each other in her bosom, and would fain have had the mastery of her also. After a time, however, when she had preserved her apparent calmness long enough to deceive completely those around her; when she had drawn, with a hand full of grace and fancy, the groups of flowers which were to serve as patterns for her maiden's embroidery--had struck the chords of her lute with a careless but skilful hand, and talked for some ten minutes on a butterfly--she desired to be left alone.

Then however, when, with the door closed and the arras drawn, there was no eye upon her but that of Heaven, she once more gave way to all she felt. "Oh, God! Oh, God!" she cried, clasping her small hands, "to be thus treated by one whom I have so deeply loved--for whom I have done so much--for whose sake I sacrificed my nights and days, scattered my fortunes, left my state and station, took on me menial offices, put my life in peril, and even my good name to risk--and more, far more, for whom I forgot and pardoned those errors that women forget least easily, and loved him still, even when he sported with my love as a thing of nought! Oh, God! oh, God! that he who, if ever man yet believed the love of woman to be a pure and holy thing, should have held the feelings of my heart most sacred--that he should dare to talk to me the words of shame, the vile sophisms of guilt and infamy; that he should dream that I--I who have stood alone, in the midst of a depraved court, the wonder and hatred of them all--that I should become his paramour, his leman, to be held or discarded at his pleasure--to play him sweet airs upon the lute, and sing to him when he was in the mood, and be called the Italian mistress of the gay Count d'Aubin!" and, as she called up all the images of the degradation he had proposed, she strained her hands upon one another till the clear blood vanished from beneath the small finger nails; and she raised her dark eyes to heaven, as if asking, "Is it possible that God can permit such baseness."

"It is my own fault!" she cried at length; "it is my own fault! I should have known too well what a vile slave man is--how he licks the dust beneath our feet, so long as we tread upon his neck, and turns to smite us as soon as we smile upon him. I should have known it, and with haughty dignity and distant sternness commanded the love that I have stooped to win. It is my own fault, weak girl that I am--it is my own fault! He thought that she who could go masquerading in boy's attire, and make herself the companion of grooms and horse-boys for his sake--that she who could dare the perils of the camp in a strange guise--could come and go, at the risk of question and discovery, through the gates of a beleaguered city--could bind up his wounds with her own hands, and watch for fourteen nights by the side of his sick bed,--would surely refuse him nothing--no, not her honour. Or perhaps even now, in his profligacy of heart, he scoffs and jeers at the thought of my fastidiousness; or deems that, by a cunning device and affectation of virtue, I sought to patch up a ruined reputation by a marriage with him. He may hold me as some light wanton! Out upon him! out upon him! Did he but know the heart he tramples on!" and bursting into tears, she covered her face with her hands, and remained thus for several minutes in silent bitterness of heart.

The tears again seemed to relieve her; and at length she wiped them from her eyes, and looked out vacantly upon the gay and sunny landscape that lay stretched in bright confusion from the height on which the chateau stood, to some distant hills, that, rising again on the opposite side of a deep valley, towered up, now covered with green woods, now massed in the grey distance.

However resolutely the soul may hold itself within the citadel of the heart besieged by grief, the garrison of that sad fortress will be affected by the sight of things that pass beyond its limits. Sweet sounds, though we listen to them not, will tend to soothe; and pleasant objects, though the eye appears void of all remark, will tranquillize and calm. There were lovelier scenes to be found on earth, than that which lay beneath her sight, and Beatrice had seen many fairer far: but over it the sun, now slanting down towards his rest, was casting soft broad shadows; and now and then a slow passing cloud came, like the faint and pleasing shade of melancholy that sometimes steals upon our happiest moments, and touched the bright things below with a blue ethereal hue as it flitted on above them. Nothing was seen to move in the sky or on the earth, but that slow cloud and its soft shadow; but, on a bough before the window, a gay-hearted bird carolled volubly to the evening sun, mingling, however, now and then, with its blither notes, a tone or two in a sad minor key, which made its song harmonise both with the scene and with the heart of her who listened. I am wrong; the heart of Beatrice did not harmonise with it,--her bosom was full of griefs too deep, too lasting, to assimilate with the glad voice of nature; but still the melancholy tones so far chastened the cheerful song of the bird, that she could hear it and not think it harsh, and the shadows of that cloud were just sufficient to make her feel the brightness not blighting. She sat and gazed; and though neither her eye nor her ear marked anything with precision, she fell into a dreamy fit of musing, and that musing was softer and less bitter than it had been.

True, she thought of the course of her love, and of that love's blight. She knew that for her joys of life, the dreams, the hopes, the imaginings--all the green things of a happy heart, in short--were withered, and blasted, and shrivelled up, like the leaves of a bough broken off by the lightning. To be calm and passionless, sad and solitary, were the brightest aspirations which her once ardent bosom could harbour now; but still to think over such a state, was peace, to the bitter paroxysm that went before. Did she ever think that hope might revive in regard to him she had loved? Never! For though her love was not over--ah, no! and she would have given her fortune and her life to have blessed him; yet so lost was all her esteem and all her confidence, that could she have thought her heart would ever betray her into one weak fancy in regard to him, she would have torn it out to trample it beneath her feet. She loved him still, she knew, she felt she loved him; for her heart was as a pile of incense which that passion had lighted, and the fire could only be extinguished by the end of her own being; but still the dream, the bright and golden dream, of happiness was over; and not even love--that ardent and undying love, which was now an indivisible part of her being and her soul--could have bribed her, by the brightest promises of hope, to see that man again, or hear his lips pronounce one other word. No! bitterly, but fully, was she convinced at last of his unworthiness; and though she still loved the erring and earthly being whom her own imagination had purified and adorned, the dream of hope was at an end--the voice of the syren was mute: and yet a consolation gradually stole upon her heart, soothed the anguish and disappointment, and did away the indignation and disdain. On it, too, she framed the scheme of her future life, as she paused and thought of the coming years. That consolation was the conviction, the certainty, the indubitable assurance, that she was beloved; that he who had insulted and injured her--who had repaid her tenderness with ingratitude, and her confidence by baseness--still loved her deeply, passionately, and alone. What then was her resolution? Not to watch him farther, even through the eyes of others--not to seek for tidings of his actions, or to dream that he would amend; but on the contrary, to fly him far and for ever; to shut her ears against every rumour from the land in which he lived, and dead as he was to her, to consider him no more amongst the living; but still, as the balm and the comfort of the long after-years, to remember that she had been beloved--that, impure and dark as was the flame that had been lighted upon the altar of his heart, still it had been kindled, and had burned for her. This was to be the theme of memory--the occupation of her long, lonely hours--the matter for the immortal working of thought--the balsam for her wounded heart--the light of her long night of maiden widowhood,--that she had been loved by him she loved!

As she thus thought, and as she thus determined, the bitterness of her grief diminished. Dark and melancholy, indeed, was the fate that she pictured for herself, but yet it was relief, for it offered her tranquillity at least; and she had learned, amidst the strife of hope, and fear, and passion, to value God's best blessing--peace. Her meditations had been long, and had not exactly followed the even course in which they have been here detailed; for tears were not wanting to chequer them, nor many an angry and a bitter thought to struggle hard against the not unsound philosophy with which she sought to preserve, for future years, all, out of the bright harvest of her hopes now blighted, that had escaped the storm. But the tears grew less frequent, and the bitter pangs of disappointment waxed fainter, as the minutes flew; and at length, when she had determined how to shape her course through the rest of life's long and dangerous voyage, she raised her eyes once more to the heaven above and the landscape below; and the objects which met her gaze were more marked and noted now, than they had been not long before.

The change upon the scene, however, was but slight--the same bird was still tuning its unwearied throat in the tree hard by--the same unmoving stillness dwelt over the whole view--and not a living object was to be seen upon the solitary road that wound away through a thinly peopled part of the much-depopulated realm of France. But the shadows had grown longer, and the little stream which had lately glistened in the sunshine, now rested scarcely visible in the brown shade of the hills; and those changes, slight as they were, to a quick and imaginative mind like that of Beatrice, might well speak of time's rapid pace, and man's slow resolves. Stretching forth her hand to a small silver bell, she rung is sharply; and when the girl Annette appeared, bade her call Bartholo instantly.

It was not long before the dwarf obeyed the summons; and though he entered with that air of deference and respect, which was habitual to him in the presence of Beatrice, yet there was a gleam of satisfaction in his eye which he could not quell; and which, had she been in her usual keen and observing state of mind, would not have escaped the glance of his mistress. But Beatrice scarcely saw him as he stood before her; but sat with her eyes bent upon the ground, and her busy thoughts straying sorrowfully over the past.

"You sent for me, Madam," said the dwarf at length; "and I come joyfully, because I have not been thus honoured of late so often as I used formerly to be, when Bartholo's scheme, or Bartholo's advice was well nigh his lady's oracle."

"I have somewhat distrusted thee, Bartholo!" said Beatrice, gravely. "Many of my plans have failed in thy hands----"

"But by no fault of mine, lady!" cried the dwarf, eagerly. "What have I done to be distrusted? How have I deserved to lose your confidence? What secret have I betrayed? How have I acted to frustrate anything that you proposed?"

"Those, Bartholo," replied the lady, "those who suffer themselves to be discovered in their art, by open acts or heedless words, are politicians of a different stuff from that of which thou art made. But there are such things as looks, and smiles, and frowns, and curlings of the upper lip, which, to the eye of Beatrice of Ferrara, are often as legible as a book fairly printed in the language of her native land. I have somewhat doubted thee; but I may have been deceived--and God send it may be so! for I would not willingly believe that any one whom I have nourished with my bread, and have rewarded not only with dull gold, but also with inestimable favour and affection, would deceive or betray me; far less could I wish to think, that one who has known me from infancy, and on whom my parents, as well as myself, have rained benefits, would wrong my confidence."

"Lady!" replied the dwarf vehemently, "so help me Heaven, as I would sooner die than do ought that you do not wish, except for your own good!"

"Ay, there may we bitterly fall out, good Bartholo, if we speak farther!" replied Beatrice. "What I require is service, and not judgment of my actions; and henceforth let me but see that you even waver in obeying, or fulfil not my behest, whatever it may be, to the very letter, and I will send you from me never to return again. However, I somewhat doubted thee, and therefore have not trusted thee in matters where I required uninquiring promptitude and exact obedience. Those matters now are over, and a smoother trodden path lies out before me."

Bartholo started, for he had heard and marked much that had passed; and yet she spoke so calmly, that he deemed it impossible one of her passionate nature could bear the blight of all her hopes so meekly. "It has wrung my heart, lady," he said, in a tone of deep despondency, that touched Beatrice more at this moment than it might have done at any other, because grief is credulous of grief. "It has wrung my heart, lady, to have been distrusted by you for an hour, though the wound would have gone deeper had I deserved it. But you know not, lady, what it is, when one has been brought up from boyhood near so bright and good a person as yourself; has been habituated to watch your every word, to obey you, and to hasten before your wishes to please you; has become keen of wit and daring of execution for the sole service of your behests; and has watched you expand from loveliness to loveliness, like a flower in the spring tide--you know not what it is to be looked coldly on, even for a moment; to be distrusted by her whom one would give the inmost heart's best blood to serve."

The tone touched Beatrice, for it was unlike the dwarf's ordinary cynicism: but there was something in the words, though they were respectfully spoken, which did not please her; and she might have replied more coldly than the kindness of her heart approved, had not the dwarf gone on rapidly:--"At your birth, lady, I was little more than twelve years old; and from that hour to this, I have followed your fortunes and obeyed you in every word, even to quitting you when you bade me quit you, and taking apparent service, once with a man I hated, and once with a man I despised; and now I find that you have distrusted me, you have looked cold upon me, you have kept me from your presence! Lady, I beseech you, do not so again; rather as you say, send me from you for ever. Call me to you, and say, 'Bartholo, thou pleasest me no longer, get thee gone, and take thy stinted and misshapen form from before my eyes; let me see no more thy apish countenance! Despised of all the world, thou art despised of me also; and though the dwarf has been my sport and mockery, has stood in the place of parrot, or lapdog, or marmoset, I am now tired of the goblin; so get thee hence!' Say this! say a thousand things more biting and bitter still, but never, oh never, lady, distrust me again."

"Nay, Bartholo, nay!" replied Beatrice, better pleased with his last words than those that preceded them. "Thou goest too far, in the bitterness of thine anger. I have never contemned, I have never despised thee! and have felt pity for thy fate, less because it truly deserved pity, than because it grieved thee. As to the past, thou ownest thyself, that if thou hadst deemed my interest required it, thou wouldest have betrayed my confidence; I was just, therefore, in mistrusting thee; but it was thy vanity I doubted--vanity that must judge of my happiness better than I can myself--and not thy love, Bartholo, which I do verily believe would seek that happiness for me at the risk of life."

"Oh! never, never doubt that, lady!" cried the dwarf, casting himself at her feet, and kissing her hand; "never, never doubt that; for your utmost trust therein can only do me scanty justice."

Beatrice withdrew her hand. "Enough, enough!" she said. "We understand each other for the future. You always remember, that I am the best judge of my own happiness; and I----" He shook his head with a mournful look, and clasping his hands together, cast his eyes upon the ground. "What mean you, knave?" cried Beatrice, for his action interrupted her more than words could have done. "What would you by that gesture?"

"I would ask, lady," said the dwarf, in a firm but melancholy tone,--"If you have lately proved yourself so good a judge of your own happiness? Pardon me, my noble lady! Pardon me! but did I not long since predict all that has happened? Did I not tell you, when first you fixed your love on one whose name I will not pronounce, so deeply do I hate him for his conduct towards you----"

"Hate him not, Bartholo!" interrupted Beatrice, fixing her bright dark eyes upon the dwarf as she spoke--"hate him not, Bartholo; for I love him still! and he loves me!"

A bright flush played over the pale cheek of the dwarf, like a gleam of summer lightning upon the twilight sky, and his nether lip quivered; but for some moments he made no reply, except by again clasping his hands together, and gazing down upon the ground, as if in deep meditation. "Lady!" he said at length, "you love him still! I doubt it not; for yours is one of those firm hearts, on which a line once engraved can never be effaced. But alas, alas! he loves not you; and all your sad experience will not convince you, solely because you still love him."

"Not so, Bartholo," replied Beatrice. "All my experience convinces me that he does love me; and I thank God for it, though most likely I shall never see his face again. Do not interrupt me! For once I condescend to speak to you of my past and my future actions; but after this, we mention such things no more. I am not the weak being you believe me. I placed you in the service of Philip d'Aubin, now years ago, not that you might act as a spy for me upon each pitiful and insignificant occurrence of his life, or note every failing or every falsehood he committed against the vows he had plighted to me; but, on the contrary, to satisfy myself on two great points, whereon my future happiness depended, first, whether he loved me, and next, whether he might not become worthy of my love. When he left Paris and retired into Maine, shaken by still greater doubts, I determined to watch him myself more nearly, and made you prepare me an entrance into the family of his uncle; but it was still for those two great objects that I risked so much. Circumstances rendered this scheme nearly fruitless: the death of his uncle, his return towards Paris, his separation from his cousin, all thwarted me; but still, step by step, and little by little, his character developed itself before me. At length, hoping and confiding still, I had the man I loved, followed by my emissaries, traced from place to place, withdrawn from the fatal battle which ruined the cause he had espoused, and brought hither as thou knowest. Here I watched him from sickness unto health. Here the last trait of his character displayed itself. All is open--all is clear! My two questions are resolved! I am satisfied. He loves me, Bartholo! He does love me! But he is unworthy of my love!"

She spoke rapidly and eagerly, but she had by this time regained her command over herself; and not a tear rose in her eye, as she briefly touched upon the various efforts which love, deeper, stronger than even she herself believed, had urged her on to make, and upon the sad result of all her endeavours. As she ended, indeed, she raised her eyes to the sky; and, led away by memory, forgot the presence of the page and the conclusion of her speech, and, gazing out for many minutes, remained in silent but painful meditation. Still she gave no way to grief; and, after awhile, again turned towards the dwarf, saying--"Well, Bartholo, so much for the past! Now for the future. For eleven long years have I sojourned in this fair realm of France, but my stay therein draws towards an end. The last tie that bound me to this place is broken! My soul yearns towards my native land. Bartholo, I am about to tread back my way to Italy."

"Indeed! indeed!" cried the dwarf, his whole face brightening. "Then all is right, indeed. But when, lady--oh, tell me when?"

"I knew not that thou wert such a lover of thy native land!" replied Beatrice, as she gazed upon his small features beaming with a sort of triumphant joy. "I have heard thee call thyself a citizen of the world; and vow that nature, when she made thee smaller than the common race of other countries, by unfitting thee for any, had fitted thee for all alike. But I see that, smother our feelings however we may, the love of our own land will not give way so long as memory binds us to it with the thousand ties of sweet associations and early happiness. Well, be thy mind at ease! Eight days, eight short days, and I am on my way hence, unless some unforeseen event delay me. I have but to withdraw my poor girls from Paris, at least those that like to follow me; to place the somewhat wasted wealth which I have here under the protection of the laws, if the laws, indeed, can give protection now-a-day; to make sure of one point more, which will soon be settled, and then to depart."

The face of the dwarf, which, during the whole of his interview with his lady, had been agitated with strong feelings either of mortification or of joy, now at once resumed the look of calm bitter cynicism, which, though perhaps more natural to his features, was, at all events, more habitual. "Ay, lady!" he said, "so it is ever! There is ever one point more to be made sure of when a lady's love and her judgment lead her different ways; and that one point more will very surely keep your steps from Italy. So I will e'en go and sing."

"Knave, thou art somewhat too bold!" cried Beatrice. "I have pampered thee too much, and made thee insolent; but thou shalt be better taught in future!"

"Not so, lady, not so!" cried the dwarf, in a deprecatory tone. "Forgive the first outbreaking of my disappointment. I thought our journey to Italy sure, when suddenly came that '*one point more;*' and I know human nature all too well to doubt, that upon one small point love can raise up such mighty prison-walls, that the best climber, ere he could escape, would break his neck in the attempt to scale them."

"Like others who fancy they know human nature well," answered Beatrice, "thou cheatest thyself with thine own imaginations. That one point more will not detain me here; but whether thy curiosity regarding it--and which I clearly see--originate in folly or in policy, it shall not be gratified. Content thyself with what I choose to tell thee, and ask no more! And now listen to my commands. Make every preparation for a journey; and in regard to this house, on which I have wasted so much wealth that might have been better spent, take order that, if possible, it be guarded against the chances of these civil wars till peace be again established. You understand what I would have. When law is once more recognised in France, perchance it and the hotel in Paris may be sold, and I have nothing more in a land that I no longer love. Now get thee hence and leave me; but let all things be done quickly."

The dwarf replied nothing, but retired at once; and Beatrice, after following him with her eyes to the door, sat for several moments in silence, with an air of anxious thought. "I doubt that imp!" she said at length. "I doubt that imp! There has of late been a fire and an eagerness in his words when he speaks to me that I love not; and I have remarked that his eyes, when he thinks that mine are not on him, have a somewhat bold familiarity with my person." And as she thus thought, a slight shudder passed over her. "I doubt him," she went on; "and he is bold, and cunning, and politic, to a point rarely reached by those whose communion with their fellow-men is more extended than his, and who, consequently, find a thousand things to call their attention from their darling schemes. I doubt him, and will have him watched! I fear he may have betrayed me already, but he shall do so no more. Annette!" she cried aloud, "Annette!"

The girl appeared, and her mistress bade her send Joachim to her. Some minutes then elapsed; but at length appeared the old man who had so skilfully managed the little comedy which had enabled Beatrice and Eugenie de Menancourt to pass the gates of Paris. "Joachim!" said his mistress, as he entered, "have a strict watch put upon the dwarf Bartholo: I doubt him; I doubt his faith and honesty."

"And so do I, lady," replied the man. "I myself heard you command him not to show himself in the sight of the Count d'Aubin, and to my certain knowledge he visited him alone in his chamber."

"Indeed!" said Beatrice, thoughtfully; "indeed! That may mean much! But have him watched, without making it apparent. Quick, Joachim! You, at least, I can trust."

"You may, dear lady!" replied the old man, laying his hand upon his breast; and then, bowing low, he left Beatrice to long, deep, anxious thought.

CHAPTER XXXIII

There be many hearts that, in the full fruition and delight of what they have obtained by evil means, know not remorse, and taste such happiness as gratified passion can bestow. There be also those firm and constant hearts which in the midst of trouble and adversity shake off one half of calamity's heavy load by the strength of conscious virtue and integrity; and there be some so dull and so obtuse, as, under any circumstances, not to see and appreciate the worst portion of their fate. But the curse of curses, the deepest earthly retribution that can be poured upon the head of the wicked, is to find their schemes frustrated, and their desires disappointed, by the very evil means which they have taken to accomplish them. Such was the case of Philip d'Aubin at the moment he left Beatrice of Ferrara; but passion, and mortified vanity, and angry pride, combined to support him for the time, and to shut his eyes to the stinging certainty that his own vices had produced his own misfortune.

For an instant he gazed after the fair girl he had lost for ever, as she turned from him in beautiful disdain; and he felt tempted to follow her, and casting himself once more at her feet, to acknowledge his errors, and throw away his faults in repentance. But with her anger there had mingled a look of scorn, against which the worst weakness of his nature rose in arms. Her indignation, her reproaches, her wrath, he could have borne, but the contempt that curled her lip roused vanity against repentance; and setting his teeth firm, he muttered "Never! never!" and took another path to the chateau. Passing hastily to the apartments which he had occupied, he bade the servant that he found in waiting, summon the *maître d'hôtel* to his presence, and questioned him on his arrival in regard to what part of the baggage with which he had joined the army of the League at Ivry had been brought thither from the field, and where were the soldiers and attendants who accompanied him.

"Neither baggage nor attendants of your own followed you here, sir," replied the man. "You were carried off from the field insensible by four or five of my lady's horsemen, and came hither still in your buff-coat and part of your broken armour. The purse which was on your person, sir, and its contents, are in that closet, if you have not taken it. Your horse is well, and in the stable; but your troops and your attendants were all dispersed;

nor have we heard aught of any of them, except that some found their way to the Chateau d'Aubin; for which, and for your lands in Maine, we learn his majesty the king, at the request of Monsieur de St. Real, has granted an immunity, lest they should be plundered in the war."

There was a dryness in the man's tone that displeased the Count d'Aubin; and eyeing him with a somewhat frowning brow, he said, "Well, then, I will go forth from your lady's dwelling as I entered it, alone. Order my horse to be saddled: doubtless a countryman can easily be hired to guide me on my way to my own lands. How far is it hence to Vibraye or La Ferte?"

"Some thirty leagues, sir, by the road," replied the *maître d'hôtel*; "but if you cross through the woods and by the hills--where the way is not bad--the distance is hardly more than half as much."

"Well, then," said D'Aubin, "I will take the shortest; seek me a guide;" and while the man was gone upon that errand, he walked up and down the room with his hands clasped, and his eyes bent upon the floor. Even then his better spirit whispered that it was not yet too late; but the fiend rose against such counsel, and setting his teeth hard, he took his purse from the spot where it had been placed, and descended to the court-yard. His horse was already prepared; and one or two of the innumerable retainers that thronged a great mansion in those days were loitering about below. The *maître d'hôtel* returned in a few moments with a guide, riding on one of the small horses of the country, and D'Aubin, putting his foot in the stirrup, slowly mounted his charger. As he did so, he ran his eye over the many small windows of the building; but nothing like a female face was to be seen at any of them; and, turning to the attendants who stood around, somewhat marvelling to see him thus depart alone and unnoticed, after all that had lately passed, he bestowed upon them half the contents of his purse, and then, with a slow pace and frowning brow, rode through the gates into the country beyond.

There was a well of bitterness in his heart, which kept him silent as he rode on; and more than half an hour passed ere he even asked a question of the guide. Nor was his a mind to be soothed or comforted, or rendered better or wiser, by thinking over events in which his own follies had acted so principal a share. Too much a spoilt child of vanity willingly to examine his own conduct with steady and impartial eyes, he felt himself injured, rather than reproved, and meditated chiefly how he might heal the wounds which had been inflicted on his pride. At length, however, the sight of a distant town recalled to his mind the state of the land through which he travelled; and he remembered that it might be absolutely necessary for his own security to ascertain the exact political situation of the different cities in the vicinity. The guide, to whom his questions were of course addressed, was shrewd and intelligent enough; and from his answers D'Aubin found that the track, through which his road lay, thinly peopled, and possessing few places of any importance, had known, as yet, but little of the evils of civil war. A body of troops had, indeed, occasionally crossed it. One or two of the defensible chateaux were held for the king or for the League; now and then, too, a troop of plunderers attached to one of the parties would appear, carry off what pillage they could collect, and then retire; but no regular force was known to be in the neighbourhood, except indeed a company of horse arquebusiers, stationed at the small town of La Loupe, on the part of the king, in order to keep open his communication with Maine and Touraine. The guide, himself, was a strong Royalist; and as the Count d'Aubin soon ascertained that fact, he neither gave him any information in regard to his own party and opinions, nor trusted too much the man's reports of great successes attending the king's arms, and of the return of peace and prosperity, wherever the country heartily resumed the virtues of obedience and submission.

Having now, by the questions necessary to ascertain the state of the country, broken the dull and sullen taciturnity which had bound him for some time, after quitting the chateau of Beatrice of Ferrara, D'Aubin continued the conversation, as a relief from thought; and many was the subject on which he needed information, as during the last few weeks he had given up all his thoughts to happier topics, and to brighter dreams, than either war or policy could supply. Curiosity of every kind had seemed dead within him; but now he learned much from the answers of his guide, and guessed more from many a vague distorted tale, which the man had heard, concerning the late movements of the armies;--tales which, indeed, contained in general less truth than falsehood, but which were easily rectified, by the previous knowledge and better judgment of the narrator's auditor. Much, too, did D'Aubin hear of Beatrice of Ferrara; of her habits of life since she had quitted Paris; of those kindlier virtues and gentler pursuits which a capital suffers not to show themselves; and of the ardent and enthusiastic love which the peasantry around had learned to bear towards her. He listened and mused, and good and evil purposes struggled hard together in his heart; but the evil was still predominant; and though a lingering inclination to cast himself at her feet, and sue for pardon, would make itself felt, more often still did he ponder upon the means of teaching her, who had so bitterly rebuked him, to repent in agony of spirit the resolution she had formed against him. Ever and anon, too, with a feeling of still unconquered triumph, he thought, "She loves me still! she loves me still! and the man who possesses a woman's love holds her in bonds that it is difficult to break."

Thus past the hours; and towards seven o'clock the guide stopped at the poor *auberge* of a small open village, in order, as he said, to give the horses rest and provender. The scene was wild and hilly; and D'Aubin now began to recognise the country around, which was little more than twelve French leagues from his own paternal dwelling. His recollection was vague, however, and not sufficient to justify him in dismissing his guide; and, anxious to proceed, he took no refreshment himself, but urged the man to hasten on, hoping, ere night had completely fallen, to reach some spot, whence he could go forward alone on the following morning. But the people of the *auberge* were slow, and the guide, who was their acquaintance, still slower; inasmuch as, finding himself in comfortable quarters, he had predetermined to take up his abode there for the night. He looked out towards the west, declared that the sun was lower than he had thought for; looked out towards the south, and predicted a sharp storm. But D'Aubin was neither of a disposition, nor in a mood, to be delayed at any man's will and pleasure; and, in consequence, he urged such cogent arguments in regard to the payment of his guide's services, that the man did at length bestir himself, and the horses were brought to the door.

"How far is it to the little village of Neuville?" demanded D'Aubin, after they had ridden on about a mile.

"Four good leagues, Monseigneur," replied the man; "but before we reach that, we come to the chateau of Armençon, which has ever held out stoutly for the king, and we are sure of a hearty welcome there, should need be;" and as he spoke he looked up to that part of the sky which rested, as it were, upon the edge of the high hilly bank forming the southern boundary of the steep, narrow valley, or rather dell, up which their road led on into the forest. D'Aubin turned his eyes in the same direction, and beheld, what is very common in the valleys of the Seine and the Eure during summer, large leaden masses of cloud, in the shapes of rolling columns and sharp cones, rising up from behind the hill, clear, defined, and harsh upon the sky, like the side-scenes of a theatre. These are the invariable precursors of a thunder-storm; but often they roll on for many hours, changing from one fantastic shape to another, ere the fire within them breaks forth, and the strife begins. The Count paid them no farther attention than was evinced by slightly hurrying his pace. The track upon which he was now entering was broken ground, forest, and hill; but still the road lay on through the same dell, skirting the banks of a small stream which fell at no great distance into the higher Eure. The uplands on either side hid the sun, and afforded a shade which would have been pleasant in that hot season, had not the closeness of the atmosphere, and the want of the slightest wind, rendered the whole air equally oppressive. The day rapidly declined as the travellers rode on, and the clouds stretched wider overhead, while every now and then a faint, shifting, electric light played between the detached masses, and showed that the warfare of the elements was about to commence. D'Aubin was not a little anxious now to hurry on; but ere he had accomplished more than two leagues of the appointed way, night had fallen, and the storm had begun. The lightning D'Aubin heeded but little, though his horse would every now and then start and rear, as the bright glare gleamed across the narrow road; but he knew the violent deluge of rain, in which those storms generally end, would not be long ere it followed; and feeling himself far more fatigued than he expected, he loved not the thought of prolonging his journey under the outpouring of the watery sky. They had now reached the summit of the hill: the trees afforded but little shelter; and a few large drops began to patter upon the leaves. "Ride on, my lord, ride on," cried the guide, who saw D'Aubin's lately acquired strength beginning to flag; "the chateau of Armençon is not above a league off."

"But I do not intend to stop till I reach Neuville," replied D'Aubin, "Think you if we pause here under the shelter of some of the thickest trees that the storm may not pass off?"

"Not to-night, sir, not to-night," replied the man; "but why not stop at Armençon?" he continued with more eagerness, as the rain rapidly increased: "they will show you all hospitality there; and if you be just recovered from a sickness, as the *maître d'hôtel* told me, it will kill you to ride on for two or three hours more in a night like this."

"Two or three hours!" exclaimed D'Aubin. "What! to travel three leagues!"

"Ay, sir," answered the man, "even so. We are not here as if we were coursing a hare over the plains. We shall have to go up and down twenty steep hills ere we reach Neuville; but we shall be at Armençon in three quarters of an hour."

"But I do not choose to stop there," replied D'Aubin, hastily: and for a moment or two the man paused without reply. The next instant, however, he said in a respectful tone, "I guess how the matter is, sir: you are one of Mayenne's friends, and if so, good faith! you are right not to go near Armençon. They shot the captain's brother in cold blood, not long since, in Paris, and, by my soul, it would go hard with any of the Leaguers if they were found within the chateau walls."

"I had nothing to do with the death of his brother," said D'Aubin, "but still I will not trust to an angry man. Tell me, however, my friend, can I trust to *you?*"

"On my life you may, sir," replied the guide; "and I would not take you now into Armençon for my right hand. But it is coming on to pour: your cloak will soon be wet through; and hereabouts there should be a hut where the wood-cutters live in the spring and autumn. That will give better shelter than the trees; and most likely you may find a bed of rushes, and some pinewood to dry your cloak withal."

"That were luck, indeed!" replied D'Aubin: "let us hasten on then, my friend; and if you can meet with this hut, I will pay you for its shelter better than ever *aubergiste* was paid."

The memory of the guide was exact; and their search was not long. The hut was, indeed, but four walls, thatched with stubble and plastered with mud; and the door, which was made of straw, interwoven with boughs, was lying detached upon the ground: but it was soon replaced; and the frequent flashes of lightning enabled them to discover the bed of moss and rushes which the guide had expected, and a small store of dried fragments of the resinous pine, which, lighted by a flint and steel, soon shed some better light upon the interior than was afforded by the fitful glare without. The interior was too small to admit the horses also; but D'Aubin satisfied himself with placing his own beast under a tree, and mentally saying, "He will do well enough," returned to the shelter of the hut, cast off his dripping cloak, and seated himself upon the pile of dried herbs.

Still the storm continued, and still the incessant pattering of the heavy rain bade the travellers be contented with the refuge they had found. For awhile D'Aubin endeavoured to occupy his thoughts by asking a number of questions of his guide, and listening to the long-winded stories which the other, feeling the moments of inactivity as tedious to his own restless and wandering nature as they were to the Count, willingly poured forth for the sake of doing something. At length, however, his stock exhausted itself; and an hour more passed in silence and expectation; but the storm still went on.

The guide's patience now gave way. "My Lord," he said, "you will be starved here, if I can find you nothing to eat. You took neither bit nor sup at the *auberge*, though you had ridden many a league; but amongst the houses that lie under the chateau of Armençon, I have a cousin, and can, I doubt not, procure a piece of meat and a flask of wine. I will say that it is for an old lady, whom I am guiding through the wood, and who cannot come on for the storm."

D'Aubin did feel exhausted, and in need of food; but still he hesitated to let the man depart, for in those days acts of treachery were not uncommon; and his life might depend upon his passing the castle of Armençon unobserved. The guide, however, insisted; and as there was no means of staying him without showing suspicions, which often produce the very evils they point at, the Count at length suffered him to depart, and remained alone, determined to try whether he could not sleep away the time while the peasant was absent.

The attempt was vain; and, stretched upon the bed of moss where the hard limbs of honest industry had enjoyed many a night of comfortable repose, the gay and glittering Count d'Aubin strove in vain to banish from his bosom the torment of thought. Memory rested on the past, and conscience knew her hour, and seized it with relentless power. His gone existence was spread out before him like a map; and the upbraiding voice within proclaimed each stage of folly and of vice through which he had proceeded, and still read its sad comment upon every act, showing his gradual downfall from honour, wealth, splendour, reputation, happiness, and love, by his own errors and vanities. The long procrastinated examination was forced upon his heart at length; and oh! with what minute agony the moral torturer wracked forth the inmost secrets of his bosom, and then broke him upon the wheel of despair. His fortune irreparably injured; he himself bound by large debts to an unfeeling mercenary; the party which he had joined against his conscience ruined and falling; his baffled schemes holding him up to the laughter of his light companions; the woman whose wealth was to have repaired the consequences of his own extravagance flying him with horror, and avoiding him with success; and the only woman whom he had ever really loved now regarding him with what had once been affection, changed, by his own infamy, into hatred and contempt. Such were the terrible matters on which reason, and conscience, and remorse had to comment during his hours of solitude; and, from the first moment that those thoughts arose, he felt that it would be a madness to deem that he could sleep. The agony of his mind affected his body too much even to suffer him to lie still; and starting up, he sometimes paced the narrow limits of the hut like a tiger in its cage, sometimes cast himself down in his fury, and cursed the hour that he was born. He reproached, he reviled himself for everything; and, in the torture that he felt when alone, exclaimed, "Fool that I was to let the boor leave me! even he were better than no one, in this gloomy, accursed place, with the lightning flashing eternally in my eyes, and the melancholy rain pattering over head."

As he thus thought, the sound of horses' feet splashing through the wet ground made itself heard in the intervals of the thunder, and the moment after, D'Aubin could distinguish that there was more than one traveller upon the road. A suspicion of his guide instantly crossed his mind, and was immediately confirmed by hearing his voice exclaim, "There, in that hut! You will find him there!"

The Count loosened his dagger in the sheath; and partly drew his sword, while, stepping back to the farther side of the hut, he watched for the opening of the disjointed door. A moment or two elapsed, during which D'Aubin could hear the stranger on the outside speaking as if to his horse, while he tied him under a tree; and then the matted screen was pushed back, and the diminutive figure of Bartholo, the dwarf, stood before him. Without uttering a word, Bartholo advanced towards the Count, and cast himself at his feet with a look of imploring deprecation that D'Aubin did not understand. It was explained in a moment, however. "My Lord," said the dwarf, earnestly, "my Lord, I find that when last I saw you I deceived you; and, by the counsel that I gave you, I have brought insult and disappointment upon your head. My fault was involuntary; but I deserve to be punished; and I have sought you myself; that you may wreak what vengeance upon me you like."

D'Aubin too well knew that to the counsels of his own perverse and pampered heart he had listened more than to those of the dwarf; but he was glad, nevertheless, to find any one on whom he could heap a part of the blame; and while he snatched eagerly at the opportunity of accusing another, he felt a degree of gratitude for the relief which mitigated the bitterness of self-reproach.

"Alas! alas! my poor Bartholo!" he said, "you did deceive me, indeed! But I am willing to believe that you deceived me unwittingly; and I seek not to punish one who wished to serve me, though he failed."

"You are noble and generous ever, sir," replied the dwarf; "and though she does not know the value of the heart she tramples on, others do, and I will conceal it no longer. You little know, sir, how much art, intrigue, and exertion were made use of to estrange from you a heart that loved you, and rob you not only of your promised bride, but of her affection."

"How say you?" cried D'Aubin, eagerly. "Speak more clearly, good Bartholo; I do not understand."

"I know not whether I ought to speak more clearly or not," answered the dwarf; "for although it is her pleasure and her pride to sport with your love, and trample on you, yet it would wring her heart to hear that, notwithstanding all her wiles, you had been successful with her rival; and though to you she may appear but as a cold coquette, to me, who have known her from her childhood, she has ever been a good lady and a kind."

"Bartholo!" cried D'Aubin, sternly, "you have in one thing miscounselled me, and rendered me miserable. You but now professed a wish to atone for that error; and I call upon you at once, to clear away the obscurity which hangs over all these transactions in which I have been engaged, and to let me see how I really stand between Beatrice of Ferrara and Eugenie de Menancourt."

"I will, sir! I will!" cried the dwarf, "let it cost me what it may. But I must be quick, for the tale is intricate, and your guide, who directed me hither, as I was following you to Armençon, will soon be back. Listen, then," he continued, while his face resumed all its bitter cynicism. "Think you, my Lord, that a girl, all gentleness and sweetness, like Mademoiselle de Menancourt, could in a moment be converted into a being as stern and resolute as an old warrior, without some very potent magic? Think you that she who once loved you to all appearance as much as a young maiden ever ventures to show, would all at once affect hate and detestation towards you without some very mighty cause? Think you that a girl who knows nothing of the world, and is as timid as a young deer, could alone find means to cheat hard-judging Mayenne and keen Madame Montpensier, and pass a blaspheming Huguenot soldier off for a Catholic priest, frustrate you and all of them by a false marriage, and then effect her escape from a beleaguered city, where a thousand eyes were upon her; and all this by the simple exertion of her own courage, ingenuity, and daring? Pshaw! One would think to hear it, and to hear that you and Mayenne believed it, that the warriors and the politicians of this world were changed into old women. My Lord! my Lord! Eugenie de Menancourt loved you, loves you, will love you still; and only now weeps the perfidy which my noble lady--thinking, as all women do, that everything is fair in love--taught her to fancy that you had committed against her. Had not Mademoiselle de Menancourt learned to think, from the first moment she set her foot in Paris, that your whole heart and soul were given to the Lady Beatrice, and that you sought her hand only on account of her wealth, she would at once, on her father's death, have flown to your arms for protection. But, day by day, and hour by hour, that idea has been strengthened and confirmed in her mind by a voice whose eloquence no one knows better than you and I. Another time I will point out how; but at present you will trust me--for your wits are not darkened enough to doubt so apparent a fact--when I tell you, that the carrying off the priest, the false marriage, and the escape from Paris, are all owing to the fertile brain and daring courage of Beatrice of Ferrara. She it was who robbed you of your bride; and she it is who now conceals her within three leagues of this place, weeping that Philip d'Aubin is false, and resolving to enter a monastery as soon as she hears of his marriage to another."

"But St. Real!" exclaimed D'Aubin, "St. Real! I have more than suspicions there."

"Pshaw!" cried the dwarf; "she thinks not of him. He may love her, perhaps, but she thinks not of him, but as a brave good-humoured lad, with wit enough to lead a score or two of iron-pated soldiers. But, once convince her that you love her, and that those who have told her you loved another were interested deceivers, and you will soon find the ice will melt, and all the coldness pass away. And now, my Lord, I have told you all. I have given you the key to the mystery; and though, God knows, there are few men in this world that can comprehend clearly anything beyond a schoolboy's sum, done upon a broken slate, yet the matter here is so simple you cannot well mistake. Now I must leave you; for if I be not back ere morning dawn, and my lady discovers my errand, I may chance to die by an earlier death than I have calculated on."

"But stay, stay yet a moment, good Bartholo," cried the count; "you have not told me yet where I may find this fair lady. Think you my marriage with her will touch your mistress so deeply then?"

"That is what I fear, my Lord," replied the dwarf, assuming a look of sorrow, "that is what I fear. I owed you atonement, sir; and I have made it at the risk of mortifying all the proud feelings of a lady and mistress that I love; for I know that she calculates upon seeing you again at her feet, and pouring forth upon you more of her scorn and indignation, before she leaves you for ever, and returns to Italy. She was laughing over the scene with Annette just now."

"It is a scene she shall never see!" said D'Aubin, biting his lip. "But tell me where dwells this fair fugitive--this Mademoiselle de Menancourt? She is, indeed, as beautiful a creature as the eye of man ever yet beheld. One not difficult to love."

"Oh no!" cried the dwarf; "where is the heart that would not be envious of the man who wears a jewel such as that upon his hand. Her dwelling, I have said, is not far off. You know the little stream that separates the lands of Aubin from those of Menancourt. Trace it up to its source amongst these hills, and not half a league from the spot where it bubbles from its green fountain you will find two cottages, in one of which is the object of your search. It is not like the ordinary dwelling of a French peasant; for the Lady Beatrice has taken a pleasure in decking forth her friend's home after the fashion of our own land, where taste, and the love of all that is beautiful, descends even to the lowest tillers of the soil."

"I shall easily find it," replied the count; "and yon fair scornful dame shall find that D'Aubin can seek him a mate as beautiful as herself. Bartholo,

I trust you--once more I trust you! but oh! if you deceive in this also, look to your heart's blood; for I will find means to punish you, should you hide in the farthest corner of the globe."

"My Lord, I deceive you not," replied the dwarf, "nor in this am I myself deceived. But, I entreat, undertake no enterprise upon my showing, without resolving to carry it through at all hazards. If you would have the love of that fair creature you seek, spare no vows and persuasions to efface from her mind the evil impression that others have given of your conduct. Nor trust to that alone. Forget that the marriage was null. Act upon it as if she were your wife, till you have her safe in your own chateau; and then let the ceremony be performed again. Neither must you seek her alone, and unattended by a sufficient force to assert your right, should it be opposed. I know that five or six of my lady's bravest followers are always watching near that spot; and there may be more. Stir not a step, without fifty horseman at your back. At all events, remember, my noble lord, that if you undertake this enterprise without sufficient strength and resolution, the failure must not be laid to me. As I hope for life and happiness, I believe that you may be fully successful."

"I am not apt to want in resolution, Bartholo," replied D'Aubin. "Hence I shall speed to my own dwelling without a moment's loss of time; but it may take long in the present state of affairs to collect such a troop as fifty men."

"Yet time is everything!" replied the dwarf. "'Tis more than likely that changes may take place, of which I cannot inform you; and if the lady be removed from her present refuge, our scheme is ruined. To be bold and rapid is the best road to success, after all. Who can tell what even to-morrow may bring forth?"

"True!" answered D'Aubin; "and, if possible to-morrow's sun shall not set ere Eugenie de Menancourt be mine. Then let your mistress and her maids laugh over the scene of my supplications if they will! But I must be guided by circumstances. At present my purse is but lean, my good friend. Nevertheless----"

"Speak not of it, sir! speak not of it!" replied the dwarf. "I came to do what I have done, in order to make atonement for an involuntary error towards one who was to me the most generous of masters; and who never could accuse me of giving him false information before. I sought not gold, and will not take it. But if you succeed, and if you be happy, sometimes remember the poor dwarf when he is far away."

Thus saying, he kissed the hand of his former lord, and departed, drawing the matted door after him. The next moment D'Aubin heard his horse's feet; and, again left alone, he once more cast himself upon the bed of moss, and gave himself up to thought. His feelings, however, were now very different from what they had been an hour before. Although, as we have before shown, the idea of wedding Eugenie de Menancourt, repairing his wasted fortune by her wealth, and triumphing proudly over her who had scorned and rejected him, and made him the common jest of Paris, had never quitted his mind, even while yielding willingly to his passionate love for Beatrice of Ferrara; yet the repulse he had met with, from a being on whose love and compliance he had counted with full confidence, the bitter scorn that she had displayed towards him, and the keen disappointment that her rejection inflicted, had, in spite of all the Titan-like struggles of pride, so abased and overwhelmed him, that he had lost courage, and looked with hopeless eyes upon all the daring schemes on which, at other times, he would have entered so boldly. The words of the dwarf, however, had revived him, not alone by showing him the easy means of accomplishing one part of his purpose, but by pointing out a new end to be obtained, a new object of desire, and that, too, of a nature to give the only alleviation which his heart was capable of receiving in the pain he suffered--the alleviation of revenge. He felt that Beatrice was already unhappy; that his conduct was--must be--a source of misery to her; but that feeling, far from making him pity her, roused up his suffering vanity to strive for means of avenging upon her the insult which her purity had offered to his baseness. The dwarf had pointed out the way; and to dream of wringing her heart by his marriage with Eugenie, while he silenced for ever the stinging laughter of his former companions, was a relief--perhaps a pleasure. At the same time, a thought crossed his mind that the tale of his having dwelt many weeks concealed in the dwelling of Beatrice of Ferrara, joined to his reputation for gallantry, might, perchance, leave her proud reputation for virtue somewhat sullied; and, as he thought thus, a smile, mingling vanity and pride and vengeance altogether, passed over his lip, and gave his fine features the expression of a demon; and yet this was the bright and fascinating Count d'Aubin: whom we have seen so full of light and harmless gaiety in the beginning of this volume, and such was the creature he had, step by step, become.

Before the visit of the dwarf he had tried to sleep in vain; but now he felt the gnawing pain at his heart relieved by a new purpose; and, after the return of his guide with wine and meat, he ate and drank, though sparingly, and then, casting himself down once more, slept undisturbed till morning dawned.

CHAPTER XXXIV

Leaving the Count d'Aubin to pursue his schemes to their conclusion, we must now follow Bartholo home to the chateau of Guery. Few were the friends which the page possessed amongst the servants of his mistress; but in that number was the old warder at the gate, who, warned beforehand of the dwarfs absence, hastened to give him admittance without noise on his return. Bartholo stabled his horse and rubbed him down with his own small hands, and then, entering by a side-door, passed through the great hall, which was lighted by one of the large paper globes of the time--not at all unlike a Chinese lantern--and picking his steps through the midst of the straw mattresses upon which, as was then customary, several of the inferior servants were sleeping, he made his way towards a staircase leading to the room which had been appropriated to himself during the illness of the Count d'Aubin, and he had now resumed. Opening the door, he entered, congratulating himself upon not having been seen, when suddenly he was seized on either side, and held fast to prevent him from using his dagger, while some one at the farther end of the chamber drew a screen from before a concealed lamp, and Bartholo found himself in the hands of the major-domo and two stout grooms, who, with little compassion and less ceremony, proceeded to bind him tightly hand and foot.

The dwarf asked not a question, and said not a word; and the old *maître d'hôtel*, though loving him but little, refrained from any expression of triumph, merely directing the grooms to watch him well and not molest him, and then left him for the night. Early the next morning the cords were slackened upon his ankles, and he was brought into the presence of his mistress, whose quivering lip and flashing eye told how much her anger was roused against him.

"Bartholo, you have deceived me!" she said; "you have basely deceived me!"

"Those who suspect without cause," answered the dwarf, doggedly, "will always be deceived in the end, and will deserve it."

"And do you think me so weak a being," asked Beatrice, sternly, "as to believe that he who could practise the piece of knavery which you executed last night is innocent of foregone deceits? No, poor fool, no! and even were it not that--as is ever the case with favourites in disgrace--the whole household is pouring forth tales of thy former treason now that it no longer avails me to know it, I should still feel as certain of your guilt as I am of living and breathing, and should only daily look for the instances of your knavery. I seek not, man, to make you own either your former or your present baseness; all I seek to know is your motive. Tell me, were you bribed to divulge my secrets and thwart my plans? Were you hired to betray the mistress that trusted and befriended you?"

"No man does anything without the hope of recompense," replied the dwarf, "nor woman either."

"I should have thought," answered Beatrice, in a tone of bitter but sorrowful reproach, "that no recompense would have been sufficient to bribe you to sting the hand which cherished you when all the rest of the world either scorned or forgot you."

"You mistake me, noble lady," said the dwarf, "I see you mistake me. There are men and women both that sell their honour for gold; but I am not of them. There are still more, both men and women, that pawn their virtue for less solid payment, ay, and sell even their souls for vanity; but still no bauble was my bribe. It was neither title given by some profligate king, nor words of flattery spoken by some vicious lover. I had--I own it--a motive before my eyes, a recompense to look forward to; but I choose not to speak it before these gaping fools. Should I ever again have your ear alone, to it I may tell the cause of all that is strange in my behaviour--if aught be strange in the actions of man. But till then I am silent."

"Leave me!" said Beatrice, looking towards her attendants, "retire to the ante-room--no farther!" Her commands were instantly obeyed; but still there was many an ear eager for the sounds of what passed farther; and those who dared, advanced close to the door, which was not entirely closed. The dwarf's voice was heard speaking quick and long, but in tones so low, that the eavesdroppers were all at fault. At length, however, the voice of Beatrice exclaimed, "Madman! dared you to entertain such a hope?"

"I entertained no hope," replied the dwarf, aloud--"I entertained no hope, but that I might never behold you in the arms of another!"

"Here, Joachim, Annette!" cried the voice of Beatrice, and in a moment the room where she sat was again crowded with her attendants. They found her with the eloquent blood glowing in deep crimson through her clear fine skin, and dying her brow and temples and neck with a blush almost painful to behold. "Take him hence!" she cried, pointing to the dwarf with a look of irrepressible disgust, which, as his eye marked it, turned him deadly pale. "Take him hence!--and yet stay," she added, addressing him--"I suppose it is vain to question you as to what you told to him whom you went last night to visit."

A change had come over the appearance of the dwarf, which it were difficult to describe. The paleness that had followed Beatrice's last words remained--even his lips were blanched; and though with his white upper teeth he bit the under lip unconsciously, no mark appeared after, so bloodless was his whole countenance. He replied, however, with a voice of unnatural calmness, "It is not in vain, madam, to ask me anything you seek to know. Life is over with me,--at least, life's hopes and fears; and I may as well tell you all, as conceal anything. The moment that what I have dared to do was discovered, that moment I knew that the game was lost; and it is in vain now to play a few moves more or less."

He then, as shortly as possible, repeated the substance of what had passed between D'Aubin and himself, in regard to Eugenie de Menancourt's abode, and the means of securing her person, and that concluded, calmly suffered himself to be led back to the room where he had passed the night, and where he was now left alone.

In the meantime, Beatrice, with a hasty hand, wrote a few words on several sheets of paper, and ordering horses to be saddled instantly, gave the letters to the servants who were first prepared. "This to La Loupe," she said, giving one, "for the captain of the arquebusiers; and bid him mark within the king's own hand to the command. This to the chatelain of Armençon. Tell him, if he cannot spare many, to send, if it be but twenty men, well armed end mounted. This to the Lady Eugenie, with all speed! Away, away! This purse to him who does his errand soonest. Now, Joachim, now! you gather together all the men that we have here, and all that are in the neighbouring town; arm them to the teeth, and make speed! Tell me when all is ready, and lose no time!--Away! for we must endeavour to be first on the spot, and carry off that poor timid dove from her dovecot, ere the kite pounces upon her. If we are too late to save her from danger, we must do our best to rescue her, whatever befall."

Beatrice's orders were as rapidly obeyed as given; but we must deviate a little from our general plan, and quitting the persons with whom we have begun this chapter, turn once more to the efforts of the Count d'Aubin; efforts which were unfortunately but too successful. The sun had not risen half an hour ere D'Aubin was again in the saddle; and though his horse was somewhat stiff from having passed a night in the open air, in the midst of storm and tempest, the Count urged him on at full speed, and never drew a rein till he was within sight of his own paternal home.

There are feelings touched by the view of such a place, so interwoven with all the texture of our being, that even the coarse hand of vice, or the more cunning touch of worldly-mindedness, can hardly tear them out; but it was not any such emotions that caused D'Aubin to stop and gaze round him as he approached the dwelling of his fathers. It was that, in a field close to the chateau, he beheld a man, dressed in the costume of a German soldier, sauntering idly about, and talking to some women who were weeding the ground. An undefined apprehension of danger made him pause; but the next moment he spurred his horse furiously on, and rode into the court-yard. It was filled with reitters, who were sitting round in various attitudes, eating their morning meal in the early sunshine. The apparition of a single horseman, for the guide was some furlongs behind, did not seem to disturb in the slightest degree their German phlegm; and D'Aubin was suffered to cast his rein over a hook, and push open the great door of the hall without one of the troopers ceasing from his pleasant occupation, to ask the business of the intruder. The first object the Count beheld in the hall was one of his own servants; but the next, which rendered all question unnecessary, was a large breakfast-table, covered with loads of meat and flagons of wine, at which sat Albert of Wolfstrom, and one or two of the officers of his troop. The apparition of D'Aubin was certainly unexpected, for the party of the League believed him dead; but it required no lengthened explanations to make him comprehend that his friend, the captain of the reitters, had hastened with as many of his men as had escaped the bloody fight of Ivry to take possession of the lands and chateau of Aubin, in order to pay himself some certain thousands of crowns, won by him at play, ere the next heir of the supposed dead count put in his claim, either by the sword or otherwise.

As he was well aware that no party would permit of his holding long possession of the lands, the mercenary leader had employed means to raise the sum he claimed, which now caused some sharp and angry words to pass between him and the count,--words which might not have ended bloodless had D'Aubin at the moment been prepared to expel the Germans from his dwelling: but his own retainers and domestics were dispersed; and not above two or three of his old attendants were to be found within the walls of the chateau. The thought of his fine old trees felled to supply the greedy craving of the mercenary, his crops and cattle swept away, his peasantry half ruined, did enrage him almost to striking Wolfstrom where he stood; but in the midst of his anger he remembered that there was but one way to clear off this and many another similar claim upon him, and to emerge into greater splendour and power than ever; and in that dim and misty dream of splendour and power he fancied that the voice of conscience, and remorse, and disappointed love, would never be heard.

"Well, well, Wolfstrom," he added, abruptly breaking off the angry vituperation he was heaping upon the chief of the reitters, "you might have waited a little longer; you might have proceeded a little more moderately; but now send out and order all to be stopped instantly, then lend me your full and active aid for this one day, and you shall receive every farthing in gold before a week be over."

"Ay, indeed! how so?" demanded the other, somewhat doubtingly; for Albert of Wolfstrom had nothing very confiding in his disposition. "As to waiting, you know, sir count, that was out of the question entirely, for we thought you dead; and as to proceeding more moderately, you know I was obliged to make haste, for on the one hand Mayenne might call me to Paris in a day, at any time; and on the other, the Bearnois and your cousin might come down and turn me out; so that I was obliged to make good use of my time. But how can I serve you?"

"How many men have you here?" demanded D'Aubin.

"Why, not many, on my life," answered Wolfstrom; "only a hundred and fifty. All the rest were killed or taken at that cursed Ivry. But what do you want us to do?"

"Listen!" said D'Aubin. "I last night learned, Wolfstrom, that by a foul scheme my promised bride was persuaded that I did not love her, and that it was thus she was induced to fly immediately after our marriage."

"But do you know, Monsieur d'Aubin," interrupted Wolfstrom, "that the good folks in Paris vow, that marriage of yours was no marriage at all; that the priest was a mad Huguenot soldier, and that----"

"Never mind all that," replied D'Aubin, "I have here a priest in the neighbouring village who has done me some services already, and he will bind me in half an hour to Eugenie de Menancourt by a knot that can never be untied, without asking any questions or listening to any objections. Only let me once have her safe within these walls!"

"Ay, but how is that to be done?" demanded Albert of Wolfstrom.

"That is what I was about to tell you," answered the count. "The same person who informed me of the means which had been used to estrange her affection from me, informed me also of the place of her present dwelling.

It is within six leagues of this castle, and all that is necessary in the present case is----"

"To carry her off by a *coup de main!*" cried Wolfstrom, clapping his hands at the sound of a project which combined, in a degree peculiarly adapted to his palate, villany and adventure. "Bravo, sir count I bravo! Let us about it immediately."

"Thanks, thanks, Wolfstrom, for your ready aid," replied D'Aubin. "All that we have to do is to mount fifty men, and to lose no time; the first, because the girl has some guards stationed round about her, and more may be sent; the second, because the keenest eye in France is upon her and me, and she may be removed."

"Well, well, to it at once," cried Wolfstrom, moving towards the door; but ere he reached it he stopped, and, turning to the count said, in a low tone, "Of course you will give my men a day's pay."

"And you a thousand crowns to boot, if we succeed," answered the Count, who knew that there was nothing comparable to gold for quickening his comrade's energies.

"We had better take a hundred men at once," said Wolfstrom, when he heard that they were to be paid; "they are as soon mounted as fifty, and we are then more sure. Fifty can stay to guard the chateau."

D'Aubin made no objection, and Wolfstrom proceeded to give his orders, which were rapidly obeyed by the well-trained veterans still under his command. A fresh horse was provided for D'Aubin, and another for the guide, who, without his consent being asked, was ordered to lead the way, with a trooper on either side, to the spot which D'Aubin described. Two old but nimble jennets from the stable of the Count were led in the rear; and thus the cavalcade issued from the gates of the chateau of Aubin, and took their way towards the dwelling of the unfortunate Eugenie de Menancourt. Scarcely had they proceeded a league, however, when, from the edge of a gentle slope, they perceived three horsemen galloping quickly on a road in the plain below, as if towards the castle they had just left.

The keen eyes of Wolfstrom instantly marked them; but, after gazing at them for a moment, he said, "They are two of my reitters whom I sent yesterday to keep a watch on Armençon; but they have a third man with them, and must bring news. We must take care that our retreat is not cut off." Thus saying, he detached a trooper to intercept the horsemen by a cross road, and bring them to him, and then halted till they arrived. Two proved, as had been supposed, ordinary reitters of Wolfstrom's band, but the third horseman was an armed servant; and D'Aubin instantly recognised one of the attendants of Beatrice of Ferrara. He was tied upon his horse, and the troopers brought him up pistol in hand. Their report was soon made; they had found him galloping, they said, with such speed towards the castle of Armençon that they thought it right to stop him. He fled like the wind, and they pursued; but at length he was overtaken, and they found upon him a letter, which, not being able to read themselves, they were now in the act of conveying to their leader. The paper, as may be already seen, was the letter of Beatrice of Ferrara to the chatelain of Armençon, and it served to show D'Aubin that his movements were suspected, if not discovered. The servant, however, was now in such bodily fear, that he at once informed the Count and his companion, that another messenger had been sent for troops to La Loupe.

"What force have they there, Wolfstrom?" demanded D'Aubin. "Do you know?"

"Certainly not two hundred men!" replied the leader of the reitters.

"Then there is, first, the probability that the commander will not listen to the request of this wild girl," said the Count; "next, he will certainly not dare to detach more than fifty men, and we are here a hundred. Even if she send her own armed people, too, they cannot amount to more than thirty, so that we shall still have great odds. But let me see," he continued, as if a sudden thought struck him, and turning to the servant, he asked, "When did the messenger leave Guery for La Loupe?"

"At the same moment that I left for Armençon," replied the man.

"Then," said D'Aubin, "we shall be there full four good hours before a soldier from La Loupe can be within a league. Let that fellow go, Wolfstrom. You, my good man, ride back with all speed to your mistress, present the Count d'Aubin's humble duty to her, and tell her he is her most devoted slave! Do you hear? There is a piece of gold for you--away!"

The man seemed doubtful if his ears heard true; but at length convinced, he took the gold, cap in hand, and rode slowly away. In the meantime, D'Aubin and Wolfstrom again put the troop in motion; and riding briskly on, calculated once more between them the distance from Guery to La Loupe, and from La Loupe to the spot whither their steps were now directed. D'Aubin was found not to have judged amiss; for even supposing the troops mounted and the captain willing, it appeared that the reitters must arrive at least four hours before them. "When we come up," said D'Aubin, as they concluded, "let your men surround the house, at such a distance as not to be seen; yourself and five or six others come nearer, so as to be within call; and, after ascertaining that there is no force actually present to oppose us, I will go on and plead my cause myself. It were better to persuade her gently, and without frightening her, if possible; but if I find her still obstinate, we must use a little gentle compulsion: for I am resolved," he added, with a smile of triumph, "that by the time the troops from La Loupe reach her late refuge, Eugenie de Menancourt shall be in the chateau of Aubin; ay, and irretrievably the wife of its lord!"

CHAPTER XXXV

What was once a poor farm-house, in a woody and remote part of the hills in which the Eure and Loire take their rise, had, under the touch of taste and affluence, been transformed into a beautiful little habitation, half rustic cottage, half Italian villa; and all this had been done as easily as the genii built the palace of Aladdin. The wood-work had been painted green, so that the heavy planks which, when shut, closed the windows, looked light; the thatch had been nicely clipped and trimmed; the inside had been hung with arras, and decorated with paintings in the fashion of the day; and along the front had been carried a portico, consisting of unpolished trunks of trees for columns, and a light trellis-work of boughs to soften the strong sunshine. The face of the house was turned towards the south; and it might have commanded, from its elevated situation, a beautiful view over the greater part of Maine, had the tall old trees which screened it in front been partially cut away: but those in whose possession it now was had carefully abstained from the axe; not alone from reverence for the ancient trees, but because quiet concealment was with them a great object of desire. No place, in truth, could have been better chosen for that purpose. There was, indeed, one horse road, which came within a few hundred yards of the house, but it went no farther than to a small isolated village not more than a league distant, and there ended. Another, passing a little farther off, led away to the chateau of Guery, at the distance of three leagues on one side, and to the small town of ---- on the other; but even this was merely a bridle path, upon which there was scarcely any traffic in the best of times, and much less now that civil war had stilled all commercial spirit in the land.

It was in the little portico, then, which we have noticed, that on the evening of a warm clear day in June, occasionally shaded by the masses of a broken thunder-cloud, which, during the night, had poured forth a tempest on the earth, sat the fair Eugenie de Menancourt, into whose cheek the warm glow of health and youth had returned, during a long interval of peace and tranquillity. Hither, after many wanderings, had she been brought by Beatrice of Ferrara, as soon as it was known that the Count d'Aubin was no longer in the neighbourhood; and in order to be sufficiently near her, to give her every sort of aid and protection, without calling further attention upon her retreat by living with her, the fair Italian had retired to the chateau of Guery which she possessed in the neighbourhood. The time had, as we have seen, passed without bringing molestation to Eugenie; and she now sat with an open letter in her hand, gazing out upon the woodland scene before her eyes, and seeing those mixed visions of romance, and tenderness, and melancholy which are so often present to a woman's eyes, and are the more dear, because she is taught to hide that she beholds them. Before her were those dark old trees; on her right a thicket of shrubs of many a varied kind; behind her the room in which she was wont to sit--then called her bower, and on the left, some fields screened again from the road by other trees. It was a calm sweet scene; and Eugenie felt not unhappy, though there might be other things she would have fain brought in, to form her picture of perfect felicity, and although the letter which she held in her hand from Beatrice of Ferrara, by telling her not to be alarmed at anything that might happen, for that friends were near, had, in some degree, created the apprehension is was intended to relieve.

As she sat thus and gazed, she thought she heard the tramp of horse; but the sound, if sound there were, ceased, and she believed that her ears had deceived her. A moment or two after, a long ray of sunshine that found its way between the bolls of the trees, and spread a pencil of light upon the green turf at her feet, was for an instant obscured, as if either a cloud had come over the sun, or some dark object had passed among the trees. Eugenie's heart began to beat quick, and the next minute a rustling sound in the thicket to her right made her start up; but ere she could retreat into her own chamber, the boughs were pushed back, and Philip d'Aubin was at her feet. With a face as pale as death, Eugenie sank into the seat that she had before occupied, and gazed with eyes expressive certainly of anything but love, upon the Count as he knelt before her, and pressed her hand to his lips.

"Eugenie!" said D'Aubin, "Eugenie! I have at length found you, then. My Eugenie! my wife!"

"Oh, no, no!" cried Eugenie, struggling to overcome her terror: "oh, no! not your wife! No, sir, I am not; I never have been; I never will be your wife! Death were preferable--ay, the most terrible death were preferable to that!"

"Hear me, Eugenie!" said D'Aubin. "Eugenie, you must hear me! for this house is surrounded by my soldiers; you are utterly and perfectly in my power; and if I have recourse to reason and persuasion with you, it is alone from tenderness and affection towards you, and because I would rather induce my bride to accompany me willingly and tranquilly, than use towards her those means of compulsion which I have a right to exercise in regard to a disobedient wife. Eugenie, will you hear me?"

"I have no resource, Sir," replied the unhappy girl; "but still I repeat that I am not your wife. In the first place, I have at the altar refused to pledge a vow towards you; and by this time you must well know that the man who read the vain and empty ceremony which you are pleased to call a marriage was not one invested with that sacred function which is requisite to render a marriage legal, even with the willing consent of both parties."

"All I know is, that the marriage ceremony was performed between us," replied D'Aubin, "and that it is registered in the archives of Paris. That you are my wife, therefore, there is no doubt; and that I have the right, as well as the power and the will, to take you home and regard you as my wife, is equally indubitable. Still if you require it, the ceremony shall be performed again; but hope not any longer to avoid taking upon you the duties of the position you hold in regard to me, for, as I told you, I have a hundred men within call ready to obey my lightest word! Shall I make them appear?"

"Oh, no, no, no!" exclaimed Eugenie, wringing her hands. "What, what shall I do?"

"Merely listen to me, Eugenie, my beloved!" cried D'Aubin. "With the power to compel, a thousand times rather would I succeed by entreaty; and instead of seeking to command you, let me at your feet seek to persuade you. Hear me plead my cause, Eugenie, in language that you have never heard me use before, because I was ignorant of the motives which actuated you, and attributed your conduct towards me to mere caprice, whereas I now know it to have been just, excellent, and wise, and like yourself. The same ignorance has made me harsh to you, and unjust towards my cousin St. Real; and I will not rise from my knee till you have heard my exculpation, and fully know how much we have all been deceived."

"Indeed!" said Eugenie, "indeed! yet I am at a loss to guess what you can mean."

"Well may you be so, Eugenie!" replied D'Aubin; "well may you be so! For it was only yesterday that I learned the elucidation of the mystery myself. You have been cheated, Eugenie; you have been deceived; you have been taught to believe a man who loved you, and you alone, a heartless profligate. But first hear me, Eugenie, when I declare that I have never loved any one but you; that from the first moment your hand was promised me by your father, the idea of your young charms has ever been present to my mind, and the hope of soon possessing them been the consolation of my whole existence."

Eugenie coloured deeply: "I am grieved, sir," she replied; but D'Aubin interrupted, saying,--

"Hear me, Eugenie, to the end: I have but given you a picture of my own feelings towards you. Now let me display all the base and crooked means that have been taken to alienate your affection from me, and then tell me if it be right and just to let those means still have effect, when you are convinced of their falsehood and iniquity. Only yesterday did I discover that at Paris you had become acquainted with one of the late Queen Catherine's train of ladies--a train which, I need not tell you, was and will remain marked with infamy to the eyes of all posterity!"

"Perhaps so!" cried Eugenie eagerly; "but the name of Beatrice of Ferrara will always be excepted. The daughter of a sovereign prince, she was always as distinguished by her virtues as by her rank; and my father on his death-bed told me that I might always confide in her, for that, in the midst of the terrible trial of universal bad example, no one had ever been able to cast a reproach upon her fame."

"It may be so!" replied D'Aubin; "it may be so! but doubt not, Eugenie, that she has passions and weaknesses too; and the confidence you gave her was misplaced. All has been revealed to me. I know everything that has passed, and therefore I am justified in saying that she has made us both her tools. Did she not tell you that I loved her--that I had vowed vows and made protestations at her feet? I know she did. I know that both by open words, and slight insinuations, she poisoned your mind against me; that she taught you to believe me profligate and base--"

"Never! never!" cried Eugenie, "never, upon my word."

"No matter," cried D'Aubin, "she made you credit that I loved her, not you; that by vows and promises I was bound to her. She it was that always crossed me in your esteem; she frustrated the arrangements for our marriage; she laid the scheme, and executed the whole of your flight from Paris. Is not this true? and do you think she had not a motive? Eugenie, I tell you she had. It may make me appear vain in your eyes; but, to exculpate myself, I must reveal that motive. Eugenie, she has loved me from our first meeting; she has loved me with all the ardour and all the fire of which an Italian is capable; but so to love unsought, is never to win love. She has teased me; she has persecuted me with her affection. But do not mistake me, Eugenie; I have never loved but you--you alone have I sought, you alone have I sighed for. To her I have turned a deaf ear and a cold heart. I care not for her, I love her not, I have never loved--ay! and though I scruple not to say that, no later than yesterday, I might have made her mine on any terms I chose--"

There was a slight rustle in the room behind--a quick step; and Beatrice of Ferrara stood by the side of Eugenie de Menancourt. D'Aubin started up from his knee. "Liar! traitor! villain!" cried the beautiful girl, with eyes from which mighty indignation lightened forth like fire bursting from a volcano;--"Liar! traitor! villain!" and as he rose, she struck him what seemed but a slight stroke upon the bosom with the quickness of light. D'Aubin grasped his sword, then let it go, and raised his hand to his eyes; a stream of dark gore spouted out from his breast; he reeled, and murmuring "Jesu, Jesu!" fell at the feet of her he had so basely injured.

Still holding the dagger tight in her grasp, Beatrice stood and gazed upon him; and Eugenie too, with her hands clasped, and turned as it were into stone by fear and horror, remained straining her eyes upon the fearful sight before her.

At that moment, the furious galloping of horse was heard along the nearest road, then came the clashing of steel and pistol shots; and Joachim, the servant of Beatrice, glided from the room whence his mistress had issued, and drawing her by the sleeve, exclaimed--"There seems a large force coming up, madam! save yourself, ere this be inquired into. The horses are still where we left them, at the end of the lane."

But Beatrice, without reply, continued to gaze upon the corpse of him she once so passionately loved, apparently unconscious of aught else but the terrible act she had performed. The next moment, the voices of several persons approaching were heard; and through the trees appeared two gentlemen on foot, followed by half a dozen soldiers dragging along Albert of Wolfstrom, with his hands tied.

"We are in time, fair lady, to do your behest," cried Henry IV. who was at the head of the party, speaking in a joyous tone, as, as the distance of the trees he caught a sight of Beatrice without seeing the object at which she gazed. "Your letter reached me, as I marched along, and though addressed to my *locum tenens* at La Loupe, I made bold to break the seal. But where is this perverse and rebellious Count d'Aubin?"

"There!" cried Beatrice, in a voice which had lost all its music. "There he lies! never to be perverse or rebellious again! Oh, Philip, Philip! thou hast trod upon a heart that loved thee--cast happiness from thee--sought destruction--and found it from a woman's hand!"

"Indeed!" cried the king, hastening forward with St. Real, who was his companion. "In God's name, what is all this? Pardie, 'tis too true! There he lies, indeed!" The king's eye then glanced to Beatrice, while St. Real gently led Eugenie away from the scene of blood and horror in which she had been made an unwilling sharer. The dagger was still in the hand of the fair Italian, though that hand now hung by her side as if it had never possessed power to strike the blow which had laid such strength and courage low;

but her sleeve was dyed with blood; and a slow red drop trickled down the shining blade of the poniard, and fell from the point to the ground.

"From your own speech, lady!" said the king, after a momentary pause, "I learn that you have just committed an awful act, especially for a woman's hand. Nevertheless, I cannot but believe, from all that I have heard, that this was an act of justice! He was a rebel, too, at the moment of his death, in arms against his king; and, therefore, this deed is not to be too strictly investigated; otherwise--although as the head of a sovereign house you are armoured with immunities--it would become me to refer the inquiry to my council. As it is, Philip Count d'Aubin having been slain in arms against his monarch, in the commission of an illegal act, and by your hand, of course justice withholds her sword from avenging his death, yet I think that it is expedient for you, lady, to quit this realm with all convenient speed; and to insure your safety, a party of my own guard shall accompany you to the frontier. My words seem to fall upon an inattentive ear! May I ask if you have heard me?"

"Yes, yes," replied Beatrice; "I have heard, my lord--your majesty is lenient! My crime is great; but be it as you will, I am ready to go! My thoughts, to speak the truth, are not so clear as they might have been some half hour since--I thank your majesty! All I ask is a prisoner's diet, bread and a glass of water,--for I am thirsty, exceeding thirsty! Then I am ready to set out.--Philip, farewell!" she added, gazing upon the corpse: "we shall meet again! Our deeds unite us for ever! Alas! alas! where shall I go, my lord?"

"Her brain is troubled," said the king, in a low tone, turning to one of the officers who followed; "go in with her, call her own people about her; but treat her with all reverence. She must be sent forth from the kingdom as speedily as possible. Madam, this officer will conduct you. Set a sentinel at the door," he added, in a low tone, "as if for honour; but let her people be with her, and lay no restraint upon her, except in watching whither she goes."

"Will no one give me a glass of water?" said Beatrice, moving towards the house.

"It shall be brought in a moment, lady," replied the officer, following. "Where are this lady's attendants?"

"Well, St. Real," said the king, turning to the young cavalier as he issued forth again from the house just as Beatrice entered. "Pardie, we are too late in one sense, after all, though not too late to prevent the mischief these fellows meditated. Ventre Saint Gris! but this cousin of yours was an ungenerous villain; and I am sorry for that poor girl, who, to my thinking, has driven the dagger deeper into her own heart than into his. Well, there he lies, and one of the conspirators against our fair heiress of Menancourt is disposed of; now to despatch the other. Martin, bring forward the prisoner."

"Sir Albert of Wolfstrom," continued the king, "it seems to me that your name was once enrolled amongst the troops of my late cousin, Henry III. and that you chose the chance of a halter and better pay on the part of the League. Traitors against myself, God help me, I am fain to forgive, leaving them to God and their consciences for punishment; but traitors to the late king I forgive not, and, therefore, I shall turn over your case to my good friend De Biron, who is not merciful, but just. Your own heart, therefore, will tell your fate: if it condemn you, be sure that ere to-morrow's noon you will be lying like him you stare at with such open eyes."

"Cannot I take service with my troop?" demanded Wolfstrom, with undaunted effrontery. "Your majesty suffered the Swiss at Ivry to come over to you."

"They were only enemies, not traitors," replied the king; "I can have traitors enow without paying them, sirrah!--What is that outcry within, St. Real? No more tragedies, I trust!--What I have said, Sir, is decided," continued Henry, again turning to Wolfstrom, while St. Real entered the house to ascertain the cause of the sounds of lamentation that they heard. "If your conscience tell you that you deserted the late king, bid good-by to the world! By my faith there must be something the matter there!" he added, as the tones of grief came again from within; and turning hastily, he himself entered the house, and advanced to a room from the open door of which the sound proceeded. The sight that presented itself needed little explanation. In a large chair, near the centre of the room, sat Beatrice of Ferrara, with her head supported upon the breast of her faithful old servant Joachim, while kneeling at her feet, and weeping bitterly as she clasped her friend's knees, was the beautiful form of Eugenie de Menancourt. Around were a number of female attendants, filling the air with lamentations; and on one side stood St. Real, gazing eagerly in the face of the fair Italian. But that lovely face had now lost the loveliness of life, the bright dark eyes were closed, the colour of the warm rose no longer blushed through the clear white skin, the lips themselves were pale, and the dazzling teeth showed like a row of pearls, as the mouth hung partly open. Her right hand was still clasped upon a glass from which she had been drinking; and rolled away upon the floor was a rich carved *bon-bonnière*, from which a small quantity of white powder had been spilt as it fell. Throughout the whole room there was a faint odour, as if of bitter almonds; and Henry, who well remembered that same perfume, when some of the noblest in France had died somewhat suddenly, exclaimed at once as he entered, "She has poisoned herself!"

"Too true, I fear, my lord!" replied St. Real; "but a leech has been sent for."

"In vain! in vain!" said the king. "She is dead already, St. Real! That is no fainting fit; and even were she not dead already, no skill on earth could save her from the tomb. I know that hateful drug too well. Come away, St. Real! Mademoiselle de Menancourt, come away! Nay, I command! You do no good here!"

Thus saying, Henry took the fair girl's hand and led her to another room, where, after speaking a few words of comfort, he added, "But I must to horse again and forward towards Le Mans. You, St. Real, I shall leave behind with your regiment, for the protection of this one fair lady, though those that persecuted her are no more. His body shall be carried to his own dwelling, and lie beside his father's. That I will see to. And now, though this is a solemn moment, and the scene a sad one, yet Mademoiselle de Menancourt, I must put it out of fortune's power to persecute you farther, for the treasure of this fair hand. Nay, nay, I must have my will!--Take it, St. Real," he added, placing it in his. "If I judge right, you value it highly; and, as you well deserve it, I give it to you now, lest any of my many friends should crave me for the gift hereafter. I would rather say to those who ask it that it is given, than that I will not give it. To your love and sorrow, lady, I leave the last rites of yon beautiful and hapless girl. Hers was a hard fate, and a noble mind; for, cast by fortune into the midst of corruption, with a heart all warmth and a fancy all brightness, she came out still, pure as gold refined in the fire, which, Heaven forgive us, is what few of us can say for himself. Amidst all the falsehoods and follies of the late court, never did I know the breath of scandal sully her fair name! She was, indeed, *one in a thousand!* Conceal the manner of her death, if possible; and let such honours as the church permits convey her to her last long home! Now, farewell!"

CHAPTER XXXVI

Of all the many personages which have figured in this tale, there are but few of whom it behoves us to give any farther account. The lives of some stand written on the bright and glorious page of history, never to be effaced till the waters of time have rolled long over this portion of the globe, have levelled our dwellings and our monuments with the sands, have washed away our learning and our records, and blotted out not alone the sweet domestic memories--on which each succeeding generation sets its foot, trampling with all the insolence of youth the withered flower just dead-- but have also razed, from the hard tablet of glory, the few names that are really worthy of eternal consecration. When such a change has taken place,- -and who shall say that it will not?--when Europe shall be called the land of forests and of barbarism, and some prying strangers alone shall come from their happier lands, and try to trace upon the desert shores the mouldering remnants of arts and sciences and nations long gone by, perhaps the name of Henry IV. of France, and those who resemble him, may be forgotten, but till then they have a glorious existence separate from the rest of men. The Duke of Mayenne, too, ambitious and intriguing, but generous and often wise, has a share of the page of history; and all those who continued to play a conspicuous part in the days of Henry Quatre, either for good or for evil, have their record in the annals of the time. This tale can alone take farther note of those whose fate it has depicted in the preceding pages, and who at this point separate themselves from the general course of history, either to fall into the calm repose of sweet domestic life, or to seek a refuge from unhappy fortunes in the tomb.

The body of Beatrice of Ferrara being removed from the cottage where Eugenie de Menancourt had dwelt so long, was borne to the chateau in which she herself had spent the last hours of her own existence; and with curses and imprecations upon his head, the tale of what his machinations had wrought was told to the dwarf Bartholo by the more faithful yet less attached servants of his late mistress.

He listened to the whole in sullen composure, and even a smile played upon his lip as he heard of the death of the Count d'Aubin; but when the last sad event was mentioned by the narrator, and he learned that Beatrice herself was dead, he struggled with the bonds that tied him, and then cast himself grovelling on the ground, which he dewed with his bitter agonising tears. He strove to tear his flesh with his teeth; and when they took him up, more to gaze upon his torture, than with any feeling of compassion--for no one loved, and no one compassionated him--he raved upon them with frantic and incoherent words, and again cast himself down in raving despair. For several days he refused all food; but at length pity touched some one, and a leech was sent for, who bled him largely, which produced a change. He no longer raved, he no longer refused food, he took what was offered him, did what was bid him; but it was with the slow and sullen stupidity of an idiot. The fire, too, had left his eye; his activity was gone; his witty sauciness at an end; and he would sit for days gazing vacantly upon the floor, without hearing what was said to him, and without addressing a word to any one. At length, the body of Beatrice of Ferrara was conveyed to Italy for the purpose of being interred amongst her princely ancestors; and then, though none knew how he escaped, it was perceived that the dwarf was gone also. It was not, indeed, extraordinary that he had disappeared without notice; for after his frenzy had terminated in idiocy, no one had paid him much attention.

How he travelled so great a distance, and how he supported himself by the way, are equally unknown; but some three months after, the wretched being was seen wandering about in the long vacant streets of Ferrara, enduring the scoff of the schoolboy and the peasant. He remained in that part of the country for several years; and those who had known him when first he had entered the household of the princes of Legnano, often gave food and money out of charity to the poor dwarf, whom they now despised and had formerly hated. At length, one morning, when the sacristan took his early round through the chapel in which the dead of that noble house slept in the cold marble which was their place of last repose, he was startled by seeing something curled up at the end of the new monument erected to the Princess Beatrice. He touched it, but it stirred not; and, familiar with the dead, he carelessly raised up the head, and beheld the lifeless features of the dwarf Bartholo.

The Count d'Aubin lay with his ancestors; and the noble estates of which he had been once the improvident possessor passed to his next male heir, the Marquis of St. Real. To St. Real it was pointed out by skilful and honest lawyers that, as the creditors who had claims upon the late Count could not easily prove their right, his estates might be rendered clear by a very simple process of law. But St. Real preferred a simpler process still; and from the funds accruing from large and well-managed lands discharged the debts, and freed the inheritance. The claims which were the most difficult to arrange were those of the heirs and successors of one Albert of Wolfstrom, who having been executed, under a judicial sentence regularly pronounced by a competent tribunal, for various transactions which did not even permit the harlot compassion of public excitement to attend his end, it was more than doubtful whether any of the demands which were made upon St. Real in his name were really to be sustained. There were some through which the young Marquis at once struck his indignant pen, and others which, though equally illegal, he paid at once; but in the end, as so often happens, the debts which had seemed overwhelming to him whose bad management had incurred them, were easily liquidated by a more provident though not a less liberal lord; and the estates of Aubin made a splendid addition to those of the Marquis of St. Real.

The young lord himself saw Eugenie de Menancourt reinstated in her ancestral halls, and wandered with her for a few days through the scenes they had both loved in childhood--scenes where the memories of the past, both dark and bright, blended into a solemn, but a sweet and soothing light, which, shining mellow and calm upon the happy present, gradually brightened into hope as the eye turned towards the future. It was like the twilight of the summer sky in a far northern land, where the night and the day mingle together in the west; and the soft and shaded, yet radiant, sunset continues till the dawning of the morning appears on the opposite horizon, so that the beams of the past and the future day meet in the zenith of the present.

It might be said that the experience which Eugenie de Menancourt and Huon St. Real already had of the past was sufficient to have justified their immediate marriage. But Eugenie had her scruples, and St. Real had a confidence derived from higher sources than either the usual happy fortunes of his house, or the promising turn which the war had taken. An old female relation was sought to bear the young heiress company for the next six months. To her Eugenie's education had been principally confided during her youth; her instructions had greatly tended to render her what she was, and St. Real thought that the society of no one could be better for her he loved till the day of their marriage at length arrived. In the meantime, he rejoined the king's army, and took part in the various events of the war which ultimately placed Henry IV. in possession of the capital of his kingdom, and put an end to the troublous times by which his reign began; but it will be remembered by all persons well versed in that portion of the history of France, that the part of the country in which the estates of Eugenie de Menancourt were situated never fell again into the hands of the League. Various detached towns in Normandy and Maine that faction did indeed continue to hold for some time, but the progress of the king after the battle of Ivry was uninterrupted, though gradual, till peace crowned his efforts; and his people learned to love, nay, almost to adore, the monarch against whom many of them had drawn their swords.

At length, six months after the death of Beatrice of Ferrara, Eugenie de Menancourt gave her hand to him whom she was not now ashamed to own she had loved from her earliest youth. Henry signed the marriage contract; and when the young Marquis, having seen him firmly seated on the throne of his ancestors, took leave of the monarch and his court, resolved to spend the rest of his life, as his fathers had done before him, in the calm tranquillity of his paternal domains, Henry placed round his neck the order of the *St. Esprit*, saying, that as he well knew he should but seldom see his face again, he was resolved to give him something whereby to remember the days he had passed with Henry Quatre.

Do we need to inquire how St. Real and Eugenie passed their after life? It sometimes happens, indeed, that two people who have loved well and truly in the first burst of youthful passion, crossed, disappointed, and soured, persevere against all opposition through long years of withering anxiety, till they meet together at length, with tempers irritated, and hearts no longer the same; and find nothing but misery in that union, from which they had anticipated nothing but happiness. Not so, however, St. Real and Eugenie de Menancourt. They had long loved without knowing it; and had chiefly had to struggle with the opposition of their own principles to their own wishes. They had been thwarted, but not disappointed; they had been grieved, but not irritated. Their sorrows had served like the black leaf on which the diamond is set, to increase, not tarnish, the lustre of the happiness they now enjoyed. But happiness will not bear description. It is the calm stream that neither foams nor murmurs; and theirs continued flowing on like a mighty river, which, troubled and obstructed at its source, soon overbears all obstacles, and then, having once reached the calm level of the open country, flows on increasing in volume, though it loses in brightness, till the full completed stream falls into the bosom of the eternal ocean.

FOOTNOTES

Footnote 1: The passion for dwarfs as attendants in great houses was so universal in France at this time, that the most extravagant sums were given for them. Henry III. is reported to have had no less than nine at one time; and at his court there was a regular *tailleur* and *valet des nains*.

Footnote 2: This speech of the dwarf applies to various modes of travelling then known in France, which it might be tedious to explain more fully in this place.

Footnote 3: The Duke of Guise, who held the throne of Henry III. and was afterwards barbarously assassinated by command of that monarch, had been his bosom friend in youth.

Footnote 4: In English, a mortgage. This sort of encumbrance was but too frequently created in France during the wars of the League and the epoch of debauchery which preceded, accompanied, and followed them.

Footnote 5: I have, in another romance, published long since this work was written, given a description of the phenomenon here mentioned, and have in that tale attempted to depict it as it appeared to the Royalists.